THE KINGDOM AND THE POWER

LITURGY OF WORLDS BOOK 3

NATHAN HARTLE

To my sibs, all my love

PROLOGUE

THE GUARDIAN HAD LEARNED he could still feel fear. He walked the corridors of his citadel, his footsteps ringing in the corridors though he could have moved with a mere thought. He gave himself a face, hands, and a set of spectacles to fiddle with. The ages had taught him, to his despair, that habits were the essence of being.

He had failed to stop the invaders. One of his prisoners, the Goddess Huire, had summoned her people to her rescue, and they were coming. He refused to let them free her—refused to be beaten.

His citadel was a powerful place, able to influence the dreams of any who meant to approach it, no matter how far away. One of the ancient minds who had built it might have twisted the invaders' dreams to break their resolve or even their sanity. But those minds far eclipsed his. He was small, feeble by comparison. Once, he had even been human.

He could meddle more aggressively with the forces the citadel commanded, calling on powers greater than mere dreams, but those powers might escape his control once summoned.

The citadel either did not sense his weakness or did not care. It flooded his mind with the invaders' dreams. They battered him, pulling him this way and that, filling him to overflowing.

If the worst came to pass—if Huire's people freed her and the other gods—the Guardian would have one means of avoiding whatever hideous fate awaited. An escape hatch of sorts.

If he had the courage to use it.

"Not yet," he said. The throat he had given himself uttered the sounds aloud. Another habit.

He would think no more of escape for the moment. Instead, he would lose himself in the invaders' dreams. Maybe he would learn how to stop them.

Or maybe, being creatures of flesh and blood, they would destroy themselves.

1

EMBERLY

CAPTAIN EMBERLY HAD NEVER imagined anything so large.

The tower loomed on the horizon when the Ronian company stepped through the gateway onto the planet. Gateways to other worlds dotted the flat desert landscape, and the tower was just one more object among them—until Emberly looked at it twice.

Private Merin, the company's astronomer, turned his telescope toward the building and gaped. When Emberly demanded information, Merin shook his head haplessly. Grabbing the instrument with a scowl, Emberly looked through it and understood.

The tower was farther than the gateways—much farther—yet it seemed taller than them. In all that vast empty land, Emberly could find no familiar object to compare it with until he saw the thin band of clouds girding its middle. Higher up, thicker banks of clouds blocked the building's top from view.

Emberly shivered.

The men had fallen silent. The captain lowered the telescope and turned to find them all watching him.

Lieutenant Roark was closest. He asked, "What should we do, Captain?"

Emberly looked again at the tower. Then he scanned the landscape. It held few places where someone could hide—or where an abducted person could be hidden. Whoever had taken Shada would be found in that tower, and she would be found with them.

If she was still alive to be found.

If the kidnappers had not taken her through one of the hundred gateways dotting the land, vanishing forever to some far corner of the universe.

Both those possibilities would mean failure and despair. Failure for the company's mission and despair for Ronia, their city. Emberly refused to accept either.

"She is there," he announced, pointing at the tower. "And we're going to find her."

⸻◆⸻

First things first, he told himself. *Don't get killed.*

As they approached the tower after an eternity of walking, Emberly told the men to carry their weapons openly but not at the ready. The company numbered a few dozen experienced soldiers, three holy men, and a number of unarmed convicts they'd rescued from the last world, Caidfell. Whoever lived in the tower, the Ronians could hardly expect to match them with strength of arms. Attempting to hide their rifles might seem deceptive, while carrying them ready to shoot would be to declare war.

Emberly took painful comfort in the state of the company, which trailed behind him like a snake dying of thirst and heat. They did not look like an invading army. They hardly looked like a threat to anyone.

The men plodded along, filthy and disheveled, carrying the company's wounded on their shoulders or on stretchers. Caidfell, the world from which they'd come, had taken almost everything but their lives, and it had taken some of those too. The rocky underground passage hiding the gateway through which they'd just arrived had forced them to abandon their wagons and beasts of burden. At first, Emberly had hoped to excavate the tunnel, opening a passage wide enough to let the vehicles through, but when Shada disappeared through the gateway, the captain had known the company must follow quickly to find her. So they'd gone, carrying what supplies they could on their backs.

Shada. If—when—the captain saw the young woman again, he would weep for joy then strangle her. She was the heart of the company and its mission: to find Huire, lost goddess of the city of Ronia, and return with her to save the city. The Lady, the divine messenger sent by Huire to lead the company, would speak only to Shada. Hell, she mostly wouldn't even appear to anyone else. For reasons Emberly would probably never understand, the Lady had chosen Shada, a domestic servant, as her representative and would deal with no one else.

That made it all the more infuriating when Shada put herself in needless danger. She had insisted on entering the gateway to this world alone, before Emberly and his men could even scout it. She'd claimed it would demonstrate their faith and trust in the Lady, who had apparently insisted on the gesture.

So she had entered the gateway, and she hadn't come back.

Her claim about the Lady must be true. The captain could not imagine why else Shada would enter this world alone. She seemed honest. Her lack of a personal agenda unnerved Emberly, tempting him to trust her less.

Maybe the Lady was the one he didn't trust.

A frightening thought, one he'd had several times. She insisted on staying in that box of hers—except when she disappeared without warning. She refused to help the company when it was in danger, insisting blood and courage were the price of finding Huire—but she had intervened once on Caidfell to save Shada. If someone had abducted Shada, the Lady had let it happen. The more the captain knew of her, the less he liked her.

He wondered if that was allowed, if it was a sin to dislike a servant of Huire.

It was a sin against the company, that was sure. The company's existence and survival depended on the Lady. The men would hardly be helped by hearing that their captain distrusted the being in whom they'd all placed their faith.

He wouldn't share his doubts with the holy men, either. Bishop Arumin, their leader, would burst into flames of rage if he knew. Even Brother Nor, the monk, would surely be shocked. Nor's rebellious tendencies did not go as far as blasphemy.

Emberly mumbled a prayer for forgiveness to Huire. Then a prayer for aid.

Frantic motion erupted at the base of the tower. Someone had seen them.

This close, the tower attained dimensions that rendered words meaningless. It was as wide as a city and far taller than it was wide. The soldiers walked with their faces turned up, mouths open. Its size was overpowering, then numbing, then oppressive.

It soon became part of the landscape, and the eye focused on smaller things. The shiftless track on which the company walked joined others to form a packed road. The road shot ahead across the waste toward a staircase leading up to a pair of doors set in the tower. Compared to the rest of the structure, the stairs and doors looked like they'd been built for mice, but as they grew near, Emberly realized with a jolt that the human figures rushing in and out of them were as small as ants in comparison.

No army emerged to meet them. A crowd had formed before the stairs, but it was a shapeless mob, buzzing and waiting. When the company at last came within shouting distance, the crowd surged toward them.

Sensing his men raising their weapons, Emberly ordered them to stand down.

The mob was wrapped in robes and scarves of every color. They came on, men and women, shouting and bearing goods of all kinds for the travelers—jugs of water, livestock, baskets of food, and casks of drink with taps for pouring straight into mouths. Rugs and jewelry hung from arms. They intercepted and surrounded the company, holding forth their wares.

"Take nothing!" Emberly commanded his men.

Waving a palm, he wearily refused a man trailed by several women. The company might barter for critical goods, but if soldiers started grabbing, nobody had any way to track purchases, and the merchants could claim whatever cost they wanted.

Worse, but unsurprisingly, the Ronians didn't share a word of common language with the strangers. Conversation descended into slow and deliberate speech then into gestures and facial expressions.

Finally, an elderly man raised his hand, and the crowd gradually fell silent. He stepped forward and met Emberly's eyes. Unlike the others, who were burdened with heavy goods, he held only a fist-sized red fruit. Pointing past the company into the waste, he swept his arm across the horizon.

Emberly turned. Gateways stood near and far across the flats. The captain was embarrassed to realize that he could sooner sprout wings than point out the gateway from which his company had emerged.

Instead, he pointed up the stairs to the tower's doors and asked the question on the minds of every person in his company. "What is this place?"

He had little hope of an intelligible answer. But the man seemed to understand, at least in part. His eyes glinted and fell briefly, once, to the pistol and saber at the captain's waist.

He made a sound too deliberate to be anything but a word: "Om."

He offered his fruit with a forceful bow. Emberly relented and accepted it. Then the man pointed at the fruit, slapped his own chest with a smile, and turned to ascend the stairs, leaving the travelers to find their own way.

2

EMBERLY

ONE OF THE GREAT doors was open a crack, as if a giant had forgotten to shut it. It was the tower's only apparent entrance, and Emberly led the company through it and into a thriving marketplace. Crowds swarmed them once more, and he forged ahead, repeating his order to buy nothing.

They stood in a sea of people pushing and moving. Many were of the Changed, those peoples whom the gods had altered in countless ways. The press of bodies, rows of booths, and piles of wares funneled the company down a thoroughfare. Beyond the edge of the market stood buildings of all shapes.

Emberly could almost have forgotten they were no longer outside. They were in a room the walls and ceiling of which were so far away as to be abstractions. He wouldn't have thought that so much space could be captured within man-made borders, that one could be indoors without the feeling of being indoors. Om, the trader had called it.

But he had little time to gaze at their surroundings. The confusion of the marketplace and the city around it raised the nightmarish possibility of the company becoming divided. He led the column down the avenue, avoiding side streets while he thought about what to do.

"It's from the old world, isn't it? This place," Lieutenant Roark said beside him. His long pale hair was tied back, sweat running from underneath it.

Emberly muttered, "Whoever among the worlds nowadays could build this, I don't want to meet them."

Roark's question was preferable to the ones that had been pressing on his mind since they passed through the doors. *Does this city fill this whole place? How will we ever find Shada?*

Until they found the woman, they could not continue their quest. The Lady had vanished days ago, following some dispute with Shada, who had ventured through the gateway in an attempt to regain the Lady's trust. He could only hope that if they found Shada, they would find the Lady. If they didn't, they would have no idea which of the hundred gateways to travel through next.

Catching Roark staring upward, Emberly dragged himself back to the present. "Lodgings first," he said.

Among the vendors and opportunists pestering the column were several children, begging and selling. Emberly heard a soldier shout at one of the hangers-on. Sergeant Orund, he marked the man.

Then he saw that one of his people had fallen. Trotting over, he found it was Carrowy, the young private who had been wounded almost fatally on Caidfell. Orund and another man had been bearing the private on a litter when a child had gotten underfoot. Orund had tripped and dropped Carrowy on his head.

"All right, Private?" Emberly asked as they shifted Carrowy back onto the litter.

The man's face was red, and he was sweating. "Not sure, sir."

Dr. Staubel had just reached them. "He needs more time to rest." His thin beard could not hide that he was even more of a boy than Carrowy.

"That's not enough," Carrowy said, his eyes watering. "Goddess, it hurts. Haven't you got anything else you can give me?"

"I'll see what I can do, Private." The doctor's face was bright, though Emberly wondered how deep his optimism went.

Carrowy groaned. "Some grog, at least."

"Don't I wish, Carrowy," Staubel said. He stayed to walk beside Carrowy's litter as Emberly returned to the head of the column.

When he got there, Roark growled, "So much for avoiding attention."

Emberly was becoming irritated by the lieutenant's fondness for the obvious. "When was there any hope of that?" he asked and a moment later added, "Someone must rule this place. Who do you suppose it is?"

"I suppose anarchy is too much to hope for," Roark replied.

Emberly smiled.

They had come to an intersection. Here and there around his feet, Emberly could see spots where the smooth stone underfoot was less dented and stained. He glimpsed what it had once been: a floor of polished white like marble. It gave him the feeling that they were all walking over a lake of ice that might soon break under the city's weight.

Calling a halt, he stood on his toes to see above the crowd. The bazaar seemed to have no end. When he came down on his heels, pain sliced up his back like a knife. His body had not yet forgiven him for falling from the fortress wall on Caidfell.

He pressed a hand against his spine and felt the sting on his bandaged arm where, desperate to stay awake, he'd cut himself during the battle. He was a wreck, and so was his company. He prayed for a reprieve. *Let me simply close my eyes and open them in a bed somewhere.*

Nearby, feet pounded the road in familiar rhythm. He knew the sound so well that he didn't notice it at first. Looking around again, he saw a troop of armed and uniformed soldiers approaching down the cross street.

"At ease," he called to the others.

He would rather not encounter this force without knowing who they were, but his company could not escape through the madness of foot traffic.

To his surprise, the fifty or so men marched past without sparing them a glance. Emberly stared at them as they went, hardly believing his company had escaped their notice.

The soldiers' uniforms were blue like an afternoon sky, decorated and ornate. Their hair was long and braided, and they were clean-shaven.

The captain looked at their weapons most of all. Each man had a rifle of dark metal, slim and plain. The rifles had none of the hand-forged character of the Ronians' guns—no wooden handles, no curves, no aesthetic sense.

"Sameness," Emberly said to himself.

Though he could not put a name to what he was feeling, Roark felt it too. "We ought to get off the street, sir."

A pair of little boys had been keeping pace with the front of the Ronian column, watching and amusing themselves. Struck by an idea, Emberly waved one of them over and knelt to his eye level. After sweeping a finger to encompass the entire column, he folded his hands and laid his face on top of them in a gesture of sleep.

The boy knew what he meant before he had finished. He motioned for Emberly to follow.

"I hope he accepts fruit as payment," the captain said.

3

EMBERLY

THE DERELICT HOUSE LAY behind a heavy door on a shadowed street. Emberly would have refused outright to enter had they not already tried several inns and found that no one would let them stay without coin in hand. As things stood, they had little choice other than sleeping in the street.

The place had its advantages, its anonymity first among them. It was one unmarked door among dozens, located on one narrow street among hundreds.

The few squatters in the place scattered at the sight of a troop of armed men entering. The company soon had the building to itself. It smelled of urine and neglect, and the company had to pack in to fit everyone inside, but it had walls and a roof.

Seeing their satisfaction, the boy who had guided them there held out his palm. Emberly had nothing of value that he was willing to give. He offered the small red fruit, but the boy refused bitterly and left scorning him.

With him went the convicts, who saw the crowded conditions and decided to stay together elsewhere. Fortunately, the boy was still willing to help them despite his outspoken opinion of Emberly. The groups exchanged encouraging words as they parted. Emberly knew he bore some responsibility for the convicts, and he felt he should help them, given the chance. They had lost their home, and he did not know what they would do.

Once Emberly had assigned the men to the various desolate rooms, he called a meeting in his. He was joined by both his lieutenants, both their sergeants, and the company's holy men. They gathered around a small rickety table with several intact chairs, sitting or standing as they could find space.

Another man stood in a corner, a man to whom Emberly dared not speak in the presence of others. A strong-minded, sensible Ronian was not supposed to see ghosts, let alone talk to them, but there stood his dead brother, Rayan, looking as smug and confident as he had in life. A terrorist, Rayan had ruled the convicts on Caidfell with manipulation and treachery. In the end, he had tried to sell Emberly's people and his own into slavery to keep them under his control.

The price he had paid was evident during his frequent visits to Emberly: a gaping wound on his broken face where the captain had shot him.

Thankfully, Rayan stayed quiet and listened as Emberly spoke to his men. The room's single candle cast them all in gold and shadow. Darkness fell early within the great structure called Om, despite the many oblong windows in its outer walls. Much light was lost on its way to this room's single window.

"We know our purpose," Emberly began. "We have only to decide on our means. We must find the caretaker." He used Shada's title to give the meeting formality despite their grubby circumstances.

"And the Lady," Bishop Arumin said.

"Of course," Emberly agreed, concealing his annoyance. "But where we find one, we will find the other, I think."

"How can we know that?" Lieutenant Iwan asked. He left out "sir," a habit of his so persistent that Emberly almost failed to notice. Iwan was too perpetually absorbed in thought to observe niceties. "The caretaker may not have found the Lady. She may have come here on her own or been taken."

"Or she might not have come here at all," said Brin, the young priest. "She might have gone through any of the gateways nearby."

Brin rarely spoke in the presence of the captain, who was grateful for it. The two had been on Caidfell together long before—a time Emberly wished he could forget.

In the corner, Rayan smirked with what remained of his mouth. He surely remembered those days, too, and he never tired of reminding Emberly of that fact. He knew secrets Emberly could tell no one else. He remembered the night when Emberly, a young soldier, had grown so disgusted by the brutality of the prison colony that he'd released Rayan from his cell in a fit of pity and despair. He remembered, and he loved Emberly for it.

"We have no reason to believe she would," Bishop Arumin said, correcting the priest. He and Brin were close, closer than most would dare speculate aloud, and Brin had the gall to look annoyed at Arumin's words.

"Indeed, we do not," the captain said quickly. He lacked patience tonight and intended to keep the meeting moving. "So we will search here."

"And how long will we stay?" That was Sergeant Orund, an aging, bearded trooper. The question was forceful, as though long contained.

Emberly let a second or two pass before answering. "Until we find her."

"And if we don't?" Orund shot back.

A deep silence fell on the gathering.

"We must. There is nothing else, Sergeant."

"Aye, there is. We could go back."

The captain was a little relieved. Here was a protest so absurd that it was easily dispatched. "Back to Ronia?" he asked. Best to pretend he did not understand, to let the man try to explain himself.

"The men aren't well, sir," Orund announced. "They hide it as best they can, but they're not well. We lost more than a few brothers on Caidfell, and that so soon after Gallobraith."

Emberly addressed the earlier, easier point. "Let's suppose returning to Ronia was even thinkable. How would we do it? Do you propose we fight our way back across Caidfell?"

"We might not have to, Captain. We gave those wraiths a good scare. I expect they would leave us alone." Orund seemed genuinely hopeful.

"They're not the only danger. The planet itself barely spared us. The trees themselves wished us dead."

"By the Goddess, sir, it would be better than this madness."

After a stir, multiple voices rose.

The bishop shouted, cutting through them all, "No, it wouldn't! You would abandon the Lady? Give up the

Goddess Huire for lost? The hope of our people, Sergeant! Surely our lives are worth that."

Orund was uncowed. "I'm not sure, your Eminence. And I'm sorry to say so. But I'm a soldier, responsible for the man beside me. Help your fellow man—that's what the Goddess teaches."

Emberly had had enough. He spoke coldly. "A soldier's responsibility is to his mission. If you were not prepared for sacrifice, you should not have joined this crusade. But since you have joined it, you had best change your way of thinking."

Brother Nor interjected. As usual, his milk-white eyes made his mind hard to guess. "We all vowed to finish this task or die trying, Orund. In exchange, our sins have been forgiven. This is a holy crusade, and we are crusaders. Are you prepared to go back on that? To take all your sins back?"

Sergeant Orund chewed on his lip. "You're one to talk about vows, monk, the way you look at the caretaker. No wonder you don't want to leave her behind."

Nor knocked the table over as he stood. Others intercepted him and Orund before they reached each other. The captain pushed into their midst and shoved them back with a shout.

He spoke to Orund first. "Leave the room, Sergeant."

The sergeant said hoarsely, "And he can stay, is that it?"

"Get out!" Lieutenant Roark screamed. His voice was a crack of thunder at which the others jumped a little. His hand was on his saber.

Orund walked out with deliberate slowness and left the door ajar.

"And you," Emberly said to Nor. "What kind of holy man gets into brawls like a schoolboy? I can hardly expect civilized behavior from my men when I can't even expect it from you."

Nor had backed away from the table and was standing alone. He breathed heavily and looked at the wall.

"Have you anything to say?" Emberly asked.

Bishop Arumin's deep voice resounded in the little room. "Brother Nor's actions are not becoming of him. I'll make sure he gives us no further problems."

Nor nodded at the bishop's words. He looked at the door, which still stood open. "Orund was right," he said. "I should leave also."

"Go," the bishop said. "Remain in your room. If you run into Orund, don't so much as look at him."

When the monk had gone, those who remained righted the table.

Then Emberly proceeded. "In the morning, we will begin our search for the caretaker. We must assume for now that she's in this city. Comings and goings are observed here, so someone must know something."

"We'll need a way to speak to people," Iwan said. "A drawing of the caretaker would be useful. Anyone who sees her will remember the markings on her face."

"What about the soldiers—the patrol we saw on the street?" Roark asked. He had not entirely calmed down from his words with Orund. His hands hung at his sides, alternately relaxing and clenching into fists. "Who are they?"

"Whoever they are, if they are running the place, they cannot have been here long," Iwan replied. "None of them were stationed at the doors of the city."

Roark shook his head. "But the crowd seemed used to them. We attracted more attention than they did."

"If I may speak outside of my expertise," the bishop said, "I don't think it matters a damn who they are. Outside of this city are more gateways than I've ever heard of in a single place. Far more than in Ronia, even. There must always be someone or other passing through. If we are discreet, we ought to be able to find the Lady without ever meeting them."

"Let's hope the bishop is right," Emberly told everyone, "but if we don't find the caretaker or the Lady, we may need their help."

The bishop's eyes widened. Emberly saw the same feeling, though more controlled, on a few other faces.

Arumin asked, "Are you proposing that we contact them? Draw their notice deliberately?"

"Not yet," Emberly said. "But it may come to that."

"Pardon me, sir, but that would carry quite a risk," Roark told him. "If they rule this city and they discover a unit from a foreign military has entered…" He let that thought finish itself. "We don't have the strength to overcome any sizeable force, especially now."

"We need not tell them who we are, Lieutenant, or show them our numbers."

"Are you sure we could conceal those things?"

"Of course I'm not sure!" Emberly snapped. "And we won't try until we must. But if we cannot find Shada and the Lady, we will most certainly try." He nodded at the bishop, who eyed him warily. "The hope of our people is worth the risk."

No one said anything else until Emberly dismissed them with orders to sleep if possible. Even those who were sharing that room with him stepped out—the captain said he needed a moment alone. That might have seemed strange, but he was past caring.

They left him by himself, or so they thought. When the last of them closed the door behind himself, the captain was left staring at Rayan's shattered face, now directly in front of him. Insects crawled on his skin. Inhaling the sickly sweet smell of death, Emberly gulped.

He spoke aloud to what part of him still suspected was an empty room. "Well, what do you think? I suppose you have advice for me."

The ruins of Rayan's mouth curled upward. "Oh, yes."

4

Nor

Nor awoke from vivid dreams to find a flame hovering above where he lay. An old woman dressed in rags was kneeling beside him and pressing a finger to her lips.

She was one of the squatters who had fled the house when the company arrived. Nor looked around. A few of the sleeping forms nearby stirred, but no one seemed awake. The woman waved her hand, telling him to follow.

Seeing the frightened, desperate look in her eyes, Nor got up. She could not explain herself to him in words, but her expression said enough. Something was badly wrong. Maybe they were in danger. Whatever was happening, she must have had reasons for waking him and no one else. As he stood, she pressed her finger against her lips again.

As he followed her into the hall, sleep clung to him, making his mind foggy and his steps unsteady. He could not remember having lain down for the night, and the blank spot in his memory made him uneasy. He wrung his hands, still scabbed from wrestling predatory vines on Caidfell.

Nothing that he remembered gave him much comfort. He had encouraged Emberly to let Shada enter that gateway, sure the Lady had really asked her to do it. He had been certain that show of faith was needed to restore the Lady's trust in the company, and he'd been willing to risk Shada's life in the process.

Then Shada had disappeared, and her absence had left an enduring pit in Nor's stomach. As a monk, he must show love to all, but she had been the only person in the company he liked and trusted beyond the limits of his responsibilities. Every thought of where she might be, of what might have happened to her through the gateway, scared him.

With the fear came guilt. He had liked her too much. He had known it even before she disappeared. He had been drawn to her not as a fellow child of Huire but as a woman. His vows forbade him to even harbor such thoughts, let alone act on them. But harbor them he had. Without meaning to, he had misled her into thinking something more than friendship was possible. When she had finally broached the subject, he had panicked, surprise piling on disbelief piling on—he had to admit it to himself—excitement. He had coldly deflected her gesture, then he had felt her pain.

That was just before she disappeared. His final impact on her life had been sorrow and confusion.

Not final, he reminded himself. She had survived. She must have. The Lady valued her too much to let her die. She had shown that when she rescued Shada in the swamp, leaving the safety of the box where she lived to do so.

Since Shada's disappearance, Nor had carried the woman's few meager possessions, hoping to see her again. They included the Lady'sbox, a lantern-shaped metal container. He could not share all Shada's burdens, but he could share this.

He would see Shada again. And when he did, he would see her only as the caretaker. No more confusion. She had her role, and he would play his.

That might prove the hardest thing to accept. When he'd encouraged her to go through the gateway alone, risking her life, he'd done *the right thing*.

Doubts wrestled in his belly as he followed the woman down the dark hall. Just ahead, a pile of bedding on the floor shifted and turned into a man. A face turned upward, and Nor recognized Private Merin, the astronomer.

"Brother Nor," Merin whispered in greeting.

Nor stopped. The old woman immediately became anxious and urged him to continue, but he held up a hand to quiet her. "Merin, what are you doing out here?"

"There was no more space in the rooms."

That did not make sense. Emberly had been certain everyone would fit.

"Why don't you take my spot, Private? It's empty now."

"I needed air, Brother."

Nor frowned in the candlelight. He wondered if this was some punishment of Emberly's. Merin and another private, Hulgar, had been poisoned on Caidfell by one of the many toxins on that planet that could sway the mind. Under its influence, they had tried to betray the company. That was hardly their fault in Nor's view, but Emberly had apparently been furious. Not even the privates' later heroics in battle had redeemed them in his eyes. The captain was too prideful to change his mind, even when he was proven wrong.

"Are you sure?" Nor asked Merin.

He had hardly finished the question before Merin said, "Yes. No, thank you."

The woman seemed nearly frantic. Nor nodded and resumed following her. As he did, the gravity of the situation struck him again. She might know of some threat to them. She might be in some danger of her own.

Or she might be leading him into danger. She might be planning to rob or kill him. She was a complete stranger whom he had decided to follow.

In any case, stopping for a conversation had been stupid. Sleep must still have a hold on him. He quickened his step to match hers.

The woman entered a narrow spiral staircase and instantly vanished down its throat. As Nor entered that tight space, he wondered what his father might have thought of this moment. His son was willingly entering a place that looked like the innards of the Worm.

Try as he might to focus, to feel properly afraid of what the woman might be leading him toward, other thoughts intruded, clouding around him. Seeing Merin had jogged his memory of the previous evening. He remembered his scuffle with Orund, after which he had gone to his room as ordered. There, he had sat and fumed until sleep crept up on him.

With an ill, sinking feeling, he realized he had forgotten to visit the wounded. The injured men were kept together, and Nor had been checking on them at least once each day.

Some had little interest in speaking with him. His dislike of the Ronian Empire and his troubled history with its soldiers were common knowledge. But others were glad for the company, to be prayed for and with.

He had missed only one visit, but for those like Carrowy who were suffering immensely, an evening of unbroken boredom and self-reflection could be a terrifying mountain to ascend.

Suddenly, the tight stairwell felt like a trap. They had been descending for what seemed like hours. Surely, they were underground already.

His guilt and doubt reached a crescendo, and he felt something was stalking him down the stairs. He knew it well and had a name for it: the silence. It had hunted him on other nights, prowling the shadows, hoping to lock its jaws on his throat and cut off all words. He had not felt its presence in a few days and had even dared to hope it had left him.

Meanwhile, it had been waiting here, in this stairwell on this world, knowing he would come. He wished the woman would hurry. The stairs seemed infinite.

Preferring a useless question to the dreadful silence, he asked, "Where are we going?"

She stopped, and he nearly collided with her. She turned toward him and pressed her palms together, fingers pointing up. After saying a few words, she continued on her way.

It had looked like a gesture of prayer. She might have guessed his role in the company. Maybe she was seeking some spiritual aid or guidance. Nor knew firsthand that confusion in those areas could scare a person quite a bit. Nor had failed in his duties twice that night. Maybe the Goddess Huire had granted him a chance to do something right. It was the least frightening possibility for where they were going.

The stairs ended at last, and they entered a cellar. The woman sped along a path between stacks of crates and bags. The air was cool, and the ceiling was high and flat, supported here and there by massive beams and stone pillars. Their movements echoed through expanses beyond the candlelight. Above, Nor supposed, was the stone floor upon which the city was built.

They climbed a rough wooden stairwell that shifted and whined as it led them through a hatch in the ceiling. A chill greeted him—the night air of the desert, passing through the gates and windows of Om.

He pulled his cloak close and put his hands in its pockets. His fingers touched the envelope Abbot Cadmon had given him on Ronia. It was an unwanted reminder. Within it lay the answer to the quandary the abbot had given Nor. Whether Nor answered correctly would determine whether he became an elder in the mystics' order.

What are the gods made of? He pondered the quandary for the thousandth time. Yet he was no closer to an answer than he had been after the first.

They were in a yard surrounded by iron fences a little taller than a man. Beyond lay narrow avenues and the silhouettes of buildings. The fences were topped with points that looked deliberately and unpleasantly sharp.

Their feet rested on grass, of all things. Someone had covered the space with soil and seeded it, not to mention keeping it watered in that arid place.

Around them stood ungainly shapes of aged stone. Some were waist high and flat, others loftier and guarded by carven beasts. They looked like tombs, long cared for and maintained.

Back along a winding, well-trodden path stood the largest of these, a hexagonal building with a domed roof. The woman made for this. Through the tomb's small barred door, Nor saw a light.

Thoughts cascaded within him. If this woman was indeed seeking spiritual help and the forthcoming scenario involved speaking to the dead, he would refuse to participate. The Temple taught that once a spirit passed over the great divide, there could be no reaching back. To pretend otherwise would be a lie.

Even entering a tomb built at the word of an alien god felt close to sin. As long as he kept his crusader's vow, his sins would be negated, but he must not take that as a license to act however he wished.

The gate creaked and swung aside. The woman led him in, passing comfortably beneath the low door. With a final thrill of fear at what might wait inside, he ducked his head and followed.

The light within was flat yellow. He could smell the stone. He stood at the end of an oblong room with small doorways on either side. In the center was a sarcophagus raised on a bier.

The stone features of the face on the box's lid were disintegrating. At its highest, the lid was level with the waist of a small woman, who stood behind it. She was examining a stack of papers that rested on the chest of the sarcophagus. Just beside the papers was a small lantern that emitted the room's yellow glow. Its light was eerily steady, and Nor saw no flame.

She was quite young, he thought at first, but on second glance, he was not so sure. She was mousy and plain in a way that made her appearance seem unimportant. Her clothing was loose and drab.

"And you are Brother Nor," she said. It was not fully a statement or a question. "I was hoping to meet you."

Nor stopped cold. The fear returned, racing down his spine.

She had just spoken the imperial tongue, the language of Ronia. Here, unspeakably far from Ronia, was a woman who spoke the Ronian language as cleanly as a native.

He didn't know what that meant, where she had come from, or what was happening, but something made him want to run. He turned to the old woman, who minutes ago had pleaded for his help. He turned just in time to see her shut the gate from outside, closing him in. She would not meet his eyes.

5

NOR

As he looked at the strange woman, Nor fought back his fear and willed himself to think clearly. But his mind had become murky.

He was not good at hiding his feelings. His voice wavered as he demanded, "Who are you? How do you know this language?"

After greeting him, she had busied herself with writing. She spared him a glance. "Oh, that doesn't matter."

Nor looked around. The gate behind him was not locked. He could run. But the woman's complete lack of concern made him hesitate. At the least, he must try to find out who she was. No one with friendly intentions would have tricked him into coming here.

"It certainly does," he said. "I must call you something."

Still writing, the woman replied, "My name is Ren, but that will do us little good. We will not be speaking for long." She finally fixed her eyes on him. "In the house with you are a number of associates. I will need their names. I also need to know where you are from and why you are here."

He stared at her. His empty white eyes often unnerved people, and he hoped they would have that effect on her. "Whom do you work for?"

Her gaze was empty. Meeting it and trying and failing to read her intentions, he thought he understood, for once, how people felt when they locked eyes with him.

She replied, "I won't say. I am here to gather information, not to give it."

Anger flashed through his fear. "I'm here for neither. If you won't tell me anything else, I'll leave. We'll exchange fact for fact. You must be fair."

She set her pen down. "That's not true at all—that I must be fair. Don't say it again. You are a stranger here. I've come to decide whether you are a guest or a trespasser."

Nor took a breath to watch and listen before he answered. In the empty spaces of the tomb, air moved and sighed. *Is that breathing in the next room?* "Are you the ruler of Om?"

She sighed as if resigned to answering the questions of a child. "No."

"Do you serve those who rule it?"

Her mouth twisted, and she shook her head. "You would get no satisfaction from knowing these things. Indeed, if you knew them, you might wish you didn't."

Nor's body surged with the desire to run. He wondered what would happen if he tried. The woman must have been armed.

"I doubt that very much," he said, unsure if it was true.

She said, "Very well. We'll have to rely on the word of our first visitor." She turned her head toward one of the doorways. "Bring him."

Three men ducked through the opening. The first and last were all in black. They wore no signs of rank or honor. Though their garments covered all but their eyes, those were a sight by themselves—a shade of yellow richer and darker than the light of the tomb, with narrow pupils like slits.

Nor had seen men like them before, but his mind was a tumult. Before he remembered, he noticed the third man and gasped.

Between the black-clad men was Private Carrowy, bent and tattered. His arms, gripped by his captors, groped for a bloody patch on his shirt over his belly. A tree on Caidfell had impaled him in that spot, and merely existing had been agony for him since. The wound must have reopened.

Carrowy had clearly been crying. He didn't seem to realize Nor was there. The center of his whole bearing was the strange little woman with her papers.

"Mr. Carrowy," Ren said, "Mr. Nor is a member of your company, yes?"

Turning his gaze on the monk at last, Carrowy nodded.

Nor met his eyes but saw little recognition there.

Ren continued, "And your company is from a place known as Ronia. Is that a planet?"

"City." Carrowy looked away from Nor and seemed to forget him. The private's nose was running, but he did not seem to mind.

"Ronia is a city?"

"Yes." Carrowy pressed his lips together hard then said, "I'm sorry. I'm sorry."

Nor realized with a start that Carrowy was talking to him. The private's eyes had turned toward him a little, as though he dared not look at him directly.

"That will do," Ren sharply said. "We'll get all of this cleared up, I'm sure." She looked at Nor. "From here, I'm afraid Mr. Carrowy's tale descends into gibberish. I'll need you to clarify some things."

Still reeling, Nor wondered how much Carrowy had told her. He pointed at the private. "This man is not well. Why is he here?"

"So he is a member of your party?"

"Yes."

"We thought so. We found him here, trying to climb the fence. He has been terribly hurt, as I'm sure you are aware, and the task was too much for him."

Nor thought furiously. If Carrowy had told Ren about the company's true mission, they could be in terrible danger. No one could say how an outsider might react to the possibility of finding the gods. Many would likely see a chance to gain enormous power.

He must convince Ren that Carrowy was wrong. "The pain has driven him out of his wits. That, and the medicine he has taken. You must not take him seriously."

Carrowy heard that and shook his head vigorously.

"So this 'Ronia' is not your home?"

Nor remembered one of the crusade's cover stories that fit such circumstances. "It is. We are traders."

Ren moved another page to the top of her stack and glared at it. "I see. We have a problem. Mr. Carrowy here told me something far more elaborate and fantastical. Talk of gods and whatnot. So those things are not true?"

Nor shook his head. "Traders, as I said. We've met with many troubles and lost most of our valuables."

"You're quite well armed as traders go."

"The ways between worlds are treacherous. If I had my way, we'd be better armed still."

"I see." She looked at the private. "That is quite a story you told me, Mr. Carrowy. I scarcely could have believed it. Still, I hoped there was a logical explanation."

Carrowy shook his head again, faster. "It's not... not a story."

"Mr. Nor seems far more collected than you do, sir. The fact is, I trust him." She shook her papers. "You swore to me these things were the truth. We've talked about what it means to lie. Do you remember?"

Carrowy began to cry.

"It means you have a long road ahead, sir. As a welcoming gift to our new friends from Ronia, we will take you into our care."

The men holding Carrowy's arms moved toward the exit, dragging the private with them. Carrowy screamed for help.

"Wait!" Nor stepped in their way, winding up eye to eye with the foremost of the black-clad men.

When turned from the light, the man's pupils gaped, nearly swallowing his yellow irises.

"Where are you taking him?" Nor demanded.

A smile lit Ren's face. "This is the finest day of Mr. Carrowy's life. He will be awakened."

Carrowy moaned. The bloodstain on his shirt was spreading.

"Speak plainly," Nor said. "What do you mean?"

She shook her head, still smiling. "People like you and I won't ever truly understand, Mr. Nor. We're already awake. It is only those like him—the beasts—that must be taught."

Nor glanced at the door and wondered how to get himself and Carrowy through it. He had no idea what "awakening" meant. If it was some kind of torture, he could not let it happen. He'd suffered torture himself on Caidfell, and it had darkened his mind in ways he didn't yet fully understand. "You don't have to do this. If he's done something wrong, our people should be the ones to punish him."

"Punishment is for humans, sir. What has he done to deserve that consideration? It's for the likes of him that mercy exists. He will be blessed, and it is our pleasure. He wronged us, too, after all. If you see him again, you will not know him."

Carrowy babbled. In the midst of that torrent, Nor heard his own name.

Ren swept her hand toward the exit, and the men stepped forward. The one in front collided with Nor and began to push through him like a door.

Nor's fear melted into outrage. He shoved the man back. "I forbid it."

The woman screamed at almost the same instant. It sounded like a word. She leapt over the sarcophagus and rushed to the man, who had stepped back a pace or two. She spoke more words into his ear. He was still, and his yellow eyes showed nothing.

Ren looked at Nor, her eyes wide. "I wish you hadn't done that. My command over these two is absolute but narrow. Until he forgets, it will be a task to keep you alive."

"That will be as it must." Nor took a deep breath. "But I will stop you from taking this man if I can."

Ren shook her head, looking worried for his sanity. "You can't. If you hear nothing else I say, hear that."

Nor's mouth was dry. "I can see that your people are powerful. But so are mine. Killing me will only begin the violence. Our peoples should start out well, at least."

"These things cannot be undone, Nor. It is beyond any of us."

"It's not too late. No one's been hurt yet."

"I meant Mr. Carrowy. His lies cannot be untold. We higher beings are distinguished by our courage—courage to face the truth. He's no longer one of us."

Nor looked at Carrowy. The private looked at the ground, in a dream.

Nor thought of all his failures then said, "He's not a liar. I am."

Ren looked at him for what felt like a long time. "And Mr. Carrowy's extraordinary tales?"

"All true, probably. You should let him go."

She looked at her papers. "Well. Now, I have two men I cannot trust." She turned her empty eyes toward Nor. "What proof can you offer that you are a liar? Tell me, what am I to do now?"

6

EMBERLY

EMBERLY'S ROOM HAD COME to life once again. Once the officers and the bishop were awake and assembled, they heard what Nor had to say. Rayan stood in a corner, unseen by all but Emberly.

Carrowy sat beside the monk, who had guided him into the room and to a chair. Dr. Staubel had come to deal with his freshly opened wound, but the private had refused him, preferring to nurse a silent grief.

When the monk finished, the captain sat back in his chair and tried to understand what he'd heard. He said, "Well, if we're to have visitors in the morning, we should be prepared. We'll maintain the present watch and guard the stairwell to the basement—lest anyone else decide to wander."

All eyes fell on Carrowy, who shrank back. Emberly asked him what he had to say for himself.

The private's eyes moved about aimlessly. He crossed his arms and sank his nails into his skin. "Nothing."

"Nothing at all? You have been accused of desertion and treason."

That wasn't the first time Emberly had used those words on the journey. Privates Merin and Hulgar had let themselves be swayed by some potion into betraying the company to its enemies. The captain had not just raked them across the coals—he had ordered them to kill themselves before letting such a thing happen again. He felt far more sympathy for Carrowy, but he wasn't sure why.

"Like I said, nothing," the private replied. "The monk did his best to help me. But I can't be helped, sir."

The room's tension transformed into genuine discomfort. Suddenly, Emberly realized why Carrowy had tried to climb that fence, and he prayed he wouldn't have to say it aloud. "You can be helped," he said, "but you choose not to be."

Carrowy bent, his face red. He wheezed in pain but still managed to grin. "You know what I'm talking about, don't you, sir?"

So much for his prayers. As little as Emberly wanted to talk about a person's private affairs in public, Carrowy had invited it.

"Nightshade," Emberly said.

Shifting and muttering—everyone had heard that word, the terror of Ronia's streets.

Emberly pursed his lips. "How long since you've had… a dose?"

Carrowy shut his eyes. "Not since we left Ronia."

The captain nodded. He'd used nightshade, too, though no respectable gentleman would never admit it, and Carrowy must have used it far more. He must have been desperate indeed to search for it, or something like it, in the streets of an alien city.

Emberly phrased his words carefully to sound ignorant. "Several days ago, then. As I understand it, you should be feeling better by now."

Carrowy laughed bitterly. "That's not how it works, sir. And this"—he placed a hand near his wound—"just brings it all back."

Emberly wished to the Goddess that he'd sent the others out before starting this conversation. "I'm sorry for your troubles, man," he said, "but it's nothing you can't get through."

In the corner, Rayan frowned.

Carrowy gave the captain a savage grin. "You have no bloody idea what it's like."

Voices were raised, but Emberly silenced them. "That's enough. You'll be under guard for the time being. I'll withhold further punishment until you've recovered your health."

Rayan rolled his eyes.

Carrowy sat back and released a miserable breath. "I'm not going anywhere, Captain. I think I've proven that."

"As for your giving up military secrets, I assume you were tortured. Your injury made you vulnerable, and—"

"No, sir. I wasn't tortured. Not as you would think of it, anyway." The private's gaze settled on Emberly, and his eyes shone. "I think you'd better finish me off now, sir. Whatever you plan to do to me, do it. I'm guilty, and I would sooner face whatever end than go on like this."

"Watch what you say," the captain snapped, his voice heavy. "No one speaks that way in front of me. I will never hear that from you again. Understand?"

Carrowy's expression did not change, but he nodded.

"Speak up!" Lieutenant Roark cried.

"Yes. I understand. Captain."

"Doctor," Emberly said, "take him away, and look after him."

The two men left, Staubel with a look of righteous disapproval that made Emberly want to strangle him.

"What about tomorrow, sir?" someone asked into the silence.

"What about it?" Emberly asked, running his hands through his hair. "When this woman returns in the morning, we'll meet her and whoever comes with her. We won't assume hostility on their part."

"Not even after what happened to these two?" Roark asked, nodding at Nor.

"What seems savage to us may be merely prudence, a show of strength on their part, whoever they are. How would our superiors react to an armed force that entered Ronia in disguise?"

"They didn't," Iwan said. "They didn't even know about them. And look what happened."

The captain realized that a day or two had passed since he had thought directly about the bombings on Ronia that had nearly destroyed their company. *How is that possible? Have our experiences since been so all-consuming?*

"They knew," the bishop rumbled, breaking his uncommon silence. "The Unheard had declared war on the Temple, but still the army tolerated its existence—until it was too late. Your superiors lacked both heart and stomach, and many died for it."

Emberly interrupted before the conversation went down the road of Ronian politics. "Regardless of blame," he said, "Iwan has seen my point exactly. Our situation here hasn't come to blows yet, and given our numbers, we'd damned sure better see that it doesn't. There's an opportunity here: Brother Nor's new friends may help us find what we've lost."

"Or what has lost us," Iwan said.

"And what does that mean, Lieutenant?" Arumin asked. The sound of his voice froze them all.

Iwan, who paid little heed to social cues, was unfazed. "I mean that if the Lady meant to ever return to us, she would have done it by now."

"Where would she be, other than watching over us?" the bishop asked a little more loudly.

Iwan interlaced his fingers. "Perhaps she's taken the caretaker and gone. She may have decided our company is unsuited to her purposes after all and found someone else. If that's true, we'll have to accept it at some point."

Arumin rumbled, "We'll do nothing of the kind. Let us all mark Lieutenant Iwan's words and listen for more of the same. He may be the first to fall victim to our true enemy: the loss of faith. If we are damned, it won't be by the Lady but by ourselves."

Iwan frowned at him. "You can't really think I'm the first to say these things."

Though Emberly braced himself for Arumin's eruption, the bishop merely looked at each of them and said, "We have not been abandoned, and anyone who thinks we have must leave that notion behind. We have witnessed miracles, and now, we are being tested." He settled back and looked at Emberly, who realized that his participation was expected.

"Indeed, we have, and we are." He had expected Arumin to say more but could think of nothing else himself.

Iwan, undeterred, moved to another subject. "I suppose our unknown hosts know of the convicts as well."

"I don't see how they couldn't," the captain said, "but we'll say nothing about the convicts yet. Until we know more about this woman and her associates, we must tell them nothing that they don't yet know. Also, this house is being watched. If any of us tries to slip out and warn the convicts, we may end up giving them away.

"Which reminds me—Carrowy. Someone must talk to him, alone. He may be more open when speaking to only one person. We must find out everything he told Ren."

"I'll do that," Nor said. "I'll speak with him early tomorrow." Still standing, he moved toward the door.

Emberly raised a hand. "Stay a moment first."

He issued a few last instructions to the others and sent them out so that he could talk to the holy men alone. Rayan remained, of course.

When the door closed, Nor hesitated before saying, "I shouldn't have followed that woman."

"No, certainly not," Emberly said. "Not without talking to someone."

"Merin saw me go."

"Someone other than Merin," Emberly said quickly. "But this is the bishop's affair, not mine. I will say that I'm glad you went. If you hadn't interrupted, who knows what Carrowy might have told them."

"I don't blame him, Emberly. He's not in his right mind."

"We're all aware of Carrowy's problems. The moment I let such things excuse wrongdoing, this company will begin to unravel. Out here, far from home, that simply cannot happen."

"I should've handled it differently," Nor said. "But I don't know how. Agreeing to meet tomorrow seemed like the only way to save Carrowy."

Emberly looked at Arumin. He had expected the bishop to pronounce some judgment of his own, but he was stone-faced and quiet.

The captain said, "You did the right thing, monk."

"I couldn't let them take him," Nor replied. "Whatever they were going to do, he didn't deserve it."

"Carrowy may yet be punished. But he's one of us. Come to me tomorrow, and let me know what he tells you."

Nor waited for the bishop to add something, anything. But the old man ignored him until he left.

Emberly sighed. "I take it your opinion of Brother Nor has not improved, Bishop."

Arumin had sunk into his chair. He would have seemed relaxed if not for the look in his eyes. "He's the least of my worries, Captain, or yours. I'd adopt Nor as a son if, in exchange, I could learn who our opponents are."

His civil tone took Emberly aback. The bishop and the captain had hardly spoken since Caidfell, when tensions and a mutual lack of trust had led to a shouting match. Emberly doubted the bishop had forgiven or forgotten. He must want something.

Emberly said, "Whatever we must know to find the caretaker is all I wish to know. But I think we'll learn, whether we want to or not."

"I fear you're right. What do you make of it all, Emberly?"

The captain's surprise deepened. The bishop had rarely sought his opinions so directly, despite having striven to enlist Emberly for this journey.

Emberly replied, "Probably nothing you haven't guessed. Our encounter with that patrol in the street was timed rather well to be a coincidence. Someone may have been testing us, watching to see how we reacted."

Arumin sat up. "Yes, that's it. By the Goddess, Captain, you couldn't have said it better: a test. But there's something else—the part that frightens me more than all the rest. I'm surprised you didn't mention it in the meeting."

Emberly frowned. "Go on."

"How far do you suppose we've come? Since we left Ronia, the gateways we've passed through—how far do you think we've traveled in cosmic terms?"

"Caidfell was the edge of any map, except for that bit of speculation you had drawn up. And the stars are very different there. Now, who knows? I doubt even Private Merin could tell us—if he could even see the sky in this city."

"The answer to my question is, a long damned way. Farther than any Ronian has ever gone."

"Lost expeditions aside, perhaps."

Arumin snorted and shook his head. "Listen. What are the chances, as far as we have come, and through an undiscovered gateway at that, that we would meet someone who speaks our language? Even some of Ronia's colonies barely speak the imperial."

Emberly crossed his arms over his stomach, which had tightened. He wondered at himself. He and all his officers were in one place, yet no one had seen it. Maybe they were all half asleep. Or maybe they hadn't wanted to see it.

"We may be closer than we thought," he managed to say. "This world could be nearer to Ronia than Caidfell is. Perhaps one of those gateways in the desert leads to a Ronian colony."

"Look at this place." Arumin waved at the window. "If we were close enough to Ronia that our language had preceded us, we would have heard of this city. No, Emberly, I think we are far indeed from our home. And yet, that woman spoke to Brother Nor with no trouble."

"How could it be?" Emberly's stomach was turning. "Could she be Ronian? Could she have followed us somehow?"

"I can't imagine how—and arrived here before us, no less."

Emberly shook his head. Pieces were falling into place, though he almost wished they wouldn't.

Arumin leaned toward him. "I thought a man of your status would have at least one other guess."

Silence followed.

After a moment, the bishop continued, "If that doesn't alarm you, this might. I think our unseen enemy has taken Shada. We must assume they know everything she knows."

Emberly clenched his jaw. "I still hope they may not be our enemy. And I won't make them one until I must." Though Arumin opened his mouth, the captain spoke first. "If you're right, though… if she's been tortured… I won't forgive them, Arumin. She is in my care. I don't suppose your Lady will help her."

"'My' Lady?" the bishop exclaimed. "She is yours, too, Captain, and she is our true leader whether you find that convenient or not. If we have to, we'll stay here and search for her until we grow old and perish."

"Easy for you to say," Emberly snapped. "You'll go first."

The bishop rocked with laughter. The captain, surprised, permitted himself a smile.

Arumin stood to leave, groaning as he did. Caidfell had punished him as it had everyone. He steadied himself, and his mirth vanished as he looked down at his feet. "That woman spoke our language, and she wanted us to know it. She knew who we are and where we are from. And what's more, she was not afraid in the slightest."

The captain rubbed his cheeks. Puzzle pieces kept shifting. "What are you suggesting?"

"You truly don't know?"

The bishop was turned partly away. Emberly stared at his dim profile and said nothing.

"Never mind," Arumin said. "If you have no idea, then I'm probably wrong, and I'm glad of it. As for your plan, I think it's right to meet with them."

He walked to the door. "Shall I send your men in, Captain? They'll be wanting their beds back."

"Not yet," Emberly said. He needed to talk to Rayan.

If his answer sounded strange, Arumin did not say so.

7

EMBERLY

WHEN ALL THE REST had left, Rayan stood and said, "Astonishing." His voice emerged clearly from his broken face. "You both know who the enemy is, but you won't say it, even to each other."

Emberly had his suspicions, of course. First, the attempted abduction of the Lady in Ronia. Then the bombing in Victory Park and the battle afterward. Then Shada had been attacked on Caidfell. Now, the woman in the tomb. Pieces, falling into place.

If Arumin shared Emberly's suspicions, as he'd hinted, that only made them more probable. *But...*

"I don't know for sure. Neither does the bishop." Emberly spoke quietly, aware that men might be just outside. His brother, of course, could scream from the rooftops, and no one but Emberly would hear a thing.

The remainder of Rayan's mouth smiled. He'd thought of something that would get under Emberly's skin. The captain remembered well what the rest of that grin would look like, and his cheeks burned with old fury.

Rayan said it: "Why do you fear the bishop?"

Even though he'd known it was coming, Emberly still got angry. He forced himself to answer calmly. "He has power over men's souls. There is nothing greater."

Rayan wagged a finger. "But you have power over their bodies, and there is nothing more urgent. He fears you, too, and he is right to. What about that other man, the pitiful thing who tried to run—why did you let him defy you?"

"I didn't let him do anything."

"Of course you did. You were even easier on him than on that insubordinate sergeant, Orund."

"I've heard your feelings on Orund, and I've made my choice. As for Carrowy, he humiliated himself, and I made him feel it. But his health is frail. Any harder punishment will have to wait."

Rayan laughed. "In other words, you'll do nothing."

"What should I do? Have him flogged? We've got a long way to travel yet." Emberly would be within his rights to have Carrowy whipped, even killed. But such a thing could not be undone. Killing one of his soldiers could poison the entire company against him. Moreover, Emberly did not want to be that sort of leader.

"It seems we do," Rayan replied, "which makes your meekness worse. Unless you stamp out these little mutinies, you'll have a big one on your hands."

Emberly glared. His brother's terrible wound was becoming easier to look at. "I never thought you would remind me of my old drill sergeant. What did you do on Caidfell when your criminal friends defied you? Nothing violent, or so you claim. Huire knows what subtle torments you came up with."

Rayan moved closer. "My means are not yours, Cyril, and thank the Goddess. Look what happened to me. Peace cannot be achieved through peace. I've accepted that much, brother, and I learned it from you. On Caidfell, you asked me to stay with you. Why?"

Emberly shook his head miserably. "I don't know."

"Don't lie. Not to me." Rayan squatted to the captain's eye level. "You need me to guide you. I'm here to show you the way! Your half measures will ruin everything. 'I made him feel it.'" He repeated the captain's words mockingly. "Your gifts aren't in oration! You're a predator. Don't forget—you set me free."

Emberly shivered, thinking of the night he had unlocked Rayan's cell. And of the bloodbath that had followed. "I don't want to talk about that."

"Why not? It showed me the man you can be. Do you want to save Ronia? See your wife again?"

At the mention of Charlotte, Emberly shut his eyes. "You know the answer."

"Then be that man." Rayan paused. Air hissed through lips that could no longer close. "Tell me one thing, brother. Tell me the name of our enemy. The soldiers in the street, the woman in the tomb. Say their name. I want to hear it from you."

"I don't know for sure. Every officer in Ronia's army has heard the rumors, of course. Clearly, Arumin has too. But we shouldn't assume it's them."

Rayan shook his head. "You stand no chance against them, you know. Not if you won't even say their name."

Emberly's jaw tightened. "Our enemy is—maybe—the Shining Realm." Rayan was right, he realized instantly. He had been scared to say it. Saying it made it real.

Rayan nodded. "It's a start, but only a start. If any of you are going to survive this, we've got work to do."

8

SHADA

THE LAMP IN SHADA's room had been lit for maybe an hour when she heard the Lady's voice again.

The day had begun like the last few. The lamp, a glass bauble fixed in the ceiling, burned yellow and steady, with no visible flame. When it flared to life, a silver tray slid through a slot in the door. On the tray was the usual array of delicate bowls and plates with steaming food, unfamiliar but good.

She ate gingerly. Her throat was still raw from the smoke she'd breathed on Caidfell, and her skin was tender here and there from the stings of that world's plant life.

She sat on the floor while eating, spurning the table with its lace cloth. She followed that bit of rebellion with another, shoving her hand through the slot as far as she could and feeling the air outside the room.

Her hosts had shut her in here days before. *Has it been three?* She needed to keep track. At first, she had shoved her arm through that slot almost to the shoulder, scraping the skin off her arm trying to find something, anything that might free her. It was hopeless but better than despair.

The speed with which she had begun to cooperate alarmed her. She ate the meals they gave her, which were the best she had eaten in her life. When she got tired, she slept in the room's four-poster bed. She flipped through the books on the little shelf, histories and novels from Ronia, some of which she recognized from her old friend Mathias's bookshop.

But she told them almost nothing about herself. She held onto that bit of power, at least.

However, maybe even that was an illusion. The Lady had given her little choice.

Ever since Shada met her captors, a troop of blue-uniformed soldiers who had approached her in the desert, the Lady had been strangely quiet. Shortly before that meeting, Shada's continued questioning and defiance of the Lady had brought tensions between them to a head. The Lady had forced her immaterial body into Shada's mouth and nested a part of her body in Shada's throat, where she could suffocate Shada at will. As Shada would later realize, the Lady's body also formed a greasy film that coated the inside of Shada's mouth and covered her face all the way to her ears, where she could whisper and threaten Shada to her heart's content.

Brought to her knees, strangled almost to death, Shada had no choice but to submit to the Lady's will on pain of death. She expected to hear the Lady's voice every waking moment, commanding and intimidating.

Instead, the Lady hid from the approaching soldiers. She became uncharacteristically quiet, almost reticent, breaking her silence only to forbid Shada from telling the men where she had come from.

The blue-garbed soldiers, meanwhile, had been flawlessly warm and courteous. Their officer had welcomed her with great cheer to the Shining Realm. Still dazed and terrified from almost choking to death, she did little but nod and grunt until it became clear he meant to take her back with him to the great tower on the horizon.

She began to refuse—she had to get back to her company—but a sharp pain jabbed her throat, and she started choking again.

The Lady whispered, "Say nothing of the company or Ronia. Go with him."

The officer had just summoned a pair of men to accompany her. They were black-clad soldiers with yellow eyes and a silent way of moving. When the Lady choked her, the officer saw her freeze and touch her chest and assumed the two men had frightened her. He sent them away and, after a moment's thought, invited Shada to have lunch with him.

He had been right about the soldiers frightening her. She had seen men who looked like them before—in the market in Ronia, when they had saved the company from an attack by terrorists. These couldn't possibly be the same men. *Could they?*

Afraid to refuse the officer's invitation, she coughed and nodded. The men produced a blanket and basket, and she sat with that officer under an umbrella in the middle of the damned desert and shared his sandwiches and tea.

Still almost mute from fear, heart still pounding, Shada listened as the officer regaled her with her good fortune at meeting them and his own delight at meeting her. She'd rarely known men to act that way unless they were courting her, but he made no advances. In the course of his chatter, she realized he still meant to take her back to the tower, which he called "Om." She wondered what would happen if she refused outright, but she was too scared to try. Upon finding her voice, she asked his name, but he had gone right on chatting without revealing it.

When the moment she dreaded arrived—he asked again what world she came from—she could think of no better response than "I'm afraid to say."

Smile unblemished, the officer put down his tea and leaned forward a little. "I understand," he said.

"Good," she murmured ridiculously.

"You're alone in this place, and I am a stranger. Who knows what my intentions are? I would be frightened too." He interlaced his fingers and stretched out a leg. "But I must insist, Shada. For the Shining Realm to embrace a new brother or sister, there is knowledge we must possess."

Trapped, afraid of being strangled again, Shada said, "I can't."

He sighed helpfully. "Shada—"

"No." Being blunt was unwise, but she was so tired.

His smile faltered. "I see." He sipped his tea. "Your choice is your own, of course, and we won't take that from you. But we must take measures to protect ourselves."

He somehow continued the conversation as if the tension she had sensed did not exist. When the time came to leave, she joined him on his riding beast without complaint. She could think of no way to resist without angering the Lady, and she'd had no desire to test these strangers' patience any further.

Then the city. Then this room.

They had placed her in here without a single break in their politeness. At no point had she passed a threshold of hostility that would make her think she was a prisoner. Yet she was. Despite the room's finery—she had worked in mansions that looked shabbier—the door was locked. Food slid under the door a few times a day, and a toilet stood in one corner.

At first, every minute in this room—this cell—had been as long as an age. Shada raged then cried. She even tried to talk to the Lady, but the Lady had silenced her, insisting that their hosts might be listening. Finally, Shada grew numb, and time passed more quickly. Days had passed by now, she was almost certain.

Many times, she wondered how long the Ronian company would wait before coming through the gateway after her. They must have come through already. *Then where are they?*

The truth was they could be anywhere. What she'd seen of Om was vast. She couldn't imagine how they would find her.

The thought of them waiting for her could drive her mad if she dwelled on it. They might decide she had run away. Hell, she had even considered it for a moment after passing through the gateway alone. But she had been unwilling to leave them.

Nor most of all. Despite her idiocy at harboring romantic notions for a monk, he had been kind and sympathetic.

She was humiliated when he rejected her overtures, but he had entirely sensible reasons and was gentle about it. *Does he think I abandoned him and the rest?*

She would probably never know. Even if the Ronian company learned where she was, they lacked the numbers and strength to free her from the forces she'd glimpsed. Some might be brave enough to die trying, but the thought of that made her feel worse.

Small acts of rebellion, like eating on the floor, were all Shada had left—that and the Lady, who had taken up residence in her body and had hardly spoken since their imprisonment. The bitter truth was that she was a prisoner without and within.

She had been given a new gift, however. Her captors, in what could only be an act of mercy, sent a pair of visitors.

When she finished her breakfast that morning, she remembered they were coming again that day. Just when her heart began to rise in her chest, the Lady spoke.

Her voice was a chorus of whispers in Shada's ear, a humming that always lay on the edge of hearing. It grew and formed words: "They will be here soon."

Shada nodded.

The Lady continued, "Remember, tell them nothing."

"I'm sure you'll remind me." Shada said this thoughtlessly, and she felt a quick, painful swelling in her throat.

"Speak softly," the Lady said.

Shada whispered, "I'm alone. And so what if they are listening? Why does it matter?"

"They already suspect you are insane. You've told them almost nothing—"

"That was your choice."

"I have reasons, but this will require delicate handling. They must decide that you're useful as you are. If they don't... I don't know, Shada."

"What does that mean—'as I am'?"

"All I can do is guess. I ventured out once as you slept—"

"You did?" Shada asked, forgetting her frustration in her surprise. "Are you no longer afraid of being seen?"

To keep interrupting was dangerous. A punishment might follow. But instead, the Lady's voice became softer.

"Of course I'm afraid. The universe is a dangerous place for one like me. But I was tired of knowing nothing about our enemies. I heard sounds that alarmed me. I was gone for only a little while, and I rushed back. Shada... they are quite different from others of your kind. I've never met the like. If they want to listen to us, they will find a way to do it. You must believe me, for your own sake."

"Why do you care about me all of a sudden?"

"I've always cared about you!" the Lady shot back. "I did not want things to be as they are between us. It pains me to hurt you. But you failed. You chose not to trust me, regardless of all the wonders that you witnessed. You have done this, not I."

Shada could think of no response that wouldn't cause the Lady to hurt her again.

The Lady continued, "They are not patient, regardless of how they seem. They will move quickly. Whatever happens, remember to say nothing of Ronia."

Shada sighed with exhaustion. "Why not?"

"Because if they learn that Ronia exists—"

There was no warning, no footsteps from outside or voices in the hall. The bolt simply moved, and the door swung open. Startled, Shada scrambled back.

Two small figures stood there, side by side.

When she saw them, Shada smiled and opened her arms. "Girls!" she said.

The little girls squealed and rushed upon her. She wrapped her arms around them as they shouted her name.

When the frenzy of greeting was over, the older one fiddled with the hem of her dress and said, "Father said we could come play with you again."

"I thought he would." Shada smiled. "He must be a very kind man."

The girl nodded.

Shada looked around and saw little in the room to entertain children. "Well, what would you like to do today?"

"We'll hide, and you look for us!" the girl said.

"I think we have enough space for that." Shada looked at the younger of the two and spoke delicately. "Delia, does that sound like fun?"

Delia nodded. Fingers interlocked, she looked at the floor. She was beautiful, perhaps even more than Lani, her sister. The first time the girls had come to play with Shada, their looks startled her. She wondered if the strange dreams that had plagued her on Caidfell were returning.

But she did not awaken, and the girls did not disappear. Like the room itself, with its bed so wide that she could not reach both edges at once, they had seemed entirely true.

They played for a while. Shada grew tired before the girls, but she kept playing for fear that they would leave. Afterward, they sat and talked. Once or twice, Shada felt a pinch in her throat—this occurred whenever she might have said something about her past.

The girls were strangely reticent as well. Whenever she asked them about their parents or family, they would fall silent for a time. Then she would make a joke or some immediate observation, and they would come to life again.

Lani seemed increasingly preoccupied.

Shada finally asked her, "What's on your mind, dear?"

A cloud of shyness descended on the girl. She touched Shada's hand and said, "Father wants you to come to supper."

9

—·—

NOR

Waist-high, golden grass. The endless plain. Above all, the baking sun.

These images filled Nor's mind as he trudged back to his bed. He would never have imagined he could sleep after the night he'd had, but the thick, heavy dreams of the past few nights were waiting, and they would not be denied.

Something else was waiting too. He had glimpsed a man in his dreams, a man whose tall body shone from a thousand bright facets like shattered glass. Remarkable as he was, Nor mostly only thought of him when he was falling asleep.

In what remained of that night, Nor dreamed he was a boy again.

He was watching and hiding in a grove of boulders. The rocks were half buried in the ground, smooth except for where they had broken and splintered over the ages.

From his hiding place, the ground sloped softly down to a river running past the midsummer encampment. His family and clan had pitched their tents a respectful distance from the water, the animals penned on the far side. In the empty space between the river and their momentary homes, nearly everyone he had ever known stood watching. Before them, Nor's father extended his hands, and a much older man, the oldest among them, gave him a small wooden box.

Nor's father was bare chested, as was most everyone on their side of the river. His hair was long and black, giving way to gray. The others all bowed to him. He placed one foot and then the other into the river. The box rested on his open palms.

Across the stream, the invading chieftain of Ronia did the same. Empty-handed, he was white of hair and entirely covered in decorative fabric, and he wore a sword at his waist. He stepped cautiously, unsure of his footing on the stream's rocky bottom.

Nor had never seen as many people as stood on the far side of the river. It was an army out of dreams. He was confused that only a few were mounted—and stunned that they all dressed almost identically.

"You look unhappy, my friend," someone said nearby. It was a young Ronian man. He had come through a crevice that formed one of several entrances to the stand of rocks. His hair was cut short, like many of the strangers', and the fabric of his clothing was even finer up close, but he walked differently. His shoulders were not slung back with pride like those of other Ronian warriors.

Nor understood his words without much difficulty. The language belonged to a clan that was distant kin to Nor's, though they were enemies as often as they were friends. The man spoke it well, and Nor wondered how far in the past the Ronians had conquered those relatives.

He did not answer the man's question. The answer was obvious. Below, his father and the strange chieftain waded toward each other.

The young warrior spread his coat on the ground close to Nor and sat on it. He glanced through the split in the rock from which Nor was watching the ceremony.

He carried a pipe, from which came a smell Nor could not place. "Don't tell them I'm up here," he said. He snapped one eye shut and open again—a gesture that Nor found perplexing and alarming. "I couldn't bear to see this up close. I'm as miserable as you look."

"What is your name?" Nor asked warily. Seasons had passed since he had spoken this tongue, but the words came easily enough.

"I'm Hob. A friend, or I hope to be. Sit down." The man gestured to the dirt.

A command from a strange adult would have inspired violent defiance in many of Nor's peers. Nor found a defiance of his own in obeying the warrior. Sitting with his legs crossed, he looked the man up and down with the boldness of the very young.

"You have no rifle," he said. He had not yet seen a Ronian without one.

Hob made a face like he had tasted spoiled meat. "I never do, when I have a choice. You're lucky your folk don't have such things. There, I've told you about myself. Now tell me, why are you angry?"

Midway across the stream, Nor's father met the Ronian chieftain. He removed the top of the box, which was full of gray dust. Ashes, some of which had been in the box since time began. Someday, a bit of Nor's father would be in that box, and a bit of Nor's eldest brother. His father raised his face to the sky and spoke. His long hair trailed in a wind that carried his words downstream to the land where waters gathered.

When he finished, Nor's father handed the open box to the newcomer. The Ronian looked at him. Then he looked over Nor's clan, crowded on the bank. He dipped his aged head and spat. A spot of shapeless white foam fell from his mouth into the box.

Nor clenched his teeth. He looked at the stranger, who had become absorbed in the scene despite himself.

"We should be building the fires," Nor said. "We always do at this time of year."

"I've heard of them," Hob replied.

"Each family builds a huge fire," Nor continued. "So big that even the dead can see them from the sky."

Hob exhaled as he watched the ceremony. He spoke, smoke pouring from his mouth like an upward-facing waterfall. "That sight must comfort them in their eternal wars. It must be beautiful."

Nor had never thought of it as beautiful.

Hob shook his head. "Who could blame you for preferring that to this?" He pointed toward the river. "Honestly, I wish you could go and take me with you. All this pomp. I'd rather be anywhere than here."

When he blew smoke, Nor caught the scent again. It made him think of spices, but it contained more than that.

Hob eyed him and said, "Your people have pipes of your own, do you not? You might be smoking one now if you were at these fires."

"Yes."

In the river, the Ronian gave the box back to Nor's father, who knelt to receive it.

"What is your name, little brother?" Hob asked.

"Norhim."

"That's good. Do you know what I think?"

"No." Nor did not understand the question.

"I think you and I are already better friends than any of them." He waved a disdainful hand at the ceremony. "Your clan has surrendered, but there are many others. The fighting will go on for a long time yet. Who knows if anyone believes a word of what they're saying down there? I would take what you and I have over that any day." He reached into his pocket. "I want to give you something, Norhim. You can use it when you build your fire." He produced a small, round bag closed with string and handed it to Nor, who stared at it, nonplussed. "That's something from my home," Hob told him. "It's finer even than this." He tapped the bowl of his pipe with a grin. "It's a gift for you to share with whomever you like, someone else who misses those fires."

Nor's father rose and returned to the bank. The chieftain of Ronia whirled to face his own people, who let out a great cheer.

Nor shoved the little bag at Hob. "I don't like pipes."

Hob did not take it back. "Then don't use them." He looked into Nor's eyes, and his smile was gone. "Never let anyone tell you what to do. Even if they force you, be sure your spirit remains free." He closed his mouth around the lip of the pipe then opened it and puffed. The smell was enchanting.

"I have to go before they miss me," he said. "Please keep my gift. Even if you don't want it, perhaps you know someone who will."

Nor held the little bag to his nose as he listened to the Ronians cheer. "I will give it away. There isn't enough to share."

Hob stood and extended his hand. Nor took it and felt its calloused strength. He gave it a shake as he had seen Ronians do. The motion was awkward but satisfying.

Hob laughed warmly. "Don't worry. If you run out, I can find more. Take care of yourself, Norhim." He slung his coat over his shoulder. Peering out at the scene by the river, he slipped away from the rocks.

Someone else left too. Nor felt a presence depart the scene and glimpsed a tall figure that shone like glass. Then he awoke.

10

EMBERLY

THE RONIANS LINED UP in the narrow street at the appointed time. They heard it approaching in the distance, whatever it was. A deep rumble contained a glimmer of the power of artillery.

The sounds of tramping boots were smothered by the rumble until they were very close. Then they appeared around a corner: blue uniforms with rifles, a few abreast. Within their ranks lurked a low, hulking shape, and from there the deep noise emanated.

When the men parted to let the thing through, the captain's legs became rubbery and ticklish. It rolled forward of its own accord, humming with noise and fury. It had wheels like a wagon, but they were thick and stout. Its body was smooth and black, and in its hollow bed were seats and two men. Behind it was another one of similar design.

Emberly looked at Nor, the only one in his company who might understand such a thing's inner workings. The monk's order had a mandate to delve where others were forbidden.

He wondered what Nor was thinking. Earlier that morning, the monk had cornered him and demanded to speak privately. Busy and irritated, Emberly cleared the room.

Nor looked down and bit his lip, clearly unsure how to begin. "Emberly, these people..."

"Well?" The captain glanced at the door to the hall where his officers waited. He had no time for Nor's dramatics. Wherever the monk's need to be difficult came from, he would have to set it aside for all their sakes.

Nor shook his head and spat it out: "I want to remind you that Huire is on our side."

Surprised, Emberly frowned and nodded. "Yes. Thank you, I know."

"I'm serious," Nor said. "It's easy to forget, so far from home, that we're going to win. But we are."

The words hissed against Emberly's annoyance like drops of water on a hot stove. Of course Huire was with them. He could hardly have forgotten. Yet upon hearing Nor's message, he felt a little cooler.

He nodded again. "Thank you, Brother Nor."

Still avoiding Emberly's eyes, Nor had turned and left. Maybe the monk felt embarrassed by his own behavior the previous night. Or maybe his dislike for Emberly made him dislike such intimate conversations between them. If the latter was true, Emberly could sympathize.

He wondered if Nor's confidence still held as they all watched the animate coach, which moved of its own accord, roll toward them.

The coach halted, and a man sprang out of the rear seat. He wore a dark, stately vest and coat and a wide hat. Approaching Emberly with a light step, he removed the hat.

"Captain!" He seized Emberly's hand with a laugh and gave it a single brisk shake. He was wiry and had a face of glowing youth, though the corners of his eyes were creased, and his hair had mostly lost its color.

"Yes. Captain Cyril Emberly. And your name, sir?"

"You may call me Ganet. I'm a general or the next closest thing." The man replaced his hat and gave Emberly a smile that crackled with energy. He spoke the Ronian vulgate with the arching notes of one who had spoken the high imperial first. "I am delighted to meet you, Captain. You cannot know how much."

Emberly could not overlook the fact that Ganet's name was also Ronian. "Whom do you serve?"

"'What,' not 'whom.' I have no king. I serve the Shining Realm, which is to say I serve us all."

"How is it that we speak the same language?"

Ganet laughed again, a causeless sound. "There is no easy answer to that. Come along in my coach, and I will try to explain."

Emberly looked doubtfully at the machine, which continued to growl. "Where will we go? My company must remain together."

The general's smile flickered. "We have arranged lodgings for you and your men. You will prefer them to these." He linked his hands behind his back and stood straight, shorter than the captain. "You'll have to excuse me, Captain Emberly. In my excitement to meet you, I've forgotten how many questions you must have. Let this suffice for now: you need fear nothing. Not now or ever again. We are all a family. Ah, here they are."

A deeper rumble had struck the walls of the alleyway. A line of larger coaches appeared at the corner. They would hold many more passengers than Ganet's coach. The blue-clad soldiers pressed against the building fronts to give the things room to pass.

"Shall we go?" Ganet asked.

Emberly looked at his men and met Roark's eyes. "Give me a moment," he told the general.

He conferred briefly with the officers and the bishop. As he expected, Roark strongly disliked the idea of the captain accompanying their new friends alone. Emberly cut off his protests. Their conversation was not private.

Then he told Roark to accompany him in the general's coach. The arrangement comforted both men, though the presence of one additional soldier, even Roark, would offer little security. The mechanical beasts dominating the street had convinced Emberly that armed conflict with Ganet might well be a hopeless affair.

He met Nor's eyes as he stepped toward the coach. The monk gave him a nod—still confident, then. Though he carefully projected the same, Emberly wished he actually felt it.

Entering the coach was unnerving. It trembled underneath him, alive with tension. He sat in the back seat, and the general sat next to him. The thing moved, and Emberly clenched his fists helplessly.

Ganet had invited Roark to take the seat next to the driver. There, the lieutenant sat ill at ease, one ear constantly turned toward the back seat.

"Now that we are alone, I must apologize for something," Ganet began. "You received a visit last night from a woman who called herself Ren. She is truly exceptional, but one cannot act on one's own that way."

"Indeed," Emberly replied as the carriage rounded a corner and thundered toward one of the larger streets. Ganet's disapproval of Ren tempted him to breathe a little more easily. "She threatened a pair of my men, one of them quite severely. She wanted to take him away, and I heard nothing of it until afterward."

"So I have heard. I can only be thankful you are giving our friendship another chance."

Emberly looked at the general. "Well... need I still worry about her?"

"Oh, I think not. She represents only one of the two hands of our people. I represent the other."

The captain stared at Ganet's profile until the other man shifted to face him. Then Emberly said, "Norhim—one of our holy men—seems to think she means him harm."

The general shook his head and deflected Emberly's concern with a wave. "He is correct, I think. But, in the end, Ren and I want the same thing."

The carriage rolled into the street, slowly but remorselessly forcing other traffic to make room. Joining the flow, it moved a little faster than the rest, and a way opened before it. The captain looked back at the alley from which they had come and saw that none of the other vehicles had yet pushed into the street.

"Shouldn't we stay with the others?" he asked the general.

"There is no need for that," Ganet said. He smiled, lips shut tight. "My men know the way."

"But mine do not," Emberly said. "Please, stop the vehicle for a moment."

Roark turned his head to look at them.

The general shifted a little, red-faced, smile unbroken. "Why do they need to know the way? You are with friends now, Captain."

Emberly straightened. "I insist."

He hoped his fixed gaze, combined with Roark's forceful presence, would decide the matter in his favor. Still, he was not sure whether to be pleased with Ganet's response. Another flicker passed over the general's face. He laid a hand on the driver's shoulder and spoke a few words in a language unlike any Emberly had yet heard in Om.

Turning back to the captain, Ganet said kindly, "They should join us in a moment."

The other carriages were already entering the street, bringing traffic to a halt, while passing livestock and beasts of burden reacted with predictable anxiety. None of the riders or pedestrians on the road looked twice at the convoy, but beneath the growl of the engines, Emberly thought the street had gotten a little quieter.

When the rest of the convoy reached them, Emberly and Ganet's carriage lurched forward. Though the street was cramped, the captain could see the wide expanse of Om's ceiling far above. "Did your people build this place?"

Ganet's eyes tilted upward. "I must be honest, Captain. We did not."

Emberly thought that a strange thing to be embarrassed by.

The general continued, "We are new here also, though not quite as new as you. There is much we don't understand about Om, and we cannot yet build anything to match it. Our achievements are not measurable in quite the same way."

As Emberly replied, he could see Roark was listening closely. "This place must be ancient, then. Do you rule it?"

The general draped his arm over the back of the seat. His smile was dreamlike. "When you say things like that, you teach me about the differences between us. What is it, to 'rule'? Who is wise enough to rule, alone, over others? A person of the Shining Realm does not think in such terms."

"But you must have leaders."

"Only those we must. Ultimately, we all serve."

"Forgive me, but it's a hard thing to imagine."

"Many others have said the same. How does that strike you, Captain? I mean the way people accept tyrants. It doesn't seem healthy, does it?"

Emberly's eyes were caught and held by a structure that had been hidden behind leaning rooftops. 'Structure' hardly seemed an adequate word—had the thing fallen over, it would have smashed a large part of the city.

Around a central pillar of chilling circumference, a road wound like a corkscrew. Emberly tilted his head up as far as the pain in his back would allow and saw where, far away, the pillar disappeared into the ceiling.

"We are going there?" he asked, feeling like a child.

The general grunted warmly.

The road around the pillar was thick and wide, with no visible support and with ramshackle structures built all up its length. Many of the buildings stood, with breathless gall, on the very precipice of the road. The whole structure, raised above the city's dust and filth, was laced with ornate patterns that matched similar dimly visible decorations on Om's walls and ceiling.

They reached the base of the spiraling road and began their ascent. Huts and booths lined both sides of the street, with enough room between for two wagons to pass each other. Emberly held his breath repeatedly as the realm's carriages whipped without fear around the blind, endless curve.

The general had been twitching and moving his lips. Now, he said, "It's sad, wouldn't you say? The willingness of our species to be ruled." He seemed to find speaking a relief.

"It is sadder to be ruled than to rule, certainly," Emberly replied. "You must be one or the other. History has taught my people that."

"And yet, why must we be prisoners of history?" These words burst from Ganet. "I refuse, simple as that. I believe in man."

Emberly let the silence hang until Ganet's unease became palpable. "An admirable aim. But not a thing one can achieve alone."

"No, indeed." The general sat up, excited. "But an entire people? Perhaps."

"If you succeed, you will be the first."

"But we have succeeded, Captain. We are succeeding, even as we speak. And eons from now, we may look on today as one of our greatest victories."

Emberly looked at him and said nothing. The carriage was approaching Om's ceiling, which stretched away like a flat horizon. The patterns in the ceiling comprised simple shapes that overlapped to form webs of vast complexity.

The lines that formed these shapes were sunken and as wide as roads.

Here and there, the ceiling sank to form hanging towers, like stalactites in a cave. Emberly could discern no pattern to the towers' placement, though he was seeing only a fragment of the whole ceiling.

Through gaps between the buildings, he saw the ground was far below. In the distance were other pillars circled by ascending roads. They supported the structure of Om while providing a way up—*to where?*

He ducked without meaning to as the road met the ceiling. They entered a tunnel that continued the road's spiraling trajectory.

The carriage slowed a little in the relative darkness. They passed shadows that moved and shapes that looked human. Echoes came from invisible recesses in the walls, and now and again, Emberly glimpsed a fire far back somewhere. A glow appeared on the walls and grew with a speed that hurt his eyes. The tunnel's far end appeared like a beacon, and he wondered if he was seeing the sky.

When they emerged from the tunnel, he felt a prickling dread while another part of him relaxed, suspecting he was in a dream.

Here was another chamber much like the first, phenomenally huge. Near the tunnel's opening, the pillar they were ascending continued upward, accompanied by another road.

They were in a crowded promenade surrounded by buildings. This part of the city was so grand that Emberly might have called the level below its outskirts. Here stood solid, ancient walls exceeded by spires and minarets that jostled in the sky for pride and splendor.

"How does it all keep standing? The weight of it..." Emberly said.

The general laughed. "And yet it stands. Someday, we will build things like this. And more."

Emberly tried to remember what Om had looked like from the outside, but the interior had confounded his memory and sense of space. "Is there more above this?"

"At least two more levels. We've not seen the whole thing yet." Ganet smiled. "Being newcomers."

"I wonder who lives at the top."

"It's an understandable question," the general replied, "but there are better ones. I will have to teach you some."

Despite the situation's magnitude, Emberly felt a petty irritation. "I'll try another, then. What will happen when we arrive? My men need rest and healing."

"We assumed as much. As soon as we spotted you coming out of the desert, we began to prepare. Here we are."

He was looking at a high stone wall on their right. Its blocks were large, each as tall as Emberly's knee. Near its center was an arched opening wide enough to drive through. The carriage shouldered its way through traffic and passed under the arch.

Filling most of the space enclosed by the wall was a pyramid, as wide at its base as a city block. Its sides were smooth and pale red like the desert. Little windows perforated its stone surface.

Its pinnacle was glass of some sort. Diamond bright but clear, it directed focused daggers of light that seared the air this way and that. Four slanted away at the angles of the pyramid's slopes. The last was pointed straight up, spreading a little to cast a multifaceted gleam on the ceiling, so far off it might have been the sky.

"You and your people will be comfortable here," Ganet told him. "Some of our soldiers are quartered inside as well."

The carriage stopped before a wide opening at the pyramid's base. "Your lieutenant here can organize things in your stead, I trust," the general said. "You and I have urgent business to discuss."

Roark turned around, mouth open to speak. Then he thought better of it and looked at Emberly, waiting.

"If you are tired, Captain, we can wait until this afternoon," Ganet said. "You have come a long way."

Emberly couldn't bear such talk. "No. I need answers."

11

ARUMIN

THE INSIDE OF THE pyramid was riddled with halls and chambers that made the structure seem less solid than it had looked from outside. Arumin marched into it like a commander inspecting his fortress before a siege.

He stood straight, doing his best to hide the pain of his aching bones and wounded chest. That seemed to work—the Ronian company followed him without hesitation. Since his heroics in battle on Caidfell, the men had held him in new esteem. They almost seemed to have forgotten the acts of military cowardice for which Arumin was publicly known.

The time was coming when he might learn just how willing they were to follow him.

He had been dismayed to learn the company would share the space with soldiers of the Shining Realm. Since learning his suspicions of these strangers' identity were correct, his imagination had blazed to life, filling every shadow with treachery and every cloak with hidden daggers.

The name of the Shining Realm had floated about the upper echelons of Ronian society for some time. He had failed to find out where the whispers had come from or who had started them, but when a gateway on the planet Dervil, on one of the empire's far borders, had been suddenly blocked from the other side without warning or explanation, the whispers had intensified.

Surely, Emberly was not as ignorant of them as he had acted the night before. More likely, he had feigned being a simpleton to avoid sharing what he knew with Arumin. The bishop tried to thaw their icy relationship to learn more, but the captain kept silent.

Then, moments before, Emberly had left with Ganet, with no notice. The captain's tendency to act without consulting the bishop was a continuing problem, as was his persistent questioning of the Lady's authority. Arumin had recruited him for the crusade in the hope that the captain's fame would add to the project's credibility, but he had assumed the captain would be more malleable to his aims. He had given Emberly charge of the company in military matters, but the captain had mistaken this for absolute command. Worse, Emberly had refused to correct or even recognize his mistake. He was thinking wrongly and was keeping secrets.

Arumin might need to remove him from command. He had begun preparations for that, just in case.

His boots scraped dust as he passed through the pyramid's halls at the head of the company. The Shining Realm's soldiers had done little to make the place homey. Here and there, odd stretches of fabric hung over doorways as curtains, the building having no doors to offer privacy. Candles and lanterns lit the hallways carelessly, many resting on the floor and against walls. The lanterns gave off a steady yellow light that was perhaps meant to be comforting.

Following the cloaked figure of one of Ganet's people, the Ronians came to a high oblong room, a sort of great hall, with several wooden tables. There, more of the Realm's soldiers were gathered, some sitting alone but most around a single table near the middle, where they shouted and laughed. Their language was high and quick like a song played on a fiddle, their words seeming to leap around in the air.

Most of them did not notice the Ronians' presence until Arumin, Brin, and their guide were already in the room, with Emberly's soldiers close behind. When the outsiders became known, a profound quiet fell on the chamber.

Arumin hoped to pass through the great hall before the two groups of soldiers had a chance to exchange words or glares. The thought of being housed under the same roof as this unknown rabble, and with no doors to boot, was alarming. The less contact the Ronians had with them, the smaller the chance for spying or foul play by the enemy.

Their guide stopped just before the Realm's soldiers. She pulled away her hood, exposing blond, almost colorless hair. Even at his extreme angle, Arumin was struck by her features. Her beauty exceeded even that of the braided, clean-shaven soldiers she faced.

She said a few words, and they rose. Their eyes shone with wanting, even adoration, as they looked at her—not the feelings of a lover but those of a puppy. Then they looked away from her, one by one and with painful deliberateness, to stare at the Ronians. The bishop found that one man out of the crowd was looking straight into his eyes. The man's expression was so vulnerable that Arumin caught himself trying to look away.

The moment passed, and the men's gazes withdrew. They returned to their seats and to their conversation, which was now low and private. The bishop looked back at the Ronians. Those close enough to have been captured by the gaze of one of their hosts were shifting uncomfortably, seeming relieved the experience was over. Only Brin's eyes were steady and straight ahead.

Arumin turned, not trying to hide the action, and saw the guide was the one who had captured Brin's attention. Her smile was faint almost to nonexistence, but it changed her entire appearance. Playful, it might have been called.

"This way, sirs," she said and led the Ronians to the end of the room and into a quiet hallway.

Arumin's jaw ached, and he realized he was clenching his teeth. His relations with Brin were worse than those with Emberly. The young priest looked to Arumin as his protector—as well he should because the bishop had protected him since finding him on Caidfell as a child—but occasionally, Brin encountered the fact that Arumin's first duty was to Huire. When that happened, arguments and quiet nights followed.

On Caidfell, the bishop had made that choice definitive. He had left Brin during the battle to take up arms for Huire. The young man was safe in a shelter, and the fight had restored Arumin's closeness with Huire, whose absence he had felt like a bottomless black pit. But all Brin knew, all he would let himself know, was that the bishop had abandoned him. It didn't matter that Arumin loved him, loved his warm presence and his touch, almost as much as he loved Huire. It didn't matter how hard the question had been. What mattered was the answer.

They had hardly spoken since. That was becoming a pattern in Arumin's life.

And now, Brin was flirting with some little tart. Maybe it was to hurt Arumin. Maybe he was actually drawn to her. Arumin wasn't sure which would be worse.

In a few paces, they came to a series of doorways lining both sides of the corridor.

Their guide stopped at the first, which was lit by a small flameless lantern—a wonder in itself—and said, "The largest will be yours, Bishop, for your convenience."

Her suggestion of a smile burst into full being, and though Arumin had no interest in her, he felt that he swayed back a little at the force of it. He was sure he would soon dislike her tremendously, fairly or not.

"Thank you," he muttered and gave her a stillborn smile in return.

These people were not their allies, no matter what Emberly wanted, and the bishop would greet their attempts to befriend him with the same contempt the Goddess Huire showed for all lies.

No sooner had he stepped into the room and dropped his baggage than he found himself alone. The young woman was chattering just outside. Brin's voice answered.

Arumin looked around the room for traps or tricks, but of course nothing was there to see, and he felt foolish and infuriated. He had forgotten to arrange a time for the men to reassemble. Damn that fool Emberly for leaving so suddenly.

One voice now dominated all others in the hallway. It was Roark, one of Emberly's lieutenants, whom the captain had left in charge of the troops. For the first time, Arumin recognized the lieutenant's barking with relief. Roark would whip the men into some kind of order.

Arumin had unpacked his bedroll and arranged it to his satisfaction when Brin returned, flanked by the girl.

"Your Eminence," the man said with a little bow. His eyes were cold, as they always were lately. "Ilis has invited us to accompany her to one of the temples of the Shining Realm."

That jostled Arumin out of less productive thoughts. "A temple?" He looked between the two young faces and settled on Ilis. "I was told your people knew no gods."

Her smile returned. "A temple indeed, Bishop, though not the kind you're used to. You will find no gods there, and you may find you don't miss them." She spoke with such unabashed warmth that a lesser man might have excused her boldness, if he noticed it at all.

"How kind," Arumin said. "I'm afraid we have much to attend to here. Tomorrow, perhaps."

Seeing the consternation on Brin's face, the bishop found a pleasure of which he was not proud.

"What must you attend to, your Eminence?" The lightness of her voice made it sound like the most natural question in the world.

Praying a time might come when he could tell her to mind her own damned business, Arumin said, "We have many wounded men here. I am recovering from some injuries myself. We must have some rest, at least."

He had not hidden his irritation well enough. "Pardon me," the girl said, her light dimming a little. "I only asked so I might see to your needs. You're our guests, and though there is healing to be done, you need not do it alone. My people will be along soon, and you may be surprised at what they can do in a short time." She looked cheered by the thought.

Arumin blinked at her. "I have no doubt."

"But for you, your Eminence, and Father Brin, I think greater healing will be found with me. You might call it restoration."

"A temple, you say." He squinted.

"And she is one of its priestesses, your Eminence," Brin added, bouncing a little on his heels. He had probably hoped to be gone already.

"I must be clear with you, miss. The men of Ronia will worship no god but our own."

"No worship will be asked of you, Bishop."

"Then it seems this visit can wait."

Her smile broadened, her excitement swelling. "Oh. Bishop, if you could only see—"

"I'm tired." Though within the bounds of civil conversation, the words were a bludgeon whose echo hung in the air.

Ilis's mouth widened, her laugh politely but poorly concealed. Brin snorted. He ducked his head, hand over his mouth.

Arumin's eyes darted between them as they shared their private amusement. He wondered if Brin had been telling her about him—about what a funny old man he was.

The bishop's growing rage and humiliation met an opposing force, one that was old and sad. The two wrestled in his chest until he said, "But since you assure me your purpose is urgent, we'll come with you. Please, don't keep us any longer than you must."

"Oh, thank you, your Eminence!" she cried sweetly. "But we are still missing someone. The man who rode with us, Norhim."

The surprise on Brin's face matched the bishop's. "That's impossible, I'm afraid," Arumin told her. He'd hoped to leave Brother Nor out of every important event and decision from that point on. The young monk had stopped him from publicly forcing Captain Emberly to confess whatever dark secrets he was keeping. Hell, Arumin had originally refused to let the young monk join the crusade at all. Only sharp pressure from Abbott Cadmon, Nor's master and Arumin's old enemy, had convinced him to do so.

"I must differ, your Eminence," Ilis said brightly. "Converting you has restored my faith in myself. Norhim shall not resist me. I'll reckon I can undo whatever knots are keeping him tied here."

"Brother Nor is not fit to accompany us. We have learned that he cannot be trusted." Even as he spoke, the bishop cursed himself for revealing their internal divisions. He must truly be tired.

Ilis was not disturbed in the least. "It sounds like he needs this more than any of us. And he really must come, you know. He is important."

"Important?" Arumin's face twisted.

She had to realize how insolent she seemed. She might have been simply clumsy, but he doubted it.

"How, and to whom?" he demanded.

"To all of us!" Ilis replied.

The bishop waited for more, but she seemed finished. He became aware of something he had already unknowingly decided—he could not tolerate Nor's presence much longer. The monk would never be anyone's servant but his own, and even that loyalty was wavering by the moment. Nor might have to share the captain's fate.

"If Nor is invited, Bishop, we ought to bring him," Brin said, his respectful facade crumbling as quickly as it had appeared. "We must please our new friends if we hope to convert them to our faith."

The corners of Ilis's mouth twitched. Her smile broadened just a little. The boy was joking, of course, and doing it for her sake. But for an instant that Arumin was too embarrassed to reflect on, he had thought Brin was serious. Arumin's anger took on a cooled, blackened quality. The wound in his chest howled, and his bones creaked.

"Let's find Brother Nor, then," he told them.

Ilis nodded. "If he resists, I will show him the error of his ways," she said, her face and voice jolly.

When she turned to leave the room, Brin raised a hand hurriedly. "Allow me. I will speak to Nor." He spat the words one atop the other, as if dismayed by something. Recovering quickly, he told her, "Nor and I understand each other. I can be helpful in that way."

By sheer will, Arumin smiled. The enemy was closing in.

12

— · —

CARROWY

PRIVATE CARROWY COULD NOT imagine how his pain was getting worse. He had moved beyond dread to simple disbelief. When the tree on Caidfell had stabbed him, he had not thought that feeling could ever be equaled, yet now, hours after his disastrous escape attempt, he rather missed its brevity and simplicity.

He'd joined the crusade in another escape attempt—an attempt to escape from need, a need like nothing he had ever known. As long as he stayed in Ronia, he would never be free of nightshade. He had even managed to find it during the company's time on the hellish world that was Gallobraith. He had been left with what seemed the only remaining option—to run away from Ronia and keep going until he found a place so far away that no one there had ever heard of nightshade. When Emberly asked for volunteers for a crusade across the universe—and a chance to have his sins forgiven in the bargain—it had seemed like a sign from Huire.

That seemed like a joke now, especially after last night, when Carrowy met Ren. That woman had told him things he couldn't bear thinking about. Things from the present and, most of all, from the future. Things she would do to him. Hearing them, he had cried like a child, and thinking of them now, he felt like crying again.

Doctor Staubel leaned over him. The private observed him as if from the bottom of a pit. The doctor's presence had meant little in the last few days. Staubel was a child, younger than Carrowy even, and as he failed to slow the spread of death in Carrowy's body, Carrowy's attention had fixed upon his age.

"It's not helping, man," the private said. His words were clear to himself, but others found him increasingly difficult to understand.

Undisturbed, Staubel continued to work. "It's helping, Private, though I know it doesn't feel like it. You're better off with new bandages than without."

"Can't you just let me die? If this is it, why wait?" Carrowy wasn't sure that he meant this, but it felt good to say.

"For one thing, you have a job to do, like the rest of us. I don't intend to let you off if I can help it."

"For Goddess's sake," snapped Private Tabard, sitting up on his bedroll. He had lost a thumb on Caidfell and was cradling the bandaged hand in his lap. He and Carrowy occupied a corner of one of the rooms that housed the company's wounded.

Staubel did not acknowledge him. "Our hosts seem well supplied. With a force as large as they have here, they must have doctors."

"Can *they* help?" Tabard asked.

"Medicine is what we need," Staubel said. "And I'm going to find it."

Carrowy was tired of listening. "Fine."

The curtain over the doorway shifted, and Brother Nor entered. After him came Father Brin. Their arguing voices had been audible in the hall.

Nor nodded to them all. "Gentlemen."

"Can I help you, Brother Norhim?" the doctor asked.

"I've come to pray with Private Carrowy. Tabard, too, if he's willing."

"I've told you everything, Brother," Carrowy said. His voice sounded harsh, and he was glad of it. "I have no more sins to confess."

Nor frowned and shook his head, white eyes impenetrable as always. "I'm here to pray, Private, not to hear your confession. I owe you a prayer after missing last night." He looked at Carrowy then Tabard.

Tabard returned his gaze. "You seem regretful, Brother Nor," he growled. "I wish you wouldn't. You owe me nothing unless it brings back my hand."

Staubel interrupted. "Well, I'll leave you to it." He made for the exit without waiting for a reply.

Father Brin took him by the arm. "Good news, Doctor. The Shining Realm is sending healers to aid you. You need not go scouring the city for supplies."

Staubel's mouth twitched into a smile that his eyes did not match. He left without a word.

"That ought to comfort you as well, Nor," Brin said, wrapping an arm around Nor's shoulders. "It means your obligations here are fulfilled." His tone was familiar, almost conspiratory, as if he and Nor were alone.

Nor replied, "I can't. We can learn about your new friends' schemes later. There is work to be done now, here."

Brin seemed pained by the word *schemes*. He glanced at the curtained doorway. Carrowy wondered if someone was standing there, out of sight. If it was Ren, he might not be able to contain his panic.

Brin said, "They are indeed friends, or hopefully will be soon. They've certainly welcomed us kindly."

Nor answered loudly, maybe addressing that same someone outside. "If you'd been with me last night—"

"Be sensible!" Brin cut him off, eyes wide. He took a breath before continuing. "We're strangers to them too."

"I doubt even that."

"There's only one way to find out. They could force us to go, but they're not. Let's take advantage of that."

Nor glanced at the soldiers. "I'm staying here."

"What good can you do for them?" Brin cried, pointing at Carrowy. "They know the prayers as well as you do. Does it matter if you are here or there?"

Nor shook Brin's arm loose from his shoulders. "Go."

Brin took a step back, looking genuinely alarmed. He leaned in as though to whisper, but when his voice came, it was scarcely softer than before. "You can't keep pushing him like this. Please, Nor."

The monk turned to face him. He spoke quietly, though in that close chamber, no secrets could be kept. "Should I be worried, then?"

"He's not your enemy unless you make him one. But that's what you're doing."

"Nothing Arumin can do will scare me."

"Don't be so sure. I've known him for a very long time."

"And whose side are you on? If it comes to that?"

Brin spread his hands and giggled in exasperation. "Why must there be sides? Do you like living this way?" He took Nor by the shoulders, and the monk did not shake him off. "Come with me right now. I will help you with him."

Brother Nor stepped back, out of Father Brin's grasp, and shook his head.

Talking to Staubel and Nor had pulled Carrowy partly out of his lonely pit of agony, but he began sinking again. He roused himself to speak. "You should go, Brother Nor."

The men jumped. His voice must have been louder than he thought.

Nor hesitated for a long moment. Maybe he was more curious about the Shining Realm than he'd let on. "Are you sure, Private?" he finally asked. "I would not leave if you need company."

"Company isn't what I need," Carrowy answered, which was both true and false.

Nor looked at Tabard, who said, "I couldn't care less."

The monk glanced once more at Carrowy, frowning as if trying to see past the private's pain-wracked eyes. "They won't keep me long," he said loudly, speaking again to whoever waited outside. "I'll visit you as soon as I return."

He gave Carrowy a nod that the private lacked the wherewithal to return, and he followed Father Brin from the room.

Carrowy took a deep breath that was audible as a gurgle.

He heard Tabard laugh and turned his head sharply, ready to curse the other man for mocking him, but Tabard was shaking his head and paying Carrowy no attention at all.

"What is it?" Carrowy spat. Anger was welling inside him, with Tabard the only available target.

Startled out of his thoughts, Tabard looked at him, and a grin twisted his face. "It's not you, friend. It's all of this."

Carrowy relaxed his neck. His head lolled back, and he wound up looking at the ceiling. He heard Tabard shifting and gasped to find the man looming over him.

"It makes you think," Tabard said, his voice soft and whimsical. "Doesn't it? What future can a man have? You do what they tell you, and when you get hurt, they're finished with you."

Carrowy wished he could sleep.

"You've given me an idea, friend," Tabard went on. "When these healers come, I'll see what they can do for me. After that, maybe I'll see what I can do on my own."

"Run away?" Carrowy asked, louder than he'd meant to.

Tabard glared and pushed a finger to his lips.

"You're mad," Carrowy told him. He had been mad to try it himself. The need for that one thing had possessed him, and he had set out to find something to fill the hole it left. Emberly had every right to kill him. Maybe part of him had hoped to be caught for just that reason.

He regretted his escape attempt. Yet since then, he worried he might become mad enough to try again. He did not need this bastard's encouragement.

Perhaps he hadn't lied to Nor after all. He wanted the monk's company, sure. Anything to relieve the monotony and Tabard's gloom. But he could do without it. He needed a real bloody doctor, certainly, if he hoped to live. But in his darker moments, these all paled next to that one thing—a thing worth risking all the rest.

13

NOR

A MOTORCAR AWAITED THEM outside the pyramid, but no driver waited with it. Nor was surprised to see Ilis get into the driver's seat herself. As fantastic and dreadful as the machines were, driving them seemed a task reserved for people of lower rank than her.

Far above them and away, where the distant walls of Om stood in place of the sky, he saw oblong stretches of light taller than any building. They were windows, rectangular at the bottom but topped with a graceful point. He guessed that it was afternoon in the world outside the walls. But even in full daylight, twilight reigned in Om's interior.

The ride was brief but full of turns. Walls and buildings rose high on either side, making it hard for the passengers to guess the distance or direction they traveled. Their route seemed so indecisive that Nor grew frustrated, becoming certain that a simpler way ought to exist. He was reminded of when, as a novice in the order, he had been instructed on manuscripts by clerics who knew little more than him.

Maybe he should have listened harder. Some who seemed ignorant weren't, and some who thought they knew a lot had a lot to learn.

He was a fine example. Brought into Huire's Temple and raised as a veritable son by Abbot Cadmon, he had repaid the old man with rebellion, misbehavior, and endless questioning. Whenever he encountered a question with no easy answer, he had assumed he had found yet another crack in the Temple's façade of wisdom.

Then he threw away everything by maiming a Ronian soldier in a brawl. But instead of throwing him to the wolves that were Ronia's civil authorities, Cadmon had bought him a chance to escape justice: a place in the ranks of the crusade. The journey would take him away from Ronia, delaying his trial so that he could focus on the other half of the grace Cadmon offered, the envelope in his pocket.

It contained the answer to a question. Nor needed to decide on his own answer before opening it. If he opened it and found his answer was correct, he would instantly ascend to a position as an elder of his and Cadmon's order. There, if he ever returned to Ronia, he would be permanently out of reach of the law. If he answered wrongly, the law would be waiting, caring nothing for the forgiveness of sins the crusade offered.

It was at this point that the young monk who thought he knew better had met his match: a question with no apparent answer. The question he must answer was "What are the gods made of?"

Nothing Nor had said, done, or thought since leaving home gave him any clue what the answer might be. There were flippant responses, of course, but those were useless. The answer to the quandary—which is what such questions were called—should feel right. At least, that was what he had heard from other monks. No answer he had considered felt anywhere close.

Cadmon's faith in him, not to mention his excessive faith in himself, seemed to have been misplaced. Not only had he failed to find an answer, but he didn't even know how to proceed toward finding one.

The envelope waited in his pocket, always feeling a little heavier than it should. It had been battered, soaked with water, and nearly lost, but it had always come back to him. Through the Lady's actions, he had seen Huire's grace demonstrated in such marvelous ways that he could no longer doubt she would preserve the words inside, undamaged, until he was ready.

Still wondering at how long the ride to the temple was taking, he leaned forward from the back seat and asked, "Have we lost our way, madam?"

Ilis had been chatting amicably in the direction of Arumin, who sat beside her, mostly silent. Over the noise of the wind and the engine, Nor had understood little of their talk.

The woman turned her head a little and smiled as she called in reply, "You may call me Ilis, if you please, Brother Nor. I'm too childish for anything more."

"Ilis, then." The name emerged from Nor's lips reluctantly. Usually, he thought formal titles were a nuisance, but their absence here felt like a violation—of whom, he was not sure.

"We must stick to certain routes," Ilis continued. "The city is nearly lawless, and we don't know our way around yet. We'll be a long time untying this knot."

They came to a broad, quiet avenue full of closed doors. Ahead, it ended at a wall pierced by a tall set of wooden doors shaped like the windows Nor had seen in the sky.

Nor knew instantly that they were approaching their destination. His chest tightened, and he forced himself to sit still. In an effort to stay calm, he tried to put names to his feelings. He was afraid and happy but also felt more than that. His mind and his chest contained a *bigness*, and if it kept growing, he would burst.

Whatever waited, he knew one thing: he must keep faith. That was what the Lady's miracles had showed him. And just when he had begun to forget, along came his dream from last night—his dream of the day his people surrendered to Ronia.

In a burst of enthusiasm, he had almost told Emberly about the dream, but he decided at the last moment that it would sound ridiculous. His words could not hope to mimic its power, and a man like Emberly—a man who placed his faith in guns and swords, who was proud of the empire his city had built with those weapons—would be too arrogant and worldly to understand.

So when Nor confronted Emberly, he had stumbled and told him to remember that Huire was with them and that they would win. Those things were true, but they were not the most precise truth. What he really should have told Emberly was the thing he had learned watching Ronia, with its Temple, overturn his entire world as a child.

He should have looked into Emberly's eyes and told him, "Huire wins."

He sat up straight as the carriage reached the doors. The doors opened—someone inside was waiting. They rolled into a courtyard. Looking forward, Nor gasped. The swelling feeling became more like terror—a cousin of terror, one he had never met. *Keep faith*, he told himself.

A Ronian temple towered over them, filling the space inside the gated walls. It would have been among the tallest temples even in Ronia itself. Nor surveyed its curved structure, which looked like the prow of a ship placed on its end. It seemed to lean forward, ready to topple and crush them.

"What is this?" he asked, too softly for anyone to hear. Arumin said something at the same time that Nor did not catch. The car swooped around to stop at the temple's doors. Ilis fiddled with the controls, and the noise and shaking of the engine died away.

She stretched her arms toward the building, presenting it like a gift. "Do you like it?"

She opened her door and sprang out of the car. Nor and Brin followed, the former cautiously, not quite trusting his eyes. For a moment, Bishop Arumin stayed where he was. He stared at the temple then looked down at his knees.

"I hope so," Ilis continued, speaking mostly to the bishop. "Getting it ready has kept us quite busy."

Arumin turned his face toward the building. His mouth was set and firm, but his eyes were wide with a look of pleading. He pushed open the car's door and placed a hand on the edge of his seat. Holding the fabric in a white grip, he boosted himself out of the carriage.

Ilis was there, offering an arm. Nor had never met anyone who thought the bishop needed that sort of help. Arumin took it nonetheless, and they set off toward the grand doors.

Sitting next to the doors was a man so small he might have been mistaken for a decoration. He was wiry and elderly, and his eyes were covered by a blindfold. As the visitors approached, he lifted a basket toward them. "Your weapons, sirs," he said in an accent like Ilis's.

A few seconds passed as everyone waited for the bishop to answer. But Arumin's mind was elsewhere, and finally Nor answered for him. "None of us is armed."

"No, of course not," the man said with a curious smile. "A strong man like yourself."

The beggars who guarded the entrances to Ronia's temples, though frequently blind, often possessed a striking awareness of visitors' manners and appearances. Still, Nor had seldom received a compliment from one of them. And he had never seen a beggar of such vitality. The man's skin was smooth and almost free of blemishes. His thinness spoke of health rather than malnourishment.

The man lowered his bowl. "Enter, my friends." He looked at Nor. "I have only one request. Please, bless me."

Nor wondered where the man had come from and whether he really wanted the holy men's blessing. Hesitantly, the monk raised a hand just over the man's scalp and said, "Great Mother—"

"Touch me, if you would, sir, and kneel with me. I'm afraid it won't work otherwise."

Arumin and Brin were already moving on toward the temple doors. Nor knelt in front of the man, trying not to appear rushed. He placed his hand atop the man's head and finished the prayer, a common plea for wellness and charity.

Then he stood again and found the others standing at the small, human-sized doors set into the mighty doors intended for the Great Mother. No one had yet touched the handles to enter. The bishop, in front, was staring at the doors and seemed lost in thought. Wishing to be away from the guardian, Nor took it upon himself to open one of the doors and hold it for his companions.

Arumin proceeded after prompting from Ilis. He glanced back at the guardian, looking fearful, and disappeared inside. Ilis followed Brin and thanked Nor as she passed.

The temple's interior lacked the hazy familiarity Nor had expected. It was well lit by torches, and the carven figures represented a wilder, more expansive vision of creation than those in a typical Ronian temple. Some of the groping shapes closest to the door represented creatures normally too small to see without the microscopes possessed and guarded by his order. Some were round and studded with protrusions, while others were twisted and had legs or whip-thin appendages. Over Brin's head leaned something like a fattened coil of living rope.

Ahead, the walls burst with more lifeforms, splendid and grotesque. Close to where the carvings converged behind the altar, Nor saw humans in all their varieties. In the midst of these, directly beyond the altar, was the flat, empty space where the Goddess belonged and would someday stand. This blank spot was wider and shorter than it was in most temples, and it bore a faint set of vertical ridges.

Setting aside such imperfections, which must be unavoidable in a temple built by nonbelievers, Nor still felt uneasy in the place. It was new. The expansive prayer rug before the altar was entirely intact and unworn. He smelled freshly cut timber.

He could stand it no longer. He turned on Ilis and said, "You knew we were coming. You know *us*."

"Of course," she replied, her innocence unbreakable and intolerable.

"How? And why would you build this for us? You don't believe in any of this."

He followed her gaze to Arumin, who had walked onto the rug. Each step was careful, as if he expected the floor to give way.

Ilis watched the bishop for a moment longer before answering. When she looked at Nor again, her smile had fallen and her eyes with it. "We built it because we like you. We think your people—the Ronians—are extraordinary. I am honored to be among the first in all the Realm to meet you."

"Why?" Nor asked again. His voice was angry, and the sound was grim and satisfying. "What makes us special, exactly? Why would anyone say that? Ronia behaves as people with power always behave." His teeth closed on his tongue, and he stifled a yelp of pain.

She watched him until he continued, calmer.

"So, your people are in Ronia. How long have you been spying on us?" he asked.

There was a thud and a grunt from the front of the temple. Arumin, sinking to his knees to pray, had fallen on them instead. Brin looked at Ilis, wide-eyed, and ran to the bishop. Ilis started to follow, but Nor took her by the arm. His grip was just hard enough to stop her in her tracks.

"Don't worry about him," he told her. "Answer."

For the first time, her eyes showed an unguarded feeling: alarm. "Spying?" she said with a stammer.

"What other explanation could there be, for this?" he replied. "Since you won't be honest with us, we must speculate as best we can."

Her chest swelled as she inhaled. A few seconds passed before she breathed again. The fright in her face was the second true thing she had shown him. These glimpses of genuine life made her acting more unbearable.

She looked around. Brin, unable to relieve the bishop's pain, had resorted to simply and silently placing a hand on his shoulder. The old man had crossed his arms over his chest and bowed his forehead to the ground. He mumbled a prayer.

"This is my fault," Ilis said. "I was so excited to meet you all that I haven't told you everything you need to know. Brother Nor, you should not accuse someone of lying unless you're prepared to defend that claim with all you have." She looked at him pointedly. "And you should search your own soul first."

"I didn't say that you lied. But you've told us as little as you can. Is that what your people call friendship?"

Ilis raised her hands toward their surroundings. "We've gone to great effort to show our good faith."

"But you haven't really told us anything."

"We will give you entire worlds," she replied, a harsh power creeping into her voice. "In return, you must give us trust. There are things I'm not permitted to say, things that must be left for others greater than me. But I have not lied, and I will not."

Brin had returned to them. "Ilis, I don't understand," he said, his tone plaintive. "I thought the Shining Realm didn't believe in the gods."

Her smile was back. It was hard not to be swayed a little by it. "Where did you get that idea, Father Brin? Of course we know the gods are real. We are that wise, at least. Where we differ from you is in our relations with them."

With visible effort, Brin tore his gaze from her face. He looked at the bishop, who had pulled himself to his feet and was shuffling toward the altar. "And that's okay with you, then? That we are different?"

"Look around," she said. "We made this place for you. We've been expecting you. We hope you will come around to our way of thinking someday, but until you do, this place is yours. Here, you can visit your home." She folded her hands.

Brin swallowed and replied, "You see, this matters a great deal. The bishop is very worried. He fears that you, the Shining Realm, aim to ultimately end his beliefs—ours."

Arumin stood before the altar, looking at the empty space on the wall. He was standing entirely, unnaturally still.

Brin continued, "He's wrong, isn't he? I hope so."

"He will not be forced to change," she said. "He will choose to."

"Yes, but suppose he never chooses to? Or I don't, or Nor doesn't? Will they force him to stop praying?"

"No." This answer, absent her usual elaboration, sounded different—truer, maybe—than her other replies.

Brin let out a breath. "That's good. Thank you."

She dipped her head. "We believe in you Ronians, you see. Your Goddess left long ago, and you have made your way in the world without her. We hope that you will eventually come to appreciate how special you are."

Arumin gasped. He had made his way around the altar to stand directly in front of the empty patch of wall and had placed a hand against it. Now, he stepped back.

"There can't—" he said and let out a cry that reverberated from the ceiling. Rounding the altar, he crossed the prayer rug with the force, if not the speed, of a warhorse.

"Bishop?" Ilis asked uncertainly, seeing that he was coming toward her.

He stopped just short of a collision. "What have you done?" he demanded, mouth twisted in a snarl.

Brin stepped partway between the two, facing Arumin. Words rushed from his mouth. "Bishop, what's the matter? I'm sure we can—"

"Hold your tongue, you bloody child." Arumin's eyes dug into Ilis, whose countenance was unbroken. "No gods, eh? How gullible I was."

Ilis's delicate face was impenetrable. "I do not understand," she said.

He whirled to the altar and stabbed with his finger at the empty space behind it. "What is that?"

Her eyebrows perked. "That is the place reserved for Huire."

"And what holds that place until she comes?"

She blinked. "What?"

"What is in that space right now?"

"Nothing—I don't know."

"Of course you don't!" He circled behind her. "You've never really looked. You came to our city, peeked into our temples, and thought you grasped all our simple minds contained."

He put a hand on her shoulder and pointed toward the wall. "Tell me this: what do you see there?"

"Nothing."

"Nonsense! You're still not looking. You see those ridges?"

"I think so," she said, squinting.

"You see the shape of the space? Round, broad at the top and narrower farther down, with lumps at the bottom.

Then there are those vertical ridges in the lower half. What does that look like?"

Brin's face had changed. He still looked fearful, but his present fear might have been that his master had cracked. Nor was flummoxed as well at first. Then, all at once, he saw what Arumin saw. His pulse quickened.

Ilis shook her head. "I don't know. Perhaps the artist made a mistake. Why must the surface be completely flat?"

Arumin leaned close to her. "Because, dear, that surface is a void. Not a mere empty space, not even a vacuum. It is the total absence of being. When the Goddess left us, you see, there was nothing to take her place. Our very existence, the nature of reality itself, was lessened. You can't fill such a void at all, and certainly not with that." He pointed again at the ridges.

She set her jaw. "You tell me, then. What is it that you see?"

"A hand, girl, a human hand! The tips of its fingers begin at the bottom, with the palm above it."

"I see it, I think. It's very faint."

"Certainly. You couldn't make your intentions obvious. By the time we saw it, we would have been worshipping the wrong God—yours."

She sank into open exasperation. "I don't know what you're talking about! We have no gods. That hand means nothing to me."

"Then what is it doing here, in our temple?"

"I don't know about these things." She shrugged helplessly. "Others have studied them. I know what I've been told."

Arumin laughed, the cackle of a scavenger. "Well, either you're lying, my dear, or you're being lied to. In either case, there's no point in continuing this conversation. I'll be waiting in the carriage." He strode toward the doors.

"Now, hold on, Arumin," Brin said, following close behind.

The bishop turned and shoved the priest back with one hand. "I won't ask you to come, Father Brin. No doubt you and your friend have words to exchange."

Brin watched him go then faced Ilis again. "Is it true, what he said? About a hand?"

"I'm sorry. I just don't know," she replied. "I'm learning too."

The priest glanced back and forth, looking torn. "I have to go to him. He'll tear our arrangement apart unless I convince him otherwise."

"Brin," she said, "you can help more by staying here. Listen to what we have to say, then take it to him. Stay with me, just for a little while."

He sighed and shook his head. "It's about more than that. He needs me. I'll be outside." He left.

As the door shut, Ilis gave Nor a faltering smile. "And you, Brother Nor? Will you be waiting outside?"

Nor's face had hardened like dried mortar. He should leave. He had wounded men to get back to. Shada was out there somewhere. The Lady was still missing. And after the previous night, only a fool would trust these people.

But he was a fool. He always had been. Yet Huire had decided to use him in this quest. She had brought him to this building for a reason. He had this woman alone—maybe this was a chance to confront the mysteries facing the company.

"No. I'll stay," he answered. "But only because I have questions for you, Ilis. If I stay, will you answer them?"

"As best I can," she said, staring at the door. "So far, my role has been more difficult than I expected."

"Can you blame them for being upset? They never expected to see a temple again, and now this. Maybe you don't realize what a statement that hand on the wall is, but someone must have. That means someone here is not to be trusted."

She spoke suddenly, as though not wanting to hear any more. "There's a person I'd like you to meet," she said. "This isn't how it was supposed to happen, but we must do as we must."

A little bell rang in Nor's mind. A voice he might have called common sense cried out once more. But maybe the Lady had chosen him because he rarely listened to common wisdom. She had needed a fool—a fool willing to lean on faith.

"Let's get on with it, then," Nor said.

He followed her to a corridor that led through the back wall. In most temples, the area behind the sanctuary included a small office and little else—larger gatherings occurred in the sanctuary itself or in the subterranean levels. This temple was different. They came into a hallway that stretched some distance ahead, where it turned and apparently continued. Doors lined either side, all identical.

Ilis stopped at one of the doors. With her hand on the knob, she said, "I'm sorry I couldn't help more. Here, you'll find what you need."

She opened the door and invited him in with a gesture. From where he stood, he could see only the nearest wall inside. He wondered if this was a test. Ilis might want to know how far he trusted her. Or maybe Huire did. In either case, he had already followed this far. This was one more door, one more like any other.

He passed through. There, in a room that was otherwise empty, sat the mousy woman he had met the previous night. She was sitting in a chair, and an identical chair faced her.

"Good afternoon, Brother Norhim," she said briskly. "Please sit down."

The door closed behind him, and he knew without looking that Ilis was no longer there. Despite himself, his heart thumped.

He resisted the urge to obey the woman. "Ren, isn't it?"

"Yes. I suppose you will need to know that after all." She bunched her faint eyebrows at the delay. "Sit."

He glanced at the bare walls. "You've been waiting in this room for us?"

"For you, mostly," she said in weary admission. "You are here sooner than I expected, which is just as well. We had better get started."

"Started with what?" he snapped.

His heart was pounding so hard that he could hear it. The idea of sitting in the room with that woman scared him. It scared him more than death, and he didn't know why. Not knowing made him angry.

"With our work together," she said. "You lied to me, sir. Your man Carrowy told me the truth, and you contradicted his word. You deceived me and placed him in terrible danger. Now, that danger is yours. I demand satisfaction."

Nor's knees tickled. "Satisfaction? You threatened us. I owe you nothing."

She listened and shook her head. "I feel for you, Norhim. If you could only hear yourself. It is the mewling of a beast."

Nor considered sprinting from the room. His body almost did it without him. But running would accomplish nothing. She knew where to find him.

And the answers to his company's questions, and his own, were here. Increasingly, he was sure of it. The questions of how to find those who were missing, of how to confront the Shining Realm without violence—maybe even of the one in the envelope in his pocket. He thought of all his failures, his excessive faith in himself. The time had come to put his faith in Huire.

"I have many questions," he said, "about you and your people. If I stay and cooperate with—whatever this is—will you answer them for me?"

She began speaking almost before he finished. "Absolutely not." She shook her head dismissively. Though impatient, her voice entirely lacked hostility. "Do not mistake your situation, sir. If you return to your companions, it will not be soon. If you see them again, they will not know you. But your life will be worth living. You will have grown—grown into a human being."

14

ORUND

THE LOFTY GREAT HALL where the men of Ronia gathered was already occupied. The soldiers of the Shining Realm were still there, gathered mostly around one of the long tables. As the bored and aimless Ronians filtered in, they hung together, collecting at another table near the door where they had entered. There they brooded and watched the Realmsmen, who paid them little mind beyond an occasional glance and snicker.

Sergeant Orund couldn't help gawking and wondering at the strangers. Though they were all younger than him and born of a frightening, alien society, they were fighting men, and their lives could not be very different from his.

Yet he could not imagine sitting among them. Their long, sleek hair, clean chins, and mustaches reminded him of the advanced disrepair of his own grooming. Their uniforms were blue-and-gold finery, while the Ronians wore only anonymous traveling clothes. Looking at the strangers, Orund felt he had misplaced something long ago.

The Realmsmen crowded around a cask on their table. The loudest and most red-faced among them had appointed himself bartender and was pouring draughts. As the celebration gathered force, their jolting shouts and shrill laughter became more irritating.

Orund's men glowered. Private Hulgar ran his fingers through his beard and clenched his teeth. Almost no words had passed between the two tribes, whose native tongues bore no resemblance, but Orund feared that wouldn't last.

Emberly was still gone, as were his lieutenants. Iwan's disappearance was no surprise as the man was prone to wandering off. But it was out of character for Roark, who would typically have loomed nearby, dispensing curses. Orund would normally have relished the absence of officers, but at that tense moment, he was left feeling vulnerable. His men were exhausted, and some were in outright agony.

In Orund's mind, the men were *his*. He was old enough to have fathered many of this lot, and given their troubled lives—a happy man with a clean conscience didn't volunteer for a journey like this—he could hardly have done a worse job than their real parents. Sergeant Orund had no other family.

The men were wounded, inside and out. Gallobraith had left them as shadows of themselves. Caidfell had been almost worse. Being their surrogate father meant protecting them—from enemies who wished them harm, from officers who wished only for career advancement. Most of all, from traitors in their midst.

Brother Nor had never really been one of their company—that much was true. But he was among them, praying with them, pretending to care, all while hoping they would forget about the Ronian soldier he'd made half blind. He was from Bodhan, and he made no secret of bearing an unending grudge against Ronia. And Emberly and Arumin had made him a crusader, giving him power over these men's souls, and they had given him a chance to have his own sins washed away. As if he had never put a broken bottle in a soldier's eye.

Orund wouldn't forget even if all the rest did, even if the Goddess herself did. That was what family was. He had tried to move against Nor on Caidfell, during the confessing ceremony, but that little shit of a priest, Brin, had found an ounce of courage for once and stood in Orund's way. When Orund, carried away by anger, had pointed out that everyone knew what Brin and the bishop got up to behind closed doors, he had stepped on the wrong toes.

Arumin himself intervened, all holy fury, and Orund had backed off to fight another day. Laughing at the bishop behind his back was fun, but few had the stomach to confront him directly. Orund was not among those few. He wondered if Arumin was still angry with him. If so, he might be living on borrowed time.

A shriek of laughter from the Realmsmen startled him from his thoughts. Nearby, Hulgar had had enough. He put his fists on the table and pushed himself to his feet. Everyone around him was sitting, making him look even more terrifyingly large than usual. He lumbered straight for the Realmsmen, who went still and silent.

Orund did not intervene right away. Roark would have been shouting at Hulgar already, but the sergeant decided enough of that sort of leadership was afoot in the company. *Best to wait and watch.*

The strangers were drinking from small metal cups. Hulgar snatched one straight out of a man's fingers. He held it to his nose, wrinkled his nostrils, and tossed the drink down his throat. The Ronians chuckled then roared when he spewed the liquid from his mouth in a geyser and flung the cup against the wall. The metal vessel clucked as it ricocheted, dented, from the stone.

The Realm's soldiers pressed toward the private, who spread his arms in a gesture of innocence. Another cup sailed from the back of the crowd, aimed at Hulgar. It splattered his face and chest.

Orund hurried to the scene before matters could escalate further. Palms up in mock surrender, he inserted himself between Hulgar and the crowd. Hulgar's smile had first shown amusement, but it now showed gleeful anticipation.

The sergeant held out his hands for a cup. A moment of uncertain silence followed, then the red-faced bartender pulled a cupful from the tap and pushed past his fellows.

Looking at the amber liquid, Orund sniffed it from a safe distance. Grunting in surprise, he placed his nose right over it and inhaled again.

He looked at his men. "It smells like a damned garden." He let a few drops fall on his tongue, and his impression was sustained. Rather than the acrid potion that Hulgar's disgust suggested, the drink tasted like honey and water. It was like no alcohol he'd ever had. He could drink buckets of it and not miss a step.

He drained the cup and shoved it into the bartender's hands. His men allowed themselves a cautious laugh. The strangers' faces were caught between surprise and a much slyer amusement.

Orund waved his fingers for another round. The sudden brightening of his mood gave him a hint of foreboding, but with so many watching, he could not hesitate.

Smirking, the bartender bowed as he handed over the second cup.

Orund lifted the drink and threw back his head. Dizziness descended on him, but he refused to turn back. He finished the sweet liquid and slammed the cup down, rattling the table. He turned to his men and let out a whoop, and they cheered.

The turn was what did him in. His head kept spinning after his body stopped, and he felt the room tipping. One of the strangers, laughing, offered a supporting hand, only to pull it away at the last instant, and Orund collapsed onto a chair that toppled backward.

The Realmsmen laughed themselves almost sick.

Orund's men rose from their seats, unsure how to react. He felt them watching him.

He thrust himself upright with a mighty heave. Swaying like a tree in a storm, he called to the Ronians in a voice distorted by grog, "Hell are you looking at? Come on, if you can do better."

The tension was released in a storm of laughter. The Ronians crowded around Orund, accepting his challenge, and the amused Realmsmen clapped him on the back. Feeling his age, he found a seat and stayed in it.

15

EMBERLY

BEFORE EMBERLY'S FEET WAS a ledge, and beyond that yawned an immensity of thin air. Even from that height, the brittle wasteland outside Om was not featureless. The late-afternoon sun revealed dunes far away in one direction, and the gateways scattered everywhere appeared as arches and slivers of color.

The captain had never been so high off the ground or seen anything at such a great distance. Like much of this world, the vista filled whatever room was left in him for awe.

Their road there had been long, taking them through a set of ascending tunnels within one of Om's mighty walls. The crowds and refuse of the city thinned, and the general lighted a lantern mounted on the front of the car. The tunnel was passable by carriage but was nonetheless low and roughly hewn from the rock. Like the city they had passed through, it seemed to be a later addition to

Om rather than part of its original construction. Here and there, the lantern's light fell upon openings to tunnels filled with spiraling stairs, and Emberly wondered if the tunnel's switchbacks were taking them past the same staircases again and again.

The general stopped at the end of the road, which was a path of smooth red stone with staggering drops on either side. The ledge was as long as several city blocks and broad enough to fit several carriages end to end. It formed the bottom edge of one of the great windows that could be seen from the distant streets of the city. The captain and the general were ants on a windowsill.

He joined Ganet on the sill's opposite edge, which overlooked the city. When they arrived, he was surprised and dismayed to see numerous gateways of various sizes dotting the streets and squares below. He'd had the dreadful thought that, if the next gateway his company must take was somewhere in that sprawling maze, the Lady might be unable to locate it, assuming they ever found her.

A blasphemous notion, surely. The Lady was in direct contact with the Great Mother, was she not? Memory would play no part in it. Though Emberly had long before lost confidence that Huire guarded the physical well-being of her faithful, he still subsisted on the hope that she did. The ruts of his thought were worn deep in the realms of the strictly mortal. All else was in her hands. He did not know how one could function otherwise.

The captain reminded himself of what Nor had said: *"We're going to win."* It felt like a silly platitude, especially in the face of grandeur like this. Rayan would have mocked it mercilessly, which made Emberly want to believe it even more.

The captain wondered where Rayan was. He had kept expecting his brother to appear in the carriage's back seat. Surely, Rayan would have advice to give at such a momentous instant.

Emberly turned back from the edge. A few paces away from the abyss stood what he could only call a throne. The seat was grand, carved from the same rock that lay beneath it. Its size betrayed the simplicity of its design. A small dais raised the sitter a few more unnecessary steps above the rest of humanity.

"Why not higher?" he asked the general. "You say there are other levels to Om even above this one. So why didn't the builders put the throne at the very top?"

"Those were different times."

"Antiquity, you mean?"

"The people of the old world lived in the shadows of gods. You don't imagine they built this place themselves, do you? Higher powers were at work here." He said the last sentence with flippant whimsy.

"If only they were still here."

"One must learn to walk sometime," Ganet said. When Emberly did not answer, he continued, "I suspect the seat is here because the air starts to become cold and thin higher up. The god—or gods—who built this place might have managed despite harsh conditions, but the humans for whom they built it could not. I'll bet the upper levels are not inhabited by anything we would want to meet."

"But the humans still wanted it to be built?"

"Different times. People could have whatever they wished. They had only to say it. They might not have known they could never live in the top of their palace until it was too late."

"They could overcome such things."

"Their gods could. Perhaps the humans lost interest."

Emberly turned his head to look out over the city. "So," he said. "Let's begin."

"At your convenience," the general replied. The wrinkles by his eyes deepened. His face held a warmth and comfort Emberly could not fathom.

The captain began, "Not long ago, a planet just outside the boundaries of the Ronian Empire fell silent. The gateway leading there was blocked off, and we have heard nothing from them since. Your Shining Realm is responsible, yes?"

"Yes."

So this was it, then. This conversation had been bound to happen someday soon. Emberly had never expected to be the one having it, not with the high command's displeasure at his actions on Gallobraith. But here it was, falling to him and his thirty-some battered and hobbled men, far out of reach of their home.

"You are conquerors, then," he said.

Ganet answered, "We help the peoples we meet become better. Stronger, wiser."

"So long as they are obedient."

"Each according to their purpose. And purpose is what we give them. We give far more than we take."

"And Ronia is next."

"Captain..." Ganet began in protest then checked himself. After a moment's thought, he said, "I am to blame here. Life in the Realm has its comforts. I have not lived your life or had to think the way your people must have to survive and advance yourselves." He laughed, a sound like a little cough. "Forgive me. You will come to see that such ideas—conquest and tribute— are antiquated in the Shining Realm's piece of the universe. As the Realm grows, those things recede. It may be hard to believe that, but when you do, it will be a fine feeling."

"But you've been spying on us. You must have, to know our language as you do."

"That is true."

Emberly focused his eyes on a single small building amidst the thousands below. "Did you set off the bombs that exploded when we left Ronia?"

"Dear me, no. That was your native terrorists, the Unheard. We tried to stop it, in fact. We knew of the plot, having befriended a very important woman from their ranks, and thought we had foiled it. When they learned of her betrayal, they grew desperate."

"How can we trust you?"

Ganet smiled, but his eyes were sad. "You can trust us to make choices with great care. Wouldn't your people have done the same? I'm sure your military has been desperate to know who we are."

"Your accent is high imperial. How long have your people been in Ronia?"

"You would be surprised. I spent ten years in the city myself."

Emberly controlled his expression but thought his face might be losing its color. "Ten years," he said softly.

"Many of us have been there—those who have been preparing for this day. No one has stayed as long as me, though. I found reasons to remain and learn. I took a special liking to Ronians as soon as I met them."

The captain's voice was slow and staggered. "All of this is hard to believe. I don't know a better way to say it. I'm not a diplomat."

"I am glad of that. Well, what else can I tell you? When I came to Ronia, I spent the first few years in Undertown. That place let me keep a low profile while I learned your language. Then I worked as a stonemason, and I saw all parts of the city. Tell me, does your family still live on the upper hill?"

"What?"

"Of course I've heard of the Emberly clan. I might have helped build an addition to your house, now that I think of it, and regardless, everyone knows the old families. Now, how about that house? It was glorious."

Emberly felt terribly numb and simple. "We lost it."

The general nodded. "I'm sorry to hear that, but after your brother's treason, I feared it might be the case. Still, I thought that, given your heroics on Caidfell, you might have..." He trailed off. "But we are straying from the point. I was offering you our friendship."

"In return for which we will be your vassals."

"Captain, that is simply not true."

"Let's drop these pretenses. I hope you realize I cannot negotiate on Ronia's behalf."

Ganet leaned back, peering at him from a new angle. "Why not?" he asked.

Emberly said, "I do not have permission," and saw Ganet wrinkle his nose just visibly. "Even if you and I came to some sort of agreement, my city would not consider it binding."

"The Shining Realm will."

"But that is not enough, don't you see?"

"Who ought to decide, then, in your view? Your king?"

Emberly laughed. "I think you know that our emperor lost his power long ago. His line goes on, of no consequence."

"The noble families, then."

"Yes, nowadays. The council of families."

Ganet looked away and smiled, abashed. "You ought to know, if you don't yet, that my people place a great weight on the truth."

Emberly snorted. "Mine place a great weight on honor."

"You have nothing to prove here, Captain. There is no need for violence. I ask you merely to be honest with yourself. Don't answer me if you don't wish to. Ought Ronia to be run by its nobility? Have they earned the right to rule your city?"

"Perhaps you've forgotten that you are speaking to one of them."

"I haven't forgotten. And yet I wonder how true it is. You've got your family's title back, certainly. The nobles invite you to their parties. But will it last, now that you've been down in the mud? What will happen to you when they tire of your war stories?"

"What happens to me is not important. That's not what duty is."

"Of course. Because you are a good soldier." Ganet leaned close. "But it's not just about you, is it? Doesn't that make a difference?"

"My family will have nothing to worry about if I don't come home. Neither will my men's families." He immediately wished he had not mentioned his family.

"And if you do come home?"

The general was still close to the captain's face. Emberly wanted to shove him away but feared that might be an act of war. He heard Nor's voice again: *We're going to win.* He saw the words waving as if on a banner, fading into the distance.

When he spoke, he realized he was grinding his teeth. "You want to be our allies." He took a breath. "What does that involve, exactly? And what if Ronia declines the offer?"

Ganet stood up straight and folded his hands behind his back. "I have told you much, Captain. Before we proceed, I must ask you to return the courtesy. What is your purpose here?"

The captain took another breath to buy time. If the Realm really knew all about the goings on in Ronia, surely Ganet knew about the crusade. Maybe he was testing Emberly's trustworthiness. Or maybe he was bluffing. He might have chosen his words to appear to know more than he did.

Emberly made a huge decision then. "We are on a mission to make contact with Huire, our goddess."

The general did not laugh. He spoke with a kind of awe. "Is that true?"

Emberly felt Ganet's eyes close on him as he answered. "Yes."

Ganet watched him, nodded, and said, "What an undertaking."

Emberly said, "We went through a terrible ordeal before we came to this world. We need time to recover."

"You'll have that time," the general replied without hesitation. "But in return, you will have a decision to make."

"I cannot make it alone. It is not my place to decide."

"Yes, it is. I am giving it to you."

"I do not accept it, General."

"I would rather you called me by my first name: Talis. What is yours?"

"Cyril." Emberly smiled grimly. "Talis... Even your names are Ronian."

"They are now. I and a few others have left our old names behind. We are who we must be. But back to the matter at hand. Cyril, things are in motion that I cannot control—that no one can. We have a moment in which to change things for the better."

"I must have time. Such a choice cannot be made on the spot, regardless of risk."

Ganet peered at him, his face dark and puzzled. "If you must, then you must. Shall we meet tomorrow?"

Emberly almost looked around for Rayan but stopped himself in time. "Agreed."

The general let out a great breath as if freed of a burden. He said, "Thank your goddess for that."

Placing his hand on Emberly's back, he gently led the captain closer to the ledge overlooking the city. "Now that we know each other better," he said, "I will entrust you with one of my more eccentric theories about this place. I suspect Om was not originally the home of men but of one man. A single person."

Lost in thought, Emberly took a moment to reply. "Why would anyone build this for himself?"

"To be alone."

"One is hardly alone here. I've never heard of so many gateways in one place."

"It could not have been that way at first. The first human to arrive on this planet found it an empty strip, a waste-land. Here, he found a god waiting for him, ready to be his wet nurse, who built him the grandest palace he could dream up. And here that man chose to stay. Later, other people arrived. If that first man was still alive by then, he learned there is no escaping other people."

Ganet pointed at the city. "All of that, down there, was made by people. By us. It is not as grand as Om yet, but it is ours. That makes it honest."

16

NOR

IN THE SMALL, BARE room, Nor felt alone even though he decidedly was not.

"I hope this isn't a surprise, Norhim," Ren said, fiddling with a pencil and watching him closely. "You knew the danger of lying, yet you came here alone. Is it so shocking to find me waiting?"

Nor prayed silently, trying to master his fear. He said, "A little. You've lured me here under false pretenses—as you lured me to the tomb last night. These are lies in themselves."

Ren tilted her head. "I think we both know that your deception was quite different. Stalling will only make this process more unpleasant."

She was probably right, at least about the second part. Still, he wanted to test the boundaries of their arrangement.

He asked, "What's to stop me from leaving?"

She scrawled some words on a sheet atop a book on her lap. "Go," she said with a flick of her hand, not looking up.

He stared. "You would let me go back to my people?"

"You can't," she said. "The city is a maze, and it's too large. You'll never find the way back. Knowing this, you won't leave. What need have I to stop you?"

Ilis must have gone, then. Nor paced again, taking a breath to calm himself. "You told me that I might see them again but that I'd be changed."

Ren stopped writing. She rested her forearms on her legs and interlocked her fingers. "I should have specified: you'll only see them if the thing I'm talking to now has any hope of becoming a man. One as learned as yourself may decide whether he has that hope."

Nor stopped in his tracks. "Is that so? You never gave Carrowy that choice."

"Soldiers, along with others of the lower orders, must have these things decided for them. But you, sir, are different. You approach sentience of a higher kind."

"If I leave—if I just walk away into the city—will you come after me again? Your threats sound serious."

"I've made no threats. I've only informed you of your situation." She wiped her forehead wearily. "For now, I'll assume your dishonestly is a trait personal to you. If you leave and I'm unable to study you, I will be forced to consider it representative of your company. I will have to study them as well."

Nor's smile was grim. "And that's not a threat?"

"No. I have no use for threats. Consider this, Brother Nor: you are still here. You are afraid, but you are not running. That gives me hope that there is remorse inside you. Before you entered this room, a part of you wanted to meet me again. You wanted a reckoning. Am I wrong?"

Nor thought about Shada. He wondered whether she had entered Om, whom she had met, and what choices she had made. "Let's say I stay here. There are things I wish to know."

"This is not a trade, Norhim. However, when you are finished, you will be one of us. Whatever knowledge we have, you will have."

His knees shook, and he thanked the Goddess he was wearing a cloak. "What will you do to me?"

"We'll do only a few things *to* you. Most, we will do together. The awakening is an entirely different experience when it's done willingly. The less you know now, the better."

Moments before, Nor had been determined to accept her offer. He didn't know what he was waiting for. Something about her surety, her sense of entitlement, angered him. He wanted to make her work for him. Before he agreed, she would have to give him *something*.

"What will I do once I join the Realm?" he asked. "Will I have a job?"

"Yes. I'm told your religious order studies the technology of the old world."

The fact that Ren knew such things frightened Nor as much as more tangible dangers. Carrowy had confessed to telling her their company's origin and purpose, but he'd said nothing about revealing their personal histories. People of the Shining Realm had visited Ronia—that much was clear. But the depth of their knowledge was increasingly horrific and confounding.

"Yes," he said slowly. "We studied that, among other things."

"*Studied*, you say? Have you left the order?"

It was a curious slip of the tongue. "I'm one of them until I tell you otherwise."

She continued unperturbed. "It happens that my people have urgent need of such knowledge."

"Really? Why? Your machines are far more complex than ours."

She had begun writing again and did not respond.

"Is this why you chose me?" Nor asked. "You're asking me to reveal secrets I've vowed to protect—you're asking me to lie. Also, I suspect, to aid in the destruction of my friends and my city."

She looked up sharply. "Ronia is your city, is it? That surprises me. You have shown little love for it in the past."

"What..." Nor began then realized what she must know about him. His fingernails bit into his palms. "If you are trying to impress me, you might as well stop. It doesn't matter to me what you've found out."

She sat back. "It sounds like you want to tell me something. What is it?"

"It sounds like you already know."

"I know some things. I won't know what you are thinking of unless you tell me."

"You must think you're damned smart." He put his hands on the back of the chair and secretly tried to break it in half, though it could not have cared less. He was determined to find Ren's vulnerability. "You're damned good at sneaking around and lying to people, that's for sure."

She sighed. "I've decided your freeness with that word is another personal quirk. I'll ignore it for now, but we'll have to break you of it. As for what you said, I don't think about myself much. I am not trying to get any confession out of you, Norhim. I'm just surprised at your loyalty to

Ronia, which has been less than kind to your people. Your years in that monastery must have changed you greatly."

"Not really." Nor looked at his knuckles and smiled. "I might as well tell you, since everyone else knows. Not long ago, I brawled with a couple of Ronian soldiers. They broke my arm, but I hurt them, too, one in particular. My arm has mostly healed, but that man's eye…" In his drive to pierce her façade, to get under her skin, the words he spoke tasted good. "I had a bottle, and I made him half blind with it." He gripped the chair so tightly that his arms shook. It moved under him, and he imagined flinging it into the wall or into her. "I ought to do the same to you."

He might as well have threatened a brick wall. Her frown was merely curious.

"Why did you do it?" she asked.

"Not because they were Ronian. Well, not just that. This was on one of Ronia's border worlds. They were drunk and so bloody loud. I saw them first on the street, but I didn't do anything then. Then I saw them again later, and they had a boy with them. They were giving him drinks. A local boy. He wanted to be there, to be their friend, but he was scared too."

Nor's mouth was dry, and he swallowed. "He was trying so hard. Drinking and getting sick. They made him drink more, and he took it, but he couldn't keep it down. Finally, he fell over. He didn't even know where he was. So they started pouring it in his mouth." He looked into Ren's face, trying to set her ablaze with his eyes. "I wanted them to stop."

Something had changed. Her eyes were alight, and she seemed genuinely fascinated. Her papers were forgotten. "I see. You had a reason for telling me this. What is it?"

He spat, "I wanted to scare you." It was the truth, and he was embarrassed, having clearly failed. But she seemed to know every damned thing else. He could not hope to match wits on that front. So he would be truthful, a witness for Huire.

But a smile touched her lips. "You did, a little." She tilted her head. "Are you glad to hear that?"

Part of him recoiled from the question. It was barbed, poisoned. But to refuse would be to trust his own instincts. He was Huire's fool now. "Yes," he admitted.

Her smile grew. "Nor, I think you know that Ronia is not really your home."

"No. But neither is wherever you're from."

"Where I am from, there is a place for everyone. Even you."

The words touched Nor deep in his chest. He gasped in alarm and reminded himself she was the enemy. He would stay, but only because he must.

Her smile vanished, and she stood. Though she was much shorter, she seemed to match his eye level. "I know more about you than you know. I know what you want and what you're afraid of. And I am very sad for you."

He shook his head. "I don't know what's truth and what's a lie." He would need to know if he was going to defeat her.

She took his hand in hers. Her fingers and palm felt cold, bloodless. "Just wait," she said.

Her touch chilled him, but he let it happen. "Why me?"

She squeezed his hand. "Because you're weak."

Every demon and hostile voice inside him boiled up until he nearly burst. His blood rushed in his ears. He managed to tamp it all down, to keep his feet in place and his voice steady. He must stay.

"I accept," he said. *Huire wins.*

She nodded and sat. "Very good." Her voice was once more brisk and abrupt. She took up her papers and started writing. "You've spared yourself and your people tremendous pain. To be sure, much suffering lies ahead, but it will all be for the better. Speaking of which—"

She stopped writing and reached under her cloak. "I am not a liar, but I do have something to confess."

Her hand emerged with an envelope.

Nor managed to say, "What is—" Then he stopped.

The envelope was wrinkled and discolored as though it had been carried across planets. It had been roughly torn open along its top edge.

Nor touched his pocket, disbelieving, and found it empty.

As he stared, blood draining from his body, Ren reached into a hidden pocket and produced a stack of papers. They were tattered and folded in thirds, having been in the envelope since Nor left Ronia.

17

—·—

MERIN

MERIN FOUND HIMSELF IN the broad entrance corridor of the pyramid with no particular direction that he cared to turn. One of the Realmsmen, perhaps not noticing the other Ronians' cold behavior toward Merin, had given him a cup of the yellow honey drink.

He knew better than to stay in that room, where men would soon be drunk and tongues would be loosened. His comrades hadn't forgotten the betrayal he'd committed on Caidfell. His heroics in the battle that followed had briefly overshadowed their resentment, but their memories were long, and their mistrust ran deep. Jokes and pranks had followed, shoulders in the halls and muttered insults, and they showed no sign of stopping.

Whether or not his betrayal was his fault made no difference—not to the captain, not to the men, and probably not to Huire. The lifeform that had entered his and Private Hulgar's bodies that night had driven them to open the doors of the company's shelter, exposing them all to myriad dangers in the jungle outside. Neither man had been able to resist the urge. Whether he could have resisted if he had tried a little harder was a question Merin would ask himself as long as he lived.

Afraid of being around the others while they drank, Merin took his cup and wandered. He thought of leaving the pyramid to roam the streets for a while, but someone would be guarding the entrance, and he didn't want to be accused of desertion.

So he sank down against the wall in the corridor, trapped between perils. If he waited there long enough, people would fall asleep, and perhaps he could sneak back to the room he shared with several other men.

But he would not be safe even there. While he slept the night before, one of his roommates had pissed on him. After fleeing to the hallway, pursued by their laughter, he had slept out there on the floor. He had since rinsed out his clothes and hair, and the smell of urine seemed gone.

As he huddled against the wall, footsteps approached outside. Bishop Arumin appeared with Father Brin on his heels. The bishop stormed down the hallway without sparing Merin a glance. Brin's eyes met the private's and, seeing nothing of interest, moved on. The holy men disappeared into the shadows.

Watching them go, Merin missed the woman's arrival until she sighed loudly. Turning, he saw her silhouette against Om's twilight afternoon.

She entered slowly, staring straight ahead, following the path of the holy men but without energy or purpose. Her arms wrapped around her body as if for warmth. It was Ilis, the guide who had led the company here.

"The bishop is inside," Merin said.

His voice boomed against the bare surfaces. She took a quick step away from him, hands raised. He cringed, regretting not speaking up earlier.

He had always had trouble looking people full in the face. The experience was too revealing. That was especially true with women—not because he didn't like women but the opposite. Their feelings mattered terribly much.

Thankfully, Ilis did not seem angry at being startled. When she got a look at him, her whole manner changed, and her face glowed. She giggled. "Where did you come from?"

He ought to have made a joke in response, but he could not think of any. "In there," he said, pointing to the hall that led to the rooms.

She nodded. "You look lonely."

Merin gulped. "No, I'd just rather be out here."

"Would you mind a companion?"

His inner reaction to the question was too complex to understand. He dreaded speaking to her, the nerves and embarrassment, but he also longed for it. Any of his comrades would have welcomed her company, but he was not like them.

Also, he was a traitor. He had betrayed the company once before. If they found him consorting with one of the enemy, the men might become violent.

But they were all consorting—right then, in there. If this lovely thing wanted to sit with him, she could, and he wouldn't stop her.

"Yes, please," he said. He would have plenty to say to himself about that response later, but he had no time now.

She laughed, not unkindly. "Good." She sat next to him and smiled, her eyes and body terrifyingly close. "Are you upset with your friends?"

How he must have looked, sitting alone on the floor with a cup of grog. "They're not my friends," he said, wishing his voice held less venom.

Her eyebrows furrowed. "Well, I can't imagine that's your fault. You seem quite nice."

"Yes. Well, I don't know. Who knows why these things happen?" Her proximity was freezing the words in his throat. His skin prickled.

She pressed her lips in thought. "Sometimes, people are just afraid. They see someone who isn't like them, and they worry. What if that person is better than them? Or just more special?"

He felt himself blush and instantly grew suspicious. His memory contained no reasons why someone who looked like her would want to speak to him. He was the picture of pity, sitting here alone. But maybe she wanted something. She was the enemy, after all.

But those dark possibilities mattered remarkably little to his body, which had different ideas. He was starting to sweat. He needed to say something and thought frantically. "Well, what can you do?" That was him, the rebellious outsider. *Women like that, don't they?*

"What happened?" she asked.

Her words were so plain, her face so open, that he could not bear refusing to answer. *So what if she is a spy?* All the Realmsmen drinking with the Ronians inside might have been spies, and that wasn't stopping anybody. He assured himself he wouldn't say anything the enemy could use against the company.

"It's not always fair, is it?" He took a breath, and more words tumbled out. "I did something terrible, and I won't deny it. But I've done good things too. You might even say I saved us." He tipped his head back against the wall, and memories paraded before him. "Shouldn't that make up for the bad things?"

She listened, looking thoughtful. "I think it should. We all need second chances because we all make mistakes. You pile up good deeds until people forget."

Merin continued. "Another man betrayed our company, just like me. But everyone's forgotten he did anything wrong. He's one of them again."

On an impulse, he finished his drink in one gulp. The amount of liquid in the cup surprised him, and he almost choked as he swallowed. He put the cup down gently beside him.

"Can't he help you?"

Funny—she wasn't acting like he'd imagine a spy acting. Maybe he had worked too hard for too long, convincing himself no woman could like him. "I think he's forgotten I exist. He's like that with people."

For a moment, Ilis seemed concerned, and her smile dimmed. Then she shook her head, and all hint of sorrow fell from her like a cast-off cloak. The smile returned in its full glory. She said, "There must be someone at home whom you think about. At times like this."

Amazed by her transformation, he felt sadness creeping into his heart. "Not really," he replied.

She leaned against his arm playfully. "Oh. Well, why would you? A soldier's life must be so exciting. You must have women all over waiting for you to come back."

He squinted at her in the gloom as the drink warmed his belly. Maybe she really wanted to be here with him, flirting and smiling. Or maybe she was laughing at him.

"No," he said flatly. "Some soldiers want you to think that, but really, it's mostly boring. Then, every once in a while, it's terrifying."

Her face softened, and her next words were believable again. "Those boring times must be a lot worse when you're alone."

She seemed closer than before, though distances were hard to judge, and the drink was rushing to his head. "Yes," he said, but that answer seemed incomplete. "Of course," he added.

"So by that logic, a man ought to enjoy good company when he finds it. Or when it finds him."

She turned to face Merin. And just like that, he couldn't bear the fear anymore. This conversation could end only one way, with her leaving, so that might as well happen right then.

He realized with terror that he didn't know how to exit the conversation in any way that wasn't catastrophic. Paralyzed, panicking, he let his eyes drop to her chest. He left them there for several seconds, long enough to make her angry.

When he finally looked up at her face, he found it unchanged.

He despaired. He would never know what was happening behind those eyes. He just wanted her to leave. "But I'm not good company myself," he said at last. "Can't you see that?"

Impossibly, she touched his face. Her skin was cool from the stone floor, but it burned like fire, and the flames consumed his body.

She said, "Is it so hard to think I might know I've found something special?"

He felt her face coming closer and wondered what kind of world this was, where the old rules no longer mattered, where enemies were friends and spies could be lovers.

Heartbeats passed, and he realized that she was very still. She sniffed.

She asked, "Are you... all right?"

He had thought the urine smell was gone. Maybe he had just gotten used to it.

He pulled his face back from her. The world was crumbling.

"No," he said, finding it hard to continue drawing breath. "Of course I'm not."

"I didn't mean to offend you. But I smelled something, and I only thought that—"

"Oh, Goddess. Leave! Please go away."

She did not. "What's your name?"

"I don't want to tell you." He pressed his fingers into his eyes.

"Really, what is it?"

"Stop! I won't tell you. I know why you're here." He was breathing fast and felt tears coming.

She frowned. "Why is that?"

"To learn what you can from me and take it back to your masters. Do they pay well?"

Her face turned cold.

"Am I wrong?" he demanded.

She shook her head. "I'm sorry you're so angry," she said. "So angry you can't trust anyone."

"Are you going to leave or not?" Anger rising, he didn't wait for her answer. He stood. "Fine, then! I'll leave myself."

Still sitting, she grabbed his leg, and despite himself, he stopped.

"Please don't," she whispered. "Come with me. There are rooms upstairs where we can be alone."

Then the worst thing of all happened. He became excited.

She saw it instantly. "I think I have your answer."

"No!" He pulled away.

Ashamed a dozen ways, he hurried down the hall.

Her words, spoken softly, echoed after him. "You think your life is bad?"

18

— · —

EMBERLY

TRUE NIGHT HAD FALLEN by the time the captain returned to the pyramid, dropped off by the general in his carriage. The two men had spoken their final words some time before, and when the carriage halted, Emberly disembarked without saying anything. Ganet's silence seemed entirely congenial, and he gave Emberly a final neighborly nod that the captain curtly returned.

Emberly was grateful to feel the ground under his feet. His back ached with his change in posture. Behind him, the infernal machine at the heart of the carriage roared in triumph and faded as the vehicle drove away. The captain hurried toward the pyramid, but his steps felt impossibly slow next to the carriage's speed.

He found Roark near the pyramid's main door. Worryingly, an officer of the Realm stood next to him.

Seeing Emberly, Roark straightened with needless formality. The other man smiled handsomely at the captain.

"Good evening, sir." He placed a hand on Roark's shoulder and left without another sound.

Emberly and Roark waited until the man was out of earshot, then both spoke at once.

"Wake the officers! I have news," the captain said.

"Where have you been?" Roark demanded. He pressed on before Emberly could answer. "You've been gone all day. The men are worried, and none of these people would answer my questions."

Emberly glared. "I've been negotiating." He ran his thumbs over his knuckles. "Who was that?"

Roark glared back. "One of their officers. I didn't learn his name."

The captain took a breath. His body had become a knot of tension in Ganet's presence. "Be careful who you talk to. They may use their rank-and-file men to learn about us."

Roark's eyes grew menacing. "I know that, Captain."

"Just don't forget it."

The lieutenant seemed to bite down on a reply.

The captain nodded toward the darkened entrance of the pyramid. "We must meet with Iwan and the sergeants right now. Are the men asleep?"

Roark shifted uncomfortably. "I'm not certain. I've been waiting for you."

"What, since I left? Out here?"

"Not quite that long. Iwan is inside, I believe. And the others."

"Is that so? And how much confidence do you have that they'll keep order?"

As far as Emberly knew, he was the only person who could make Roark feel trapped this way. The lieutenant's eyes shifted from one shoe to the other. "Not complete confidence, Captain. But I was very worried for you. I had a bad feeling..." The sentence trailed away feebly, but he tried again. "I would soon have taken a party to search for you, sir."

Emberly glanced at the tops of the surrounding walls and listened to the vastness of the city. If he was returning to chaos, he needed to collect himself. "In Huire's name, I wasn't gone that long, was I? You can't neglect the men like that, especially not the ones we've got here."

"You're right, sir."

Emberly had more to say but stopped. The lieutenant already felt ridiculous, and Emberly needed all the allies he could get.

"Let's find Iwan and the others. Meanwhile, you can tell me all that's happened."

Roark knew more of what had happened outside the pyramid than inside. Arumin had visited a replica of a

Ronian temple—eye-opening news in itself—and found some oddity there, but he had told Roark little about it.

Entering the great hall, they found it mostly empty. A few soldiers of one side or the other slumped in chairs or slept on tables. Sounds of revelry floated down the corridors. Looking at the room, in which chairs were broken and a table overturned, Emberly felt a weight settle on his shoulders.

Footsteps echoed from the Ronians' rooms.

Arumin entered and said, "The celebration has moved elsewhere."

He advanced on the captain until they were close. His eyes were watery. "Where have you been, Emberly?"

"Speaking to the general. What happened here?"

"Isn't it obvious? Now that you're here, you can end this madness." The bishop looked at Roark and snorted. "It seems you're the only one who can."

Emberly rubbed his eyes. "I need to meet with my officers right now."

Arumin's head tilted, making his face look like a gargoyle's. "Why? What did Ganet say?"

Emberly had been unaware, until that instant, that he was out of patience for questions. "He said a lot of things!"

The bishop's eyes widened, and his voice went cold. "From your choice of words, Captain, I take it you don't mean to include me."

Chewing his lip, Emberly realized that was indeed what he meant. He dreaded the idea of meeting with Roark and the others, saying the things that needed saying, with Arumin watching and disapproving every step of the way.

"Your Eminence..." He chose his words with care. "This is a military affair. There are matters of strategy that will not interest you."

The grin that came over Arumin's face was grotesque. "Boring stuff, is it? Thank you for your concern. But no matter is purely military anymore."

Emberly had no real answer and could not be bothered to find one. "Pardon me," he replied instead, "I thought perhaps you weren't feeling well. When I heard that you walked out of your own meeting in a temple built in our honor, I knew something must be terribly wrong."

Arumin's lips closed over his teeth. He nodded. "Ah. I see. Pulling rank. I'm not one of your soldiers, Emberly. You are one of mine. One of Huire's."

No one said anything for a moment. Emberly looked up and down as if gauging the bishop's height.

At last, he said, "And are you well, your Eminence?"

"No," Arumin answered, shaking his head. "No, I'm not well. Your man here told you about the temple, yes?"

"What about it?"

"He hasn't told you everything, then. Do you know what they did?" He did not wait for an answer. "They declared war."

Emberly's heart jumped. "What do you mean? All I heard was something about a hand."

"They put that hand in the place of the Goddess. When she returns, she will find that temple already occupied. If the Shining Realm is allowed to build such things in Ronia, they will do the same there."

The air in the room became thin. A Ronian soldier sleeping nearby lifted his head from the table.

"We shouldn't suggest such things lightly, Bishop," the captain said, leaning close to Arumin.

He glanced around the room. Private Merin wandered through the doorway where they had entered. His arms hung at his sides, loose and purposeless.

"Get out of here!" Emberly shouted.

The private must have been lurking in the corridors somewhere, and they had passed him in the dark. Barely noticing the shout, he disappeared down the hallway toward the rooms.

As the private's footsteps faded into the shadows, Arumin asked, "Suggest what? That Ronia may fall?"

Emberly threw up an arm, silencing Roark before he said something that would require punishment. To Arumin, he said with finality, "That will not happen."

"You're not that big a fool, Emberly," the bishop answered, his voice rising. "You've seen the things these people are capable of. The things they know." He was yelling, nearly prompting Emberly, in his horror, to cover the old man's mouth with his hands. "I don't know what you were talking about with General Ganet for several hours, but I know you understand exactly what I mean!"

"Be quiet, Bishop!" Emberly, knowing he was being a fool, shouted this sacrilege almost as loudly as Arumin had shouted his.

In the silence that fell, Emberly thought he had finally gone too far. The bishop would denounce him, cast him from the Temple, do whatever he had the power to do. But when the old man spoke, he was calm.

"You seem uneasy, Captain. Shall we talk elsewhere?"

Emberly readily agreed. He sent Roark to find Iwan and the sergeants, then he followed Arumin's shuffling form to the room the bishop shared with Father Brin.

On the way, Arumin asked, "Shouldn't your lieutenant keep control of the soldiers, Emberly? Goddess knows why your sergeants haven't."

Emberly did not share his dark suspicion that his sergeants were as drunk as the rest. As for Iwan, the captain felt both unsurprised at his absence and baffled as to where he might have been. Such were the men the crusade's voluntary nature had saddled him with.

He resented that the bishop felt entitled to comment on the subject. "No," he said then added, "I'll deal with them later."

Arumin looked back at him but made no other answer.

To Emberly's relief, Brin was not in the room. The young priest still brought back memories of Caidfell that the captain did not want to recall. Stepping through the curtain, Emberly noted that the bishop's and the priest's bedrolls lay on opposite sides of the narrow room.

Arumin returned to their conversation without preamble. "You're right about one thing, Captain. We cannot afford to act rashly. But neither can we let them deface a temple. On that, we cannot budge." He pulled at his beard, which still held knots from their trek through Caidfell's wilderness. "Don't let the general flatter you, Emberly. They think we're fools. They thought they could make a change like that and we wouldn't notice—or care. Sadly, they were nearly right. Nor and Brin might have missed the perversion if I hadn't pointed it out. We make things too easy now for the young.

"It's a fine line we must walk. But we cannot deceive ourselves about what's at stake. With that bloody ghoulish hand in the temple, they said all that needed saying."

Emberly shook his head. "We mustn't assume that war is inevitable or that we are simply doomed."

Arumin glared. "Of course we're not doomed. On the contrary. If we do as we should, we cannot fail. If that means fighting these bastards toe to toe, then so be it. I look forward to seeing how we win."

Despite himself, Emberly was impressed. "Bishop," he said softly, "I will never have such faith as yours."

"Perhaps that's why you are on this journey. Faith can be built. It can also be rebuilt. As for war..." He shrugged. "If nothing kept us here and we knew the way, we'd gladly flee this city. But here we are. It's simple."

Emberly's face burned, and he began to sweat. He felt a trap closing. "Bishop... my job, and that of my men, is to escort Shada..." A painful silence came and went. "Escort her and the Lady to the Goddess and her divine court. If we're going to succeed, we must be strategic about when we fight."

"What strategy can there be here? What is left to us? I would bet my life that your general made the choice clear to you. Fight, or sell ourselves and our world."

"I need time. I'm meeting with the general tomorrow."

The bishop shook his head in disbelief. "Why? What will more time gain us?"

"A chance to find Shada and the Lady, that's what! We can't go on without them."

"Neither can our ends be accomplished through corrupt means. The Lady will only return to us if we act rightly, and the only way to fail is to turn away. This is not a burden—it is a release. We have only to plan our attack with some degree of care and execute it."

Emberly took a small step backward. "What attack?"

"Before we leave this city with the Lady, we will destroy that abomination masquerading as a holy place."

With a measure of calm, Emberly said, "Destroy the temple the Realm built for us?"

"It's not a real temple, Emberly. It is an evil joke."

"It's real as far as the Realm is concerned."

"Even if that were true, why in all the worlds would it matter?"

"Because..." The captain steeled himself. "I am not prepared to go to war."

The bishop looked at him with a somber lack of surprise. "Ah. We come to it at last."

"Your Eminence, I wonder if you truly comprehend our situation."

"It's not hard to understand. We are vastly outnumbered. Our enemy has turned out to be the Shining Realm, just as you and I feared. They've been spying on us, and somehow, they were here on this world, waiting for us. They've got us trapped in this building, and we can't leave without the Lady in any case. And they intend to invade Ronia."

Hearing the facts so plainly stated, Emberly fought despair. "They will do just that, I believe, if we refuse to negotiate."

"We will refuse."

"I cannot agree so quickly, Bishop."

"You frighten me, Emberly. On Caidfell, you were all too willing to do what the moment required. What's happened since then? I wonder where your values truly lie."

"I've learned from my mistakes. Let me add, you're not the only one who is frightened."

Arumin pointed at the ground beneath their feet. "This is a test of our mettle. To see if we will sell our world—and our Goddess—in exchange for our lives."

"But keeping the peace won't just buy our lives. It will buy the lives of many Ronians."

"What value is a man's life next to his soul?" Arumin cried, spreading his hands. He raised an index finger. "What are a million lives compared to a single person's eternity?"

Emberly gasped. "It's not a million lives, damn it! It's not an eternity! It's a carving in a bloody wall, and no one is going to die for it!"

The whole building seemed to fall silent. If anyone in the corridor or the great hall had been talking, they were listening instead.

The bishop's eyes were bright, his mouth hard. "If that is how you feel—"

"That is, absolutely, how I feel."

"Then you had better leave. You and your men have business to attend to."

"Yes, please. I respectfully suggest you get some rest."

"I don't get much rest nowadays, Emberly. Perhaps it's my age. With your men running wild, I suspect sleep will be difficult."

Emberly had not turned even halfway toward the doorway before Arumin blurted, "These things—little things—they matter, Captain. You will come to see that." His eyes pierced Emberly. "I know it."

19

— · —

ARUMIN

TRUDGING THROUGH HALLS HE did not recognize, places haunted by the wayward and the drunk, Arumin did not trust the pervading sense of calm. The Ronians and the men of the Shining Realm were scattered about the pyramid's insides, mingling, sitting in small groups and speaking low.

Soon, he came upon a larger gathering, half a dozen men from both sides of the coming war. They sat in a misshapen circle that blocked the corridor, one speaking and the others listening. As the bishop came closer, he recognized that the man was singing, softly and poorly. Yet when the others looked up at Arumin, their eyes were wet.

He knew the Ronians' faces but not their names. "I need to find Robir," he growled.

His voice was grim and dusty, and it echoed. Something broke inside the group of men. A bubble of feeling had been growing among them, and they burst into laughter.

Their mirth was not cruel or jeering. It was the unaffected amusement of children.

The bishop had grown used to the newfound respect the men had been paying him since Caidfell. Feeling it slip made him angry, whether it was caused by alcohol or something else. "Pull yourselves together!" he shouted.

The effect was immediate. The men grew sad and wide-eyed.

"Forgive us, sir," one said, and the others murmured similar things.

Arumin wondered what he would have done if they had kept laughing. After a brief struggle to remember why he had come, he asked again for Robir.

"Ah," the spokesman answered as a ripple of laughter dared to bounce from man to man. "He won't be among this rabble, sir. He's in the rooms. Asleep already, I expect." He looked at Arumin with a frightfully open face. A smile came upon it, though he visibly fought to keep it away. "I'm sorry, Bishop," he said. His eyes shone with mischief as he assessed Arumin's face. "It's just, you see, I never realized..." The sentence crumbled before it was finished, and the laughter won.

With the men in rolling hysterics, Arumin cursed at them and hurried out of their sight. Their laughter stayed with him, fueling his rage. By the time he found his way back to the Ronians' rooms, he could have dismantled the pyramid with his bare hands.

He found Robir alone, awake, and on his knees. The private faced an empty wall, his forehead close to the ground. He did not look at Arumin.

The bishop cleared his throat.

Robir continued to pray. As Arumin waited and watched, the private straightened inch by inch and stood, rising from his knees with frigid grace. "Your Eminence."

"I'm glad to find you awake. I was told to expect otherwise."

"I haven't slept much since Ronia, Bishop."

"But you're not drinking with your friends, either."

"I've had enough drink for this life. Anyway, I had a feeling I ought to stay in here."

Arumin tipped his head. "A feeling?"

"Yes." Robir's gaze grew hard and certain. "Surely, what's happening out there doesn't seem right to you."

"It does not," Arumin replied. "Though some might argue the men deserve to relax a little."

"What, like this?" Robir nodded toward the corridor. "There's no such need, sir."

Pleased with that response, Arumin said, "After Caidfell, they're lucky to be alive."

"Indeed. Whose fault is that, would you say?"

Surprised at the man's openness, Arumin allowed himself a moment to think. He expected Robir to wait, but he was wrong.

"I hoped you would visit me soon, Bishop. I was afraid, very afraid, that my confession had been just a dream."

Arumin nodded. On Caidfell, Robir had asked to confess his sins to the bishop. Instead, he had poured his suspicions about Captain Emberly into Arumin's ear. Robir was convinced the captain was reckless and corrupt, unfit to lead the crusade. Emberly's behavior on Gallobraith supported the "reckless" part, but Arumin was less convinced the captain was corrupt.

The bishop was far more concerned by Emberly's lack of faith and obedience to Huire's will. Those things concerned him to the point of moving against the captain, violently if necessary. In that, Arumin and Robir had common ground.

The bishop said, "Private, if you had another confession to make, you could have come to me."

Robir did not answer. For a few seconds, he stared intently at the bishop's chest. Arumin realized belatedly that the private was listening for sounds in the hallway. Then Robir spoke without moving his eyes. "This cannot work that way, Bishop. We must take care. I cannot be seen frequently visiting you."

A thrill spread through Arumin's chest. He had worried about saying too much only to realize Robir was a step ahead of him. "How do you suggest we proceed?"

"We must decide as much as we can now. We won't talk again until something changes or we are ready for mutiny."

Hearing that last word, the bishop's heart quickened. "All right. We must organize swiftly. Soon, things may become irreversible."

Robir's brow sank. "Is Emberly back, then? What did he say?"

"Too much to recount it all. Will you trust me when I say you're right to fear him?"

"I trust you, sir. But I wouldn't need to trust you to believe that." He looked at the bare wall toward which he had been praying. "I'm afraid for us. For us here and for all Ronians. Not for our lives but our souls."

"Each of us can but save himself. Others can come only afterward and only if they want to."

Robir stood straighter. "Tell me what to do."

"I'm certain there are others here interested in saving themselves. I need you to find out who they are and gather them. Enough to overcome those loyal to Emberly. He'll have fewer allies the longer he dawdles, but we can't wait."

"I have a few in mind. Most of this company were with Emberly on Gallobraith. They remember how he acted."

"Good." Arumin sighed. "This will be difficult, Private. We must be ready when the time comes—if it comes. I must be clear: I haven't completely given up on Emberly. He may yet make the right choice."

"Your faith is greater than mine, Bishop."

"In any case, much will depend on you."

"If you're with me, your Eminence, then so is Huire."

"I don't know how much help I can practically be, Robir. The men admire me more than they used to, but they'll never forget my past. They fear me as a man of the Goddess, but they'll always wonder if my courage will hold out."

"You're a good man, your Eminence. Any who don't respect you will have to deal with me."

20

SHADA

"THERE IT IS!" LANI called, and her hand tightened around Shada's fingers.

Her voice was high and careless, and Shada's heart jumped at the thought of what might be out among the trees, listening. She reminded herself that nothing was there that her captors did not wish to be.

The smaller girl, Delia, left her sister and Shada behind, racing alone up the rounded hill that rose above them as they emerged from the trees. Somewhere along the wooded path, Shada had nearly forgotten that they were in a park, but here, paths converged to meet a set of garden terraces. Her eyes moved naturally up the hill to a lawn with a cottage at its center.

Though it was the size of a house, it was inescapably a cottage. It had a timber frame and whitewashed brickwork, and its roof was alarmingly steep.

As they climbed the hill, Shada could see a distant stone wall that enclosed the park. It looked much smaller than it was. The treetops, which rose to perhaps half its height, made it seem like a line of bricks around a yard filled with lumpy moss. Beyond rose the towers and spires of Om.

The girls were bringing her to supper as promised. They had taken her from her finely decorated cell into a hallway just as palatial then outside. There, she had found herself in the park, an expanse of tree-lined walks and flowers of surreal radiance. Upon stepping outside, she had winced and stopped in her tracks, covering her eyes against the withering light. Looking around, she realized she had been living and sleeping inside a wall of immense proportions, perhaps miles in length. When she could finally look upward, she saw in the sky patterns and lines in geometric shapes. She was still in the city, then.

Since they were going to supper, she assumed the time was late afternoon. Spending most of her recent days in nearly pitch dark had left her unmoored and despondent.

Glimpsing the cityscape of Om once more made the feeling worse. She could have no hope of the Ronian company finding her, or she them, in a place this size—not unless her captors wished it—and she could not broach the subject without revealing the company's existence to a potential enemy. She might be alone forever among strangers.

When she left Ronia, she had thought she'd accepted the idea of dying on some faraway world, of never seeing her father again. The Temple had promised to see to his care, which alone made this journey worthwhile. But it made the prospect of losing him no less miserable.

The walk through the park had been long, and her legs were wobbly and ticklish with disuse. Without the pressing walls of her cell, she felt terribly exposed even when hemmed in by trees. The garden loomed in its age and majesty, and she was thankful the girls were with her. In her present state, being out there alone might lead her to panic. Having something worse to contemplate helped: the thought of Lani and Delia alone in those woods.

"What's your father's name?" she asked Lani.

The girl didn't answer. Shada had to repeat herself before the reply came.

"He wouldn't like us to tell you that."

They reached a set of stairs that ended in a small terrace before the front door. Shada said, "Well, I hope he doesn't mind my clothes. I have none to change into." It was an absurd concern in her circumstances but a concern nonetheless.

"He won't mind at all," Lani said.

Delia was waiting by the door, bouncing on her toes. "You should see what he wears sometimes!" she cried.

Shada stopped by the door as dread rushed upon her. In a matter of moments, she had begun thinking of herself as a guest instead of a prisoner. How easily the truth slipped away.

She decided to hurry before fear got the better of her. The door opened as she raised a hand to knock, and she dropped her arm, feeling foolish. When she saw the person behind the door, her heart raced, and her legs ached to jump.

He was male—his wide jaw and thick neck made her almost sure of it. He had no hair or eyebrows. His skin had once been burned, fully and all over.

Shada collected herself as quickly as she could, but she feared her surprise was obvious. The man would be awfully good at noticing such things, she suspected.

"Come in," he said. His voice was so dry and scratchy that hearing it was painful.

She obeyed. Before she thought to introduce herself, he closed the door behind them all and walked away without a word. The girls nudged her waist, urging her to follow.

They passed through an entry hall. Walls of soft white were hung with tapestries featuring stars and planets, made larger and simpler than they would have been on a map. Their borders and backgrounds teemed with living things. The girls caught up with her, and each took one of her hands.

As they entered a corridor, a clatter echoed from the farthest room, and it dawned on Shada that the burned man was not the one she had come to meet. They reached that door and entered to find someone waiting.

She could see only part of him. He was not quite middle aged, older than Shada but younger than Captain Emberly. He was very tall, towering over a wide painter's easel that faced away from the visitors. The room had a high ceiling and plenty of light, with tall windows looking out over the hill they had ascended and the forest growing close to the other sides of the house.

He was painting with a loose and quick hand. When he heard them, he looked up, bowed, and smiled. "Pardon me. I thought I would have more time. I've made a mess, you can see." With his foot, he tapped a cup that had recently fallen to the floor, spilling brushes and water mixed with black paint.

His eyes fixed on her. "Will you do me a favor, miss?"

She was oddly surprised by his attention. "Yes."

"Stay right where you are, please, and keep looking at me. I've nearly finished."

He looked at the canvas and back at her. The realization that she was his subject came slowly and dreadfully. She had never seen an image of herself that she hadn't regretted allowing.

"Have we met, sir?" she asked.

"Not yet. We shall in a moment."

"Are... you painting me? You've only seen me for a few seconds."

"A little longer than that." Without looking away from the canvas, he pointed out the window with his free hand. "I watched you and my daughters come up the path. Thank you for bringing her, darlings," he told the girls.

"Yes, Father," they said together.

He looked at Shada with wide, bright eyes. "I'm afraid you may be disappointed when you see it. It really isn't much, just a sketch." He murmured to himself in polite unease.

"I'm sure it's lovely," Shada told him. She could not imagine why she was being so courteous.

Yes, she could—she was alone and at the man's mercy.

He stepped back from the easel and eyed it harshly. He raised his brush, but then he shook his head. "No, it's got to be finished now, or it never will be." He picked up the cup from the floor and put the brush in it. "Come look."

Shada and the girls walked to the other side of the canvas. For an instant, Shada was not sure what she was looking at. It was all black, a set of mostly thin brushstrokes that met in a whirlwind in the center of the canvas. It looked like a single letter from an alphabet of ten thousand flowing characters.

Then it changed. Not a line moved, but they all came together, and she saw herself.

"I like it," she told the man, who was watching her as if half expecting dreadful news.

"Do you really? You may be honest."

She obliged him and looked again. This time, she saw not a tangle of lines but very few. It was her in a simple portrait that captured her in fewer lines than seemed possible. It even included the markings on her face, portraying them in a new way. They did not look like a disease or a grim web of cracks but like a part of her, no more or less than the rest.

"It's beautiful, actually," she said.

He smiled in relief. "I'm glad. I tried to follow my instincts."

She could not put her finger on what she liked about it. It was not glamorous or aggrandizing, but neither was it caricature like one would buy at a fair. Perhaps it was what she thought she looked like, in her better moments. It could have been far more accurate yet less true.

She looked at him. "How did you do this?"

"Well…" His eyebrows bunched as he looked at the painting. "I would like to say it was skill. But I think not. I just had a sense of it." He smiled. "You made it quite easy."

Just like that, she was angry, so angry that she couldn't help speaking up. "How?" she demanded. "I didn't pose for this. All I did was come to your house."

Taken aback, he said, "Of course you didn't. But these things don't take me long."

She gasped and laughed in the same breath. "You've been watching me. Goddess…" She said the last word without meaning to. Pain jabbed in her throat. It was the Lady, reminding her not to mention Huire.

The man frowned. "What? What do you mean?"

"In that room where you've kept me. You've been looking at me somehow."

"No!" he said with some force.

She discovered to her bitterness that she wanted to believe him. "Why should I trust you? You kept me in a cage for days—I don't even know how long—"

He extended a hand toward her, palm down. "Your treatment has been inexcusable. I could not stop it until now. Soon, I will be in a position to ensure that such things don't happen."

She gasped, exasperated. "If it wasn't you, then why am I here?"

Biting his lip, he hesitated an instant too long for her liking. "Please," he said. "Let me explain."

"And what is this?" She pointed at the canvas. "Was this supposed to make me happy? Showing me that you can do this, somehow, when you've never seen me before?"

"Yes. I thought it would cheer you up. I can't imagine what you've been through. But if I had known it would make you feel this way, I would never have done it. I'll destroy it right now." He took the canvas from the easel.

Unable to hold still, Shada turned toward the window and back. "Of course you will," she cried. "Why wouldn't you? You can make another one any time you wish!"

"Stop yelling at Father!" This was Delia, standing close by.

The adults looked at her. Shada was surprised, having nearly forgotten the girls were there and dismayed at what they had heard.

"He wouldn't do those things," said Lani, who was still standing next to Shada.

The beating of Shada's heart made her breath short. Her gaze met the man's.

He said, "You have little reason to trust anyone, I expect. I hope you don't think I asked my daughters to say those things. Because I swear I didn't." He placed the painting back on the easel. "They're right about me, but that's because they are brilliant."

Delia beamed at that.

The man turned and approached Shada. He placed his hands on his hips, completing his resemblance to a statue in a museum. "You may not like me, and I can't reasonably ask you to," he said. "But I hope you'll do one thing for me. Stay here tonight. We've got room for one more, as you can see." He twirled his finger to indicate their surroundings.

Shada thought of the wall surrounding the park, where her cell awaited. Having seen the grass and trees, along with the girls and their father, the thought of spending another night in that dark little room could have overthrown her sanity if she dwelled on it. Perhaps she should not trust him, but the children did, and she had begun to place increasing weight on their opinions.

"My name is Jeric," the man said. "I would offer my hand, but..." He held up his fingers, which were covered with paint.

She looked again at Jeric. The effect of knowing his name was profound. As she watched, he came together, just like the painting. He was frankly beautiful, not broadly handsome as the captain was or a delicate sort of pretty like Father Brin. He was perfectly proportioned, the product of an inspired but calculating artist.

He said, "I have little say in what goes on a stone's throw beyond these walls. But here, I can protect you. Will you stay, just for a while?"

Shada paused. The sight of such beauty all around made her nervous. Some design must have been behind it all, some intention on her captors' part. Or maybe she had begun to lose her bearings entirely.

When it came to it, she had no idea who these people were or why she was there. She only knew that between the Shining Realm and the Lady, she had no choice.

She gave her answer, and the girls cheered.

21

NOR

AFTER REN REVEALED THAT she possessed Cadmon's letter, Nor felt surrounded and outgeneraled and reluctant to speak again. Whenever he talked, it seemed, he allowed her to toy with him.

Ren matched his silence with her own. She seemed to be waiting for a response, and he was determined not to give her that. They entered a stubborn silence that seemed to last for hours.

In his boredom with the resulting quiet, the standoff gained apocalyptic weight in Nor's mind. The very fate of universal justice might depend on his forcing her to speak first. Questions of how she had managed to steal the letter, how she had known it existed, and why Huire had let her take it all swirled in his mind, half formed and inseparable. He wondered whether thirst or his bladder would force him to break his silence.

At some point, he looked up and found her staring at him. Their eyes met, hers proud and somber. Immediately, the staring became part of their struggle, and he bored into her with his eyes.

But he found it impossible to lock eyes with someone like that and not feel like he knew them. Looking into her gaze gave him a feeling of intimacy that he loathed, and he finally looked away with a growl.

Once he broke the silence, she spoke. "I hope you're not too angry. You simply must accept what I am saying: things are not what they appear."

"I agreed to your terms." Nor found himself pacing and clenching his fists. "I've joined your Shining Realm. Whatever leverage you hoped to gain over me through that letter, you no longer need it."

"Leverage?" Her brow furrowed, then she shook her head. "I'm helping to set you free. You're still deceiving me, Nor. It's not a lie, not exactly, but it's too close for comfort. You haven't really joined me."

"I told you I accept. What more do you want?"

"But you haven't accepted. You've pretended to commit yourself to the Realm, all the while planning to work against us from the inside, to learn information that will help your friends. Isn't that so?"

The accuracy of her statement nearly drove him to a rage. Everything had gone wrong. He had carried that letter all the way from Ronia—*Only for it to fall into the hands of this...*

He took a breath. This was a test of faith. He needed to demonstrate for Huire his belief that the letter would reach him intact, one way or another, when he was ready for it.

It wasn't the first such test. On Caidfell, the envelope had been submerged in the swamp and soaked, and only Nor's faith had convinced him that the letter inside must still be legible. The Goddess would allow no other outcome. He had walked around ever since, certain in his conviction that the letter must be undamaged, though he had never laid eyes on it and the envelope that held it was ruined.

Having realized he was facing another test, he felt calmer. But he still had to know one thing.

"How did you get it?"

"That doesn't matter."

"Why did you take it?"

She ignored the question. "What matters is that you surrender to the awakening. If you don't, it will be much harder. For you and your company."

Nor threw up his hands. "I don't know how." He had failed to deceive her, so he must risk destroying their arrangement—by telling the truth. *Huire's fool*, he thought. "I'm not like you. I care about things"—she made a face—"I care about my Goddess. I care about my friends. I don't want them forced to join this 'Shining Realm.' How do you expect me to change that?"

She raised the hand that held the letter. "Read it."

His mouth went dry. "What?"

"Read the letter. It's all there."

"You've read it." That wasn't supposed to happen. Huire had meant the letter for him alone.

"Yes. You should too. If I can't convince you to surrender to the awakening, perhaps your friend can. This Abbot..." She looked at the letter. "Cadmon."

Hearing the abbot's name on the woman's lips chilled him. Those were private things, things not for her.

He must stay calm and keep telling the truth. *Huire wins.* "If you've read it, you might know why I can't. If I read the answers it contains before I know what they are—"

"An unforgivable sin, in your Goddess's eyes." Ren nodded. "That's exactly why you must read it. So much unnecessary suffering."

"I won't." He wondered what fate he was dooming himself to by saying that. But it didn't matter. As she had said, reading the letter prematurely was unforgivable. "Do you mean to keep it?"

"What if I say yes to that? What will you do then?"

He felt himself teetering on a precipice—of death, of damnation, of terrifying suffering. "I don't know."

She shrugged. "You could kill me and take it, I suppose. But I hope we are past that. The consequences for you and your people would be terrible indeed."

He clenched his fists and shifted from foot to foot. With nowhere to turn, he bent and roared in frustration. He glimpsed what might have been a smile on her face.

She raised the letter to her eyes and said, "Let me save your soul the trouble."

Nor straightened like a shot. "What are you doing?"

"Setting you free," she said. "If you won't read it, I must read it to you."

"No!" he shouted.

He gripped the shreds of his faith for dear life. She wouldn't read it to him. It wouldn't happen.

But if it did, it would be his fault. He had hardly thought about Abbot Cadmon's question or the envelope with its answer since leaving Ronia. Occupied with crisis after crisis, he had forgotten about this, a task far more important than any other, including mere survival. He had spared it the odd moment here and there, but each time, he had given up in frustration at the apparent impossibility of the quandary. *What are the gods made of?* He had no idea. He did not know how he could have let himself waste so much time.

In the wake of his outburst, Ren looked at him with polite weariness. "Hiding from the truth is foolish."

His composure broken, Nor's voice stumbled. "If you have it, then it must not be meant for me. I'm not meant to be an elder."

Her brows rose. "Then who is meant to have it? Me?"

"If this is truly happening—"

"If?"

"You will not read it!" he cried in mad triumph. "You won't be able to! The words will be taken from your mouth."

"By your Goddess, I suppose." She lifted the paper and cleared her throat. "It's titled 'What Are the Gods Made Of?' Is that what you've been wondering, Brother Norhim? The letter begins, 'My dear boy—'"

Nor could imagine the abbot saying those words—they were too familiar. "Stop! What do you want?"

"I want surrender." Her voice was cold and calm. "Unconditional surrender. Since you can't give me that on your own, I'm giving it to you." She cleared her throat and began to read. "'How—'"

Nor stopped thinking. He charged.

Her chair toppled as he bowled her over. He expected some defense, some counterattack, but she did not resist as he pinned her to the ground and wrapped his hands around her throat.

She said, "You know that if you kill me—"

"I won't," he growled, pushing his face close to hers. He was shaking, and his lip trembled. "I'm going to let go now. I won't resist any more if I can help it. Surrendering will take time, but I'll do it if I can. On one condition: I'm going to keep that letter. Until I'm ready, I won't read it. If you don't agree to that... I'll let go anyway, and you'll do what you will."

Her eyes gleamed. Her face shone with a satisfaction that would haunt him. She said, "Agreed. I look forward to conquering you."

Releasing her, he sat up. "I don't think you can," he said. "I can't even conquer myself."

She lay back, relaxed, looking at the ceiling. "I can," she replied, her tone whimsical. "I've already begun."

22

BRIN

The thin blanket hardly insulated Brin from the cold floor. To his disbelief, he had not awakened with a headache. The small, bright lantern nearby assured him that he was still somewhere in the pyramid.

A toe nudged his ribs. "You, there."

The face that hung over him was welcome. Ilis had dressed, but the outlines of her form brought memories of what she had shown him just hours before. He was accustomed to being awakened by Arumin's snoring and muttering.

"Is it morning?" he asked.

"Have you somewhere to be?" Her question did not seem jealous. As usual, her curiosity verged on childishness. She stepped over him, putting one foot on either side of his waist, and sank to straddle him. He remembered how close he was to being naked.

The stone floor tickled his back and legs. He said, "I thought it might have been a dream."

"Is that what you hoped?" The scarce light made her smile more frighteningly radiant.

He did not bother to answer.

"It's early," she admitted. "Still dark outside, I imagine."

He slapped her ankle. "Then why did you wake me?"

She placed her fingers on either side of his face and turned his head to one side. It was a delicate action, but he felt power in her hands. Her lips brushed his earlobe as she whispered, "There is something you need to see."

He could not have hidden his excitement if he wanted to. "And what is that?" he replied, matching her tone.

She frowned. "It's funny, but I don't know how to explain it. You will just have to come with me."

"Can't it wait?" he asked with a grimace.

"Not if we want to keep our secret. If we go later in the day, there are sure to be people there."

"Our secret?" he asked. Then he realized what she meant.

"Your master won't be happy with what we've done here, and neither will mine." She sat up and dragged her fingernails down his chest. "I'm not nearly done with you yet."

Brin looked around for his cloak before realizing he was lying on it. As he tied his belt, she stood and offered her hands to pull him up.

"It's not far," she said, picking up the lantern, "but it's easy to get lost. Watch me carefully." She spun like an ornament and walked away, giving him ample opportunity to recall the shape of her hips and back.

To his distaste, Brin found himself pitying the girl. He was not the fool she thought, and he could not recall giving her reason to think he was, but she still seemed to think she was toying with him—not that her assumption was unrealistic. He had known a number of holy men more celibate than him who, once seduced by a woman, had followed at her heels like stray pups. But he doubted if this woman had known many priests.

Unlike many of his Temple brethren, Brin had found and taken many opportunities to break his vows. Huire, wherever she might have been, had far bigger worries than his misconduct. *Anyway, what all-knowing deity could put a man next to a thing like Ilis and expect him to keep his right mind?* The Goddess knew better. She expected the most from those whom she gave the most, but surely that worked both ways.

At the moment, Huire probably could not stand the sight of Father Brin. On Caidfell, he had done something beyond the bounds of decency even for him. Desperate not to be killed by that planet's wraiths, he had bowed to one of them in a pose of worship, pleading for its mercy, praying like it was a god.

Nor had seen him do it. Were it anyone else, Brin would have worried about rumors spreading, but the monk kept himself to himself. Whatever Brin owed Nor for that bit of discretion, he'd repaid it by saving Nor from angry soldiers during the confessing ceremony. Brin had the odd notion that he and Nor were on the verge of becoming friends.

As for the Goddess... Well, the crusade meant all sins were forgiven, didn't it? Brin, it seemed, would be putting that to the test.

Cavorting with spies would not help his cause.

The Shining Realm's scheme regarding Ilis probably seemed simple enough from the Realm's perspective. Put a lovely woman among a group of men and see whom she attracted and what she could learn from them. He wondered if she had tried it on anyone else in the company before approaching him. He doubted it. He couldn't imagine any of those brutes turning her down.

That made him her primary target and the beneficiary of her attentions, not that she would get any information from him for her trouble. Part of him thought it would serve Arumin right if Brin told this woman all the secrets he knew—the old bastard had left him to die in a battle, after all. But he felt some attachment to the bishop even then, when they weren't on speaking terms. When he'd seen Arumin distraught in the temple, Brin had surprised himself by trying to comfort him. Now, Brin would keep his lips sealed and let this woman crash against him like waves in a storm.

Ilis took him to a doorway hung with a thick curtain. It was surprisingly difficult to push through, and Brin wondered what sort of heavy material was sewn inside. They entered a room with stone benches along three of its walls. The far wall was different: flat, dull metal of a kind Brin did not recognize. A large window in its center was covered by a pair of doors, each of which could slide back to allow one to look through. Brin thought he could see a glow around the doors' edges.

"What's in there?" he asked Ilis.

The air felt strange, and his ears itched. He sensed a vibration, almost silent but omnipresent.

She put a finger to her lips, asking for silence. The energy of the room was getting to Brin, and the shape and motion of her lips gave him a flash of unbearable erotic excitement. Then she pointed at a nearby corner, and the feeling drained away.

One of Emberly's men was sitting there, head bowed and eyes closed. It was Iwan, one of the lieutenants. Praying that the man was asleep, Brin took Ilis's hand and pointed toward the doorway they had come through. She tilted her head in pitying amusement and tugged him onward.

He planted his feet and would not move. She turned, the light still in her hand, and looked at him with an expression of little surprise and much regret. It was painful to look at, but to Brin, the thought of Arumin learning about this, seeing his fears confirmed, was more painful still.

"It's all right," Iwan said aloud.

Brin's heart convulsed. He looked at the lieutenant, unsure what he meant.

The man's eyes were wide and still in the lantern's light. "Open it," he told them.

Frightened and inclined to be obedient, Brin kept close to Ilis, crowding her as they walked to the metal window. She guided him to one side and took hold of a metal wheel set into the outermost of the two doors. She strained at it, but it did not turn. He stepped forward to help, but she waved him back before finally succeeding in moving the wheel a little. A clang sounded from the heart of the metal, and the wheel spun more easily after that.

When it stopped moving, she grabbed a handhold near the wheel and stiffened her body for a great effort. She turned her head away and closed her eyes. "Cover your face," she said.

Iwan had moved from his corner and was standing against the opposite wall, near the curtained doorway.

Brin shut his eyes and held up an arm to block whatever might come forth. The metal ground and whined as it moved, and its growling coincided with a sudden birth of radiance that rushed past Brin's arm and through his eyelids. Its red glow was everywhere. It would have found him even if he had buried his head in the wall.

"Give it a moment." Ilis's voice was hushed. "I've opened it as wide as my finger, which is all I dare."

"What is it?" he gasped.

"I don't know anything about it, really. Only a few can know, and no one knows all of it."

He let himself look at it gradually, first lowering his arm a little then opening his eyes. He half expected to be blinded, but the light had a peculiar quality. It illuminated the room well enough, but its full intensity was focused almost entirely into a white line that stretched from the middle of the floor up the center of the heavy curtain and partway back along the ceiling. It was a light so pure and brilliant that it might have carved the world itself in half along that thin white seam.

With the door's opening, the vibration that haunted the room swelled, digging under the skin of everything. Brin's head and jaw ached, and whenever his upper teeth met his lower teeth, they all stung.

"Close it, for the love of Huire," he said.

She laughed. "I will, but not for her."

With another grinding more unnatural than the first, the light disappeared. Ilis dusted off her hands and said, "That's what makes the light in the sky so that our people in the city can find their way back. Only a bit of it goes to that, though. It does other things, or so they tell me."

Brin still could see only that light. He wiggled his fingers in front of his eyes.

"We should have worn glasses, really," Ilis said. "They have dark glasses for when someone wants to look at it. But I like to see it as it really is."

When Brin's eyesight returned, he noticed that Iwan was gone. He felt a little sick at what the lieutenant might say and to whom—all because Ilis had wanted him to see something she couldn't even describe.

"Why did you show me that?"

"Because you need to know what we can do," she replied. "Did your Goddess ever show you something like that?"

"I've seen some things."

The glow of the lantern was now dismally insufficient. She touched something on its side, and it brightened, but her expression was still shadowy. "My masters have a lot of reasons for letting us see that light. I've done things that don't come naturally. I've given my will over to them. But when you see this, you say, 'How could people so wise be wrong?'"

"Who decides who the wise are?" Brin asked, blinking at the glowing forms that circled his head like constellations. "Nobody really knows." He chewed on his lip. "You've got doubts about your masters, then? Tell me."

She tipped back her head and gave a carefree laugh. It went on for several seconds, and he felt himself getting angry. "Oh my," she said, finishing with a contented sigh.

"Why did you laugh?"

"Because you're so honest," she told him. "And you don't even mean to be."

"Mean to be?" He snorted. "How would you know if I'm honest?"

She put her palm on his chest. "You think you're such a bad man, but you've got this big, beating heart in here. I can see it through your chest."

"Hell, why do you say that?" When the pressure of her hand suddenly prickled his skin, he pulled away.

She giggled. "You've been trying to learn about me. Squeezing me for information. Meanwhile, I've gotten to know you quite well."

He sneered. "What makes you think I care about you? Don't tell me you were hoping to tie me down."

Her eyes widened just enough for him to notice. "There's nothing wrong with it, Brin. You wanted to be a spy to help your master and all those men back there. If I was with that lot, I would want to impress them."

He cursed from the very bottom of his gut. His words were choked. "You blame me? You were doing the same thing, damn you."

She shook her head. "Now, stop that. You know I'm not blaming you. If you knew me... I'm no one to blame anyone."

He was sinking into a bog and could not seem to stop himself. "What now? Will you take me away to some torture chamber, like you tried with Carrowy? Isn't that what you do to liars?"

"Listen. My people all believe, but some of us know the world isn't simple. I lied to you, after all. Or I might as well have. I'm not going to hurt you, especially now that your game is over."

He wanted to be violent, to punch the wall or shatter the lantern that she held. "Enough of this," he said and walked toward the curtain.

"Stop!" she called.

He obeyed, hating himself.

"I don't want you to go," she said, and her voice was gentle like it had been that morning.

She approached him slowly. Frozen, he watched her like he would an advancing lion.

"I've got a new idea," she added. "You will stay, and I will say whatever I want to you, whenever I want. We will make love, and you won't want it to stop."

She was so close that he became dizzy. She said, "You can't take care of yourself—that's plain. You need me." She shrugged away the cloak she had tossed on earlier, showing him that almost nothing was beneath. "You are a priest no longer. You serve only me."

Morning was advancing, and others would soon be awake. If anyone walked through the curtain, she would be in plain view. But no one would, he knew. She stood there, not a fear in the world, and time and space shaped themselves around her.

The Goddess would have to understand.

23

— · —

EMBERLY

EMBERLY HAD BEEN SITTING in the same spot for far too long. Knowing that everyone in the little sleeping chamber was watching him, he had spent the night suppressing yawns as he passed beyond sleepiness into false alertness and bone-deep exhaustion.

They had picked that room because it was far from the great hall. Three others were there, sitting on the floor: Roark and the sergeants. The former had pulled the latter out of their stupors and dragged them not quite violently to Emberly. Roark said they had been meek and apologetic. When they arrived, Emberly looked at Orund's red face and thought he might have been crying.

Lieutenant Iwan was nowhere to be found. In fact, no one had seen him since the afternoon. As the night ground on and the officers' arguments spiraled, doing little but retreading the same ground again and again, Emberly accepted that he must consider Iwan missing. The captain teetered between staying there to rehash every detail of the company's circumstances and waking everyone to search every inch of the pyramid. He prayed that the lieutenant was alive and well so that Emberly could kill him.

At one point, the captain woke up to find the others staring at him, waiting for something he had been about to say. He could not remember what it was, and he could not hide that he had fallen asleep with his eyes open.

Roark rescued him though his comment was unhelpful otherwise. "We should be thinking of Brother Nor as well, sir."

Emberly dragged a hand down his face. "He was at the temple when the bishop left. We must assume he is still with Ilis until we learn more."

"Isn't that a concern itself, Captain?" That was Orund. He had been quiet and thoughtful for most of the night, even wistful, but the mention of Nor roused him. "If he's chosen to stay there, it's fair to doubt his loyalty."

Emberly wondered if the sergeant understood just how bald and serious a statement that was. He ought to have rebuked the man for it but settled for a sharp look. The sergeant's words might sound more ridiculous if unanswered. He silenced the inner voice that reminded him how Brother Nor despised Ronia and most of its works.

He realized their conversation had become too loud. The curtain over the door offered no secrecy. He spoke in a near whisper, as they all had when the meeting began—that felt like another lifetime. "We won't learn anything about Iwan or Nor until morning. We'll talk to our hosts about them, but to do that, we have to know our stand."

Orund's reply was a weary recitation. "There is no choice worth talking about, sir. We aren't strong enough for a fight."

"The fight's already begun," Roark countered. "It started when—"

"Stop," Emberly interrupted. He had heard more than enough. Orund didn't want a war—Roark had accepted it as inevitable. Listening to them go around again would do no one any good.

In the silence that followed, he thought he heard feet shuffling some distance away, behind the curtain. He shook his head, shoving aside his increasing confusion. "How did this happen? How have they been on Ronia for so long, and us unaware? We had scarcely heard their name..."

He stopped as the footsteps in the hallway became audible to everyone.

As the curtain swelled inward, Lieutenant Iwan emerged. "Captain," he said with a cordial nod. Looking around at the others, he had the utter temerity to yawn.

Emberly's weariness burned away as he sprang to his feet. Everyone jumped at the size of his voice. "Where have you been?"

Iwan took a cautious step back. "Sorry, Captain. I was searching the pyramid, and I fell asleep."

"Asleep?" Emberly could not properly express the absurdity of that word with his face or voice.

"Yes, sir. I sat down to think, and the last few days caught up with me. But that's not important now, Captain, believe me."

"I'll decide what's bloody important! For all that's holy! What possessed you to leave without asking me? We had no idea where you were."

"I'm sorry, as I said. I didn't mean to be gone long. This building is not really that big when you know where you're going, which I do a little now."

Emberly could not shrug off Iwan's recklessness, but neither did he want a public spectacle that the soldiers of the Realm might hear—or worse, hear about from the captain's men. "Listen to me carefully, Lieutenant. This can never happen again. We don't know what else they are using this place for."

"I believe I've seen a little of that, sir." Iwan settled apart from the others, on the floor next to the doorway. "Though I don't know what help it will be. I've seen where the light in the sky comes from."

"And?"

"It's the end of our world. We are going to lose, Captain."

Upon hearing that, Emberly's first emotion was annoyance. He shook his head. "Answer the question. What makes the light?"

"I only glimpsed it, but that was enough. It was a great light. The one in the sky must only be an offshoot of it, I think."

"I don't understand. Was it an artificial light, like in ancient times?"

"It was more than that. I doubt even Brother Nor could tell us what it really is. But you're right about one thing—it's a relic from the old world." Iwan squinted as if still blinded by what he had seen. "They made terrible things back then. And somehow, the Shining Realm still possesses some of them."

"Well, unless we know what it is, we can't say what it means."

"It doesn't matter what it is," Iwan said, waving away the distraction. "What matters is that they have the power to keep something like that and use it, as we would use a hammer. They have mastery over forces we can't dream of. Even if we weren't so few, we could not fight them and win. And Ronia cannot either."

Emberly stared at him. "What would you propose, then, Lieutenant?"

Something in the captain's face and voice finally penetrated the fog around Iwan's head. He paused before answering. "I am only trying to speak accurately, sir. As I see it—"

"I know how you see it. You've decided we're beaten already, and you wish to surrender." He did not give the lieutenant time to answer. "And you could be right." He laughed and looked around at them all. "What do you say? Let's throw down our arms!"

Roark looked dazed. "Sir?"

"We're no fools," Emberly said. "The high command won't like it, of course. If Gallobraith was worth our lives, why not something even stupider?" He stretched out his feet and lay back. He lowered his voice. "We will stay alive, at least for a little while. All it will cost is our souls. We're on a holy mission, you see, and we mustn't lose faith. So says our bishop and our Lady—who is fucking *gone*." He spewed the last word and threw out a fist. If he had something to throw, he would have. Punching the air was unsatisfying and left him a clenching, heaving mess.

The others had jerked their heads back at his spasm of motion. They waited for him to calm himself.

Then he nodded. "I think we are done here." He felt freshly awoken, almost giddy. "You can all leave. Rest if you can."

The others looked at each other.

"It's morning, Captain," Iwan said. "Too late for sleep."

"Stay a moment, would you, Lieutenant?" Emberly asked him.

No one moved.

Orund asked, "What will we do about the Realm, sir?"

"I will let you know when I've decided."

Feng, a sergeant, cocked his head. "Well, Captain, shouldn't we—"

"You should do as you're told."

That silenced them briefly. They all stood, moving slowly.

Orund was not finished. "Sir," he ventured, "The men need—"

"What did the captain say?" Roark cried. "Do your job, Sergeant."

Orund left quickly. Feng followed, his face inscrutable. Roark went reluctantly after.

Emberly looked at Iwan for several seconds, considering. Finally, he asked, "Lieutenant, how did you find this room? Did someone tell you where we were?"

"I followed the sound, sir," the man said. "I could hear you all the way down the hall."

The captain had expected as much, but that did not make him any happier to hear it. He might as well have invited the whole city to listen. "Get out," he said and watched Iwan leave.

He was relieved to be alone, away from their relentless, expectant gazes, but he also felt sick with loneliness.

He was relieved when Rayan entered. "You were listening," he said.

"Who wasn't?" his brother replied.

Emberly scoffed. "Where have you been all day?"

His brother stopped in the center of the room. His usual infuriating smile had vanished. "I couldn't bear it, brother. Do you understand? Your refusal to enforce your will..." He sighed. "Your men ran roughshod through this building all night long, celebrating with the enemy, and you didn't say a word. In Huire's name, why not? And don't tell me the Realm isn't your enemy."

"Oh," Emberly replied. He smiled. "I meant to. But with all that's happened, I forgot."

"Well?" said his brother sharply. "Are you their leader or not?"

Emberly snorted. "Idiot."

Rayan looked at him, and a word emerged from his exposed throat. "Me?"

Emberly glanced at the curtain, and his voice dropped to a whisper. "Yes, you, you damned fool. Do you truly not realize what is about to happen? One way or another, these men's lives will never be the same."

"They're not dead yet, Cyril. And while they're alive, they answer to you. Especially in a crisis." He threw up his hands. "Maybe you'll die tomorrow. What matters is the mark you make on the world. I won't see my brother go down in history as a mediocrity."

The captain stared at the floor. "Sometimes, being a good man requires mediocrity."

"Then don't be a good man. Be a great one. Great men are bastards, but history needs more of them."

Emberly chuckled grimly. "Listen to you. Who'd have thought to hear these words come from your mouth?"

"Death does things to a person. The spirit world lends a certain perspective to dead folk and to gods."

"Gods," the captain murmured. He remembered again Nor's words. He looked at Rayan. "'Huire is on our side.' Isn't that what the monk told me?"

Rayan nodded wearily.

"Arumin says if we fight, we'll win. I don't believe him. But I believe Nor. Huire is with us. I've seen too much to think otherwise."

His brother cocked his head. Something in Emberly's voice had interested him. "Go on."

"I have a plan."

Rayan's eyebrows rose. "At last. I hope it's a good one."

"It's terrible. You're going to hate it." Emberly laughed. "I'm ashamed of it myself."

24

SHADA

IN A FLASH, SHADA became sure she was lost. She ran to a place where two garden paths met, and there, she risked stopping. Looking left and right, she found the trees hid the cottage and any path that would lead there. She finally dared a terrible glance behind herself. No one and nothing was there, but that did not calm her as much as let her keep breathing.

She chose the path that led uphill and was vindicated when she escaped the shadows of the trees close to the rear of the house. Jeric was standing on the back terrace, and she rushed to him.

"What's the matter?" In his light clothes and holding a steaming cup of something, he seemed oblivious to the notion that anything might be truly wrong.

"I saw someone," she said, gasping, and pointed back toward the forest. "In there." The words sounded silly as they emerged, and she felt instantly defensive. Running to her captor for refuge was an odd experience.

He did not seem to doubt her. "Who?"

"I don't know! It was a stranger. A woman." She tried to recall the image, which had passed in a flash. "She was thin, one of the thinnest people I've ever seen. And she was filthy."

"Did she talk to you?" Jeric asked. His stance remained relaxed.

Oddly, Shada had to think hard about that. "No," she finally said. "But I think she was watching me."

"I see."

Her breath was returning. "I heard something nearby, like a rustling. I was already nervous—I've only been in one forest before this one. So I turned, and there she was."

"She meant to stay hidden, then."

"Yes, and she disappeared as soon as I saw her. But I did see her—I am certain of that." She put her hands on her hips and kept breathing.

She had woken to find nice clothes laid out for her, a pale dress with flowers, but now it was sweaty. She had thought a walk might clear her head, but that idea was in shambles.

"I don't doubt it," he said. "Sometimes, locals from the city find their way in."

"Doesn't that worry you? The girls play in these woods."

"They are harmless," he replied with a flick of his hand. "They won't dare get close to the girls. Or to you, for that matter."

"Why?" She did not understand his confidence.

"It may seem like we're alone here, but in fact, we are watched over by very powerful people. If anyone harmed one of us, they would regret it."

Shada did not know what to think. She only knew his explanation did not seem like enough. She started to reply, but something in her throat jabbed her so sharply that she almost cried out. The Lady did not want her to question him any further.

Then Jeric began speaking of other things with such will and enthusiasm that he swept her along despite herself. "I've come to love this place," he said, nodding cordially at the blooming gardens and the woods. "Delia and Lani like it too. I wish we could stay here forever."

"Who will make you leave?" She cringed inwardly, wondering if the Lady would hurt her again, but the pain did not return. "You must be wealthy, to own a place like this."

A smile touched his lips, and he looked down at his cup. "I don't own it or anything else, really. I count myself fortunate in that."

"Your world must be very different than mine."

"I dare say so."

"But you own this city, now, don't you? You and your people."

"Not as we see it. We come to a place and do what we must. In the end, things will be better." He looked at her. "Had you heard of the Shining Realm before coming here?"

"I've been thinking about that. I must have heard that name somewhere. People like me are told what others choose to tell us, but rumors drift down regardless."

She looked at his profile. The longer she looked at it, the more she wanted to look, and realizing that was infuriating. "You know where I'm from, don't you?"

His smile turned sharply upward. "Do I?"

Shada did not answer right away. The Lady had commanded her to hide her true origins, and Shada fully expected retaliation for that last question. As seconds passed and no new agony struck her, a faint hope began to grow: that the answer to her question was obvious to the Lady as well. The voice in her ears said nothing—perhaps the Lady feared being overheard in the quiet of the morning.

The extended silence must have seemed strange to him. He turned his smile on her and narrowed his eyes.

She said, "Yes, I believe so. We speak the same language—you sound like a Ronian from up the hill. So do your daughters, and so did the first of your soldiers I met. If you're not from Ronia, you've at least been there."

He finished his cup in one gulp and said, "Yes, I know of Ronia."

Shada felt movement in her throat and on her cheeks. The Lady was shifting. Perhaps Jeric's admission had surprised her.

"I know of it," he went on, "but I've never been there."

"How do you speak the imperial language so well?"

"I've been taught. So have the girls. In fact, they've seldom heard anything else. As for me, I have been learning for a long time. Many of my people have."

"Are you planning on going to Ronia?"

"Yes."

Her feet grew heavier. "So us meeting now—it's not a coincidence."

He chuckled gently. "Did it seem like one?"

Shada caught her breath in fear as a buzzing whisper filled her ears. The Lady was speaking, and her words were terse. "We must learn their plans. Go along with him."

Shada could not answer her then, of course, but she thought she followed her meaning. The Lady wanted her to try her charms on Jeric. That might have been a good idea, but after what Shada had just learned, her emotions got the better of her.

"I want you to tell me everything," she demanded. She was pleased with her tone, which sounded like Captain Emberly commanding one of his privates.

His face was grave and his voice respectful. "No. I'm sorry, Shada. I've said more than I should already."

"I don't want an apology. I want the truth." Pain stabbed at her throat, but she kept talking. "If you and your people are planning to conquer my world—"

She stopped as her windpipe was filled by a hard little ball that grew and grew. She fought back panic. It would pass—it must.

He replied quickly enough to think he was interrupting her. "No. We are not going to 'conquer' Ronia. But we are going there—to set it free." He turned to her. "I have to ask you something now, Shada."

The ball vanished just before it grew large enough to hurt her seriously. She bent a little in relief, struggling to hear and understand him.

He noticed that something was amiss and paused. She straightened and, to her own amazement, managed to give him a smile. It was partly genuine. She now doubted that the Lady could be easily goaded into killing her.

Jeric frowned but kept any questions to himself. "In the Realm," he continued slowly, "to lie is to shame oneself. Lying is what barbarians do—people without the strength to abide in a civil society. So I'm at your mercy in this. Please, don't ask me anything more just yet. I will explain it all soon if you choose to stay."

She almost forgot about the Lady. "Would you let me leave?"

"Yes! As I said, the way you were treated before was unpardonable. It was unbecoming of any human, much less a lady like yourself."

Shada knew the Lady would not let her walk away yet. Still, she looked out over the forest and took an experimental step away from the house. When Jeric did not move, she breathed aloud. "It's that easy."

He said, "I'll take you to the gates of the garden myself."

"I have no place to go." That fact kept coming back, no matter how she pondered leaving that place. Nothing else was possible. She had no hope of finding the company without the Lady, and the Lady insisted she stay there. That meant everything and everyone she'd ever known was gone from her life. The company. Nor. Her father.

Loneliness washed over her, so deep she might have drowned. "What would happen to me?" Her voice nearly cracked. She resented the weakness he made her feel and resented the Lady for not letting her truly express it.

"I'll see that you're cared for." Jeric did not elaborate. "But I hope against hope that you will stay."

She took a deep breath, trying to calm herself. "Why?"

"Because you have—" He looked down. "People like you are precious. You have come from a place where those without money or a title are forgotten. In our new world, everyone has a place, and yours is a very special one."

Again, the Lady spoke to Shada: "There is an opportunity here."

"What do you mean?" Shada asked Jeric.

He said, "I'm very selfish, Shada. I must confess that before I say anything else. This place is a shelter for me and my girls. Soon, we will be called away forever. But until then, we have a little while to make memories that will sustain us in the times to come. The girls have a few moments in which to be children.

"But I can't help them do that. There's something missing from me, Shada, and it is something you have. I don't think I can explain it better than that. You are good for them. I am not."

He turned toward the back door of the house. Immediately, his servant, the man whose face and head were a great red scar, came out with tea. Jeric thanked him warmly and caressed his face.

Battered by a storm of feelings, Shada wanted to hear his voice, anything but her own thoughts. "What's his name?" she asked after the scarred man left. "No one's told me."

"His name these days is Adney. I don't know what it was before I knew him."

Even in her wretched state, that seemed strange. "Why did he change it?" she asked, relieved to have something to think about.

"I changed it," Jeric said.

He would have said no more had Shada not pushed him. "That's an odd idea. How can you just… change someone's name?"

Jeric looked as confused as she felt. "Why wouldn't I? When someone takes on a new role and does different things, they are no longer who they once were."

"How many names have you had?"

"Two. This one and the one I was born with. I chose Jeric—a Ronian name—when I was selected to become myself."

Their conversation, the giving and taking, felt precious. When they were talking, she wasn't alone. "You chose your own name? Why were you allowed to do that when Adney wasn't?"

"For the same reason that I was given this house. Because I am different from him. He's as good a man as me—better, probably—and I love him. But our suitabilities differ. We embrace that and have peace. He was given to me partly to remind me of these things."

He looked at her with painfully open sadness. "Shada, I am flawed in many and various ways. All I have is my honesty.

"I cannot contain how I am feeling. That would be a lie. I intend to treasure this place. I want you to stay and treasure it with me."

The Lady's voice came to her again: "He desires you. Give him what he wants."

Shada froze. Her body hummed with anxiety and grief. She said nothing.

Perhaps sensing her uncertainty, Jeric frowned. He looked away toward the garden. "Do you like it?"

"It's wonderful," she managed to answer.

He turned again to face her, that time with a decisive air. "What would you have different? Tell me."

"Nothing that I can name." She was afraid and needed a moment to think. She wondered whether it would truly be so crazy, such a betrayal, now that she had no choice in her life, to let herself enjoy this place, to enjoy him. "It just seems—false." That was the best answer she could give.

He did not look disturbed. "What's false about it?"

"I don't know."

Aside from feeling trapped and suffocated, she felt stupid. Really, she had little experience with making men want her. They either did or didn't. And the Lady could hardly have picked a worse moment to force her to learn.

She sought refuge again in talking. "It's everything. The colors, even. See those flowers there? Don't they seem just... too bright to be natural?"

"I'm afraid I don't understand. We make things as we want them to be. If we want dull flowers, we will breed dull flowers. Everything is natural. It's a question of whether you embrace the power or not."

"People shouldn't have too much power. They aren't good enough."

"Only the gods should, eh? Shada, I think my people will convince you otherwise."

They looked at the trees for a while. Insects chirped in the grass, and Shada wondered who had brought the little creatures here, across the desert.

Some time later, he said, "You haven't left."

"No."

"Do you intend to?"

"Not yet." The answer was feeble but honest.

He wanted honesty, and she realized something that should have scared her but didn't: despite the Lady's interference and Shada's own desire for freedom and purpose, the idea of giving Jeric what he wanted made warmth bloom in her chest.

He smiled. "I'm grateful. As much as I intend to offer you, it won't be nearly what you offer me."

He reached out and touched her face. The motion was slow, but it still happened before she could really think about it. He drew his fingers down her cheek and to the end of her chin. On the surface, it looked like his gesture to his servant, but she knew how different it was.

In most circumstances, such an action from a man she barely knew would have twisted her stomach with anxiety. But she had no more anxiety to spend. She wanted to cry, and she wanted him to keep touching her.

He said, "These marks on your face. They aren't your goddess's work—or are they?"

"No. My mother was born on one of Ronia's colony worlds. In ancient times, that place had many gods, and each had a chosen people whom they decorated with a mark."

Jeric was looking at her face intently.

She turned away in embarrassment and said, "Most are nicer and cleaner than mine. My father was Ronian, and I look quite different."

His expression was stern. "Do you know that you're beautiful?"

She was surprised but answered frankly. "I don't feel it, except once in a while. The last time was when I saw your painting of me."

"Then I've done a good thing. You've taught me something already, Shada: if the gods gave you this face, then they can't be all bad."

"Kiss him. Now." The Lady's tone was harsh. But Shada obeyed.

As Jeric pulled her to himself, she struggled to reconcile her pounding heart with the knowledge that he could never be anything but her enemy.

25

EMBERLY

WHEN EMBERLY WALKED OUT to meet the general, only Roark came with him. Bringing more men would have increased the tension and thus the odds of violence—and violence must only happen when Emberly wanted and expected it.

At midday, the city was likely as bright as it ever got. The distant windows of Om stood out from the surrounding walls as brilliant blue swaths of chilling vastness. Two motor carriages waited for Emberly and Roark, and as they approached, General Ganet emerged from the lead vehicle. From the rear one stepped a small woman whom Emberly did not recognize. The general and his companion were each followed by a couple of brightly dressed soldiers, with a driver remaining behind the wheel of each carriage.

The general wore a wide smile, the skin of his cheeks tight enough to snap. His eyes were wide, and his hands were in constant motion. The woman was mild, and little about her seemed to warrant description. Emberly kept an eye on her and she on him.

"General," he said, briskly shaking Ganet's hand.

"I hope your evening was comfortable, Cyril."

The man's grip was so strong that it might have been meant to hurt. Emberly glanced at his hand in surprise.

"Yes, thank you." Emberly remembered that he and Ganet had agreed to address each other by their first names, after the general had insisted.

He turned toward the woman, wishing to have this all done as soon as possible. "I don't believe we've met, madam."

"This is one of my agents," Ganet said.

The woman's eyes darted to him and back.

"Her name is Ren. I believe you've heard of her."

"That's right." Emberly faced her for the first time.

"Captain," she declared, making the word a sentence in itself. "I am sure you weren't pleased with my actions against your men. But I assure you their behavior left me no choice."

Emberly looked her in the eyes.

Ganet spoke into the ensuing silence. "Only one body-guard, Cyril?" He smiled as if expecting a laugh.

"I trust you, Talis, and I don't expect to need reinforcements."

"In that case, I hope you will forgive me for bringing company. We have ways of doing these things." He looked at Roark then back at Emberly. "Speaking of which, it is time we reached an agreement. What have you decided?"

The captain looked squarely at him. For a brief time, a few seconds perhaps, his mouth went totally dry, and he thought his voice might fail him. He licked his lips and reminded himself Huire was on their side.

"I've made no decision," he told the general.

Ganet's smile was frozen, preserved behind glass. "Why not?" he asked finally.

Emberly held his gaze. Try as he might to forget about Ren, she remained in his peripheral vision.

"The situation is very complicated. I'm sorry, but I will need more time."

"We had an arrangement." The general's voice cracked.

"New considerations have arisen," Emberly said. "That is the simple truth. I look forward to reaching an accord, but I cannot do so today."

His plan, formed in the sleepless depths of the night, was terrible—so terrible that Rayan had stormed out when he realized Emberly was serious about it. But if Huire was on the company's side, even a terrible plan should suffice.

Captain Emberly would not send his men into a hopeless fight if he had a choice. That was not how a good soldier worked. He had sent many soldiers to their deaths during his career—on Gallobraith, he had gained a reputation for it—but never for a hopeless cause. When it came down to it, he simply could not face ordering his men to their deaths and hoping that Huire would stop the bullets. It was too real. If he was wrong, the bloodstains would be too permanent.

Yet he had seen miracles. He had seen the Lady and Shada save Nor from the swamp. Divine interventions did happen—he just could not bear to count on this one.

He would not start a war, and he would not surrender.

So he would wait. He would stall, avoiding a fight as long as fate and the Shining Realm would allow. He would give the Goddess time to produce one of her occasional miracles, saving the company and returning Shada and the Lady to them. He would give the men he'd sent into the bowels of the pyramid time to find some hidden means of escape.

He would save his men's lives.

Unless the Realm decided to kill them immediately. But even if his men died, Emberly would not be the one to kill them.

Utter silence reigned for a few moments. The driver of Ganet's carriage coughed. Ganet glared at the man, who looked as pale and frightened as Emberly felt. The man leaned close to the steering wheel of the carriage, stifling further coughing.

Emberly saw with terrible surety that the driver was expecting violence. He should have brought more men, and it was too late.

The general plowed onward. "This must be done soon," he blustered. "How much time—"

"Ganet, don't be ridiculous," Ren said. She took a small step forward, inserting herself fully into the conversation. "Captain, this cannot wait. You already know all that you need to know. You must decide right now, this instant, whether our two peoples are at war or not."

"I cannot do that," Emberly told her.

"Not deciding is still to decide, sir. Reject our offer, and the shooting will start right now."

Ganet's head snapped around toward her. "Wait."

She ignored him. "I doubt that many will die. I expect that most of your soldiers will see the wisdom in adopting our ways."

Emberly looked at her. He had been praying that Roark would remain calm, but now, that might not matter.

"Well, Captain? Are you a wise man?"

He said, "Do what you must."

With an inchoate cry, Ganet's driver leapt from his carriage. In his hands was a pistol of the Realm's slender make. "No one move!" he shouted as they turned toward him.

"What are you doing?" the general shouted back.

"Shut your mouth, and raise your hands," the driver said. Unlike Ganet and Ren, his accent was distinctly not Ronian. He was a young man with fairer hair and a thinner mustache than most of the Realmsmen. His eyes were wide, and he gripped the gun with both hands, whipping the barrel this way and that with nerve-racking franticness.

Once everyone obeyed, the driver announced, "This is over." With the barrel of the pistol, he pointed at Emberly and Ganet. "The two of you, get in now." He took one shaking hand off the pistol and pointed at the carriage. "Get in! Everyone else, back away—over there."

The captain looked at the general and found the general looking back. Emberly could discern little in the other man's eyes but alarm.

"What is going on here?" he asked the driver.

"A minor inconvenience, I imagine," Ren said. To the driver, she said, "What is your name?"

"Does not matter," the man said.

"Certainly it does. Who told you to do this?"

"No one!" he said quickly.

"I don't believe you. Tell me now."

"He's right," Ganet said. "It doesn't matter. He won't tell us, and I'd rather go along than get shot. Cyril, shall we?"

Emberly stepped toward the carriage, but a hand clamped onto his shoulder.

Roark said, "No."

The driver lost the remains of his composure. He shouted and cursed at Roark, and Emberly half expected him to start shooting.

"Lieutenant," the captain said sharply, "let me go. This is the way it must be."

"Like hell," Roark said. Then he spoke clearly to the driver. "Do you know what this means, son? It means war. If you take him, you are already dead, and so is anyone with you."

"No!" Emberly snapped. "We'll go. If he wanted to kill us, he would have. I'll come back soon."

Roark replied, and his voice was not softened. "You've said that before, Captain. I don't believe you."

"There can be no violence here," Emberly said.

Roark knew as well as anyone that they would lose.

"Can't help that, sir," the lieutenant said, watching the driver intently. "When the men find out about this, there will be fighting no matter what I say."

The captain felt the truth of that even as Roark said it. Though the walls of Om were far away, he felt them closing in. "Then you must tell no one. I went by my own choice."

Roark sneered, a look unlike any he had given the captain before. "And how am I to do that? Not tell your men—our men—that their captain has been abducted?"

"It's simple," Emberly snapped. "I am ordering it. You will obey."

Roark's jaw flexed, and he exhaled through his nostrils. He had reached a line he would not cross. "Very well, Captain. I will lie."

"Swear to me that you will obey."

"I swear!" Roark spat. "And if you really think I needed to, then go to hell."

Emberly turned away. The driver checked his pockets and the general's, searching with such haste that he would have been lucky to find anything. He took Emberly's pistol and saber but missed the smaller gun and blade in his boots. The captain got into the front seat of the carriage next to Ganet, who had taken the wheel at the driver's command. As Emberly sat, his decision to get in the vehicle felt horribly true and permanent. His plan, which he'd known was terrible, was collapsing around him. He wanted to jump out of the car and run for all he was worth, but he limited himself to squirming in his seat.

The driver climbed into the back seat alone. "Don't follow us," he snarled at Ren and the soldiers.

For a few seconds, the carriage's engine refused to start, and the driver bounced with panic. When the engine roared to life, he leaned toward the general's ear and shouted at him to drive away quickly.

The car howled under the arch in the wall that hid the pyramid from the street. Ganet drove with surprising aggression, forcing the carriage into the ceaseless traffic and immediately looking for gaps through which to forge ahead. Emberly wished he wasn't in such a hurry.

Ganet shouted at their captor in the high, musical tongue of the Realm. He sounded alarmed and exasperated, the notes of his words discordant. The man answered, his tone unmistakably pleading.

"What the hell is going on?" Emberly demanded.

From behind them came a storm of shouting and the bleating of animals. The second carriage had emerged from the arch and swerved into the street. Ren sat in the front passenger seat with the Realm's soldiers piled in around her.

The general shouted anew at their captor, who cried back, their words meeting like the chaotic chatter of a flock of birds. Ganet glanced at Emberly, his face blanched. "He should have disabled her car," he said. "But no use scolding him now, poor boy." Then he addressed their captor, not bothering to switch to the Realm's language. "Shoot them if they get close." To Emberly again, he said, "Cyril, it would comfort me greatly to hear that you are still armed."

"What in Huire's name are you doing?"

"I needed a chance to talk some sense into you. For that, we had to be alone."

"Did you plan this—kidnapping me?"

"Kidnapping us. I planned it, hoping that I wouldn't have to do it. I hoped you would embrace the future rather than run from it. But you have persisted in being a fool."

Their carriage was leaving mayhem in its wake. Behind them, Ren's car weaved through dazed clusters of pedestrians and wagons, using the partly cleared road to gain steadily. The chase would have seemed slow and unimpressive to onlookers while being terrifying to all involved.

The captain's carriage swerved as Ganet yanked the wheel to one side, bringing them around a herd of livestock. The little hoofed creatures fled from the metal beast, and their retreat halted traffic on the other side of the road. Collisions and near misses resulted, further slowing the general's progress.

All the while, Ren's carriage bore down on them. Their abductor—apparently a soldier of Ganet's—fired his pistol at it. His hands were shaking, and he missed cleanly. Screams and angry shouts erupted from bystanders, who began to abandon their wagons and flee. The soldier slumped in his seat as the car's motion knocked him back and forth. He was muttering, struggling to calm himself.

Emberly asked Ganet, "And you chose this boy to do it?"

The general did not spare him a glance. "This boy has just sacrificed his life, Cyril. Rather than insult him, you might lend him any weapons that you still possess. You and I cannot be seen shooting."

Emberly dug his remaining pistol from his boot and handed it over. Ren's carriage had slowed after the shot, but it was roaring back as if set on vengeance. Having accepted Emberly's pistol as a backup weapon, the soldier put it on the seat nearby and spun to fire at the onrushing enemy. He missed again. An elderly man on the side of the street staggered.

"This isn't working," Ganet said. His face was red.

The way ahead was blocked by a pair of wagons. Both drivers had tried to clear the way by steering their load beasts off the road, but their wagons were still too close by half to allow the carriage through.

The general halted the vehicle. Ren's carriage was hurtling toward them. She would soon be able to trap them between the wagons and her vehicle.

Ganet turned in his seat to face the young soldier. The man leaned in so that the general's hand could rest on his arm. Ganet said a few words. All that happened in an instant, but to Emberly, it was maddeningly slow. With the carriage halted and the enemy coming, the soldier aimed his pistol carefully and fired.

Ren's driver bent, throwing himself forward, and the vehicle stopped with a razor-sharp scream a short distance away. At that instant, Ganet leaned toward the wheel, and their own carriage roared ahead toward the wagons blocking their path.

One wagon was heavily laden with gray sacks. The other carried only a few passengers who had already leapt out onto the street. Emberly and the others were tossed forward as the carriage struck the empty wagon, pushing it partly out of the way. Its owner threw down his cloth cap and screamed at the strangers.

Ganet, in turn, screamed at the carriage. His arms shook as he squeezed effort from the engine, pushing the empty wagon away a few inches at a time.

Emberly looked back. To his relief, the other carriage had not moved. The soldiers were struggling to move the unconscious driver. Then the captain saw something that sent his heart pounding.

Ren was coming for them at a dead run. He glimpsed her face and saw utter abandon.

He could not tell if she was armed, but that didn't seem to matter. Feeling like a storm was coming that would sweep them away, Emberly shouted uselessly at the general to hurry.

An eruption of gunfire sounded from the back seat as the soldier emptied his weapon. It was deafening even in that chaos. When he stopped, he gave a cry of anguish that cut through the ringing in Emberly's ears.

She was still coming. Emberly fumbled for the knife in his boot. He had just drawn the blade when the carriage broke through the wagons. His head whipped back and struck the seat, and he dropped the knife.

Pulling himself together, he looked back. Ren was still chasing them, but she quickly fell behind. The soldier slumped in the back seat. In his neck was lodged an awful little metal thing. It was round like a wheel, and from its edges, a bouquet of little blades extended in every direc-tion. The man shuddered as he probed it with his weak fingers.

Still weaving through traffic, the carriage approached a crossroads. Ganet twisted the wheel right, and as they turned, Emberly felt the carriage's right wheels leave the ground. He hunkered down until the carriage righted itself with an ugly thump. High walls rose on either side of them, and the street was mostly empty.

As they sped along, Emberly shouted at Ganet, "Well? What did you want so badly to tell me?"

"Wait. We're not alone yet."

Emberly squinted at him then looked at the man in the back seat.

They were approaching another crossroads. There, their road met what looked like a much wider boulevard. Ren and her soldiers had not yet appeared behind them.

"This is our chance," the general said. "We must disappear."

Once more, he barely slowed down. With a sharp left turn and a jarring rise and fall of the wheels, they settled onto the new road.

But the road was not there. Emberly could not comprehend it—the street ended just in front of them. Beyond was thin air, and into that they roared.

They plummeted down a stairway as broad as the road had been. The floor of Om slanted abruptly downward toward a valley. The stairs were lined and speckled with perilously balanced stands and tents, and beyond those lay toppled ruins of far greater stature. The floor of Om had collapsed there without breaking through the ceiling of the level below. What was once a road had been carved into a rough staircase.

Airborne, the carriage soared over the stairs for some distance then plunged. Emberly clutched about to avoid being lifted from the carriage. He thought only of the stomach-rending fall and the impact to come.

When the bottom of the carriage hit the stairs, the world turned to noise and motion. The wheels were being torn apart, but the carriage was somehow still upright. Ganet still futilely clutched the wheel. They bounded down the middle of the staircase, moving too quickly to tell who or what they were hitting. The bouncing settled into a rattling slide. Looking ahead, Emberly saw the bottom, an open area cluttered with fleeing people. He let out an overdue scream.

The friction of the stairs tore away their momentum. They hit the bottom with a shadow of their original speed, but their bones were jarred nonetheless. Emberly's spine howled as the pain from his fall on Caidfell returned. The carriage slid to a halt with the shriek of a tortured animal.

Ganet moaned. The young soldier was pale and sweaty, pressing his wound. Emberly pulled himself upright and looked around.

They were in a crater of sorts. The ancient collapse had opened a space where a great many tunnels and chambers beneath the skin of Om had been exposed to the air. The walls of the valley were riddled with openings, and its slanted floors—the fragments of the collapsed surface level—held a city's worth of small buildings and makeshift dwellings. Some of the inhabitants ran this way and that. Others stood and watched the new arrivals.

The young soldier leaned over the side of the carriage and looked at its wheels. Emberly was sure the vehicle would never move again unless it was dragged.

The soldier, muttering in alarm, grabbed the general's shoulder and shook him. Ganet turned and listened as the soldier spoke quickly. The general's eyes grew wide, and he replied softly.

The soldier grew more agitated. He pointed at himself and cried out, glancing a couple of times toward the top of the staircase. The carriage had left a trail of wreckage, and crowds were gathering around injured people and flattened booths.

Emberly said, "What's he asking?"

The soldier finally tore his shirt open and shouted at Ganet. The general looked at the man's exposed skin and answered him with unmistakable finality.

The young man was fighting back tears. He climbed out of the carriage and bowed. The two men looked into each other's eyes, then the soldier turned and ran.

Ganet watched him go. Voices were rising nearby as bystanders converged on the carriage. The general settled back in his seat and turned to Emberly. "He wanted something I could not give, Cyril. No doubt you know the feeling." The lightness of his tone was unconvincing. The general seemed deeply shaken, and not by the crash.

He continued, "We'll have a moment, at least. I have to convince you to reconsider your position."

"You don't yet know my position."

"I know enough. You're a proud man from a proud people, and submission is unthinkable. At the same time, you recognize that your situation is hopeless. To send your men to death while accomplishing nothing... You're not the sort of commander who could do that without pause."

"My men have faced terrible odds since leaving home. So has Ronia, since its birth. We've survived."

"It's been a while, though, hasn't it? Since your city fought for its life. The universe must look smaller nowadays. Has any Ronian now living ever faced the end of everything?"

"Our Goddess remembers."

"And where has she been?"

"We will find out soon."

"You're a loyal man, Emberly. I admire you, though I pity you."

"I have faith. A man like you may sneer at that, but—"

"I sneer at nothing!" the general cried. "I want you to live and to be one of us. Do you know how great a risk I've just taken?"

"I will not be pushed to a decision!" Emberly yelled. "No crazed plan of yours will move me an inch. I will not be pushed! Do you understand me?"

"Then the decision will be made for you, you damned fool!" Ganet shot back. "I've protected you from your fate as long as I can. I cannot hold her back any longer!"

The onlookers had multiplied into a thick crowd. Many had seen friends or relatives felled by the carriage's mad descent. Something hit the vehicle's side—a few people had begun throwing rocks and debris. Others were shouting and pressing in on all sides. Someone shoved Emberly, and his shoulder struck Ganet's.

"This has all gone wrong," the general said. "You should run, Cyril. When she finds us, I don't know what will happen. I hope you come to your senses."

Emberly looked outside the carriage. His head jerked back in an explosion of pain and shock as a thick bald man punched him in the face. A cheer went up from the crowd, blending with the whirl of voices growing steadily angrier. Men grabbed Emberly by his hair, arm, and jacket and landed blows of their own. Others were trying to pull Ganet from the carriage by his arms.

Emberly broke free with a flurry of arms and fists. Doubling over, he spent his instant of freedom looking for the knife on the floor. Then someone got a solid hold on his bandaged arm. As they pulled him back up into the storm of punches and tearing hands, his fingers found the knife and snatched it.

He slashed at their shoulders and faces, and they let him go. Swinging the knife, he tried to drive them back. The men in front wanted to retreat, but the weight of the crowd held them in place. Emberly focused on the large bald man, poking at his face with the blade, and the man forced the mob back alone with a strength born of sheer panic.

Ganet screamed. The general had escaped his attackers' grasp long enough to pull a gun from somewhere. He pointed it at the attackers nearest him and warned them with incoherent shouting to get back. Stepping up onto his seat, he turned this way and that, letting the whole crowd see the gun.

The pressure lessened a bit. The men nearest Ganet took a step back, and the rain of blows on Emberly halted momentarily. But the crowd boiled with rage and seemed unlikely to hold back for long.

"Cyril!" Ganet snapped. "Run."

"What will you do?" Emberly was surprised to hear his own concern for the general.

"That doesn't matter. You can still stop this war. But my work is over."

Emberly opened his door and stumbled out. He faced the mob, who looked like an impenetrable wall.

"Wait!" the general called. He stepped across onto Emberly's seat and said, "Hold out your hand."

In a dream, Emberly obeyed.

Ganet looked at him and said, "My people will come to your men tomorrow. Then it will all be decided, whether you are there or not. For the love of your goddess, make peace."

He placed his pistol in Emberly's hand. It felt light and strange to the captain, but its presence awakened him in a way that words could not. He turned it on the mob and shouted at them to make way. His words were as incomprehensible to them as theirs were to him, but his meaning was clear enough. He stepped aggressively toward the crowd, and they began to move aside.

Emberly threw a last look at the general and started out. When he saw a clear path of escape, he ran.

26

— · —

GANET

ONLY WHEN EMBERLY DISAPPEARED through the mob was Ganet struck by the enormity of being alone in that crowd. The thought of its wrath focused solely on him was so dreadful that he opened his mouth to call the captain back. But a greater fear, that of humiliation, stopped him.

Since he had given his pistol away, the mob surged forward in a landslide. The general stood with one boot on each of the carriage's front seats, hoping to escape the grasping hands for an instant longer.

They came over the sides and hood of the carriage. Ganet did not draw his knife. They would get hold of it soon enough, and he didn't want to give them the idea to torture him with it.

He raised his fists and swung at the wall of people as it came. He could scarcely miss, but the blow was lost in the rush of the mob.

He was crushed among them. He hurt all over—no punch or kick could compare to the pressure of body packed upon body from all directions. He could not have fallen if he tried.

With a quiet wheeze, he began to suffocate. Then, to his surprise, the crowd separated a little. Gulping air, he decided he would not be buried under the crowd again. He made a pitiful leap to climb over them and was snatched down.

Things became indefinite. They were dragging him from the car, then the ground struck him. He huddled against it, trying to sink into its vastness. No one knew how large this planet was or what lay beyond the desert in which Om stood.

A wayward calmness came over him. *What mercy is this?* He drew his knees toward his chest and covered his head as they pummeled him. If he wanted, he could roll onto his back and accept his punishment. He wondered where that courage had come from. Perhaps he had accepted that he would be spared worse fates.

He heard gunshots but did not think about what they should mean to him. The kicks to his body lessened then stopped. He opened his eyes to a flurry of motion. His attackers were running away.

Collecting himself, he raised his head. Several Realms-men were descending the great staircase. He was relieved to see they wore the blue of his army troops, not the black of Ren's commandos. Ganet could not see Ren among them, but he was certain she was there. He settled onto his back and waited.

She soon appeared over him and spoke in the tongue of the Realm. "General, I am relieved to find you well."

From the ground, he nodded in response. Ren's soldiers pulled him to his feet, and he let his weight sag onto them.

She moved straight to business. "Which way did your driver run?"

Trembling, Ganet half listened to the question. A cloud of belated shock was descending, making thinking hard. He remembered that she was waiting and shook his head. "I don't know."

"We must move quickly," she said. "Did he take the captain?"

His eyes focused on her face. "Who?"

"Your driver," she said with passing annoyance. "Did he take Emberly when he escaped?"

Answering took some effort. "No," Ganet said. "Went separately."

His attention wandered as she issued orders to the soldiers, who were loyal enough to Ganet that they waited for his nod before obeying. They resented the presence of her and her commandos more than he did. Most of them left, spreading out to search for the driver and the captain. When she turned back to him, her eyes and tone were sharp.

"I don't understand. If your man didn't kill either of you but left you behind, why kidnap you in the first place?"

"The boy was... afraid," Ganet replied. He had planned the kidnapping in a rush—his last, flailing effort to prevent a war. He had convinced himself Emberly would surrender, so he had not given proper consideration to a different outcome. The whole thing had fallen apart, and as a final comeuppance, he was too addled to remember the story he had invented to explain it all.

"Afraid of what?" she breezily demanded.

"Death." He coughed the word. "The driver feared there would be shooting, so he panicked. He took us and left."

"Did he tell you this?"

"Yes."

"When?"

"As we drove."

Her face was alive with doubt. "But Emberly brought only one man to the meeting with him. We outnumbered them by far." She spoke with an authority that made Ganet feel like he had taken the opposite position.

She was right. He had expected Emberly to bring more soldiers and didn't understand why he hadn't.

She said, "The driver should have felt safe enough, coward or not. What happened here, General?"

"I only know what he told me. He was always strange."

"If he behaved erratically, you should have reported it."

He closed his eyes. "You're right, of course."

"What happened after the crash?"

"A crowd came and attacked us. It happened quickly. They were furious—I suppose because of the people we hurt in this rampage. If Emberly and the driver are not lying dead somewhere nearby, they must have escaped."

"'Must have?' You told me you saw them go."

Ganet let a second pass before he answered. If he made his confusion obvious, she might forgive inconsistencies in his story. "Did I?"

That gave her pause. She put her hands on her hips and leaned toward him. "Yes. Have you truly forgotten? You told me they left separately. Unless that was false, you must have seen them go."

He was losing control one word at a time. An icy feeling grew inside him. As her eyes did not leave his face, he stumbled over his words. "Then I must have seen them. I... can't remember."

"Are you injured?"

"Only a little. I can walk."

"Then how can you be *confused*?"

She wanted to make him angry or, better yet, afraid. She was succeeding, but he could not let her know it. "I'm not young like you. This was a lot of excitement."

"Are you telling the truth?"

He chose that moment to attack. "How dare you? Do you know—"

"I know exactly what I am asking. I want an answer."

He met her gaze but found it impenetrable. "Yes."

She fell silent. For a long moment, she seemed to turn inward, looking through him rather than at him. When she spoke, her voice returned to its normal restless efficiency. A dark moment of decision had passed. "Very well. You should rest in my carriage while we conduct the search."

When he did not answer immediately, she said, "We must hurry. What's the matter?"

"If you think I'm lying," he said, "please do not wait. Do what you mean to do."

She looked exasperated. "You have given me your answer, and I have chosen to believe you. What more can be said? Please, consider it settled."

She took his arm and led him to the stairs. Moving reawakened the pain lurking throughout his body. He slowed their pace, and she obliged with a poorly disguised huff.

Perhaps feeling that they were wasting time, she spoke. "Our position is precarious. This city has long been ruled by a federation of savages—warlords who have no interest in being united." She shook her head. "They each want our protection. They want to buy us, General. If they can't be taught better behavior, more vigorous measures will be needed. You must be ready for that, sir."

Had Ganet been sure he could climb the stairs alone, he would have thrown off her arm. They did not simply represent two competing hands of the Shining Realm—they represented entirely different ways of doing things. He settled for a growl. "Remember who you are talking to. I am capable of anything."

"I do remember," Ren replied. "But with your love for the Realm comes a gentleness toward those you hope will join it. Take care that sentiment does not overcome your willpower."

Angry and out of breath, he did not answer.

She allowed their pace to slow. "While my soldiers were saving you, they fired over the heads of that mob. If the crowd hadn't run after that, my men would have shot some of them. What if your Ronian friends do not come to heel? Will you do what must be done?"

"Of course I will." He said it perhaps too quickly. "But I won't have to. Emberly is on the verge of breaking."

"What makes you so sure? It seems to me that he's stalling for his own advantage."

"I'm sure," he snapped, "because I lived among the Ronians longer than anyone. I know their character. Their pride can be conquered, and when it is, it will become part of us. They are just what we need."

"We will find out soon. I will put pressure on Emberly's soldiers."

"No. The captain himself must decide."

She stopped and looked at him. "But Emberly is gone, General. Maybe forever."

Ganet was short of breath again. "We had better hope not. The Ronians are not like us. He is their leader."

"Of course. But if he is gone, they will have to accept it, and quickly. Perhaps I should have a hand in it."

"No."

"No more waiting. We must proceed immediately. If the Ronians are leaderless, then this is the perfect time. We will take them without much effort and begin to awaken those who survive."

"No!" he barked. "I told Emberly we would come to them tomorrow. Whether he survives or not, I am obligated to him."

"That was a rash thing to promise."

"It is done. We'll discuss this no further."

They stared at each other. Finally, Ganet tugged at her arm, and they resumed their climb.

"I am your conscience, General," Ren said, her tone amicable. "It is my place to advise you."

He grunted. "Advise. Consider what that word means and what it does not."

"But should you prove inefficient beyond repair, I must fulfill my second function. I dread the thought." She might have sounded more dismayed over an unexpected rainstorm.

Refusing to show fear, he let her words drift away on the air and changed the subject as though bored. "How is your other task proceeding?"

"I am coming to know Norhim quite well. His transformation will be beautiful."

They said nothing else until they reached the top of the stairs. Her carriage waited nearby, quite close to the staircase. The driver might have stopped barely in time to avoid the same tumultuous descent Ganet had suffered.

They stopped and looked out over the valley. Seeing how big it was—yet only a small part of Om—he could imagine it swallowing them all. Surely, Emberly or anyone who stepped out of sight would never be seen again.

"Any news of Jeric?" he asked.

When he did not hear an answer, he turned his head toward Ren. She was smiling. That answered his question, and though he tried to be happy about it, the amusement in her eyes curdled his enjoyment.

27

EMBERLY

EMBERLY DIDN'T KNOW IF they were chasing him. He ran among clusters of low hovels and through alleys where his boots tossed up dirt like shovels.

Close ahead rose the wall of the valley. There stood the openings to tunnels, a warren burrowed under the skin of Om. As he reached them, Emberly turned briefly to watch and listen. The chilling rumble of the crowd reached him. From his elevated position, he could see the staircase that the carriage had come down. Tiny figures of people hurried up, down, and across it, but he could not see what was happening at the bottom.

Entering the nearest tunnel, he found it lit dimly by torches and surprisingly crowded. People there must have heard about the commotion outside—they were moving with tense quickness, noticing Emberly just enough to avoid colliding with him. Their numbers and speed reminded him of the mob he had just escaped, and his heart raced. He would have fled the tunnel if worse were not waiting for him outside.

He moved ahead. More tunnels opened up on either side, but he ignored them, dreading the idea of getting lost. He thought the mob had probably killed Ganet, and he wondered if he had done the right thing by running. The few seconds he had spent in the hands of the crowd, surrounded by hateful faces, pounded and shaken by a force of geological size, had renewed his sense of how little control he had over anything.

Ganet was dead. Emberly had little doubt of that. What was more, he had sacrificed himself for Emberly. *No, not for me*, he thought. *For a chance at peace.*

"Who are you?" someone demanded from the shadows.

Emberly walked briskly, preparing to run, then turned back when he realized the voice was familiar. Of the few human shapes in the dim tunnel, none seemed to be paying him any mind. Hurrying on, he rounded a bend.

A hooded figure leaned in from the dark, almost touching his face. "What's wrong with you?"

Emberly threw up an arm out of reflex, but the figure had slipped away.

Farther on, the walls fell away on both sides, and he entered a room. People were sitting along the walls and gathered in small conversations. They were shadowed forms in dusty robes, their sizes and genders indefinite. The handful of torches cast shadows with sharp outlines, darkening stretches of the wall. The room had so many entrances that he could not see or count them all.

There, his presence drew more attention. Light fell onto cheeks and tips of noses as faces turned in his direction. But all soon turned away. Only then did he realize how he must look: torn and dirty traveling clothes, hair disheveled. He was one of them, not worth a second glance.

Only one kept watching him. It separated itself from the crowd, gliding toward him like it was floating above the tunnel floor. He watched, holding his breath, ready to fight or run, suspecting who it was, not knowing what possibility he dreaded more.

He was right—Rayan pushed back his hood, exposing his ruined face. Bloodlessly pale in the torchlight, he regarded Emberly with menace. From his open jaw, he said, "Welcome to hell."

28

— · —

ORUND

ORUND HAD NEVER FELT so old. He sat as Doctor Staubel prodded and poked him, suppressing the occasional wince when the doctor found a place that was bruised or sore.

"Not a thing's broken, sir," he said.

Staubel ignored him. Soon afterward, the doctor touched his elbow, and Orund cursed loudly enough to be heard down the hall.

"What happened here, Sergeant?" Staubel asked.

"That's where I landed," Orund said, "when he threw me."

The doctor had shown no real curiosity about the fistfight or Orund's intervention in it. Ordinarily, the sergeant would have thought little of it himself, having witnessed countless such scraps. But the context of this fight worried him.

"I don't like the sound of that," Staubel said.

The memory of the pain resounded in Orund's arm, and he flinched when the doctor reached to touch it again. "I'll rest it when I can," he said, hoping that would end the matter.

To his surprise, the doctor relented. "Do that," he said with a resigned nod. "Tell me if it gets worse."

Orund looked around the room. Larger than most chambers in the pyramid, it was mostly filled with empty beds. Carrowy and Tabard lay in a nearby corner. The former was not yet well enough to move around much, and the latter seemingly lacked the desire to move.

"You've cleared this place out, then," Orund told Staubel.

"I can't accept thanks for that," the doctor said quickly. "The Realm's healers have paid us a couple of visits. They'll be back again today."

"What do they know that you don't? Are they magicians?" The sergeant meant it as a joke but quickly wished he had kept his mouth shut.

His words had a curious effect on the boy—whom Orund could not think of as anything but a boy, especially at that moment.

The doctor took a step back and ran his fingers through his scanty attempt at a beard. "A lot, I think. As for magicians, they may be. They have medicines..." He did not finish the thought. "So one of ours fought one of theirs—is that it?"

The abrupt change of subject confused Orund for a moment. "Oh, the fight. Yes, that's what it was. A Realmsman brought a woman in from the street last night. One of our boys fancied her, and that's all it took." He gazed at Staubel, who looked away. "You should get out of here and drink with me tonight. The rest of those bastards talk too much."

Staubel smiled. Orund wondered if he'd heard a word of it.

"You're not the first to come to me banged up," the doctor said finally. "Doesn't that worry you, Sergeant?"

"Sure," Orund replied, "but what do you expect? They asked the world of these boys on Caidfell—and that's after they watched the bombing in Ronia up close. Now, Emberly's forgotten about them." He felt safe enough saying so to Staubel, who didn't seem close to the captain.

Staubel nodded. "Giving them a break is one thing. This is something else."

That was the last thing either of them said for several seconds. Having finished with Orund, the doctor stood there as though he didn't know what to do next.

When his patient's discomfort became visible, Staubel said, "I'm just going to step out for a moment. You may be on your way, Sergeant."

When the doctor was gone, Orund was distressed to realize that his discomfort was not. Looking for its source, he turned toward the two men in the corner. "Coming along, then, Tabard?" he asked.

"Seems that way," the man said. He held aloft his maimed hand, from which he had lost a thumb on Caidfell. The hand was grotesquely swollen, and its color was off. "The healers from the Realm gave me something they say will save the hand. I'd have lost it otherwise."

"Good thing they came, then."

"Yes. Our officers could learn something from them."

Tabard's injury would bar him from climbing the ranks of Ronia's army. He was not an even-keeled man to begin with, and since losing his thumb, he had periodically overflowed with understandable bitterness.

"And you, Carrowy?" said Orund. "Feeling any better?"

Again, he wished he had said nothing. Carrowy was lying flat, sweating and shivering. He looked at Orund as if the sergeant was a distant object on the horizon.

"He doesn't look better, does he, Sergeant?" Tabard said, his tone full of venom.

Orund was so struck by Carrowy's appearance that he let Tabard's disrespect pass unanswered. Something had to be done.

He knelt next to the private and spoke more gently. "Look, Carrowy, tell me what you need. The healers can get it, I'm sure."

"They treated his wounds already," Tabard said. "But they haven't got what he really needs. What he needs is out there." He tipped his head to indicate the world outside.

Orund had feared as much. Carrowy wouldn't likely find nightshade here, on a strange planet, but he might find something else to use as a substitute. "Listen, mate," he said to Carrowy. "It's hard—I know it. But it will pass. That's what I hear, right?"

"He hasn't touched the stuff since we left Ronia," Tabard said. "That's a long time. He won't find an end to his pain while he's lying here. And neither will I."

"You've got to hold on," Orund whispered to Carrowy, desperation making his tone whiny. "Can't I do anything for you?"

Carrowy's lips moved, but his voice was too soft to hear. Orund leaned in and was startled when the private's next words were much louder.

Carrowy said, "Nor. Brother Nor."

Try as he might to stop it, Orund could feel his face souring. "What about him?"

Carrowy said Nor's name again.

Tabard said, "The monk came to see him a few times. Hasn't come in a while, though."

"I see," Orund replied. "He's been making friends all over."

Tabard and Carrowy must not have shared Orund's views on Nor, though they had probably heard of them. They were both quiet.

Orund knew of more important things to say and do, but he would not let the subject rest. "I see I'm alone, then."

Carrowy stared at the ceiling.

Tabard, more dismissive than nervous, said, "Don't know what you mean, Sergeant."

"Yes, you do. I told you what he did—and to one of ours, at that. Took a boy's sight away. You were all with me at first, but now you've forgotten."

A series of noises came from Carrowy's mouth.

Orund leaned in again to hear them then reported, "'We must forgive. Huire says.'" He sighed and shook his head, meeting each set of eyes in turn. "I suppose I'm too weak a man for that."

"Please," Carrowy said, just loud enough to hear.

Thinking for a second, Orund stood. "All right, then. He was gone last night, but I'll see if he's back yet. Only because you asked for him." He doubted that Nor had returned without his knowing about it. That meant the monk had been missing for a day, but Orund was reluctant to tell the men that, Carrowy in particular.

To Orund, suspecting Nor of being a traitor was perfectly reasonable. The monk loved the Temple, true enough, but he cared not a bit for Ronia's army. Now, he had gone off with the Realm and had not reported back. The Realm had no reason to hurt Nor that it didn't have to hurt the whole company, and it hadn't hurt the company yet. Nothing was left to say.

But Orund would rather tell Carrowy just about any-thing than that Nor had abandoned them.

The area within the pyramid that the Realm had set aside for the company's use was not large, and the sergeant reached Nor's room more quickly than he would have liked. He wondered what he would say if he found Nor there. He certainly would not want the monk to think Orund was asking for a favor. He felt both better and worse when he found Nor's room empty. He looked up and down the hall, wondering whom he should ask for new information on the monk's whereabouts. But as he looked at the empty room, with its echoes of distant voices and movement, his suspicion that Nor had deserted them pressed in upon him anew.

"He's not here, mate," he told Carrowy when he returned. When the private's expression did not change, Orund wondered if he was listening. "Where's Tabard?" he asked because Carrowy was alone in the room.

The private shook his head a little, claiming ignorance.

Orund did not believe him and asked, "He's not coming back, is he?"

Again, Carrowy's head shook just perceptibly.

Orund knelt again, wincing at the ache in his own hips and ribs. "Nor will come see you when he gets back. I'll make sure of it. He likes you."

Nodding, the private closed his eyes.

"You try and sleep." Orund patted him on the arm and stood up. He no longer felt helpful, but he had to say one more thing. "You don't have to follow Tabard. Don't you go running off, you hear me? Things will feel better soon."

29

SHADA

IN THE LATE AFTERNOON, Shada followed the sounds of chatter and occasional laughter to the little study in which Jeric sat with Delia. She opened the door quietly and saw them together. The girl was sitting at a miniature desk with her father next to her, looming like a giant in his ordinary-sized chair. Two of the small desks sat in the room, but the other was not in use.

They were silent when she arrived, with Delia writing something and Jeric watching, so Shada failed in her attempt to sneak in unnoticed. He looked up and gave her a smile so warm and beautiful that she was afraid to believe in it.

He stood and came to her. "You haven't been too bored, I hope."

"Not at all."

She felt guilty and embarrassed at enjoying the sight of him. Had he not been complicit in her abduction, she would have enjoyed it yet more. But even that venomous bit of knowledge kept slipping away the second she took her eyes off it. He didn't *seem* like an evil man, and despite her best efforts, she could not quite think of him as one.

Maybe that was a trick captors played on their prisoners. But she had known a great many deceptive people in her life—most recently the Lady—and he didn't remind her of them. Maybe he was a new kind of liar, one she hadn't met before.

Such thoughts were fruitless in the end. The Lady had forced her to cast her lot with Jeric, and she would play that role to keep herself alive. Until the Lady changed her mind, Shada would cooperate. A few hours before, that had meant kissing him. Now, it meant playing along with their budding relationship. If she enjoyed it just a little, well, it was her right to exercise at least a little control over her mind and heart.

But that brought new problems. *Kissing is one thing, but what if he wants more?* She might tell herself that she would never be part of anything she hadn't chosen, but she wondered how true that was. When survival was at stake—when partnership with Jeric might even let her influence the fate of Ronia itself—she wondered what she would and wouldn't do.

In any case, she had never been sure how to act around men after a first kiss, and the endless dangers and crises she had faced since her last relationship had not changed that in the slightest. Acting too familiar seemed wrong, especially in front of Delia, and Jeric's slightly distant courtesy made Shada wonder if that morning had, after all, been a dream.

She had spent the last couple of hours in the cabin's small library, where she had been surprised and a little frightened to find a large number of books written in high imperial Ronian. Some were bound in a familiar style and, she decided, had been brought there from Ronia itself. They dealt with topics in history and the natural world—what Shada thought of as philosophy. Most were quite specific, dealing with a single battle or the ways of a particular species of bird.

Another shelf held numerous small books of a neat cloth binding and similar width. The writing in them was a single line of ink that stretched from the beginning of each page to its end, dipping and swirling on the way. It was beautiful, but she could make nothing of it.

As the afternoon wore on and supper approached, she discovered that some of the books on the latter shelf were written in the alphabet and language of Ronia. Looking at a couple of these, she found them to be awkwardly written, with phrases and words that made little sense or were curiously misused. They seemed to be translations into Ronian of works from a different language, one whose rhythm did not fit comfortably into its new medium.

She told Jeric what she had been doing, and he seemed pleased. "I hope you're as hungry as we are," he said. "We have a long meal ahead of us." He touched her hand, and to her dismay, she felt it in her toes.

"Where is Lani?" Shada asked.

She thought she saw his smile falter, but it was small and passing. He looked at Delia. "Return to work, love." The girl made a pretense of obedience but plainly continued to listen.

"She's outside," he told Shada. "Her lessons are finished."

"I'm surprised to see you two are still at it," Shada said. "It's getting late." Then she remembered that this was not a Ronian household, though it had been made to resemble one. For all she knew, children in the Shining Realm might continue their lessons into the evening.

"Delia needs a little extra schooling," Jeric said. "She's the smartest of us."

"That's interesting. It sounds backward."

He chuckled. "How is that?"

"Well, I've been a governess myself. I would think the poorest student needs the most attention." She felt a little uncomfortable talking about such things in front of Delia. Children talked, and it wouldn't do for one of them to think herself superior.

"Ah," he replied. "Yes. That's a very sensible view."

Outwardly, he was calm, but something was amiss. Shada said, "I could help to teach them while I'm here."

That did it. His exterior cracked, and for an instant, someone who was deeply alarmed peeked through. He recovered quickly but not completely. The whole thing was over in less than a heartbeat, after which he told her, "That sounds lovely."

His body still, he turned his head to Delia. "That's enough for tonight, darling."

The girl looked surprised but accepted the reprieve gladly. She put her things away and went to wash up.

"It's wonderful that you teach them yourself," Shada offered weakly. She did not know what worry she had caused him, and she immediately and selfishly wanted the other man back. For one thing, the Lady might punish her if she put Jeric off. For another thing, she liked that other man.

"Thank you. They are everything." His smile was eager. He appreciated the line she had thrown him but, for reasons of his own, would not take hold of it.

"Supper will be soon," he said. "I'll see you then." He gave a little bow and walked off at a forcibly even pace, leaving Shada with fresh and nebulous worries.

Tracking her current discomfort to its root, she was surprised to find that it was grounded not in Jeric but in Lani. She was outside alone, and though Jeric was sure she was safe, the thought of a child in the woods as darkness encroached was hard to embrace.

Shada went outside. They would eat soon, so Lani should come in anyway.

Twilight was long in Om, and darkness came early. Still, even in the fading light, she could see Lani was not in the tame garden that filled the space between the house and the trees.

As Shada observed the broad expanse of forest surrounding the cabin in all directions, her worry increased. *What if, one night, one of the girls doesn't return from play? Where would we even begin to look for her?*

"Lani!" Shada's voice sounded weaker and more timid than she expected. The trees and the quiet evening gave her the feeling of being in a huge temple, the biggest one imaginable, and shouting felt like a violation that might carry terrible consequences. Even her croak of a call seemed to draw the attention of everything nearby, air and grass, visible and invisible.

That was nonsense. Nothing harmful was there, and if there was, finding Lani would be all the more important. Shada opened her mouth and drew a breath, ready to shatter the evening stillness, but then she heard a voice.

It was Lani's, she was sure. It was toneless—not a sound of distress but not one of carefree enjoyment, either. It came from the trees a little to Shada's right.

Shada hurried down the hill by the most direct route, which nonetheless wound frustratingly back and forth. By the time she reached the trees, several seconds had passed, and she could no longer place herself in relation to the voice. The path she was on continued into shadow. She saw nothing to its sides but trees and the muted shades of a few bright flowers.

Standing still, she held her breath. She tried to listen, which seemed futile as her own heart was pounding in her ears. Then she heard it again.

The voice was indeed Lani's. That time, the girl giggled. Shada's chest tingled with relief while, at the same time, she felt annoyed. *What is there to laugh at out here?* They did not know who or what might be listening.

The laughter came from down the path. As Shada set off into the deeper evening, she tried to counter her anger with reason. The woods of Caidfell had been brutal and terrifying, and it was a blessing that any of the company had emerged alive. She still hurt here and there, and no amount of coughing would remove the lingering pain in her lungs and throat. She would not be able to think calmly about this forest or any other for a long time.

She soon saw Lani ahead. The girl was sitting on the path with her legs crossed, facing Shada. Her hands were clasped in front of her.

Shada did not believe at first that there truly was a dark shape behind Lani. Even after her eyes accepted the shrouded form crouching behind the girl, spindly hands on Lani's young shoulders, whispering in her ear, a part of her still resisted. Part of her had not yet learned that nightmares could be true. She felt herself sprinting toward the girl and the shadow, heard herself screaming bloody hell.

If she caught the thing, she would hurt it. What she would do when she held that spidery, thrashing shape in her arms—

Lani screamed as Shada barreled toward them. Behind the girl flashed a pale face with eyes of breathtaking ferocity. Then the figure was gone, off into the trees faster than Shada could conceive of following.

Stopping at the edge of the path, Shada peered into the forest, trying to decide if the woman was really gone. She saw nothing but trees and heard nothing but Lani crying.

She ran to the girl. "Are you all right? Did she hurt you?"

The shape that had loomed over Lani was the same woman Shada had glimpsed that morning. She had nearly forgotten that encounter, but she would never forget the face she had seen over Lani's shoulder.

In the shadows of the trees, Lani's sniffling was the only indication that she was weeping. "No," she said. "Did I do something bad? Why are you angry?"

Shada had knelt in front of her, and she withdrew a little. "No, Lani. Of course not. I was scared because I saw that woman..." She trailed off and wondered what she had seen, exactly.

"I wasn't afraid," Lani said. "So you shouldn't be, either." She was still crying.

"Are you afraid now?"

"A little."

"Was it me who scared you?"

"Yes." The girl stopped, perhaps deciding whether she should say any more. "When you shouted, I thought you were a monster."

"I'm sorry about that." Shada's apology felt false. She hated to see the girl crying and know she was the cause, but she couldn't have said, if it happened again, that she would act differently. "We should go to the cabin and find your father. He'll want to hear about this."

"He knows."

In a squat, Shada rocked back on her heels. Losing her balance, she fell into a sitting position. "What does he know?"

"He knows I have a friend. It's natural, he says."

"Has he seen your friend?" The woman's appearance had frozen Shada's blood, though that was not enough to judge her with certainty. The woman had not acted violently. She might be harmless, a simple lunatic. But still, to let them play together, Jeric must be out of his mind.

"I don't think so," Lani replied. She was a little calmer. Her fingers were interlocked, and she was twiddling her thumbs. "That would be a surprise."

In those words, Shada heard the repetition of a phrase Lani's father might have used. She felt more than ever they were being watched, and she wanted to escape the woods quickly. But snatching Lani up and bolting to the cabin would scare the girl more. They would return together, both on foot.

Still sitting, she crossed her legs, faced Lani, and took her hands. "May I give you a hug?"

Lani nodded. "Yes."

Shada leaned into the awkward embrace. She felt the girl shaking.

Sitting back, she said, "I'm sorry I scared you. I was very scared myself. I didn't want you hurt."

"She won't hurt me," Lani replied. She said it not in defiance but as a simple fact.

Shada looked off into the woods again. "What's her name?"

"I don't know. She won't tell me yet."

That drew Shada's eyes back to Lani's face. "What reason could she have for that?"

"We haven't really met each other yet. She and I. That's what she said. We will, though."

Shada furrowed her brow but then relaxed it. She didn't want to seem angry. "That's very strange, Lani. What do you think it means?"

Lani shrugged, unperturbed by the mystery. "She's kind. She has a home in the forest, but it's lonely there."

"Is that what she told you?"

Lani nodded.

Once again conscious of their surroundings, Shada stood and brushed off the dirt and leaves. "I want to speak to your father right away."

"He knows." Lani sounded a little impatient now.

"I don't think he knows much," Shada replied, putting her hands on her hips. "If he knew the things your friend has said, he wouldn't be happy."

"He wouldn't mind."

"We'll see about that."

"He won't, I promise." A smile crept onto Lani's face, and she began to giggle. "You shouldn't worry. My father will make you feel better."

"I'll feel better when we're back inside. Will you come with me?" Shada offered a hand.

Lani accepted. As they walked, she seemed deep in thought. She caught Shada watching her and said, "Don't be afraid."

"I know," Shada said. She couldn't help sounding a little sardonic. "She won't hurt you."

"Really, she won't. She isn't real."

Shada kept walking, but her steps became mechanical. She could think of no reply other than "What?"

"She's in our imaginations."

"'Our' imaginations? What makes you say that?"

"My father says so. It's natural to have imagined friends."

Walking faster, Shada said, "I suppose he's right about that."

When they reached the cabin, she opened the door and waved Lani through. The evening really was getting truly dark, and she was tempted to shove the child inside and slam the door behind them. It would be right then, when they were so close to safety, that whatever-it-was would lunge from the shadows and drag them back to who-knew-where.

She forced herself to close the door softly and deliberately. "Go to the kitchen, dear, and hurry. Find Adney if he isn't there," she called as Lani trotted away.

She had to find Jeric. For all she didn't know about him, she knew he was powerful, and he could set things right.

He was not in the study, where his easel still stood. She hurried down the hall and tried the doors one at a time. She opened the correct one quickly and carelessly to find him bare chested and facing a mirror.

His back was mostly turned to her, but the mirror showed what he was doing. He was holding a pair of tweezers to his chest, and just as her eyes focused on him, he jerked them away, raising a little tent of skin near one nipple. The skin quickly snapped back into place.

She stopped, breathless, and hoped without hope that he hadn't heard her enter. Then he said, in a tone that suggested he was barely breathing himself, "Come inside."

She obeyed. He turned toward her. Everything moved slowly. His face was tortured.

Then he hurried forward, throwing down the tweezers. He passed her, threw the door shut, and said, "Close the door, for the love of all."

Her eyes were drawn inexorably to his chest. One side of him was hairless. His left half, starting with his chin and divided along an arrow-straight line to his belt buckle, had chest hair, belly hair, and all the rest. His other half was bare and smooth. The only exception to the rule was a tiny bare patch around his left nipple. From there, where he had just plucked the hair, beads of blood had arisen.

He turned this way and that. He stood straight, his motions measured. His face dropped into listless neutrality. "I don't know," he said. He repeated that a couple of times.

She turned away and saw herself in the mirror—pale, mortified. Looking away from that, she let her gaze fall upon a small table next to him. On it was a little metal tin, and in the tin was a thick tuft of fine hair. The tweezers were on the floor, and the final hair he'd plucked had been lost somewhere.

Lani. She had to think of Lani. Turning back toward Jeric, Shada launched into the conversation she'd meant to have. "I found a woman with Lani. It was the same woman I saw this morning. She was telling the girl something, and I chased her away."

"That's fine." He nodded, not looking at her.

She glared. "No, it's not 'fine.' You said no one would come near the girls."

"Yes."

"You were wrong!" she cried. "Whoever you think is out there protecting us, you are wrong. You can't let your daughters wander like this."

He shook his head as if to clear his mind. "Did you say the woman was whispering?"

"Yes."

"What did she say?"

"I don't know. I didn't ask." *Why didn't I ask?*

"But she didn't hurt Lani."

"No."

"Then why were you worried? Ronia must be a dangerous place. Shada..." He paused, struggling visibly with what to say. "What did Lani say about it?"

Shada tried to remember. "Well, she wasn't afraid," she admitted. "She told me that... that you knew about the woman."

"And what else?"

Biting her tongue, Shada wondered about all of their sanity, her own most of all. "She said the woman wasn't real."

Jeric was a little calmer. He looked at the floor and ran his fingers over the lonely bare spot on the left side of his chest. "I have to say something, but I don't know how."

"Just say it."

"The mind is a powerful thing."

Shada hissed and dragged her hands across her face. "No. We both saw her."

"Lani told me about a friend she had," Jeric said. "A kind woman who plays with her. The girls have rarely been around other children. If Lani wants to imagine a playmate, I won't take it from her. She's a child."

"I saw her."

"Your travels have left you frightened of the woods, and for good reason. Might you have expected to see something? When imaginations combine—"

"Oh, hell." She felt like she was going to burst. "She was in front of my eyes. I swear she was."

"You may be right," he said.

Silence fell.

When he spoke, his voice was listless. "Supper will start soon. We both had better get ready."

Though she was desperate for the conversation to end, Shada couldn't forget what she'd seen. "What were you doing in here?"

"What do you mean?"

She took a breath and plunged. "Why are you pulling your hair out? I've never heard of anyone doing that."

"Oh." He thought about it, and a smile touched his lips. "It's nothing."

Shada looked at the dots of blood in the newly bare patch on his chest. "If you don't want to talk about it, I won't ask again. It's just that, after this morning, I think I have the right to ask you things."

His smile became warmer then twisted with sadness. "You do. And thank you. But it really is nothing." He laughed. "It's nothing."

He walked past her, picked up the tweezers, and placed them on the table. She had said she would not ask again, so she did not. Feeling sick, she decided to leave the room. Maybe, once she was out of his sight and he was out of hers, she could think clearly about how to face him next.

Before she could force her feet to move, he spoke. "I wanted to do it. That's why. I simply have to *do* something, sometimes. Something fills me, and I have to let it out."

"Something fills you? What is it?"

"I don't decide anything for myself, you see. But the mind—it needs to be ridiculous." He held out his hands and looked at them as if he thought he was answering her question. "At least, mine does. Future men, not so. I am a step on a great journey."

He turned his eyes upon her, and she felt their power.

He said, "I tried to do something good this time. Usually, I just do silly things. But I wanted you to see me soon, naked. I guess your men keep their hair."

Shada's face burned. "Couldn't you use a blade, like when you shave your face? Were you going to take the hair from your right side, too? Why pull it from only one side?" A buzzing sensation warned her not to ask that last question, but she felt lost and wanted to understand at least one thing about her surroundings.

His anger swelled, and he clapped his hands together with a startling crack. "There is no damned 'why'! Because, is why!"

He looked around, agitated, for something on the floor. Then he sank to his hands and knees to search the floorboards more carefully. The hair—he was looking for the hair.

As she stepped into the hall and closed the door, Shada murmured, "I'll see you at dinner."

30

NOR

NOR TURNED THIS WAY and that, unable to convince himself of what his eyes already knew. He was trapped. The room was square and minuscule, with the ceiling just above his head. Suffocatingly close as the ceiling was, it was almost comforting. It contained elements that he knew and to which he could relate.

It was made of a firm substance like bone. Had he touched it with his eyes closed, he might have mistaken it for sanded wood. The floor was made of the same material.

The rest of the room was something else.

He held a glowing lantern of the kind the Realm used. He did not know how he had gotten it or how he had gotten there. Having no idea how it was used, he held it gingerly for fear that its light would disappear. The warm yellow illumination fell with sickening welcome on the walls, which were dark and shiny and covered with facets like stained glass, but globular and senseless in shape.

His other hand was wrapped around a pleasant feeling. It was the handle of a knife, and when he looked down, the great, curved blade shone in the lantern's light like a sweep of fire.

Something lay underneath all of that. He did not yet know what it was, but feeling its presence, he fervently prayed he was in a dream. Even if it wasn't a dream, perhaps it could be made into one, turned unreal.

Some time before, Ren had spoken to him. Her eyes had been hard and honest like an animal's as she said, "Do what you must."

He reached out with his knife hand and brushed a couple of fingers over the wall. Its surface was cool and brittle and felt hollow. He was plainly supposed to break through it, which did not seem too difficult. He would not even need the knife.

His unease at touching the wall and his revulsion at the thought of breaking through it had roots that he could not place. The room's walls were intricate, even delicate. Something felt organic and purposeful about the shapes within them. His task, in contrast, was purposeless. If he wanted to get out of here, he had to do what Ren wanted and break what she told him to break. Perhaps the reason was simply to condition him to obedience.

He had chosen this. It was his awakening. Huire wished him to confront the Shining Realm from the inside, and until he learned her plan and the answer to Cadmon's quandary, he would follow that path.

He had assured Ren he would submit his will to the awakening, but he doubted he was capable of such sub-mission. He had never given all of himself to anything, not even to the Temple. His reticence had always held him back. Now, it was the thing that would save him, would let him subsume himself in the Realm without losing himself in it.

Meanwhile, in moments alone, moments like this, he threw himself into answering the quandary. Little snatches of time, a few seconds here and there, weren't much on their own, but he hoped they would add up to something greater.

Still, to his frustration and near despair, he didn't know where to start. He didn't know how he could ever learn what the gods were made of. Back in Ronia, merely asking to examine the Lady had earned him the rage of the Temple elders.

Standing in that little room, he prayed. *I'm here. Lead me.*

No answer. Huire said nothing.

Something flipped inside him. Anger surfaced—anger at this impossible situation, at Huire's impossible demands, her impossible silence. Even after his terrifying leap of faith in joining the Shining Realm, she was silent.

Are you even listening? He cast the words into the void, wondering if anyone heard. Regret followed immediately, and he prayed again. *I'm sorry.*

Then he realized what that something was that lay underneath everything else—the thing making him twitch and grit his teeth with growing anxiety. It was a sound, a humming that existed everywhere but most of all within his own ears. It contained various parts and pitches. The hiss of his fingers against the wall had reverberated and swelled to become part of it. His breathing did the same, as did every other movement. His heartbeat was getting louder and faster, each beat adding a layer to the tumbling behemoth of sound that kept coming and coming, always upon him but somehow always coming closer yet.

He broke through the wall without thinking. Punching and kicking, then shoving with his shoulder and hip, he felt the facets break with a crunching that made the sound worse and much bigger. Some of the facets fell to the floor, some were left dangling by filaments, and some clung to him.

The noise of the wall's destruction was deafening. He was confused but grateful to find that the next place was far quieter.

He was in a narrow space. Behind him was the wall he had burst through. In front was another wall, this one a gravelly, repulsive surface of a green so dark that it was almost black. The ceiling and floor were of the same bone-like material. Together, the two walls formed a narrow corridor with turns nearby in both directions.

He picked a direction and set out. His suspicion was soon confirmed: the green wall surrounded the little room he had just escaped, and four quick turns led him back to the same spot.

For an instant, he lacked direction, and into that instant flooded more unwelcome questions for Huire. *Why did you let Ren have that letter? How did she even get it? I'm the one who needs it*. He silenced the thoughts as soon as they arose. Huire had saved him before and would save him again. When he had the answer to the quandary, the envelope with its letter would find its way back to him. It must.

So bring me the answer! Unwittingly, he scraped his foot along the dusty floor. His heart jumped. The sound was returning, faster and louder. The outer wall's surface was riddled with tiny lumps that concentrated, here and there, in vertical and diagonal stretches. Between, the wall was scaly.

He abandoned his prayer to necessity. He kicked and struck the wall. It gave under the blows but bounced back. It was less a wall than a piece of stretched canvas.

Then the knife did its work. He stabbed the scaled surface with the odd feeling that it did not deserve such treatment. He cut it with desperate efficiency. As the growing noise again became terrifyingly loud, he tumbled through into blessed quiet.

Now wary of the sound, he climbed to his feet as quickly and softly as he could. Then he looked at the wall in front of him and nearly scrambled back the way he had come.

This wall was a little longer and seemed to surround the others. It was covered, top to bottom, with hair. The hair was thick, red-brown, and shaggy, like that of some kind of livestock.

In his shock, he mouthed a prayer. Catching himself in the act, he felt his shame return. He came to Huire for help constantly, and she answered constantly. If she didn't answer now, she must have a reason. He wondered at the empty space growing inside him—the space where his trust in Huire had been.

He didn't wonder long. Though the empty space had always been there—*Who doesn't have one?*—it had been growing since he tackled Ren and put his hands around her throat. When he attacked her, something had cracked inside him, and through that fissure, his trust was pouring. That scared him, as did his apparent help-lessness to stop it.

The fear pressed in around him. He shut his eyes and gritted his teeth. *I'm sorry! Answer me, please!*

He clenched his fists, causing the lantern to slip from his fingers.

Watching it fall, he yelped.

He expected it to break, leaving him in darkness. That did not happen. Instead, it struck the floor with a crack that could have rent the planet. It was one of the loudest things he had ever heard.

He bent over and gasped. The crack resounded in aftershocks that smashed into his ears one after an-other. He thrust out his hands, felt the fur that lined the wall, and attacked it with the knife. That exit was messier than the last, as his strokes crossed one another or missed the wall entirely, but such was his terror of the gathering noise that he plowed through the wall, leaving the lantern where it lay.

The new space was not as dark as the others. The light of the lantern that filtered through the ragged hole fell on another wall in front of him. That one's entire surface, from end to end and floor to ceiling, glowed.

He gaped. The glow must have been coming from a light source beyond the wall. Perhaps it was the last wall he would need to cut through.

The glow of the lantern left a jagged strip of light on the new wall. In that strip, he could see the new wall plainly.

He said something aloud—something unimportant, a startled exclamation. The noise came back at him like a charging animal. It was so huge that he bent and writhed, holding the knife against himself, his mouth open. The pain demanded that he scream, but the sound of that might split his head open.

The noise was relentless, but it reached an equilibrium of sorts in which he could see the wall through tear-filled eyes. The ragged patch of light told him again what he had not believed before. The wall was made of human skin.

He rose to his feet—he was not sure how—and approached the lighted patch. The skin was drab and lighter than his, and here and there on it were concentrations of short, dark hair.

Nor froze. He wondered if he could stand feeling his knife penetrate that taut curtain. *Would it bleed?*

But of course he could stand it. If he did not, the sound would soon leave him unable to do anything. And he had done worse.

He had managed, for a few entire days, not to think about the night when he blinded that soldier. But telling Ren about it had brought it all back. He recalled the river of trembling rage that he had let wash over him. The feel of the bottle in his hand, the sounds the man made, had all been terrible, but something had been there with him, helping him through it. *What is the cost of feeling such a spirit pawing at your soul and letting it enter?*

The noise was again becoming unbearable. Nearly out of his mind, Nor still felt reluctant to cut through flesh that had once belonged to women and men like him.

Am I to die here, then? The thought was outrageous. The skin was dead, no use to any living thing. His resentment of a morality that regarded such a thing as sacred, that would ask his life for such a thing, swelled. Rage bloomed in his head, at all sides and forces that had placed him in his situation, himself not least and Huire most of all.

Answer me, damn you! He thrust the prayer into the universe like a soldier would thrust a sword into an enemy.

Nothing.

The crushing noise was blurring his vision and making him dizzy. Almost forgetting to stifle a howl, he thrust the knife. The skin stretched back but quickly broke. Once open, it separated as easily as he had hoped. The knife slipped downward with a sigh. The cut produced no blood.

He had no thought of making a graceful exit. As soon as the gap grew large enough for his torso, he dove through and into the blinding light beyond. He collapsed, eyes closed, his fingers tearing at the floor.

The noise was gone. For a few seconds, he did not believe it. He held his breath for fear that the sound of his breathing might destroy him. When Ren spoke to him, he flinched. Her words resounded strangely but did not grow louder.

"Congratulations, Norhim. That was splendid."

"You... put me there?" *Idiot,* he thought. Of course she had.

"Yes. If you want an apology, then you've got farther to go than I thought."

Still lying down, he turned his eyes to the floor. His last words to Huire echoed in his mind. To his dismay, he realized he did not feel like repenting. "I did it," he told Ren. "Let's move on."

"I absolutely agree. There is only one thing left for today." She reached out to help him up.

Ignoring her hand, he rose to his knees. There, he stopped and looked up at her. "Tell me."

She moved her hand in front of his eyes. Suddenly, a small box lay in her palm. She opened it, revealing something tiny and dark inside.

He recoiled a little when it moved. It was a small insect. Its body was an unfamiliar shape, but its bulbous eyes were those of—

"A housefly, you would call it," Ren said.

He leaned in to examine the creature, wondering why it looked so strange.

After a moment, he cried, "You tore its wings off!"

Indeed, the little animal was wandering about inside the box, perhaps searching for those precious things it had no name for but knew it had lost. Nor wondered if such a creature could grieve.

Ren gave him an accommodating smile. "It will not need them anymore. I want you to smash it."

As his eyes adjusted to the light, he could see the fly's tiny features in extraordinary detail—the hairs that rose from its carapace, the many obtuse angles of its jointed limbs, the twitching multitude of parts around its mouth. Revulsion had always kept him from looking closely at such things, but right then, in the euphoria of his own survival, their very aliveness captivated him. The creature was a galaxy of complexity, an enormity of processes brought into one small space and made perpetual.

"Why?" he asked. He was angry at Huire but didn't want to ruin one of her creations for no reason. Looking at the thing so closely made destroying it seem like an act of lunacy. The very thought seemed to come from outside this universe.

"Because that is what happens next."

"You want me to step on it?" Still in disbelief, he was alarmed at the degree of consideration implied by his question.

"No, I don't think so. You've done very well today, and I think you are ready for something more. Crush it in your hand."

Holding the box in front of him, she turned it over slowly. When it was upside down, she raised her hand to tap it. Seeing that the fly would be jarred from the box, Nor cupped his hands and caught it as it fell. Its legs worked frantically, tickling his palm as it spun on its back, trying to right itself.

Ren asked, "What do you see?"

Nor did not reply.

"Answer me," she said firmly. "Describe it."

"I don't know how," he snapped. He could have watched the thing for hours. "There's so much."

"Yes, I know," she said. "And here is the marvelous thing: it is ours. We can destroy a thing, even a thing like this, when we decide it shouldn't exist. The universe has made it so."

"No," he said.

The thing was simply too splendid.

But there he was, on the path where Huire had placed him, where she had lured him.

Huire had trapped him there with no help and no answers. And she had placed this little creature in front of him and contrived his circumstances so that he must destroy it to continue with the mission she had given him. If his smashing it upset her, she had no right to complain.

He tilted his cupped hands, and the fly tumbled back onto its feet. Holding it close to his eyes, he noticed the places where its wings had been. Only their ruins remained, broken stumps. The animal was already maimed.

It was miserable. He would do it this quick favor.

He squeezed it in his fist. He did it quickly, hoping to feel as little as possible—a bit of cowardice he would regret. As his fingers snapped shut, one of his fingertips landed directly on the fly. With his newly vivid senses, he felt the little body give way.

Still on his knees, he opened his hand. Releasing a breath, he went to brush his hand against his clothing.

"No!" she cried.

He stopped.

She said, "Look at what is left."

He did. It was a moist, crumpled mass.

"That is all it ever was," she told him. "Beautiful as it was, it was an accident—the workings of dead particles. Raw materials powered by life, which is a force like gravity or any other. If such a thing came about by chance, what wonders we of consciousness may create! What we may become!"

He had never heard her sound like that. Her voice was breathy and sensual. For the first time, she was speaking of something that did not leave her brisk and impatient.

He shook his head at her words, but his refusal lacked energy. "Is that what you're doing? You in the Shining Realm, I mean."

Though he was not sure exactly what the question meant, she took his outstretched hand in both of hers and smiled. The expression transformed her face. "Yes," she said with relish. Whatever she thought he understood, she seemed thrilled and surprised. "We are becoming."

With her fingernail, she scraped the insect's remains off his skin and into her palm. "There are many more just like it, and there are many more of us. We are all tools."

"No," he murmured, unsure if she heard him. He barely heard himself.

Leaning forward, he let himself sag toward the floor, intending to lie there for a while. But she stepped forward so that he slumped against her legs. She knelt and put an arm around his shoulders.

"You've done so well." She ran her hands through his hair. "It was hard, and there is a long way to go. But you are doing it for your world and for all worlds. It will be worthwhile."

He reached out to Huire once more, a desperate grasp into empty space. Then he felt a little prick on his shoulder. He was not surprised and did not resist sleep.

31

HULGAR

LIKE MOST ROOMS IN the pyramid, this one was small, and when Hulgar slapped aside the curtain and stepped in, it was already crowded. Several men were there, more than he had expected, though no one of rank. He had followed Merin in, and the others pushed in more tightly to make room for the arrivals.

Robir was in their midst. When he spoke, the others' low chatter faded.

"You found him," he told Merin.

Merin looked surprised at being included in the conversation. He looked up at Hulgar, who offered him no help, and said, "Yes. Well, he was hard to miss."

If he was hoping for a laugh, he didn't get it. Robir smiled without mirth. "I told you he likes you. You're a charmer, Merin."

That got a chuckle. From the look on his face, Merin knew it was at his expense.

"Very well, then." Robir turned his eyes toward Hulgar, who filled one end of the room by himself.

Hulgar was used to the way men acted around him, their reticence or sycophancy. He was not accepted as one of them, but neither was he above or below them. He had no space to occupy.

Robir was a strange sort. He showed not fear but, rather, excitement. He acknowledged Hulgar's special usefulness freely. "Have you guessed what this is about, Hulgar?"

The big man's eyes darted about. Addressing the entire group, he made an obscene suggestion as to what had brought them all here together. Were he another man, the open provocation might have earned him a beating or worse.

Robir let it pass without complaint. "I don't know much about you, man. But I know that you love our captain as much as anyone here."

Hulgar snorted.

"Have you considered doing something about it?"

The room held its breath. The threshold had been crossed sooner than some of the others expected. Hulgar was in no hurry to answer. He drew out the silence perversely, waiting to see what would happen.

"Ah, another attempt at humor failed." Robir looked at Merin, and his smile at that man's bungling returned. "You're the funny one."

Hulgar's brow gathered over his eyes.

"I'd buy you a drink if they weren't free," Robir continued. "Sorry for all this bother." It sounded, to Hulgar's surprise, like he was suddenly giving up.

"What's the plan?" Hulgar rumbled.

Merin looked up at him. The others sat forward.

"We have a friend," Robir said. "One who will tell us when to act and who will take command when our work is done."

Thinking about that, Hulgar laughed. The sound was so loud that the others winced and, as it faded, listened for approaching voices and footsteps. "No," he said finally. "You can't really believe it will work."

"Of course it will work."

"With Arumin in charge? He's a ruined old sack of bones."

"Mind your words," Robir snapped.

Hulgar smiled. Robir must be confident in his plan if he would risk getting his head kicked in. "How many have you got here? Eight?"

"When we move, others will follow. We've got nine, including you."

"You haven't got me."

"What will it take?"

Hulgar's lip curled. "When the captain falls, so does Arumin."

Robir's face turned to stone. "You're mad."

"He's a snake. Preaches to us then does whatever the hell he wants."

"He's a bishop."

"What does that mean anymore?"

Meeting Hulgar's stare, Robir took a moment to contemplate the conversation's unexpected turn. "We're taking charge because Emberly is a bloody fool." He had probably not anticipated saying these things aloud. "You were on Gallobraith. He'd get us all killed if it made him feel important. We can't trust him with the Lady. Who knows where he is now? He's made friends with the Realm—"

Hulgar interrupted. "You still think your Lady's coming back?"

"Yes," Robir said firmly, though his lips had begun to form some other word.

"I'm finished here," Hulgar replied. "The answer's no. But don't be scared. I won't tell Roark about you. I'm curious how your little revolution will end."

"They've built a temple!" Robir cried. It was almost a shout.

Surely, someone had overheard them by then. A few of the others sank lower against the wall, and Merin looked like he might be sick.

"What do you mean?" Hulgar asked.

"Just what I said. The Realm knew we were coming. They've been spying on Ronia somehow. They built a temple to win us over. The bishop has seen it. He says it's a blasphemous thing." Robir's expression was calmer, but he could not hide the tight redness of his cheeks.

"If they can do something like that, it's all the more reason not to fight them."

"I don't understand you, Hulgar!" Robir's voice hit a new pitch of exasperation. He contained it quickly and forced a smile. "Are you only interested in those?"

He pointed at the brands on Hulgar's arm. Clusters of dozens of raised welts looked like the petals of small flowers. One near his massive wrist was so fresh that it had scarcely stopped bleeding. Hulgar had earned it the previous evening, wandering into the streets alone to find it.

A long time had passed since anyone had spoken of Hulgar's scars within his earshot. Someone coughed. The air in the room became thick and hard to breathe. Robir's icy visage could not quite hide his horror at the topic he had broached.

Hulgar looked at his newest scar then, out of habit, at another one near the center—the oldest.

"You know nothing about these," he told them all.

"Come on, man, it's not that hard to guess. Has the Realm gotten to you like they're getting to the others?"

Robir's accusation resounded, and its echoes bolstered the questions that he spat, one after another:

"Did they find out what you like?"

And louder:

"Do they bring you women?"

Again, like a drumbeat:

"Poor wretches no one will miss?"

The others were tense, waiting for the clouds to burst. Someone's face fell into his hands.

"You think we all don't know?"

Robir fell silent here. He breathed deeply, perhaps marveling at where he had found himself.

Hulgar felt life moving his arms and his hands. His knees and feet tingled with power. He laughed again and tapped his scars with his finger. "Have all the guesses you want about these. You will be wrong." He turned to go.

As the others sank with relief, Robir had the impossibly poor judgment to speak again. "Our sins are forgiven," he said.

Hulgar stopped.

Robir continued, "On this crusade. If we keep to Huire's path."

Hulgar turned back to them. "Huire won't forgive a thing. She's dead."

Silence. Robir closed his mouth.

"I've met the true gods," Hulgar went on. "They're in the blood. Do you know what they like? Sacrifice."

32

— · —

ORUND

ORUND LEFT BEHIND THE brightness of the great hall. From it echoed many voices, growing louder even as he retreated from them. Had he not just left the crowd behind, he might have heard that noise and thought a fistfight had erupted.

When he stepped into the darkness of Dr. Staubel's little infirmary, he noticed how full it had become. The textures of shadow moved as several of the patients tossed and turned. He wondered if noise from the party was keeping them awake.

One of the shadows was upright in a chair.

"Doctor?" Orund asked it.

When the figure moved a little, he became sure it was Staubel. "Quite a rabble you've got here," he said. "Is there a flu?"

His casual tone rang hollow and pitiful. The figure shifted and grunted. It sipped a drink and put the cup on the floor. Staubel didn't seem to want to talk, but he had taken Orund's earlier advice and found himself a drink.

The tinny rattle of the cup filled Orund with dismay. He had first thought the Realmsmen's drink was a mere sugary swill, a drink for little girls, but it had sneaked around and ambushed him. He was wiser for the experience and would approach the drink with caution. He had found it left no hangover, which worried him, in its way, as much as anything.

He tried Staubel again. "Is it too loud out there? I can do something about that." He wasn't sure he really could.

"No," said someone in the corner. "The noise doesn't matter. This lot is all dreaming."

Orund recognized Tabard's voice. "Dreaming?" he asked, not hiding the weariness in his tone. He was tired of not understanding.

"Yes. You didn't know?"

Orund hadn't known and still didn't. He was about to release his frustration onto Tabard when a realization struck him. "On Caidfell, a few men said they weren't sleeping well."

His eyes were adjusting to the dark, but he still could not identify the men on the cots. They moved, some violently. Familiar voices moaned and sighed.

"Is this what they were talking about? I didn't know it was like this."

"It mostly isn't," Tabard said. "Just a few get like this. 'Dream sick,' the men call it. If they didn't tell you, maybe they didn't want you to know." His voice carried a smirk.

Scoffing, Orund replied, "I wouldn't have judged them for it. I would have looked after them."

"Some don't like that."

Staubel's voice rang out, raw and heedless of anyone's need to sleep. "It's the drink," he said. His cup scratched the floor as he picked it up. "There's something in it. It wakes you up."

"Puts you to sleep, more like." Orund chuckled uneasily.

Hearing Staubel speak clarified just how drunk the doctor was. Staubel was a small man and young. It wouldn't take much.

Orund doubted the Realm's drink had truly cast some spell on them. Thinking to appeal to the doctor's education and rationality, he said, "Maybe we brought a sickness from Caidfell. The place was lousy with vermin, bad water."

"Ha," Staubel said. He made no further argument.

Giving up, Orund turned to his original purpose and spoke in Tabard's direction. "Being honest, Private, I didn't expect to see you again."

Though that was a rough, public way to broach the subject, Tabard seemed beyond caring. "I was going to leave," he said. "I was leaving. I stood under the gate by the street, but I didn't go farther." After the room was silent for a breath, he said, "I told him it was a bad idea."

With a creeping dread, Orund walked toward Tabard's corner of the room. Upon reaching Carrowy's cot, he knelt and extended a hand. Confirming what his straining eyes told him, his fingers touched bare, empty fabric.

"No," he said softly. It was not a denial. It was surprise, sorrow, and a stab at acceptance all at once.

"I was standing out there at the road," said Tabard, "and Carrowy came out. He could barely walk, and I thought to myself, what is he gonna do out there, work for a living?"

"You should've stopped him," gasped Orund. A worthless sentiment—Carrowy was a grown man.

"I tried," Tabard answered with a note of refused guilt. "I asked how he was going to eat. That's when I decided not to go. I'm as crippled as he is."

Orund shook off his fear for Carrowy for a moment. He might have lost him, but he couldn't lose anyone else like that, not even a piece of work like Tabard. "Are you dream sick?"

"I was," Tabard replied, "I hated it, so I stopped sleeping. I'm not going back to sleep until it passes."

Orund wondered, his spirit sinking a little further, if Tabard was losing his wits. "Is it that bad?"

"Sometimes. Some of the boys say that, when they sleep, a man speaks to them. What do you make of that? They can't always see him, but he's there. When they do see him, he's made of diamonds."

Sergeant Orund shivered. "All right, then." With a final look from Staubel to Tabard, he left the room, still searching for someone to help.

Behind him, Tabard sighed and settled back, perhaps for a long wait. "I'm not sleeping. Not unless that man makes me."

33

THE CRUSADERS

THE ONES WHO DREAMED were lucky. They might meet the shining figure who waited in their sleep, but they could pretend he was just a nightmare. The ones to pity were those who stayed awake.

Lieutenant Roark was one of them. He had stormed through the pyramid, scaring the life out of more than a few soldiers who thought their endless celebrating had finally provoked his wrath. He marched out under the false sky of Om and swore, softly and slowly, with as much bile and venom as he could muster—a curse to make the world wither away.

Finding himself as impotent there as he was anywhere else, he paced back and forth then sat down, tight as a coiled spring.

He was soon joined by the same Realm officer who had kept him company the night before. His name was Thayer, and his curly hair and oddly unblemished skin made him striking even among the soldiers of the Realm.

"Is your captain out late again?" he asked with such good-humored impudence that Roark laughed.

Thayer produced a flask and offered it to Roark. The lieutenant began to refuse, but then his resentment returned in a seething river—resentment toward Emberly, whom he adored, for leaving him again. He seized the flask with a fervor that widened the other man's eyes.

Roark rarely drank, and the sweet, comforting liquid caught up with him quickly. Thayer chatted endearingly about nothing, and his charm and heavy accent were pleasant. Once or twice, he asked Roark a probing question that provoked only hard silence.

Undeterred by these failures, Thayer at last said, "Lots of girls in there, Algir. You can have your pick, but you'd better hurry."

Angry and afraid, Roark smiled. "Not tonight." *How drunk am I?* He didn't remember telling Thayer his first name.

"Not tonight," the man repeated thoughtfully. "It can't be that hard... to say it out loud."

"To say what?" Roark asked.

His eyes crossed the distant ceiling of Om and settled on Thayer. He knew what Thayer wanted to say—*"That women aren't your taste*"—but his gaze warned the man away from the topic.

Thayer looked back at him with an intense, hard-to-match honesty and prudently changed the subject. "What is your world like?"

Roark finished his cup. "Ronia? Don't you already know?"

"No. But whatever it's like, you're here now. You don't have to be afraid anymore."

"I'm not afraid of anything," Roark replied, petulant.

"It's all right," the man said with urgency. "You're a good man. It's all right."

That brought Roark, instantly and surreally, close to tears. He stared at the cup and then at his hands.

"Algir. Please, look at me."

Roark did. The man's eyes were savage, knifelike in their beauty. The lieutenant felt both trapped and terribly excited.

During their unbroken stare, Thayer said, "No one sees who you really are, but I think I can."

Roark was frozen, his breathing quick. He hoped Thayer would not notice.

"Don't you want that?" Thayer asked.

"Do you mean..." Roark fumbled. "I shouldn't be afraid of you? Or your Realm?"

"They are connected, always. That's the truth. But it's not so bad. Actually, I think you will find that it's wonderful."

The man's eyes could have melted lead. Roark had reached a crossroads.

"You have nothing to fear?" he asked. "Really?"

Thayer's lips faltered a little. "We maintain appearances. I have a wife. But that's just the surface. We're free."

Roark didn't know what he was going to say until he said it. "I don't think you are."

Thayer's face fell in a tightly controlled way. He had come closer little by little, but now, he leaned back. After a brief silence, he said, "You'll see someday. We'll show you."

Their cups were empty.

Just when Roark was about to leave, Thayer offered his flask again. "Now that we know each other better."

Eager to face no more decisions, Roark took it and drank.

Thayer took it back and drank also. After swallowing, he said, "I don't know what will happen, even as soon as tomorrow. But I'm glad for this moment. I only hope that we'll know each other in the future. The future is holy."

Somewhere far inside, the continual din was growing louder and wilder. Roark could not help wondering what was happening in there, but he drank until he didn't care.

Just as Hulgar was getting sick of being alone, a man entered. The room was lit by a candle. Hulgar didn't trust the Realm's flameless lanterns.

"You asked for me," the stranger said. He was gray-haired and wiry, and his uniform was less decorated than those of other Realmsmen. He was stifling what looked to be perpetual amusement.

"That's right," Hulgar said, pleased by how things were falling into place.

The man waited, fidgeting.

"So," Hulgar said thoughtfully, "you're the one in charge."

The man nodded. "Here, in this instance. Is there a problem?"

"The problem is I want to know who I'm dealing with."

"Now you know," the man said sharply, still mulling over his private joke. "Any other problems?"

Hulgar smiled. "Nothing much needs to change," he said. "But I'd like it if you surprised me."

The man's eyes narrowed with distaste. "I see."

"Goodbye, then."

The man looked at Hulgar strangely. "The last one, she..." In the candlelight, sweat shone on his face. "What is it that you do?"

———◆———

Robir was also alone. He had pulled off his shirt, one of two in his possession, and torn it into strips. He spent some time braiding those into a whip, embedding it with jagged stone shards he had broken from the wall.

It was no use. When he swung the thing over his shoulder, it struck his back with hardly a sting. In modern times, such skills had been thoroughly forgotten.

Giving up on that, he knelt on the floor and felt his chest with his hands. He knew it without seeing it—the scar on his breast. The musket ball had left an ugly lump, passing closer to his heart than he could bear to forget. Never did he see the scar or feel the numb tingle of the skin around it without thinking of Gallobraith. Of course, Gallobraith meant Emberly. The two were one. The captain was that world made manifest.

He started there, digging in with his nails, raking himself.

"One more day, Goddess."

His hands became wet as the wounds lengthened. He yelped each time they slipped.

"I'm so weak."

It hurt, but he wasn't bothered, and that made him angry.

"Give me strength."

He snarled and began to bite himself. No matter what he did, it couldn't hurt enough. Enraged by his failure, he prayed for mercy.

⸎

Arumin said no prayers that night. He tried a few times, but thoughts kept breaking his concentration—thoughts of what Brin was doing, what he was saying, at whom he might be smiling. Brin had not smiled at him in days or even spoken to him.

Some thoughts, the bishop would not touch. One was the thought that Brin might leave forever. Another was the memory of a dream he often had—a dream of a dark tunnel with a thin ray of light at its end. It was not like the dream sickness the men were suffering. It had recurred to him since childhood. Each time, before he could glimpse what lay at the end of that tunnel, his mind recoiled, and he awoke.

Thinking of that dream made the mash of scars on Arumin's torso itch. It even itched through the new gash on his chest, the one he'd gotten on Caidfell, which stung as if hot ash was sewn up inside it.

His last attempt to speak to Huire, before he gave up in bitterness, was brief. "I've done it all for you. Everything. Don't leave me now."

⚜

Merin held his drink and sat by himself at the end of the great hall. He wanted to sit closer to the others, to be clapped on the back and to get sick with them. Once in a while, he laughed a little at one of their jokes, which he overheard from where he sat.

He thought of the things he had heard earlier, what Robir had said and what Merin himself had agreed to. He kept drinking, afraid his dread would bubble over and he would be sick. Through all that happened next, he sat and watched.

⚜

No one noticed Staubel at first. He wandered in drunk, with no idea what he was looking for, and he found it only slowly. He tottered toward the crowd of men holding their cups, picking up speed as he came on. Had anyone seen him in that instant, they could not have missed his frantic, swinging gait. They might have thought he was starving and had wandered into a banquet.

Sergeant Feng was the first to glimpse the incoming shape. His smile remained plastered to his face as Staubel smashed into him and he fell into a table. Staubel kept hold of his arm, twisted the cup out of his hand, and threw it.

"No!" the doctor shouted.

It happened so quickly that almost everyone missed it. As heads turned, the doctor lunged at his fellow Ronians. His hands flailed, knocking cups from hands.

For a moment, no one resisted. The others did not grasp what they were seeing. They stood in their circles, some still sipping from their cups. Finally, someone pulled back reflexively when the doctor tried to take his drink. Staubel shoved him, and he fell on his back.

A Realmsman broke the spell. He grabbed Staubel by the shoulders and held him. Staubel saw his uniform and beat his hands away furiously.

He choked out words. "Don't drink it!"

"What the hell do you mean?" Feng demanded as someone helped him to his feet. "What's wrong?"

"Something in the drinks. I don't know what!" Staubel cried. He turned toward one of the Realmsmen, a common soldier. "What are you doing to us? What is this place?"

"Doctor!" Feng shouted. The ring of authority in his voice calmed the mayhem and drew Staubel's attention.

Staubel suddenly felt abashed.

"Tell us what's happening," the sergeant ordered.

Staubel collected himself as he spoke. "That"—he pointed at a nearby cask of ale—"is poison."

"But we've been drinking it for days, man. Everything's fine."

"It's not like that," he said. "That's not how it kills you." He looked around at all the sets of eyes, and his mind raced as he tried to put his thoughts into words.

"It kills the soul," he said at last.

The roar of laughter he had dreaded did not arise, though someone unseen chuckled.

Floundering, he continued, "That's how they'll get us."

"Who will 'get you'? Will it be us?" a Realmsman asked. He was black haired and crystal eyed, likely an officer.

Facing the man, Staubel felt his momentum falling and began to panic. "Why else would you help us?"

The man's eyes widened, and his voice became sad. "Doctor, what a question."

"I mean it!" Staubel said. "You've taken us in, given us women and drink..." But nothing he was saying gave evidence of betrayal. Again, he felt the weight of all of their eyes. "And your healers..."

"Is that your reason?" The Realmsman cocked his head and spread his hands in a gesture of utmost charity. "Doctor, we can show you our ways of healing. You're held back by your lack of training, but we can make you as fine a healer as any of us."

"That's not the reason, damn it!" Staubel turned toward Feng and the Ronians. "Has the drink drowned your wits? Have you all forgotten that they tried to kidnap one of us? They threatened Carrowy and scared him halfway to the grave, and now he's gone!" His voice rose to a painful pitch. "They are not our friends!" He stabbed the air with his finger, pointing at the Realm officer.

The officer folded his hands. "Do you mean the man who tried to desert you? What did he say we told him?"

Staubel breathed hard. He said painfully, reluctantly, "Nothing."

"Doctor, the poor man was suffering terribly. And ashamed at himself, no doubt. He has plenty of reasons not to speak of what happened."

Staubel clenched his fists. "But it was more than that. He was scared."

"Of course. Think of how he has suffered, with that belly wound. How he's still suffering. Let our healers work, and learn from them."

Staubel roared in frustration. He shouted at his comrades, "Can't you see?"

In the Ronians' current state, such abstract talk barely seemed worth hearing. They were full of the Realm's ale and its abiding, possessive wistfulness.

But the sounds Staubel was making had a different effect. The way he roared from his narrow chest and the way his voice cracked when he said "see" struck a chord. A chuckle rippled through the company and grew.

As his nightmare came true, the doctor shouted, "Carrowy ran away! He's got to be found!" But his effort had already failed.

The laughter built upon itself, groping its way to new heights. He turned and looked at them all. He was growing numb, and the noises and sights were fading behind a buzz. He was as drunk as any of them, but it had not trapped him in the same way. He wondered what to do.

Then he saw the Realm officer who had offered to train him as a healer. Most of the Realmsmen were laughing, but not him. His eyes were wide with amusement, his smile suppressed into a pitying smirk. *"I tried to help you, boy,"* that look said.

Staubel drove at the man, hands extended to shove him. But the man moved quickly, and the world flipped and twisted. The doctor hit the floor on his back and bent in an ugly spasm. His breath left him with a sigh.

From the floor, he watched what happened next. As long as the Ronians were under the ale's sway, nothing he said was likely to move them to action. But seeing him thrown to the floor by a Realmsman turned their amusement sour.

A Ronian, laughing as heartily as ever, tackled the officer to the ground. As they grappled on the floor, the officer started laughing too. When the Ronian gained the upper hand and began striking the officer in the face, other Realmsmen converged on the spot, followed by the Ronians. The laughter was universal now, louder and shriller, with howls and whoops of religious intensity.

The brawl destroyed the room. Tables and chairs were smashed and heads dented by metal cups as the men beat each other bloody.

In danger of being trampled, Staubel jumped up, only to be knocked down again by someone paying him no attention. He glimpsed a face, white and red, torn between primordial drives, mouth wide, gasping for more breath with which to laugh.

He hit the floor but jumped right up and screamed. The fight swept him along and carried him where it would. Nothing hurt.

Somehow, it ended. Blows became sluggish, and energy slackened. The men withdrew, slumping in the corners and against walls. They laughed even then, but softly, at memories of what they had done.

As the last fighters looked around in confusion or wandered away, the men of the Shining Realm gathered to leave. The two armies exchanged no parting words. The Realmsmen left the room in pairs or groups, supporting the injured on their shoulders. A few were carried out, maybe dead.

The Ronians were little better off. Some lay on the floor while others turned chairs upright and fell into them. Their laughter had grown tearful, like they were hearing a sweet and funny eulogy at a funeral. Their tears mixed with the sweat in their shredded clothing and the blood from their noses, mouths, and heads.

Staubel was the first to weep outright. He curled up against a wall and sobbed louder than he would have dared before. Some followed his example, while others had not finished laughing.

The doctor wanted to be alone. Since he didn't want to stand just yet, he crawled toward the doorway. Approaching it, he arrived at a set of long, booted feet.

He turned his head painfully upward to see the bishop. Arumin looked over the room's devastation. He had gone so pale as to look monstrous. Beside him was Orund, who cursed at the scene and helped the doctor off the ground.

As the sergeant led him into the corridor, Staubel's eyes met those of Private Merin. The private sat where he always had, at one of the few tables still upright. He observed the doctor with detached interest, having only watched from the edges as the men of both armies fought their own playful little war.

34

— · —

EMBERLY

CURSING, FIGHTING DESPAIR, EMBERLY turned around for the hundredth time and marched back down the tunnel from which he'd come. This labyrinth had exits. That was a fact. He had only to wander long enough—

Dust crunched behind him. Despite his exhaustion, he picked up his pace. In the hours he had been lost in the tunnels—*Or has it been years?*—Rayan had pursued him continually. The captain made no attempt to hide his hurry. He had long since lost his fear of attracting attention. He would have been almost glad to encounter the mob that had chased him from the crash site, if only he could see daylight again. His bandaged arm still hurt where one of the crowd had grabbed it.

He had outrun the mob, but he couldn't outrun a ghost. Rayan kept pace effortlessly, and the sweet smell of death followed.

"What are you afraid of, brother?" Rayan asked. "Those vagabonds? You've got much worse to fear now."

Passing a turn, Emberly hesitated, wondering if the tunnel had been straight or had bent. He held out the torch he had snatched from a tunnel wall. He thought he recognized a figure crouched against a wall, and he chose that way.

"Don't run," Rayan said. "It's only a matter of time. You and I have an eternity."

"Shut up!" Emberly was indeed almost running. Passing a distant light, he turned his head to see Rayan floating after him, cloak billowing.

"How long will it take?" his brother asked. "A thousand years? Ten thousand? Doesn't matter. I will break you. You will look in a mirror and face what you've done. Murderer."

Emberly ran. Through his horror, he told himself the surface was just around this bend. When he was back on the street, his ragged appearance might disguise him, letting him sneak back to the pyramid, back to his company. He could be there when the Realm came for them.

Upon first entering the tunnels, he had chosen the ways that led upward, thinking he would have to arrive at the surface sooner or later. As time passed, he had fought the dawning realization that he should have reached the surface long before. Watching himself become more and more lost was maddening, and every direction he tried made it worse. Soon, his surroundings were a tangle of passageways, lit and unlit, each one both unfamiliar and like every other.

The place seemed to obey no natural laws. With that realization, a fear colder and more ancient than that of death rose and spread its wings inside him, and it had not left him since. He swayed with panic like a man waist deep in rough surf as he heard Rayan's words again: *"Welcome to hell."*

That wasn't true. He knew it wasn't. He could not have died without even knowing it. But the more lost he became, and the longer he wandered endless passageways, the fainter grew the voice of the part of him that knew things.

He had approached some of the dim figures he encountered, but most shied away, and the ones that didn't menaced him until he drew his knife and scared them off. None of them spoke a word of his language, and he spoke none of theirs.

Deciding once more that he'd chosen the wrong passage, he stopped. Rayan was gone.

Forcing himself to breathe, fearing the exhaustion that had followed each round of panic, he retraced his steps, heading for a large chamber he had seen not long before. Minutes passed, and he did not find it.

He stopped and looked around. That area was quite dark and empty, lit only by his torch, as were a couple others in the distance. He did not recognize the place.

He trudged onward. The tunnel got darker and darker.

It was all wrong. He had made it wrong.

He bent over and dug into his cheeks with his fingers. He dropped to the ground and beat on it with his fists. For a moment, he was back at Ganet's carriage, but this time, he was a part of the faceless mob, looking into the vehicle at his own huddled form. On the dusty rock where his blows landed, he saw himself.

When he grew tired, he sat up to catch his breath. Footsteps were approaching, and he listened like a man awaiting the fall of an executioner's axe.

Rayan appeared around a bend. He no longer floated.

"What's going on? Where are we?" Emberly hissed.

Rayan said nothing until he reached Emberly. When he spoke, his voice held none of it usual cruel joviality. "Those are the wrong questions. I've already asked you the right ones: Who are you? And most importantly, what's wrong with you?"

"I don't have time for your games."

His brother's eyes lit with astonishment. "This is no game. This is your life. This is the lives of your company and everyone in your city. You claim to care about them, but here you are, thinking of yourself yet again."

Emberly hissed. "If you can help me, do it! Tell me how to get out of here."

"Me, me, me." Rayan's eyes gleamed. "How you'll get out of here, Cyril, is by answering my questions."

"Goddess." Still on his knees, Emberly pounded the ground. "Enough of this! Tell me what you want me to say, and I'll say it."

Rayan shook his head. "As for who you are, that's easy. You're a human man. Like all others, you're faced with choices. Unlike all others, your choices have led you here, alone and on your knees, lost in the underworld, instead of fighting the war it's your duty to fight."

Emberly grimaced. "My duty is to my men. I can't send them to their deaths. They've never faced anything like this."

"Like what? Like rifle fire? They've faced that. One might even say it's their job. No, Cyril, you're stalling. Why?"

Barely containing his rage, Emberly struggled to think. Rayan had always loved tormenting him, and now, he had a captive audience. Until Emberly learned how to get back to the company, his brother could dangle that knowledge as bait to keep him trapped. Worse, Rayan might know nothing about where they were, but he could easily pretend he did. The sick bastard must have felt his dreams were coming true.

Emberly had to give Rayan what he wanted: answers to his questions.

And his brother was only too right. Emberly hadn't just stalled out of concern for his men's safety. Digging through the turmoil inside himself, he tried to put words to his reasons. "If I start a war," he said, "Goddess knows how many in Ronia herself will die."

Then he spoke the words he could hardly bear to think. "My wife might die. My son." Into his mind marched the armies of the Shining Realm, sacking Ronia like the heathen armies of old, pillaging and raping. Charlotte and Edmund would wait outside their family home, lined up in formal style as though greeting honored guests. Edmund's knees would tremble, his body stiff with fear. Charlotte would put on a face of brave, defiant courtesy, her lovely smile hidden away, never to return. Both would wonder where Cyril Emberly was, why he wasn't standing there beside them as they had always, patiently and courageously, stood beside him.

Emberly watched as the Realmsmen put Edmund to the sword. Then they took Charlotte—

Rayan interrupted his thoughts, his voice a blessing for once. "I see." His face was grave. Maybe he had shared Emberly's vision. He had always liked Charlotte. "Here's an easy question, brother. Are there worse things than death?"

Choking, Emberly spoke the terrible truth. "Of course there are."

"What things?"

"Damn you." The captain shook. "Don't make me say it."

"What things?" Rayan repeated, cold and merciless.

"Slavery," Emberly answered. He hated Rayan for forcing him to admit some things were worse than the vision he had just seen. In his hatred, he lashed out at his brother. "You should know. You tried to enslave your own people on Caidfell."

"I did indeed." Rayan showed no remorse, just simple acknowledgment of fact. "Let us learn from my unfortunate example. When you learned I meant to be a slavemaster, you resisted. You would have chosen death for yourself, for your people, and for mine. Now, if you did that for strangers, you could hardly do worse for the people you loved—your family, your soldiers, the Ronian people.

You would do right by them, granting them death if they couldn't live free.

"At least, that's what I thought. Something's changed. What is it, Cyril?"

Suddenly short of breath, Emberly gasped. "Nothing. I've been stalling, true. I did it to give Huire time to save us, as she's done before, through the Lady."

"And what's been the result? Ganet, the only voice of reason among the enemy, has been killed. That strange little woman with the dead eyes is in charge. Your men are flailing, leaderless. And you—you are lost, talking to a ghost."

The captain squeezed his eyes shut. *Huire is on our side.* "The Goddess may still save us."

Rayan's lip curled. "She may. But what if she doesn't?"

"Be serious."

"I am deadly serious. The Lady is powerful, I'll admit—when she bothers to be present. But it was Ganet who died for your sake just now. Aside from the Lady's word—the Lady, whom you hardly ever see—what certainty do you have that Huire watches you? That she even knows who you are?"

The words burned. Emberly answered softly. "None. I just have hope."

His brother nodded. "Hope. Very good. Hold on to that hope, Cyril. You saw what happened to me when I lost it. Hope is a gift—a gift you are squandering. You can fight. You must fight, but you won't. Why?"

"I'm a coward." Tasting the word, Emberly felt his anger rise again. "That's what you want me to say, isn't it? You've always wanted to hear me abase myself."

"Now *that's* cowardice. Avoiding the truth with easy lies. You're not a coward, Cyril. Not in that way. You've conquered your fear of death as well as anyone can. Try again."

Emberly shook his head desperately. "Ganet sacrificed himself for peace. I must honor his memory by—

Rayan's groan came from deep inside. "Oh Goddess, if I wasn't dead, I would kill myself. Ganet was a fool. A brave one, but a fool. You saw what he resorted to for your peace. What chance do you have of making peace with the woman when her own comrade failed? You saw the look in her eyes. No, no, no. You've faced death. You've sent others to their deaths. You're a killer. Now, why won't you kill?"

Something snapped inside Emberly. "Because I've killed one person too many."

"Who?" Rayan's eyes blazed.

"You!" Emberly screamed the word, which resounded down the tunnel. He shut his eyes and sank forward until his face touched the ground. His voice came as a hoarse whisper. "I put a bullet in you. My own brother. And when I asked for forgiveness, you said it wasn't yours to give. I must have it, brother, and if I can't get it from you, I'll get it elsewhere."

Silence followed his words. He looked up slowly to see Rayan gazing down on him, face pale.

"But..." Rayan began. Then he started again. "That was different. These are soldiers. I wasn't."

Emberly sat miserably on the floor and wrapped his arms around his knees. "These are all just words. What difference do words make when you're bleeding to death? I don't want to send more people to the afterlife, like I sent you."

Rayan was quiet for a time. Emberly had rarely seen him lost for words.

Finally, he said, "Cyril... what if I told you that I was a bastard, and I deserved what I got?"

Emberly sniffed. "You deserved it, maybe. But not from me."

"Yes, from you." Rayan's voice rang cold and hard. "You're their leader. You lead soldiers to victory and keep them alive when you can, and when something stands in your way, you cut it down. Even if that something is your brother." He choked on the last word. "When you shot me in the back, you showed me the man you could be, the man who opened the door to my cell. A man who makes choices. Who commits. Who takes responsibility. For all the worlds, a man who *kills*."

He touched Emberly's cheek. His death-smell was nauseating. "I can't forgive you, brother, because you don't need forgiveness. You waded into the muck and did what had to be done, and it was righteous. And you're going to keep doing it, Goddess or no Goddess. Aren't you?"

Rayan's words worked a spell on Emberly's mind. The clouds cleared. The tumult quieted. He slowly nodded.

His brother's lip twisted. "How feeble. Speak up." He leaned down. "You're going to be strong. You're going to be ruthless. Aren't you?"

Emberly looked into Rayan's eyes. He rose, and his feet felt steady, his legs strong. When he spoke, his voice was hard as steel. "Yes." He did not shout—he felt no need to.

Rayan glowed. "Good. I never stopped hoping you would."

He looked around. "Except..."

"What?"

"It's not true, is it? What you said earlier?" Emberly asked. It might be silly, but he had to know. "I'm not... dead?"

Rayan's eyes widened, then he threw back his head and laughed. It was a cackle of such wicked intensity that Emberly thought for a horrified second that it was all a cruel joke, that he was truly in the underworld. Then Rayan stopped and coughed. By the time his laugh resumed, Emberly felt his face darkening.

"Dead!" Rayan crowed. "Of course not!" After another round of laughter, he calmed and wiped his eyes. "I can't stay angry with you, brother."

Emberly bent over. His hand closed around a fistful of sand and pebbles. He bolted upright and whipped these into his brother's eyes. Rayan cried out in pain and surprise, covering his face.

He spoke slowly between. "What the hell... was that? Are... you trying to blind me?"

Emberly thought about it. "It surprised you, didn't it? I didn't want you disappearing like you always do."

Rayan rolled over and spat sand from his mouth. He sat up with a look of shock, recovering his breath. "Every time I despair for you, you give me reason to hope."

"Go away," Emberly said, closing his eyes.

"I won't. That's not what you really want."

"No. I want a way home. Back to the company."

"A gift, then, to speed you along. If you don't want it, don't use it."

Emberly heard breathing and quick footsteps. A boy stood nearby. He was small, not ten years old. He whispered something and hooked his fingers, asking Emberly to follow.

Emberly looked back to find that Rayan had left him again.

35

NOR

WEEDS AND WITHERED GRASS. The endless plain, blotted by fields and roads. The baking, unchanging sun.

In Nor's dream, it was midday, and he was a boy again, a little older this time, hiding in the same grove of boulders he had seen in other dreams. Beyond, the hill swept down to the shallow river where, a few years earlier, his father had surrendered to Ronia.

Nor had come to the rocks to hide, but he was no longer safe even there. Someone had entered the maze of boulders. Nor had climbed atop a rock and watched as the intruder, a Ronian, passed beneath. He fingered the knife in his hand and thought of burying it in the man's neck. The heavy bag on Nor's back was burdensome, and he wished he had left it on the ground.

"I should have asked your permission before I came in here," Cadmon said.

Watching through his own eyes of many years past, Nor marveled. The abbot was not the perpetually ancient man he had been when Nor last saw him. His hair was fully brown and tinged with red, and he was only mildly overweight. Nor wondered if Cadmon had ever truly looked like that or if years of retreading had distorted Nor's memory.

"This is your second home, from what I've heard," the abbot said. "I'm sorry to invade it."

"Then leave," Nor said. Like most children among the Newat, he had mastered Ronia's language beyond the abilities of his elders.

Cadmon looked upward for the source of the voice, turning his head back and forth and his body with it. He had not been spry, even in middle age. Nor leaned back out of sight.

"Your mother asked me to come," the abbot replied at last.

Nor spat. He looked over the tops of the boulders and down the hill. At the center of the town's midday bustle stood a bridge across the river. Beyond the buildings, a Ronian temple rose. The new village was mostly built of wood imported from Ronia, for which his people had accepted debt—a word he did not yet understand.

"She stopped praying to your Goddess for that long?" he asked Cadmon bitterly.

"She asked, but I would have come anyway. What would she do without you?"

"Whatever she wants. She's got you."

"I'm nothing compared to you, Norhim."

Nor stepped to the edge of the rock. He looked down at Cadmon and said, "Then go. Leave this world forever."

"Boy, even if your parents' problems were my doing, I would not leave. I would stay and make it right." Looking up at the young man, he raised a hand to shade his eyes. "I admit my complicity in evil. Corruption rules all human worlds. None of us escape that in this life unless we run away." He lowered his hand and squinted in the sunlight. "Where will you go?"

Nor had expected that question. "Into the plains."

"Even they end somewhere. How will you stand it, being alone?"

"I won't be alone."

"Who will come with you?"

"My grandmother. She hates it here now."

"She'll come along if you make her. Don't drag her into this, lad. Especially if you don't plan to go quietly."

Nor didn't answer.

"What do you think will happen afterward?" Cadmon asked. He let Nor think for a moment then continued: "It won't end with Hob, you know. If you kill him, others will follow. You're fighting the tide."

"At least I'm not like you."

Cadmon's head dropped. Perhaps it was from shame, but Nor suspected that he was simply tired of looking into the light. "Thank the Goddess," said the abbot. "You can be far better."

Nor looked down at the man's hair, which was scarcely balding. Surely, Cadmon had never really looked this young.

"To hell with your Goddess!" Nor shouted, hoping that somehow, his mother would hear.

"So you believe in the Dark now, eh? I've done something right."

Nor tried to summon the courage to leap down, knife in hand, and end the old man's life. If he couldn't even do that, he must be a coward indeed.

He began to cry. He sat on the rocks and covered his face, but sounds escaped nonetheless. Ashamed of his weakness, he said, "Our gods are gone."

The abbot was now out of sight, but his voice carried clearly. "Norhim, all of the gods are gone."

If that was an attempt to cheer him, it was laughable. Still crying, Nor gathered his breath and said, "But ours aren't watching us, are they?"

"I don't know. I know of only one who surely is."

Nor felt repulsed by that overture. "After I kill Hob, I'm going to the hills to light a fire. Maybe they will see it and come back."

"If they do, will they be happy with what you have done?"

"They will be proud," Nor said with new relish. "At least one of the Newat still draws blood."

"You've got reasons to hate, Norhim. But that's no excuse for hating. It's poison, boy."

Nor leaned over the cliff to look at him again. "I don't care."

In Nor's eyes, Cadmon's appearance shifted. He looked older for a moment—not portly, as Nor had known him, but gaunt and underfed. "If you murder Hob, they'll find you," the abbot said, "and you will be killed. I won't be able to stop it, though I will die trying."

"I don't care."

"Your people's lives will become worse—your family's especially."

Nor's mind was dark. "That's good. Everything is too easy now. Pain will wake them up."

Cadmon fell silent. Nor realized he had shocked the old man. That was something he had often tried, but now that he had finally managed it, it brought him no enjoyment. When the abbot spoke again, his voice had become more formal and familiar, like Nor's mother sounded when she scolded him.

"They will bury you," the abbot said. "You won't be burned or left to decay. You won't rise into the sky. No eternal ride through the stars."

Nor couldn't let such an idea stand. "Father wouldn't let them bury me." It was the response of a child, and his face burned. It was not worth a reply, and they both knew it.

Cadmon continued, "Your body will be embalmed, drained of fluids, and stuffed with filler. Below the ground, you will languish for centuries."

Nor swung his legs and slid down the nearly vertical slope of rock. He landed in front of the old man, who stepped quickly back. Nor brandished his knife.

"Your people are cursed!" he cried.

Taking a breath to recover from his surprise, Cadmon said, "Some of us. When the Goddess returns, we will learn who."

The blade glinted in the sun, and Nor felt dread and sickness at the thought of plunging it into the abbot.

Perhaps the abbot knew that, because he seemed unafraid. "Come back," he said. "Or go if you want. But don't damn yourself. We're all on one of two paths. Your gods would agree with that."

Nor squeezed the knife in his fingers. He must kill Hob. What that man and his "nightshade" had done to the Newat could not go unavenged. But he could not bring himself to feel the same about Cadmon.

He needed Cadmon out of the way but not dead. So he used a tactic of which Cadmon's fellow Ronians were masters. He lied.

He put away the knife with as much authority as he could convey. "I will let the bastard live."

Cadmon glared. For a moment, Nor believed the man could see his thoughts. "You must promise it."

"I promise," Nor lied again. Then he felt the need to balance his deception with a truth. After all, maybe the gods really were watching. "I promise this too: I will never come to your temple again."

Cadmon smiled. His smile had an electricity, no matter his age. It was sad, having gained a few lines since coming to Nor's world, but a deeper warmth still lit it.

"I don't believe that last promise." He turned and walked away, calling, "Thank you, Norhim. Enjoy your fire."

36

NOR

NOR DECIDED HE MUST be awake. The unnamed presence in his dreams, the man made of glass, had vanished again. Floating in darkness, Nor touched his eyes and found they were open.

Wherever he was, the Realm had put him there. They did what they wanted, commanding him, and he followed. Ever since he gave himself to Ren—maybe the day before, maybe in another lifetime—he had simply obeyed, trudging from place to place, from dark to light to dark again, drinking or eating whenever a plate or cup appeared in front of him.

The things he drank stretched and twisted time. He might have known Ren all his life. She might be his mother. She was there whenever his eyes opened.

The struggle between them had begun as a game, he realized. He had decided in a fit of vanity and madness to test his faith, to prove himself not an abject failure by giving himself a mountain to climb.

The mountain had vanished, leaving a gulf into which he fell and fell but found no bottom. Somewhere above, in the land of sunlight he'd left behind, the Goddess must be watching, shaking her head—if she was watching at all.

"If" was wishful thinking. He had called to Huire, begging her, but felt only the coldness of space. Wherever she was, she was not with him. Maybe she had given up on him long before, or maybe she didn't even know he existed. The result was the same: he was alone.

He turned his head at a faint noise and sputtered as salty water rushed into his mouth. Then he remembered. He was floating in the pool where Ren let him rest between sessions.

What was that noise? She might be coming to see him. Each time she threw back the sheet covering the pool, light flooded in, a blinding dawn with her at its center, a dark little sun.

He would almost have welcomed her. In the pool floated his thoughts like a thousand gnawing, stinging creatures of the deep. In the dark, they reigned unchallenged.

He had thrown himself into this danger like a fool. For Huire's sake, he had even called himself her fool. He had known it was a bad idea, but in his unending stupidity, he had done it anyway. Not content with Huire's crusade, he had started his own. Now, Huire was nowhere to be found, and he had separated himself from the company, the people he had been charged to care for.

He was also separated from Shada. He had convinced himself he might find her this way, using rationales that were feeling as slippery and immaterial as the water around him. In truth, he had given up searching for her, just as he had given up on answering Cadmon's quandary. Unwilling to face real difficulty, he had fled, throwing himself into something impossible, something he couldn't help but fail, so that failing wouldn't be his fault. He had thrown himself into *this*.

The thought of Cadmon brought renewed shame. Thinking of the day he had dreamt about, the day he had promised Cadmon he would never again enter a temple, he recalled the old man's smile. Cadmon had known he could not believe Nor's promises.

Nor's fury at himself grew thicker and more bitter. He had made one mistake over and over: he had believed in the Goddess Huire.

For her, he had left his people and their gods, betting his soul in a great gamble that he seemed to be losing. For her, he had given himself to Ren. For her, he had undergone torture by the wraiths on Caidfell. For her, he had accepted that damned envelope from Cadmon, the secret that now lay in Ren's hands, the secret with which he should never have been entrusted.

But it wasn't all his fault. Cadmon had guided him every step of the way. His kindness had seduced Nor into the Temple's service—*He must have planned that all along!*—which had led to this wretched end. Cadmon had failed—he had failed to see that Huire was a distant, uncaring being. Most of all, he had failed to see that Nor was defective, unfit for responsibility of any kind, much less shepherding the souls of the Ronian company through the reaches of the universe.

Nor's teethe ached, and he realized he was clenching them. His body was a knot of tension, and he forced himself to relax.

If the Goddess was not behind the miracles he had witnessed, he didn't know who was. Maybe the Lady was a god in her own right and had lied to the company, leading them on this crusade for her own hidden purposes. Or maybe the man in Nor's dreams, the man made of glass, was more than just a figment of his imagination. Time and events were washing away the lines between the possible and the impossible, the reasonable and the laughable. Maybe the glass man was real.

Finally, the darkest possibility: Private Hulgar had told the company about a dream he'd had on Caidfell, a terrifying vision in which Huire had abandoned them to the mercy of dark, bloodthirsty gods. Nor had dismissed the dream, but here in the dark, dreams seemed like the realest things of all.

Now Nor, as punishment for discounting Hulgar's vision, was drowning in his own. In eternal twilight, night and day coming and going as they would, he killed whenever he was ordered, and someday, killing would feel like nothing at all, and all of it at his captors' will.

At her will.

Ren was his goddess now.

She would keep him in this twilight until he took a form that pleased her. She had given him blessings, such as the truth about Huire, and curses, such as taking him away from Shada and everyone else that he cared about. She had even bestowed him with sacred truths:

Life is an accident—the workings of dead particles.

We can destroy a thing when we decide it shouldn't exist.

We are all tools.

In his rage at Huire, rage blackening to hate, he fiddled playfully with Ren's truths. He mouthed them quietly, waiting for Huire's response to this sacrilege, for Huire to come down and smite him or embrace him. Nothing.

Fine! he cried to the Goddess. *Maybe I'll try out these new truths. Make them my own. I've tried your way, and it's brought me to hell, far from the people I love. And those people are all that matters.*

But the joke's on you. In this hell you've sent me to, I've learned new ways. I've found a new goddess, and she's taught me that I don't need her either.

As he thought that, the blackness over him fell away like a blanket, and he squinted in the light.

The metal walls of the round pool in which he floated blocked his view of the room. The water, if that's what it was, was incredibly buoyant, holding him like a gentle hammock. They had dressed him in clothes so light and thin that he had forgotten he was wearing them. Ren leaned over him.

He trembled when he saw her. He heard Cadmon say, *Don't damn yourself.*

She noticed his trembling and smiled. "You've made it, Norhim," she said. "It's a new day." She put a hand on his chest.

He placed his hands on hers and felt her fingers slide between his. How small she was when he finally touched her. It was hard to believe.

"We are all tools," he said aloud, his voice weak from disuse.

He thought maybe her face changed then—a twitch of the lips or a flash of the eyes—a hint that she realized her danger. If so, she didn't have time to react.

He clamped his hands around her wrist and twisted his body away. She tumbled over him and landed in the water. He could not see her face, but he hoped that, for at least an instant, she was frightened.

He threw himself onto her and shot an arm around her neck. She fought like a demon, twisting this way and that without regard for pain. The water kept turning them over and over. She whipped her head back and forth, trying to slip from his grasp. Her fingernails cut his arms and reached ever closer to his eyes. She was mostly silent.

He locked her throat between his bicep and forearm. She sensed the damage he might do and froze.

They must have been alone in the room. If anyone was watching, they would have intervened.

"Don't scream," Nor said. Feeling the beating of her heart in her neck, he thought of the fly he had crushed and felt cruel joy. "You trusted me." He laughed and got a mouthful of water. "You really did."

"You've lost now," she coughed. Her voice could not rise above a whisper. "Your friends, your Goddess. You've lost everything."

"My friends never trusted me," he said. "They're wiser than you."

She spoke in choked phrases. "You can't imagine… what waits for them… now."

He didn't doubt her honesty. The knowledge that he had brought the Realm's wrath down on the company broke over him like an icy bath. He had to warn them. But first, he needed something. He squeezed her throat and asked, "Where is it?"

He stopped pressing to let her answer.

She said only, "What?"

He squeezed again, and she indicated one of her pockets. He prompted her to take out the letter and give it to him.

When the envelope rose from the water in her hand, he felt lightheaded. He had been afraid she wouldn't have it.

He didn't know why he still wanted it. Maybe it was a morbid curiosity for answers about a goddess he no longer followed. But he was determined to have them. Holding her tight with one arm, he snatched the soaked envelope.

Feeling its trifling weight in his hand, he clutched it between his fingers, clasped his hands together, and tightened his hold on her throat. He had done it, outsmarted her. *How did she come so close to making me her puppet?* She had played with him like a toy—she, who was hardly larger than a doll herself.

"What should I do with you, then?" he said. "Maybe I'll drown you. You're just a tool."

He saw her face in slight profile. It was turned up toward the ceiling, so he could not see her colorless eyes.

She said, "Do what you want."

The words chilled him. "You're a liar. You cannot care for your life so little."

"There is no life," she replied as her body relaxed. "We don't exist. We've fooled ourselves into thinking we're alive."

She moved gently, pressing her body against his. A part of him had suspected all her talk of life's emptiness was meant to scare him. Now, he was probing the depths of her belief, and he felt no bottom. Fear and revulsion rose in him, and he began to push her away. Then he realized she must not escape. He was trapped, holding her as she pushed against him in almost sensual intimacy.

"Liar!" he cried. "Say what you want. If I push you under, you'll be scared. Anyone would."

"Only a little. There is no one to scare. I am nothing," she replied. "We can... find out together."

"Goddess," he spat. He had to get out of here.

"You've come so far already," she continued. "I didn't know. I'll die so you can know the truth." She placed a tender hand on his arm. "Awaken."

Shutting his eyes and clenching his teeth, he squeezed her neck until she passed out. Doing it took everything he had, and he wanted to be sick. The last thing she did was grip his arm hard with both hands.

37

— · —

NOR

ACHING ALL OVER, NOR pulled Ren out of the water. The pounding of his heart made feeling her pulse hard, but she was breathing.

The magnitude of his own plight overshadowed all else. He did not know where he was, whether in a building or under the ground, or even what lay outside the door. His mind had been opened and tinkered with like a watch, and he remembered nothing they hadn't wanted him to. That very moment could be another dream, for all he knew. But in such thoughts lay the shortest route to insanity.

The room was empty but for the pool, glowing lanterns in each corner, and a chair where Ren had draped her cloak. He searched her soaked clothes but found nothing. Then he checked the cloak, which had pockets in its lining, and found three items. The first was a small syringe like those she had used a number of times to make him sleep. The second was a black baton long enough to reach from his elbow to his fingertips. It was light but hard and would be quite destructive in determined hands.

She carried no gun. He was strangely unsurprised. She exerted too much assurance of control to make such a concession to unforeseen events. Even carrying a baton betrayed a vulnerability that he hadn't expected.

The third thing he found was the envelope with Cadmon's letter. Ren had opened it but had kept the papers inside. He could feel them as he held it. Relief rushed over him. Strangely, his loss of faith in the Goddess had little effect on its preciousness to him. It was all he had of his old life. He was tempted to tear it open and read it right then, before anything else happened to take it away again, but his promise to Cadmon not to open it until he was ready still held sway in his mind. Maybe the conditioning word Cadmon had used to ensure Nor's obedience had actually worked. Nor had thought such things were fanciful.

After taking the syringe, baton, and letter, he set himself to the seemingly impossible road ahead. He could not bring himself to kill Ren, and anyway, killing her would not save the company. The Shining Realm seemed to work with one mind, and that mind was turning against Ronia and its people. The only thing he could do was escape and warn the company. Once again, Cadmon's letter would have to wait.

If he left that room and wandered, hoping to stumble on an escape route, he would be doomed to capture and to the torments Ren would inflict when they met again. To escape, he would need her help. But she couldn't help him until she woke up, and he didn't want to imagine what forcing her assistance would require.

Then came a gentle knock on the door.

His stomach plummeted. He glanced frantically around the room, fighting back hopelessness. He had only one idea, a desperate one. A second, louder knock spurred him to act on it.

Dragging Ren by the arms, he concealed her behind the pool, against the wall farthest from the door. Meanwhile, a man's voice called twice from outside. The first call was polite, the second much less so.

Nor raced to the door, baton in hand, and stood to its side. It was hinged to open inward, and he placed himself so that it would hide him when it opened. Another call, pitched with urgency, was speaking a language Nor did not know.

The door opened. Nor's stomach had whipped into an icy storm, but in that instant, it settled. The wait was over.

No one appeared. The silence seemed to last years. Then came the pounding of running feet.

Nor swung around the door to chase the retreating intruder and collided with a Realmsman standing in the doorway. Down a long hallway ahead, a second soldier disappeared around a corner.

Still dazed from the collision, Nor and his enemy locked eyes. Then both sprang.

The soldier threw himself toward Nor, who grabbed the handle of the massive door and swung it with all his weight. It bashed into the soldier, driving him into the doorframe before bouncing open again. Nor stumbled back with the effort. The soldier pawed at his belt, his eyes stunned and blank. Befuddled, he finally drew the pistol at his waist.

Nor was too far and moving the wrong way to reach him in time. He grabbed the handle of the door and swung it again.

That swing was weaker. The door struck the man but did not drive him from the room. Nor rushed against the door as it bounced back. The soldier flung out an arm, and the door closed on it.

The soldier's hand and forearm remained in the room. It was his pistol hand. Holding the door closed, Nor watched the weapon turn, with dreamy slowness, to point at him. He begged his muscles to stop it, grab it, do something.

Only when the barrel was pointed at his face did he remember the baton. He clubbed the man's hand with all his might as the gun's shattering roar filled the room. The weapon struck the ground. Nor had not been shot.

He beat vigorously on the soldier's trapped hand and arm. Outside, the man screamed.

After a moment, Nor opened the door. The man pulled away, wanting no more, but Nor caught him and beat him unconscious.

A profound silence fell. The hallway ahead ended in a corner, from beyond which came a tumult of voices.

Nor almost took off running that instant, but against a large part of his judgment, he knelt and searched the soldier's uniform for anything handy.

All he found was a small oblong box. He sensed it was related to the pistol but had no time to learn how. Rushing back into the room, he grabbed the pistol—no one would know it was empty.

Pistol in one hand and baton in the other, he sprinted down the hallway. The noises were swelling, and as he neared the corner, someone hurried around it.

The man was covered in black except for his yellow eyes. As he stared at Nor, the slitted pupils expanded, yawning mouths in pools of yellow. The light from the open door cast Nor's long shadow across the man.

Nor raised his gun. "Stop!"

The man's eyes flicked to the weapon then to Nor's face. He did not reach for his own pistol.

More voices came from around the corner. Nor felt a renewed surge of fear.

"Drop your weapon," he told the man.

The man said nothing and did not move. Perhaps he knew Nor's gun was empty. Nor fought off that terrifying idea. Maybe, unlike his superiors, the man didn't speak Ronian.

"You're going to help me," Nor said. "Put down your gun." He pointed to the weapon and the floor.

The man did not move.

"Do it!" Nor shouted. He didn't know if he would kill the man. Feeling helpless and sick, he began to shake. His gun's barrel wagged like the tail of a happy dog.

The man's eyes took that in, and his hand moved slowly toward his weapon.

"Don't." Nor coughed.

The hand paused then inched closer to the pistol.

"No!"

The man exhaled with a shudder. His mouth widened behind its slit in his mask.

Nor grasped slowly that the creature was laughing at him. He felt the heat leaving his body. Maybe he should throw down the gun, attack with his baton, and earn a quick death.

More soldiers arrived. They filled the space behind the first soldier, who raised his arms to halt them. Some were black clad and yellow eyed while others wore a sky-blue uniform and were men of a more familiar sort.

Nor clenched the baton, feeling its weight and wondering how many times he could swing it before they overcame him. Maybe they would not let him swing it once. He took a step backward toward the room he had come from. In there, he would have no way of escape, but he might shut them out and live a little longer. Every second he stayed out of their grasp seemed worth any price.

No one moved as he backed up several paces. He kept the gun on them, ever conscious of its worthlessness. The men muttered among themselves. The doorway must be near.

He was paying such close attention to so many things that he ignored the sharp sting in his neck. He thought it was just one more damn part of him that hurt. Then an arm whipped around his neck and pulled him back. He fell.

He writhed, Ren underneath him. She fought to lock an arm around his neck. From the far end of the hall rose a howl that might have come from hell itself. The horde charged.

Ren's syringe was lodged in him. He could've sworn he had taken it from her. Maybe he had dropped it. Maybe the laws of time and space were crumbling along with everything else.

She was weaker than she had been. Thrashing, he dropped the baton and started prying her arm off his neck. But he would not be fast enough. If she'd given him a whole dose of that potion, he would be unconscious in seconds.

A wildness overcame him. With a surge of strength, he turned his head, wrenched her arm up, and sank his teeth into it.

Blood filled his mouth like a river of copper. She screamed, an earsplitting sound. To his terror, she still held on, but with a shout, he tore her arm away at last.

He was up and running. The soldiers were nearly upon him. They had not shot him yet. He did not want to imagine their plans.

As he sprinted for the door, he knew he would not make it. He was dizzy and off balance. He felt himself tipping, tipping, and finally falling headlong.

He smashed into the ground across the doorway's threshold. His heart galloped hard enough to burst from his chest, yet each beat crawled past like the turning of the world. He rolled onto his back.

They were oncoming, towering over him, their dimensions stretched, a nightmare army of fire-eyed giants. Still holding the empty gun, he hoisted it in useless defiance.

He pulled the trigger, and the weapon jumped. The blast drowned out the roar of charging men.

The soldiers staggered, scrambling back and colliding with each other. Their leader fell to his hands and knees, bleeding from his chest. Amid the mayhem, his eyes met Nor's. Then he lurched forward, crawling like an infant.

Still stunned by the gunshot, Nor reacted slowly. He had seen the pistol fire. It should be empty. *What sort of gun doesn't need to be reloaded?*

The soldier reached him. He pulled the trigger again and again, shooting the man until the gun stopped firing. The soldier slumped, still reaching for Nor's throat.

With a final effort of his failing legs, Nor forced himself upright, limped through the door, slammed it, and threw all his weight against it. He gripped the door's handle so that they couldn't turn it. He waited.

The handle moved, and he tightened his fingers around it. Someone outside pulled it up and down but quickly gave up. They started kicking the door. Every couple of seconds, a crash rattled the big slab on its hinges, which whined at the abuse.

Nor wondered why he was still awake. Ren must have managed to give him only a partial dose. But he couldn't have long. When the door collapsed, they would have him. *She* would have him.

And the room had no other way out. *Why did I bother coming in here?*

Of course, he knew why—the letter. He could feel the envelope in his pocket, seeming heavier and heavier. He might have lost faith in Huire, but the letter remained, the answer to the quandary inside burning a hole in his mind.

Yet he wouldn't read it. Even now, when he doubted the Goddess knew or cared, his conditioning as a monk, and maybe his remaining loyalty to Cadmon, made the idea of reading it unbearable. He could not until he had answered Cadmon's quandary, and he would never get the chance now.

In his final moments of freedom, he lashed out once more at the Goddess, who didn't care. *Why did you give me this task if I'm to die before I can learn the answer? Why did you let Ren take it?*

But... had Huire let Ren take it? It was in Nor's hands now, after all. It had left him for a time, only to come back.

He could hardly complain about the path it took, as long as it ended up in his possession.

Could I possibly have lost it through my own fault? He tried to think. *Was there a moment I'd let it out of my sight? Let someone touch me?*

The answer came to him with piercing clarity. Once he thought of it, he quickly became sure. The beggar outside the temple—Nor had knelt next to the man, getting close to him, and his guard had been down. The man had seemed suspiciously hale and healthy for someone who lived on the street. The idea had occurred to Nor that the man might be an agent of the Shining Realm, but he'd had no reason to think of him again at all until now. But now, the man stood out in his memory, wily and alert, fully capable of slipping his hand into Nor's cloak when he'd had the chance and turning it over to Ren.

Those thoughts came to Nor in a cascading series, all in the space of a moment. The door continued to rattle, the invaders outside making slow progress against its bulk. They were moving cautiously, perhaps suspecting that he had more ammunition. Maybe that's what the little box was, not that Nor knew how to load the weapon.

He still felt no dizziness or sleep coming upon him. He wondered if Ren had somehow failed to give him any significant amount of her potion. He hoped she had—he would rather not be awake when the soldiers took him.

But rather than slowing down, his thoughts did the opposite, coming faster and faster. Maybe the beggar had taken the envelope. But to do that, he must have known it was there, and Nor certainly hadn't told Ren about it.

Or did I? Maybe he had revealed its existence somehow without meaning to. He had only seen Ren once before their encounter in the temple. It had been the evening before, when he found her in the tomb.

He'd had the letter with him as always. But it was hidden. She could not have seen into his pockets. But she might have seen him reach for it. He had developed a habit of resting his hand on the pocket that held the envelope. Until that moment, he had not considered how dangerous that might be. Ren could have seen his hand linger over that pocket and concluded it held something precious. Devious as she was, she might have stolen it to use in her dealings.

Those were intriguing possibilities, but other questions remained unanswered. *Why was I allowed to carry the letter this far, only to die before finding an answer?* It all seemed so pointless.

If I was to die, why come all this way at all? He might have died in Ronia, killed in the prison for which he'd surely been headed. Hell, he certainly could have died numerous times on Caidfell. If those bestial vines had torn him apart, Shada would not have risked her life to save him. That damned letter would have been lost in the muck. *Why did the Goddess let me live to see—*

He pressed his palms to his temples.

"I see it." His voice was a whispered scream.

When the envelope had been soaked in the swamp, he had nearly despaired, thinking the message inside must be illegible. But he had not opened the envelope to check. He had decided that, since the letter was meant to reach him, it inevitably would. Though the envelope had been ruined, the note within must have been unharmed, as impossible as that seemed.

And it had been. When Ren opened the envelope, she read the letter with no trouble.

Nor gasped. "Goddess." It had really happened—a miracle. The letter had been saved.

His mind a whirlwind, Nor risked removing one hand from the door to take the envelope from his pocket. He stared at it. "Goddess," he said again.

Everything was making sense. Huire might have let Ren take and open the letter so that Nor would know it was readable. So he would know his faith was not misplaced.

Or maybe not. Maybe he would die as soon as these men entered or later in some torture chamber. Even if the Goddess's hand was at work here, he might never know why she did anything. He might die not knowing.

He could not have thought this out completely in ideal circumstances, let alone while holding a door shut as men tried to break in. He wasn't smart enough. He had been getting by on faith alone, and now, he hardly had that.

What else do I have?

It struck him like a lightning bolt. The answer. He knew the solution to Cadmon's quandary. *What are the gods made of? Well, what is Huire? What does she offer, and what is the only thing, ultimately, that she asks of her wretched, bumbling children?* Nor didn't need to be smart enough. He only needed to share in the stuff of Huire, *which is...*

Thrilled beyond the fear of death, he removed his other hand from the handle and dug the letter from the envelope. He half turned to keep his back pressed against the door, and the world tilted.

The potion was working.

Tossing aside the envelope, he held the folded pages to his chest. He might have minutes, he might have seconds. He had the answer, or as good an answer as he would ever reach. He must read the letter right then or never.

No one had pounded on the door in several seconds. Maybe they were waiting for him to pass out.

Shoving his shoulder against the door, he thought of the first and oldest thing he had learned about the Goddess. He knew the answer Huire would want, the ingredient for the final submission of his will to hers. He gave it.

What are the gods made of?

"Love," he said and opened the letter.

38

The Letter

How will I give this letter to you, when I see you in a few hours, knowing what it says?

We have not talked much recently. This was my choice, and I was right. It would be pitiful to apologize now. I have been hard on you over the years, and now I must be cruel, so I should tell you the truth about myself at least: I am not a hero or a villain but a coward, too afraid to be either.

I have long thought I loved you like a son. But now, I doubt it. Love is not a feeling, after all. It is a choice, a lifelong string of choices, the same as serving Huire. All the world's warm feelings are nothing next to a single betrayal.

What are the gods made of? Damned if I know. When we met the Lady for the first time and you asked your insolent questions, you sent me down a path from which I can never return. In my selfish moments, which are ever more common, I think of who I was before that meeting, and I wonder at the final value of truth.

The order possesses documents from the old world that few ever see. Access is restricted to elders, and then only in times of rare need. These contain no hidden secrets; they are simply believed to be erroneous.

Before the Lady came to Ronia, I had seen these records only once. The things I saw have not left me, no matter how much I pray. When you questioned the Lady, something came back to me. I returned to the records.

A bit of research that I had hoped would dispel a nagging fear became a descent, step by step, into the pit. I have built, in my mind, a constellation of truths I cannot deny. Not all of the forbidden records are false, it seems. Here is further evidence of my cowardice: I confess there are moments now when I hate you. I wish it was a demon within me, one that I could carve or burn out, that does the hating. But it is, alas, only me.

The Goddess is not who we thought she was.

Even writing this makes me ill. I am so afraid. The beliefs of a lifetime linger forever.

The Temple teaches that human beings created Huire and the other gods through our love. Our love is so powerful that it brought them into being so that they could love us in turn.

This is a lie. Let me explain:

In far antiquity, men's knowledge of things reached a point of transcendence. Perhaps it was gradual—they solved one problem and then another. Their machines, once metal, became organic. They crafted living things. At first, these were beasts, simple masses of flesh, too malformed and deranged to live long. As men became cleverer with their arts, their projects grew more sound, stronger, and smaller, though not more beautiful.

Norhim, I have seen pictures of them. Diagrams. I remember when I found them—the thought of that moment—but why relive it?

Men's creatures served them, fought for them. Most of all, they loved them—men ensured that from the start. These things grew so small that they were mere specks, and then smaller still.

I fear you will know where this is headed. Please keep reading.

These things congealed into masses, infinitely changeable in shape and density. Events moved quickly after that, it seems. They could already eat and reproduce. Now, those who could fly became dominant.

They began to conceive rather than just feel. Each of the masses—"droves," men called them—bred its individuals selectively, redesigning itself. The larger the drove, the more capable and powerful it seemed, and the greater its potential for complex thought.

Through it all, their love for man was undimmed. Their love was a part of them, you see, down to the smallest.

Thus came into being the marvelous ancient world that our order studies. The droves cared for us as we had never been cared for. They grew to titanic size and built entire worlds around us. They traveled through the depths between planets, building the gateways, harnessing unguessable energies, so that we could follow.

We consented to this arrangement. How could we not? We became, in a sense, their children. They went on ahead, from world to world, preparing the way for us. I wonder how far they got before they vanished. We may never reach the boundaries of their creation.

I do not know why they disappeared. The records predate that time and give no hint of it.

Most of what I've written here is surmise. Research will never change, whatever else does. But do you remember the feeling one gets when a hypothesis simply fits? I "know" these things, more surely than I have known anything I've studied, and as much as I wish I was wrong.

But, onward. We had merged with the droves. We depended on them for every want and need. Perhaps they became gods to us, the stuff of myth, before they even vanished.

When the gods' end came, humanity found itself alone. Those of us who cared to keep living and who survived for even a little while were bereft of all sustenance, knowledge, and material possessions. They had truly been our everything. Amid the upheavals of countless worlds, each robbed of its master, unsupervised nature and geology ran amok. Somehow, humankind learned to live once more.

When I learned all this, I was faced with dreadful questions. Who is the Lady? She came to our city, claiming to be sent by Huire. But who knows if Huire ever existed, at least in the form that we think of her? If she did exist, will she ever return? There are no promises anymore. If the Lady is lying, then who is she really, and why did she come to Ronia?

Here is my greatest secret—one that, in happier times, might have made you laugh. In my desperation, I decided to steal from the Lady.

I decided to do what I'd forbidden you to do: I would take a part of her. I began to search rooms where she had been, surfaces she had touched. I gathered dust and examined it in the microscopes of the order's laboratories. For a time, I found nothing of note. I allowed myself to hope that she was the being of spirit she claimed to be.

But I did not stop searching. Your words came back to me again and again: "There have been many false prophets." If we give credit to a false idol, we harm our faith. And you were right, you arrogant bastard! You still are. If what I say below seems hard, remember that I said this.

Finally, in desperation, I dared to touch the Lady herself. I found a moment when she and I were alone and brushed against her. Some of her mass would stick to my clothing, I assumed. It was meant to look like an accident. She must have thought it was, for I am still alive.

I thought I was ready for any reaction from her. But when she struck me, I was so surprised that I fell over like a statue. She pulled me up, called me a fool, and told me I deserved worse. My feet were dangling in the air. I had no idea she was that strong. She hit me again and let me fall.

Through it all, her face did not change. She looked perfectly serene, and her tone was as sweet as ever. I have not looked at her the same way since. She is not like us, Norhim, not even in ways that I thought she was. Her face and voice do not reveal her mind—in fact, they seem like an afterthought. This looks so obvious that I am not sure how I missed it. The feeling has become familiar.

When she finished beating me, her words became kind. She said she would never tell anyone that I had done something so foolish, and that I must promise not to tell anyone, either. It would be so embarrassing for me if others knew I had stumbled and assaulted her divine form. There was no telling how troubled they might be, or what might happen. I promised.

At last, she forced me to remove my clothes. All of them. I can only assume that she suspected my true intentions. I almost refused, but I was too afraid. She lifted them in a bundle into the air, and she devoured them. There is nothing else to call it. She turned to smoke and descended on the clothing, which simply dissolved as if eaten by locusts.

Then she left me with a final warning to tell no one. Whether through carelessness or malice, she left me naked in that room.

I don't know how long I stayed in there. I didn't know what to tell whoever found me. Honestly, I hoped to forget what had happened. Perhaps being trapped in that room, unable to think of anything else, saved me from doing just that.

When some young priest finally found me, a great commotion arose. Others came, and soon, a crowd had gathered outside the room, knowing only that something was wrong with old Cadmon and he had shut himself in there. I gave them an excuse that turned their curiosity to concern and—they could not hide it—amusement.

You see, I pretended not to know where I was. I led them to think I had wandered from my room and, out of my senses, discarded my clothes somewhere.

They believed my story. It was easy enough to believe, given how I have looked and felt lately. The worrying has rather gotten to me, Norhim. There have been moments when I halfway believed my excuse. You haven't seen me much, but you must have noticed I'm getting thinner, a problem that is entirely new to me.

On the day the Lady attacked me, I was more grateful than ever that I had distanced myself from you. I was glad you have so few friends from whom you might hear of my ordeal. If word of it reached you somehow, thank you truly for not mentioning it.

When I was alone again, I took the only option left to me. I cut off part of my beard where she had struck me and examined the hair under a microscope. Soon, I found what I had expected and dreaded.

In the microscope, I saw what she truly is. There is no reason to burden you with a detailed description. It is enough for you to know that my fears—about the gods, about the Lady, about the Temple—were confirmed. I scrubbed my face and hair, frantic at the thought that millions of invisibly tiny horrors were lodged in my skin.

They must remain there to this instant, though I try not to think of them.

A couple of hours from now, when you and I meet for the last time, I will make you swear not to read this letter until you have answered the quandary. I will use your conditioning word, if such a thing really works.

Now, I must hurt you more, Norhim, though I do not wish to. The quandary is a sham. You have no way of knowing the real answer.

I fully expect you to break your word and open the envelope early. I am counting on it, in fact. Well intentioned as you are, your promises are nearly worthless, lasting only until your feelings change. But who am I to scold you?

I can only hope that your word holds until you are well away from Ronia. If the Lady behaves treacherously, as I suspect she will, the temptation to open the letter will be strong. If you learn the truth too soon and tell others in the company, the crusade might return to Ronia. Bishop Arumin would want to continue at all costs, but if Captain Emberly's soldiers suspected their deadly journey was ultimately pointless, they might rebel.

That must not happen. The crusade must continue.

Here, we come to the heart of it. The Lady has lied to us. But given what she knows of Ronia, she has almost certainly been in contact with Huire, whomever Huire truly is. Whatever the relationship between these entities, I suspect the Lady honestly intends to guide the company to our Goddess—a word I can hardly bear to use.

It may be that you will live long enough to meet Huire. The task that I give you, and which I can only beg you to accept, is this: you must end all contact between Huire and Ronia. Forever. The presence of the gods turned us into infants. We barely survived their departure, and if we fall into the arms of our own technology again, we will return to the cradle, perhaps forever.

If Huire or any of the gods have notions of returning to the human worlds, whether their purpose is loving or not, you must stop them.

I laugh as I write this. How can you possibly do such a thing? Will you agree that it must be done? How will you overcome Arumin, who will resist this plan to his last breath? How will you convert others in the company to your cause, gaining the allies you will surely need? Have you even read this far in the letter, or have you decided I am insane and torn it to pieces? I have no answers.

But if I go on contemplating the futility of what I am attempting, as well as the likelihood that the journey will cost your life, I will destroy this note myself and tell you the truth. If that happens, Arumin's mad quest might succeed, and our world will once again be dominated by beings who treat us as children and playthings rather than the capable beings I hope we can be.

The Unheard were right all along, in a way. We must do without the gods. Perhaps you should resort to violence to prevent their return. I don't know how far you ought to go. There may be no final answers.

After our meeting with the Lady and your subsequent defiance, I did what I should have done long ago: I gave up on you. Not on your life but on your future in the order. You are not a monk, and you refuse to become one. Your childhood has left you unwilling to submit to anything. Why I did not see this sooner, I will never know.

We are still companions in one respect: we have shared a way of life that is a lie. It is in this spirit, poor as it is, that I am sending you to die in a better way than I will. I hereby cast you from the order. Now, you will serve the truth, which has always been your true master. What it is, or if it exists, we may never know.

I charge you with all of this, having lied to you and tossed you onto a sacrificial pyre. It is thanks to me that you chose this life at all.

I can only appeal to your decency. If there is one thing in the universe I still believe, it is this: you are good. Goodness may be nothing at all, a pleasant fantasy, but you carry it in you, and you will need it.

What else to say?

Do not trust easily. Certainly, don't trust the bishop or his young imp.

Do not trust Shada, the caretaker. I fear her limited strength will not stand a chance against the Lady.

Do not even trust Emberly. He should be in prison, not leading men.

Make allies, not friends, and only very carefully.

I don't think you will return. If you do, I will not be here to see it. My usefulness is at an end, and I have been alive for too long.

What love I have, feeble sentiment that it is, is entirely yours. Though you will be rightly disgusted to hear it, I am sorry.

Cadmon

39

SHADA

SHADA WOKE UP LATE at night to a knock at the door. Confused and mostly asleep, she decided something terrible must have happened. After jumping out of bed, she flung open the door to see Jeric.

He wore nightclothes, a sort of gown. His fingertips clasped a candle holder, and the light from the flame made his face seem to flick this way and that.

Seeing him filled her with dread, though not dread of him. The mix of feelings that she had been attaching to his face and voice were strange and unpalatable. "Hello," she said. "What's wrong?"

"I could not leave matters between us as they were at dinner. There are things that I need to make clear."

She leaned against the doorframe. "I see." She waited.

"May I come in?"

She listened hard to the silence of the house. "I don't want the children to—"

"They're asleep." He spoke comfortably, as if expecting her concern. "Even if they weren't, they know I may visit whom I want in my own house. Provided she will have me in."

They hadn't spoken that easily since she had caught him in the bizarre ritual of pulling out his hair. She could not stop thinking of that solemn ceremony or his nervous agitation upon being discovered. She didn't want things to be cold between them. She had no one else to talk to or depend on. But this visit in the middle of the night was strange. Still, the Lady would not want her to risk losing his affection. She stepped aside.

As he entered, she shut the door as softly as she could. He put the candle down and removed his gown, letting it fall from his shoulders. He became naked so quickly and with such assurance that a moment passed before she gasped in surprise.

"What's wrong?" he asked with the same ease.

"What are..." Words collided in her throat. "I think you misunderstood me." Her instinct was to send him away at once. But the Lady cared nothing for her discomfort.

Jeric cocked his head. "If that's true, I am sorry. But I'm not convinced."

"I—" she sputtered, wondering how she could escape this encounter without provoking the Lady's wrath. "You said you wanted to tell me something."

"I wanted to make something clear." His face was solemn. "I've found my words to be inadequate, Shada. They've never been equal to my feelings, especially at this moment."

His eyes met hers without shame. Embarrassed, she looked down. His chest was hairless. After she had walked in on his private project and left, the project had continued. He noticed her staring, smiled, and said, "I cannot help doing strange things sometimes. This time, I wanted it to be something good. Something for you."

Shada faced conflicting drives. The frightened part of her wanted to scream at him to get out—had wanted that since he disrobed. But her better sense told her to find a middle way. He might not have expected her to take offence. His was a different world.

He misread her hesitation. "What do you want? Whatever it is, you'll have it."

She raised a foot to step away. She needed space to think. But caution suggested she stay where she was. She placed the foot back on the floor.

She expected him to move toward her, but he remained in his place. He was wearing a soft perfume she could not have described.

"I've been trained well," he said. "You'll love it, I promise."

She tried not to cringe. "Trained? Someone trained you... for that?"

"My life is not my own," he said, "but I am cared for."

"Who taught you? How?"

"Lots of people of different ages and sorts. They knew I'd have a partner someday and I'd need to know these things."

That image shook her. No bit of this man's life had been left alone.

"Does it worry you that I've been with so many?" he asked. "I promise I'm all yours now."

In the thick, awkward silence that followed, her frustrations rose. "What do you even know about me?" The words were sharp and not really a question. "Other than what they've told you, I mean. You and I have hardly had a chance to speak."

"I hope to know you for a very long time, Shada. But what difference will details make? I know who you are already—it's not hard to see."

Part of her had not stopped noticing his beauty. Disturbed at herself, she kept talking. "My life—the past—made me who I am."

"The past isn't real," he said. His voice was kind but emphatic, correcting a wrong. "Not anymore. Only the present, until it passes, and the future."

She thought she saw a way out, using his own words. "But then, if you give yourself to me—that will become false as soon as it's over."

"But there will be more, Shada!" he cried. He reached out and surrounded her hands with his fists. "We will look toward the future, always!"

He tugged her gently toward him. She let herself cross the distance but stopped inches from his face. She could play along no farther.

"Something is wrong," she said into his eyes. "I think we should wait."

Silence ensued. "I see," he said shortly afterward. His face took the rejection bravely, but his eyes were grim. "If that is your wish, you will have it, of course."

They still stood toe to toe. "Thank you," she replied and backed off a little.

"You should not apologize." He looked paler and sadder than the situation warranted. "But... what did I do wrong?"

She did not know how to begin really answering. Where he came from, dropping by in the night might be perfectly normal. She gave the easiest reply. "Nothing."

He pursed his lips. His eyes gazed into the distance, troubled. "I hope you're not saying that to spare my feelings, Shada. I agree—something has come between us. But if I'd done everything I should, there would be no problems."

She frowned. "That's a strange thing to say."

"No, it isn't. Attraction between sexes is the natural state of things. Absent some disruption, it should take its course." These words sounded forced, a recitation. "That means I made a mistake."

He put his hands on his hips and stepped away. He bounced on his heels a little, becoming agitated again.

"I didn't mean to upset you," Shada said.

"I should be upset!" he snapped. "Much depends on me, and much has been given to me. If I don't get this right, I shudder to think what may happen."

"What are you saying? Will you hurt me?"

He shot her a look. "No! Never!" Then he calmed himself. "But I fear for your people and my own. They've worked for a long time to create one like me. I was supposed to be the last. But if I am flawed—if my pieces don't fit together quite right—then they will replace me."

"Replace you… with whom? I don't understand."

"I know, Shada, and I'm sorry." He spoke haltingly. Breathing hard, he bent over, hands on his knees. "Why don't you want me?" he pleaded.

Alarmed by his manner, she turned the question around. "Why do you want *me*? I'm nothing special." Suddenly, she was angry. "What do you *really* want?"

He looked incredulous. "What do I want? I want you, just as I said. How full of lies Ronia must be! And why? Because I choose to, that's why. And because it's how things must be."

She closed her eyes and pressed her fingers against her eyelids. "Nothing 'must be.' Who do you think decides these things?"

After a visible struggle, his panic seemed to recede. What was left was a quiet, deeply grave man. He walked over to his gown, picked it up, and dressed himself. "I will go. I'm so sorry, Shada."

"Wait." The word was out of her mouth before she could think about it.

He stopped.

She couldn't believe she had kept him from leaving. But she wanted answers and might never have a better chance. "Sit with me."

He shook his head. As he tied the sash at his waist, she noticed his eyes were wet.

"Please," she said. Seeing him tearful and broken, she no longer feared him.

"Listen," he said, his voice as harsh and stern as she had yet heard it. It startled her enough that he saw it, and his face and voice softened. "Yes, of course."

He walked to the bed and put his face in his hands. His brief anger, if that's what it had been, had passed, and she sensed she had missed a chance to get under his surface. Hoping to recover that possibility, she sat next to him and put a hand on his back.

So there she sat, comforting her captor. Everything was strange. She even thought for an instant of what they might have been doing in that very spot, had the previous couple of minutes gone differently—an ugly, unwanted thought, but there nonetheless.

He noticed her hand and collected himself. "Yes, of course. Your question. You asked me who decides. Well, no one person makes decisions in the Shining Realm. It's the will of all of us. I'm just a tool." He wrung his hands, his upset returning. "This is so difficult and so unfair to you. But things must be as they are, Shada. You and I must become partners even if you can never bring yourself to love me."

If she had forgotten he was her captor, she would have remembered then. "If we 'must' be partners, then we aren't really partners."

He shook his head. "No one will force you to do anything, and no one should. But I will play my part in the world to come, and I suspect you will, too, because you are a good person. I told you the Realm will set Ronia free, but I might just as well say your people and mine will become one. The Shining Realm is a confederacy that includes all free worlds, and no world that is truly free can be outside of it. It is a kingdom in which the only king is reason."

She tried to absorb all that. "I believe you mean well."

It had felt like a neutral statement, but it seemed to strike him painfully. "You're right to doubt me," he replied slowly. "I've earned nothing less. But do you really love Ronia as it is? Don't you want it to change? Some people feel that way about their homes. I don't understand why, but so it is."

She laughed. "I love it, I guess. In a way. At the same time, I think it sometimes wishes I didn't exist."

His face was sad, but his voice was forthright. "We'll make it better, Shada. You'll be able to love it even more."

"What does any of this have to do with me?"

"You still haven't realized that?" He stifled his smile. "I'm sorry. I shouldn't laugh. You're so modest you don't see what you can become."

Her anger returned. "Don't toy with me. What do you want?"

"I want you to be my queen."

She swallowed as she discovered she had been suspecting this since their conversation on the terrace that morning. But she had dismissed that suspicion as incomprehensible, childish. She felt about it the same way she had felt about the Lady choosing her as caretaker. It was too big to understand.

But the more real it seemed, the more viscerally she wanted to reject it. "I don't want to rule anyone. I can't, not even myself."

"And you think those things make you unqualified?"

She dodged. "So... your people do have rulers after all."

"Freedom is a process. Release must be won, not given. Someone must guide your people. That will be you—a woman of that world, who has already rejected its belief in gods—and me, a man of a lineage bred for this time. Bred for this very moment, in fact."

This was a dangerous situation. Shada didn't know what the Lady would want and realized the Lady had been entirely silent during the conversation. Surely, she had a preferred answer, and if Shada chose wrongly, the Lady might become violent.

Shada rubbed her temple. The Lady commonly resided in Shada's ear and throat, leaving a trail of residue between the two, across the outside and inside of Shada's cheek. This connection seemed to allow the Lady to think with one mind while essentially being two places at once. One piece of her whispered in Shada's ear while the other waited in her throat, able to choke her at will. But right then, when Shada touched her face, she did not feel the expected residue. Only a situation as strange as that one could have kept her from noticing.

Is the Lady gone again? Maybe she had gone scouting as she had when Shada was trapped in the cell.

Shada tried to give Jeric's offer the consideration it deserved, but it was hopeless. There she was, entire worlds apparently laid at her feet, and all she wanted was to reject them without causing offence. In the weeks before she left Ronia, the city had seemed less appealing than ever. At several moments since then, if not for her father, she could have accepted never seeing it again.

Her first concern must be the Lady. Though the Lady had encouraged her to play along with Jeric's attraction, her entire purpose was to guide the Ronian company to the Goddess. Everything else was a means to that end.

Even if they never saw the company again, surely, the Lady would not want Shada returning to Ronia without Huire at the head of a conquering army. And Huire wouldn't want that any more than the Lady. It was even possible Huire had chosen that moment to return to Ronia because that was when her people would face the Shining Realm.

Shada's answer must be no, then. Not only was it unthinkable, taking part in an invasion that would hurt so many—Goddess, it might even hurt Shada's father—but it was Huire's will and the Lady's and Shada's own. It was even best for Jeric and his family—if Shada agreed to a marriage against the Lady's wishes, the Lady's retribution might hurt them all.

Jeric was watching her closely, and she realized she'd been silent for a while.

She had to refuse him gently. "My father still lives in the city. I won't be a part of anything that would hurt him."

Even revealing his existence was an awful risk. The Realm could take him hostage to ensure her obedience. Without realizing it, she had decided to trust Jeric with that fact.

But she still had told him nothing about her real reason for leaving Ronia—the company and its mission. If she trusted him with her father, she ought to trust him with anything, yet revealing the company's presence in the city would still feel like a betrayal. Jeric's power was clearly limited, for now. She wondered if he could force the Realm to leave the company alone.

"Of course you won't," he said. "We have difficult times ahead, and those most special to us should be out of harm's way."

"His situation is... delicate. He is not healthy." She wanted to stop there, but she needed to ensure Jeric's sympathy. "He has habits. He's dependent on certain substances, and he's nearly destroyed himself getting them."

Jeric sat back. "That must be terrifying to watch." He put a hand on hers. "I don't blame you for running away."

Her hand twitched under his. She couldn't stand him thinking she had abandoned her father. But she had no other explanation for leaving Ronia except the truth. How strange, also, that Jeric apparently didn't think less of her for leaving her father alone. *What kind of man is he, really?* The question seemed to have no bottom.

"You will see him again," Jeric continued. "We have cures for problems like his. His life can be restored—think of him at his best. That man can be made real again!"

Nothing else could have struck at Shada's heart like that image. She wondered if this was some perverse test of loyalty arranged by the Lady—or Huire or somebody else.

The idea of her father healed, himself again, was so over-powering that she could think of almost nothing else. At times, during the depths of his addiction and the heights of her bitterness toward Ronia, she would have sold the city and everyone in it to save him. Right then, those times felt not so long ago.

She could not accept Jeric's offer, and she would not. It was impossible for multiple reasons. But neither could she bear to refuse it at that moment. To say no definitively would be to snuff out that image of her father as the man he had been when she was a girl, before her mother left.

While Jeric thought she might marry him, she could continue to see the open, hopeful expression he was wearing. That face made her feel less alone in the universe. It even made her feel loved. It let her hope, faintly.

"May I tell you tomorrow?" she asked.

The warmth did not exactly leave his face. It jumped around, found it had nowhere to go, and returned. "Yes, you may." His smile, at least, was steady.

He began to leave, but in a moment of insanity, she took his head and leaned it on her shoulder.

He accepted the action without resistance. Feeling his hair on her face, she felt, against all odds, love for him—not romantic love but the kind of love Huire said everyone should feel for each other.

His breathing softened, and she realized he had fallen asleep, poised on her shoulder. She decided not to wake him yet. She could support his weight for a little while.

"Tomorrow will be the day," she whispered.

She could not afford to dwell on what might happen when she refused him. He might not mean her harm, but he was not really in command. She wondered if he ever would be, even as the king of Ronia. Others were behind, above, and around him, and they thought of Jeric, his children, and Shada as raw material.

40

—·—

EMBERLY

EMBERLY PEERED ROUND THE corner in the predawn darkness. Down the street stood the wall that concealed the pyramid. Behind him, the boy who had led him there whispered something. The captain grunted in the affirmative, having no idea what he was agreeing with.

The boy, who had appeared in the tunnels the instant Rayan vanished, had eagerly assented to lead Emberly wherever he wanted to go, especially when the desperate captain had produced his knife and offered it as a reward. The real difficulties began when the captain tried to describe exactly where he was going.

Knowing not a word of the boy's language, Emberly formed a triangle with his hands. The boy smiled, chattered, and started off immediately. The captain's options were two: follow wherever the boy led or wander the tunnels of Om forever.

The journey took much of the night and involved innumerable misunderstandings and detours. Emberly was frustrated to the point of madness, sketching the pyramid in the dust of the tunnels again and again. The boy's enthusiasm remained undimmed.

When they finally emerged from the tunnels, the pyramid was only a couple of blocks away. Dawn was touching the sky outside Om's great windows. Emberly had stopped down the street to scout the area in case the Shining Realm was watching. Peering around a corner, he saw no sign of them, but he didn't trust his eyes.

The boy said something. Emberly looked over to find the boy's hand outstretched.

With some misgivings, he handed over his knife. He nearly obeyed Rayan's whispered urgings to send the boy away without payment—he needed the blade. But he feared the boy might raise a fuss and draw attention if displeased, so he surrendered the weapon and shooed the boy away. The farther the child was from the coming conflagration, the better.

Looking around the corner again, he tried to decide his next course of action. Then he heard a voice.

"Captain." Roark stood nearby, looking at him, aghast. "Where have you been?" he demanded.

Emberly glanced around. He felt ridiculous, hiding around the corner like a spy. "I escaped," he said frankly. "Has the Realm arrived yet?"

Still looking shocked by the captain's sudden appearance, Roark stammered. "No, to my surprise." All at once, he looked less like the accuser and more like the accused. "There was an incident last night. Our fate may be sealed, sir, and it's my fault."

Emberly coughed. He had meant to laugh. "There was no escape for any of us. I should have seen it. Unless our missing people returned in the night, and someone found a hidden way out of that pyramid."

He didn't really expect either to have happened, but when Roark shook his head, Emberly swallowed anew the knowledge of how close they were to the end. "How did you find me?"

"I came out to look for you. But it seems you found your way back on your own." He helped Emberly to his feet, pausing to think in the meantime. "I had no idea you were so close and no reason to expect to find you. But it doesn't surprise me very much." He smiled, though his face lost none of its sorrow. "Do you realize the others are going to see you like that?"

Emberly realized that had anyone but Roark found him in his present filthy state, he might have combusted with shame. He wondered what it was about Roark that spared him. "Honestly, I dread standing in front of them more than anything else."

"I suppose we'll soon have trouble enough to make you forget about it. Speaking of which, we had better hurry back. The war may start without us."

Emberly caught him by the arm as he turned away. "First, I've got to tell you something." He stopped for a moment, reconsidering, but decided he was too late. "In Ronia, when I saw the list of volunteers for the crusade... I knew them all, of course. Most of them made me afraid. But when I saw your name, I nearly shouted for joy."

41

Shada

Shada left her room quietly the next morning. She feared refusing Jeric and wanted to delay it for a little while.

She looked into each room as she walked to the stair-case. Descending the stairs, she felt the air change. She knew so little about this house. When she reached the main hall downstairs, she stopped. Surveying the room, she imagined herself, for a greedy moment, being married to someone, being the lady of a house like that.

Perhaps due to proximity, or perhaps inevitably, the roles of husband and children were filled by Jeric and the girls. In another universe, they were sweet, a simple family in need, and she was the one who could bind them together. She held a magical charm that would let her take them all into her arms at once.

She banished the image almost as soon as it came, wondering what insanity had convinced her to entertain it at all.

A thumping noise echoed from down the hall. Grateful for the distraction, Shada listened. One of the girls was speaking.

Going to investigate, she found the door of the girls' bedroom ajar. Her throat tightened though she didn't know why, and she hurried to look inside.

A nightmare waited. The woman from the forest was standing between the girls' beds. The pallor of her spidery arms and the dirt and leaves embedded in her clothing were a gaping wound in the neatness of the room. Lani stood in front of her, and the woman's arms were wrapped all around the girl. Lani's arms were pinned against her white nightgown, and her face was turned toward the light from the room's single large window.

As Shada passed the threshold, the smell of the woman's body hit her like a wall. The woman had seen her already, and she released Lani from her embrace. Shada rushed at the pair of them, ever more unsure that she was really awake.

But that time, the woman did not vanish into the shadows. She pounced on Shada, claws rending and teeth searching for Shada's throat. She was everywhere, and Shada, who had not expected such resistance, found herself instantly outmatched.

She shrank back toward the door in a mindless retreat, her hands raised and flailing. Finally, the woman grabbed her hair, pulled her downward, and punched her in the face again and again. Then she ploughed forward. Shada staggered back into the hall, where she fell on her backside in a daze.

The door slammed with the girls and the intruder on the other side. Pain and icy shock filled the hallway.

Feeling herself sinking backward, her head seeking the floor to rest, Shada screamed, "No!"

She fought her way to her feet, though her weight seemed to have tripled, and she leaned against the wall. From there, she threw herself against the door, shoulder first, twisting the handle. The door didn't move, and the crash rattled her bones. Something was blocking the door.

"No!" she screamed again. She could hear nothing inside the room.

She threw herself into the door again. Still dizzy, she struck it close to its hinges. The wood barely grunted in response, and an ugly tingle passed through her shoulders.

She saw Adney down the hall, standing half hidden in a doorway.

"Help me, you damned fool!" she shouted.

He had been watching, still and quiet. His brutally scarred face was indeterminate.

She beat on the girls' door with her fists, but it only rattled. Turning her face toward the ceiling, she howled Jeric's name. *Hasn't he heard the chaos by now?*

The total silence that followed persuaded her no help was coming. She kicked the door near its handle. It shuddered encouragingly, and she kept at it.

When the door finally wobbled open, she was out of breath but almost too scared to breathe. The chair that had blocked the door toppled. Inside, Delia sat in bed, alone with an open window. Shada ran to the window and leaned into the morning air. Trees rimmed the world in all directions. Here and there, leaves shook or a branch swayed.

Pulling herself back inside, she turned toward Delia, who was looking at the empty bed where her sister had been. Shada took hold of her. "Are you all right? Did you see which way they went? Did she hurt you?"

As Shada pummeled her with questions, the girl's blank face reddened, and her breath came quickly. "No," she said finally, in answer to one thing or the other. She squeezed her hands into balls and rubbed her eyes. "I didn't know she was real..."

"Okay, darling. It's okay." The lie was so bald-faced that Shada was ashamed. She had imagined that if she ever became a parent, she would be an honest one, one who didn't hide the existence of evil from her children.

Shada picked Delia up and hurried out of the room toward the staircase. Adney had vanished. The stairs clattered under her feet, and she barged into the room she knew was Jeric's.

Still in his nightclothes, he was standing with Adney, conversing softly, his arms wrapped tightly around himself.

Shada started yelling as soon as she entered. "You know she's gone, don't you?" Then she stabbed a finger toward Adney. "Or hasn't he bothered to tell you?"

"I know." Jeric's voice was funereal. His face had drained of blood.

"Why are you just standing here? Whatever you're talking about must be terribly important." She reluctantly put down Delia. The girl waited, her world falling deeper into shambles by the second as Shada shouted at her father.

"Your man saw it happen and did nothing! We might have saved her. Your daughter—"

Adney endured the lashing without batting an eye. As for Jeric, Shada's last word made him wince. "Stop!" he cried. "There was no saving Lani. If you'd fought the woman off, she would have kept coming back."

Shada gasped. "You know her."

"Very well."

"And you let this happen!"

"Delia, darling, please wait outside for a moment."

"No!" Shada pushed her fingers through her hair. "You're a madman! You would leave Delia alone now, when an evil witch has just invaded your home?"

"Very well!" He repeated himself, sharply and with a much different meaning. "Delia, stay in this room, please. We'll talk in the hall, and no one will get past us."

"Him too." Shada stepped in front of Adney, who was moving toward the door.

She realized as they came face to face that he was much larger than her—and Jeric was larger yet. Adney's eyes were soft, blue, and deeply strange. Compared to the ruin that surrounded them, they were breathtaking.

To Jeric, she said, "I want to talk to you alone."

"Why?" Jeric seemed genuinely puzzled, though Shada was increasingly unsure who or what was genuine.

"Because I don't trust him, and you shouldn't either."

A cold spot passed across them all. Jeric said, "Shada, that is a very serious thing to say."

"I know that! I wonder if I shouldn't say the same about you."

Some impulsive retort nearly escaped Jeric's throat, but he swallowed it. "Adney is my man, and I trust him over almost anyone. You should tell me nothing you wouldn't tell him."

Shada wondered if she was losing her mind. Maybe no skeletal witch from the forest actually existed. Maybe they were humoring her until they could lock her in a cage. But Jeric's face convinced her otherwise. Its pain was so subtle and comprehensive that, if it was a lie, nothing at all would be left to believe.

"Let's go, then," she told them at last.

When the bedroom door had shut—no doubt leaving Delia free to eavesdrop—Shada, Jeric, and Adney all faced each other.

"Ask what you will," Jeric said.

"That woman..." Shada stopped for a moment. When she asked her question, she would learn whether or not she was crazy, and uncertainty had an undeniable attraction. "Is she the girls' mother?"

"No," Jeric said. Judging by his face, he did not think it an odd question. "Her name was—is—Oliva. As for the girls' mother, I met that woman only a few times, when she was brought to me. Oliva was my partner after that, but she loved the girls a great deal. Lani especially."

Shada willfully refrained from asking a dozen questions at once. "'Loved'? Do you mean she doesn't love them anymore?"

"She certainly does. She wouldn't keep coming back if she didn't." Jeric's smile was a broken one. "The odd thing is she shouldn't exist anymore. They meant for her to die some time ago."

"Why? Who are 'they'?"

"The woman who serves as my partner is expected to be almost fully human. Oliva was expected to deny her own will, at will. That includes even the more beautiful feelings when they obstruct truth: love, for one. And maternal attachment."

Shada thought she followed his meaning. "But... why would she need to deny love? Was something going to happen to the girls?"

"Questions were raised about Lani. The greater one's purpose in life, the more is demanded of one. Many are not suited to it, Shada. It's only sensible."

"What was wrong with Lani?" Shada realized she was already speaking of the girl as a thing of the past. It was maddening.

Jeric's sad frown became more thoughtful. "You must have noticed. She was not particularly bright, not in comparison to Delia. Also, she was aesthetically inferior."

Shada wanted to ask what sort of father concerned himself with those things, but she restrained herself. "And what about Oliva? Did she fall short of your standards too?"

"Oh, no." Jeric's eyes were urgent at the thought. "She was magnificent. She was everything a person should be, and I am—" He cut himself off. "But my opinions make no difference here. Surely, you understand that by now. Oliva could not endure the thought of Lani being taken away. It unhinged her. It destroyed her."

"So... what? You sent her into the woods?"

"Yes. Well—" He looked at Adney, whose attention was on Shada. "It was a terrible situation—a tragedy for all of us. For a time, I thought both Lani and Oliva would be taken away. Our present arrangement, strange as it must seem, is simply how things have sorted themselves."

Shada shook her head in wonderment.

"Things are as they must be," Jeric told her. He sounded overwhelmed, lost in a warren of assumed rationality. He began to mumble. "The dynamics of a population are such, the proportions are very delicate..."

Shada wanted to hurt him, and she knew how. "You're a liar."

Adney responded first. He moved half a step toward her, so quickly that she jumped. He stopped there, expression unchanged. She wondered if he could move that wreckage of a face at all, to show any emotion.

"Enough," Jeric snapped at them both, too late to stop Adney from reaching Shada if he had wanted to. He whirled toward Adney with a new, ferocious expression. "Don't you touch her! Do you understand me? Tell them she is mine!"

Then he turned toward Shada with a forced calm. "Please, please watch what you say. Think about everything I've ever said to you. Every word, from the moment we met. You won't find a single falsehood. Can you say the same for yourself?"

He had leaned forward farther and farther as he spoke, but now he straightened. "I am a human being, and you damned well know it. If you cannot follow my words and think honestly about what they mean and understand their implications, then the failure is yours."

Adney was drifting closer to Shada.

"Don't," Jeric rumbled, his tone utterly venomous.

Adney didn't stop. Shada refused to retreat. She faced him, her back to the top of the stairs. "Why does Jeric keep looking at you? 'Servant,' indeed. Who are you, really? And what is wrong with you?"

The air around her head seemed to crack in half as Adney slapped her. Her head jerked to one side, and pain flooded into her already bruised face.

His hand returned to his side like a knife to its sheath. She grabbed the rail at the top of the steps for support. The staircase swung long and steep below. He might have struck her much harder if he wished, and that was perhaps the worst thing about it.

Adney stood before her for an instant, then he pitched backward into the nearest wall, holding his face. Jeric came at him and hit him again, in the gut. Adney bent over. Whether he was simply shocked or had resigned himself not to fight with his master, he did not resist as Jeric took him by the shirt and threw him down the stairs.

The bedroom door opened, and Delia sprang out. She ran toward her father, but Shada intercepted her, and together, they watched as Jeric, towering, yelled down the staircase.

"We're finished with you! Understand? Tell them that! You'll never touch my family again!"

He stopped, face red. "He's gone." He turned toward Shada and Delia and took a heaving breath as if clearing foul air from his lungs. In a far gentler voice, he said, "We are in terrible trouble."

42

SHADA

WHILE THE ADULTS STARED at each other, Delia walked to the stop of the stairs. Wrapping her arms around the banister, she looked down. "Did Mr. Adney cry, Father?" Delia asked.

"Not much can make Mr. Adney cry, darling. He has been through a lot."

"You shouldn't hurt people."

"No, of course not."

As the girl absorbed that, Shada tried to collect herself. For a short time, as a child, she had known a man who worked as a courier and owned a bicycle. He let her borrow it twice—a foolhardy act, considering the thing was his livelihood and she was barely tall enough to pedal.

A few times, as she rode, she closed her eyes. It was a delicious temptation that always struck while she was speeding down a hill. Each time, her good sense returned before disaster struck, and she had opened her eyes. Now, she felt like she was racing downhill, eyes open like the sensible person she had finally become, only to be stricken blind.

Jeric looked at her in his unabashed way. *Do all the Shining Realm's people have that same look?* To him, she must have seemed closed and mistrusting.

"Thank you," she said. Maybe Adney would have stopped after a single slap to her face. Maybe not.

The gratitude seemed to embarrass him. He looked down at his daughter and ran his fingers through her hair. "Save your thanks until we learn what I've done to us."

"Would he have hurt me more?"

"I don't know. If he'd decided to take you away, you might have suffered a great deal. You still might, and us too."

"Where do people go when your leaders take them away?"

He shook his head. "There are no leaders. You must stop thinking like a primitive. Even on Ronia, someday, there will be no—"

"Please, answer my question."

"You haven't let me!" he snapped. His anger disappeared almost before the words passed his lips. "I'm sorry, my love. I was going to say that I have no answer for you."

He chuckled bleakly. "I don't know where they go. I only know what they're like when they return."

"How have you stood by and watched such things happen? And for your whole life?"

She immediately regretted asking. Ronia was hardly a paradise, and she had made survival there her business. But Jeric, she reminded herself, was far guiltier than she.

His reply amounted to a helpless shake of his head. His eyes were wide, not with surprise but, perhaps, with the understanding of dreadful new realities.

The words "my love" reminded Shada that Jeric was operating under a false assumption. This seemed a ludicrous moment to talk of such things, but no better one might occur, and he needed to know. She would have to say it in front of Delia. She would not send the girl out of their sight again.

"I cannot be your partner," she said. "It's impossible. There could be terrible consequences for all of us. I must leave."

To her surprise, the news did not visibly affect him. Perhaps he had been expecting it, or perhaps he had reached his capacity for dismal astonishment. "Where are you planning to go?"

She had no clear answer until she spoke. "First, I'm going to find Lani."

His eyes turned to the floor. "Shada, it's too late. Had you left earlier, I could have protected you, but after what just happened..." He shook his head. "They won't let you leave."

"Not even to find Lani?" Feeling trapped, she grew desperate. "We have to look, Jeric. I won't try to leave this park. Whoever's watching us must understand. She's a little girl." She couldn't believe she needed to explain this.

"I see. And when you've dragged Lani out of the forest, what then? Will you bring her back to me? I'm a villain, after all. You must think so."

Shada's heart galloped. She watched Delia from the corner of her eye, trying to imagine how much the child understood. "You're less a villain than that woman in the woods. Goddess knows what she'll do with..." She wanted to grab Jeric by the throat. "Don't you care for her at all? She's your daughter!"

"Of course I care for her!" Jeric roared. "But things are more complicated than your precious ideals. I'm not Lani's only parent, don't you see? Oliva loves her as much as me. Maybe more."

"You'd let Lani live in the woods?"

"The Realm wants to take her away. She and Oliva, they're both 'unsuitable' for a man in my place. I haven't allowed it, but after today... I may have just sacrificed my place in the Realm, Shada. I may have no more power to protect them. But maybe, just maybe, if they live quietly out of sight, the Realm will leave them alone."

She stared at him. "Then why did you hit Adney? Why bring this on yourself?"

His eyes were desolate. "Is it impossible to believe, even now, that I actually love you? I couldn't watch you be beaten or dragged off, no matter what."

Shada nodded, numbly realizing that he had been honest about something, then. "They're coming for you, aren't they, Jeric?"

He nodded. "I think so. Unless I can think of something to give them. Some way to redeem myself."

Protecting the girls was most important. To that end, Shada had a mad idea. She had been having a lot of those. "What if we all went into hiding? If Oliva has survived in those woods, so could we. We could eat fruit from the trees—"

Jeric was already shaking his head. "I'm too important, Shada. They won't let me disappear."

"Then I'll go. Let me take Delia. Maybe they'll spare us. Our chances will be better than they would be here, with you."

He rested his hand on the banister. Assured that it was really there, he sagged against it. "If I believed that," he said, "I would shove you both out the door. But they're watching this house. If you leave, they will follow, and if you find Lani, you'll have led them to her. They may not bother searching for her, but if you do their work for them..." He let the thought finish itself. "It's you and I who are in the most danger, and I think we're most likely to survive if we stay together. Delia still needs us."

She gulped. Moments ago, leaving Lani to that woman had been an unthinkable idea. Now, not only was Shada thinking about it, she found herself agreeing. The world had once seemed a logical enough place, but she was learning better.

She proceeded before she could think too hard about what she was doing. "So let's stay alive. Do you have any ideas?"

He was quiet for a time, and she forced herself to wait.

"One," he said at last, with great effort, having begun to sweat. "We must regain the Realm's favor. I may know a way."

"What is it?"

"You will marry me," he said. "No more hesitation, no more conditions. We must present ourselves in a united front, right now, as the future ruling family of Ronia. If we give the Realm just what it wants and do so immediately, they may show mercy."

Shada blinked. She felt the life in each of her fingers and toes. "We can't. I've told you already. You're talking about invading my world, my city. And there are other reasons, ones I can't tell you, but you have to trust..." She trailed off.

"If the world isn't what we want," he said, "we will make it a little better. Whoever joins the Realm changes it. We may not remake the Realm, but we can try. We have a beginning right in there." He cocked his head toward Delia.

Shada began to refuse again, but a new idea occurred to her—an ugly idea, but it was the only one she could think of.

She faced a gauntlet of terrible options. If she refused Jeric, she would doom them both. If she accepted, she would be part of the invasion of Ronia. She had only one hope.

She could play along and pray for the Lady's return.

Shada had finally accepted that the Lady would never let her go. Whenever she left, she would always come back. Whatever the source of her fixation on Shada, it was insatiable.

That meant the Lady—the cruel, oppressive Lady—was Shada's only possible rescuer from this trap.

Shada could marry Jeric and, when the Lady inevitably returned, explain the situation and beg for her help. The Lady couldn't possibly want her to help invade Ronia—that went against the Lady's entire purpose for existing. She would have to help Shada out of her bind. She must. She would take Shada away, sparing Shada from betraying her city.

What if the invasion of Ronia proceeds before the Lady returns? Shada would make that decision when the time came.

How desperate her hopes had become. Her most optimistic outlook depended on the Lady returning and taking her back into slavery.

But that was the best she could do, the best that Ronia and its crusade had left her with.

Jeric was watching her face carefully. If nothing else, he perceived that she was conflicted. "You've rubbed off on me a little, Shada. You and your world. And I hate it. It feels like I no longer fit together."

"I'm sorry." She could think of nothing else to say.

"If you want to help me, do as you've agreed. Stay. I know you have doubts. Of course you do. I've proven myself weak. I dithered over what to do about Lani. I did the same when Oliva lost her mind. I didn't pursue her when she fled into the woods. All these things hurt my standing in the Realm. But I can't do such things anymore—the Realm won't let me. You cannot trust my judgment, Shada, but you can trust my intentions, at least."

She looked at him. "How would we do it? Do you have weddings in the Shining Realm?"

He smiled. "Of a kind. 'Marriage' and 'weddings'—these are your words. We will undergo a ritual, one made especially for us. A test, you might say, though it will be nothing we can't handle. It's waiting for us at the edge of the forest. It's been waiting since you first came to this house."

She did not let herself hesitate. "Let's go now."

He nodded, and his smile faded. Each of his movements seemed incomplete, as if he were wary of falling into some trap.

They left the house a few minutes later, taking nothing but the clothing they wore. Jeric led the way onto the back terrace, and Shada followed, her hand linked with Delia's.

Jeric stopped in his tracks. She had to walk around his large form to see why.

Adney was waiting. He was standing directly in their way, at the top of a few stairs that led to the garden path. His presence froze Shada's blood. She wanted to feel relief that he had not left. It meant he might not yet have reported Jeric's attack. But none of her emotions were coming and going as they should.

"We're going to the clearing," Jeric announced. "Stand aside." Then he leaned toward Shada, and his hand closed around hers. "Walk."

They advanced toward what seemed an inevitable collision. As they approached Adney, he stepped out of their way. No one said anything.

They passed him at a distance shorter than Shada's forearm. She dared not meet his eyes, but she could not help noticing he had an ugly black eye where Jeric had hit him. Within the scar tissue surrounding the eye was a small ring of living flesh. She wondered what Oliva's punches and Adney's slap had done to her own face, which began to throb anew.

Delia passed Adney last of all, and Shada's heart sang with terror as the girl carelessly brushed past the man. Descending the steps, Shada expected Delia to be torn from her grasp at any instant. At the very least, one of them would get a knife in the back. But nothing happened.

Jeric led them to the forest. Somewhere ahead—who knew how far—were the battlements surrounding the woods. Though they had left the house behind, the sense of relief Shada was expecting failed to come. That was when she turned her head and saw that Adney was following them.

He stayed just a few paces behind, strolling in utter silence, like a loyal valet. There he would remain until the end of their journey.

43

NOR

WILD GRASS FLITTING BY underfoot. Stars watching above. A knife clutched in young fingers.

In this dream, Nor was a little older, and he was running. He was on the outskirts of the village, far from any light but the stars. Any time he strayed from the center of the road, the sides and corners of huts leaned out of the night to threaten him with a bruised shoulder or broken nose. But he refused to slow down.

He knew what was about to happen. He had been coming to it for days. He had the same dream sickness as the others and dreamed even when he was awake. Always in the back of his mind were passing sounds and images from memories. Even when his life was in danger.

Some of the memories felt like crude reconstructions of true events, but not this one. Experiencing it while awake might have dulled its pain, but consciousness held torments too deep to contemplate.

Instead, he ran. He crossed the footbridge over the spot in the water where his father had sold his people to Ronia. On its far side was the village hall. The two-story structure—once a novelty in itself—cast faint light from its windows over a little patch of the street.

No one was outside, and an uneasy silence came from within. The front door hung ajar, blurring the fundamental division between inside and out that Nor had never considered until the Ronians began to build doors. He stopped in his tracks before the vertical slab of wood, showing it a confused and resentful deference as he reached for its handle. As it opened, he took a dancer's step out of its path in the way he had learned to do.

The first time he had ever consented to entering that building had been some years before, to view the corpse of a man newly killed on a hunt. He had rarely entered since, afraid that doing so would become easier as the place worked the same spell on him that had ensnared his family and friends.

Inside, the few who were awake did not notice him. From where they lay or sat, they looked around, searching their own bodies and the floor around them for unfound things. The fire in the central pit was dying.

The rest were dormant in a way more profound and sinister than sleep. When they woke, a melancholy would descend on them all. In a side room, the waist, genitals, and legs of Nor's unconscious father leered from behind a doorway. The legs and buttocks of a woman accompanied him.

Nor wandered away across the hall like a widow on a battlefield. He found his mother near the firepit.

She was awake and smiling. Head on her forearms, she lay curled up and naked, looking across the room. Her body glistened with sweat. Ordinarily, her smile would have warmed him, but now, it soured his gladness at finding her.

He knelt before her eyes, and she slowly looked up at him. Her smile lived on undiminished, and she reached up to touch his face. Her fingers searched his chin idly, and he wondered if she was hoping to find the beginnings of a beard. The touching went on until it annoyed him.

"Mother," he said, leaning away from her hand.

Unhurt by the rejection, she dropped her arm. Her eyes and her benign smile resumed their watch over the lower reaches of the room. He was blocking much of her view, but she stretched her neck a little to see past him.

Giving up, he moved on to the hall's far end. There, only fragments of the fire's light reached. A Ronian man sat in a large chair, slouching to escape illumination. He was awake. Nor could not imagine him sleeping.

Hob smiled as Nor approached, and Nor knew that this smile, at least, was for him.

"Thought you left," the man said.

Nor shook his head.

"Knew you wouldn't," Hob continued, unfazed by the contradiction.

Nor's face burned.

"Come to me."

Not wanting to, Nor did it anyway. When he came within Hob's reach, nothing much happened. The man glowed in the distant light.

"You're a good boy," he said, unfurling a hand to Nor, palm up in offering.

Nor was tired of people reaching and fumbling at him. The hand presented no threat, but he slapped it aside.

The act must have stirred recent memories in Hob. His smile dwindled, and he asked, "Why'd you say those things? I heard."

As sometimes happened lately, Nor found himself gripped by a pure, suffocating silence. To answer the question seemed impossible.

Searching Nor's mind with wicked skill, Hob asked, "Is there anything you want to say now?"

Nor glowered.

"This is your time. I don't even feel like moving."

Bunching his fingers into fists, Nor inched them behind his back.

"What have you got there, a knife?"

Nor had indeed.

"I might not jump fast enough. You'll stick me and be gone."

Once, Nor's father had made him kill a man captured in war. The prisoner had been hauntingly calm as blood spilled from his throat. Now, Nor tried to find in Hob's eyes what he had seen in that warrior's, but Hob's calm was different. It was not earned but stolen.

"Are we not still friends?" Hob asked. His eyes had been closing so slowly that Nor hadn't noticed until then. The man yawned. The firelight caught slices of his face. He mumbled, "I'll let you decide. What do friends..."

He joined the others.

Nor had known since he saw Hob slouching there that he would not hurt the man. The urge to kill him, years in the making, was cleanly and utterly taken from him.

He drew his knife and stuck it in the floor between Hob's feet. Then he left the house at a run, letting his feet kick people as he went.

Outside, he found the blackness of the night unprecedented. He followed the trail of stars between the roofs of buildings until grass was under his feet. The moon shone on the field, and somewhere ahead, it could guide him to the pack he had suddenly dropped, the one he had been carrying out onto the steppe, never to be seen again.

Instead of looking for the pack, he turned aside. Just past the last houses was the site of a vast construction project. Wooden beams stretched into the sky, closer to the gods than living men had ever gone. Nor circled it at a distance, wary of the bits of metal littering the ground. On the far side of that new building—a shrine to Ronia's goddess—was a simple hut.

He beat on the door until it opened. He could not see Cadmon's face, but he knew it was there.

A moment passed. Nor felt the stars turning overhead.

A rumble came from the old man's chest. Cadmon, half asleep, muttered something.

Nor hadn't understood. He waited tensely until Cadmon spoke again. "Here to kill me?"

When Nor did not kill him, he said, "Welcome, then. You may sleep on the floor."

44

—·—

NOR

ONCE THE SUN, REN'S face had become the moon.

She watched from above as Nor traveled without moving. He lay on a litter of some kind, and a rumble came from underneath—one of the Shining Realm's motorized carriages.

She rode with him. Glad for the company, he examined Ren's face with a child's lack of abashment. Blasted and numb, his mind pondered little. She was the brightest thing in front of him, so he looked.

She didn't shun his attention. In fact, she glowed a little. "Despite everything, I admire you," she said.

He feared words, he realized. Words brought new things, knowledge, and he wanted no more of that. He kept staring and did not answer.

She lifted something and held it in front of him. His eyes slowly focused. It was a needle. "I've still got to give you this," she said. Her posture was slouching, informal. Even her face seemed more open. "Though we both know you don't need it."

She touched his shoulder with a cold hand. He noted the needle's brief sting with indifference. "You've been so well behaved since you read that letter. I wish you'd been like this before. Oh, Nor, why did you attack me? I would've told you what the letter said. If I'd known you were this delicate, I would've broken it to you gently, guiding you to the truth. Now, it's too late."

At that, he rolled onto his shoulder, facing away from her.

"Like a lamb," she continued. "I had hoped facing the truth would be another step on your journey. But it seems it's broken you."

Her hand again rested on his shoulder. That time, no needle came.

"But all is not lost. Do you understand me, Nor? You still have a role to play. It's not the one I hoped for you, but a role nonetheless. Don't despair—know that, even in your weakness, you have a place in humanity's great journey."

Before his eyes, the dark interior of the carriage became darker. His vision was fading though his eyes remained open. He thought of the wraiths on Caidfell, how they too could make him feel anything they wanted.

The difference was, this time, he welcomed the darkness.

"One more," she said. "To set you free." Her voice was fading also. Turning his head, he saw the glint of another needle.

He rolled back toward her. Whatever she offered, he would receive it. He hoped the darkness would continue forever.

He saw the door of Cadmon's cabin open before him, and the old man's silhouette beckoned him inside. Nor followed, as he had on that night long before.

He no longer feared. The worst had come true, and he dreaded only the light. The light would unveil it before him again, the pain before which he could only retreat toward death.

45

HULGAR

HULGAR'S COT WAS TOO small for him to sleep in, even alone. Each of his visitors had fitted it comfortably, though, so he contented himself with the floor. The courtesy had done this girl little good.

Hulgar had slept less than usual that night. He was no longer plagued by the kind of dreams he'd had on Caidfell—visions of the past that didn't end even when he woke up. But Hulgar's dreams moved in seasons, and this was their summer.

The girl was younger than the others the Realm had given him. When she first announced herself and entered the room, his first thought was that he probably had daughters her age. He felt little attraction to her, not that he had expected to. Such things made little difference.

She had arrived wrapped in several layers of clothing, too much to be comfortable in the room's stuffy air. She had held onto these garments like a fortress throughout the night, never removing a single one even when he offered to help.

She must have slept very little, certainly not more than he. She could not have, when she had so many times found him newly awake and leaning over the bed, his mass hanging above her like a thundercloud, his tears falling on her, heralding a storm. He would speak to her eagerly of Vera, placing his hands on the girl's to impress the urgency of the story. Now and again, his head dropped into her lap so that he could cry without being watched.

He had never asked the girl's name, but he did ask her how old she was. She said she didn't know, but he could guess well enough. "I asked your boss to surprise me," he told her.

Soon after she entered, her initial terror had seemed to fade. He didn't know what the others had told her to expect. The past nights had been dark ones indeed, with Hulgar's rages and melancholies coming and going like whirlwinds. Each of the women had left the room untouched but with an air of having narrowly escaped something. Each, he knew, hoped never to see him again. He could understand that.

The girl had sat on the bed at his invitation. At first, her eyes pointed straight ahead as he spoke. She must have listened, though, because she soon was sneaking glances at him. When he told her about his biggest fight with Vera, the one that had changed everything, the girl met his eyes for an instant. Closer to the end, when he got to the part when he tried to find Vera but couldn't, the girl made a little noise in her throat.

"Imagine," he said. His mouth went dry, and he paused for a moment. "Imagine—I sent Vera out onto the street. My own wife. Then she's gone, like that. Or maybe someone took her. I heard every rumor you could think of. I even heard she died."

"You were poor." The girl said that then shut her mouth tight.

He puzzled over the meaning of her words, what he should say in return, and if he would cry again. Only after a long silence did he realize that she was trying to cheer him up.

"That's what I told Vera," he replied. "Money was all I could think of. So, onto the street she went."

He sighed and shuddered. Feeling kindly toward the girl, who wanted him to feel better, he decided to comfort her in return. "Did someone send you out into this life? Couldn't have been a husband—you're too young."

"They chose me."

"I'll bet your father didn't like that." He laughed at what her father must have said.

She looked at him strangely. He did not like her expression, and he did not bring up her family again.

He listened to the halls outside. "It's morning now, love. We don't have much time."

She had relaxed significantly since they met. Now, her fear resurged. She clutched her garments tight around herself as he came to kneel next to the cot.

He sank his head into her chest. Despite the layers of cloth, he could feel one of her small breasts against his cheek. He scorned himself for noticing and began to pray.

The noise that came from his throat started as a soft whine, like a lonely dog. Then it rose and fell in pitch, sometimes forming half words. He was bitterly determined not to cry now. This girl was counting on him though she might not know it.

The Goddess would have preferred tears, but he wasn't praying to her. Once, long before, he had thought her an uncaring cosmic bitch. Only on Caidfell had he learned the truth: she was dead, dead and rotting. The new gods demanded strength, and he dared not shed tears while their great eyes were upon him.

His prayer culminated in a series of coughs, deep wet expulsions. The girl's body jerked in fear with each massive sound.

Then he withdrew and looked down on her. "You'll be safe now," he said. "I'm sure of it. You're lucky, in fact. There is a special place for women when this life is done."

She would not look at him.

"Do you believe me?" he asked, putting on what he imagined was a game smile.

She nodded. He doubted she would share her true feelings with him, a stranger.

He continued, "You won't have to be afraid. Not if I have anything to say about it."

She closed her eyes tightly for a moment. Then, to his astonishment, she touched his arm and looked right at him. "You should leave now," she said, "if you can. You and your friends must get out of here, or they won't let you leave at all."

This time, his smile was real. "You're very kind, love. But I don't think we'll be doing that. If you're willing, I've got a favor to ask. It's a message for the man who sent you."

Seconds later, she walked slowly from the room. The candle in the corner was still lit though it had burned low, and Hulgar began heating his knife over it.

A few minutes after that, the thin gray-haired man whom Hulgar had met the previous night returned. He stalked into the room, hands in fists. As he shoved his way past the curtain, he shouted, "What's wrong with you, you—"

Seeing no one in the room, he stopped. The candle was out, and darkness reigned.

Hulgar was behind him, a great mass in the corner by the door. He fastened his tremendous hands to the man's shoulders. "Surprise," he said.

46

EMBERLY

EMBERLY HAD HOPED AGAINST hope to enter the pyramid with a minimum of fanfare and face his men after he cleaned up. That wish evaporated as soon as he and Roark came within sight of the building.

Several of his soldiers were standing guard with rifles. The first one who spotted him called out, and they all trotted over. "Goddess be praised," another said. "We were getting worried."

Emberly thanked him and thought about how he must look like he had been through hell. While he was gone, Roark had obediently told no one of his abduction, instead announcing that the captain was in private, intensive negotiations with the Shining Realm. During their brief walk to the pyramid, Emberly and the lieutenant had assembled a story that would explain Emberly's appearance.

"Did you make a deal, sir?" one of the soldiers asked.

"No," Emberly replied. "The negotiations failed. I've been a hostage of the Realm."

That did not generate the shock he expected. The men muttered in anger and dismay, but even that soon died away. Roark had mentioned a brawl the night before, in which a few Realmsmen might have been killed. Now, looking into his men's eyes, Emberly knew they had realized peace was not to be.

He added, "They wanted things that I couldn't give—that we couldn't."

"How did you get away?" someone asked.

"That's too long a story to tell here."

They were accepting his return far more casually than he had anticipated. *But why shouldn't they?* Unaware of Emberly's misadventures, they had been waiting and wondering and drinking. Aside from the news of his captivity, his return meant little more than a break in the monotony of their watch.

He wanted the conversation to end. Roark had lied for him, so concealing Roark's lie with his own had seemed only fair. But the lies were bothering him more than he would have liked.

"Any sign of the Realm?" he asked the soldiers abruptly.

"Nothing yet, sir. Their men are all gone. Vanished." The man who said that glanced furtively at Roark. Perhaps he was thinking of the brawl and his own role in it.

"They won't be gone for long, I'm afraid," Emberly said. "Stay alert."

"Yes, sir," the men replied, with varying degrees of zeal.

"Can we help you, sir? You don't look well."

"No," he said sharply. "Thank you." The last thing that he wanted right then was more attention.

He got it anyway. The great hall was full of men preparing for action—loading weapons and tossing down a hasty breakfast from the remaining supplies the Realm had provided. Many were gathered around the few remaining tables, having piled the wreckage of the others in a corner. Someone raised a cry at Emberly's entrance, and the captain was quickly surrounded.

He accepted their greetings as spiritedly as he could and thanked them, all the while wishing that the moment would be over. He felt oddly appreciative of a number of men who looked up when he entered but then went back to work. Through a gap in the crowd, he saw Private Robir sitting against a wall and watching him. In the man's hand, apparently forgotten, was a red fruit shaped like a teardrop.

Emberly had dreaded having to generate some kind of uplifting speech at that moment, and he was glad when the crowd dispersed on its own. Earlier, Roark had roused them, assigned a guard, and set them in motion, preparing for a fight. That left the captain free, for the moment, to have a certain urgent conversation.

When he found the bishop sitting cross-legged on his bedroll, he explained his absence in the fewest words he could manage.

"Escaped," Arumin said when he finished. "That must have been quite an exploit, Emberly. Perhaps the greatest of your adventures. I'm glad to see you—I don't trust your man."

"Roark? You can trust him as you trust me."

"Oh, I doubt that. Who could be your equal?"

"Listen. Right now, it doesn't matter if you believe me or if you like me. We both have far bigger problems."

"Do we? Are you referring to your soldiers' days-long rampage? The reign of terror, drinking, and whoring that has held sway over this place? And the fact that you, along with the fools you call officers, have allowed it all to happen?"

"I'll be damned if I excuse myself to you. I've failed, but at least I've tried. Now, unless you know of some way we can escape this place and find Shada, there is nothing left to do but make war."

Arumin stood, and Emberly remembered how tall he was. "Well, Captain, it's a grim time to find that we finally agree on something. But here it is. There is only one piece of business left before we settle this."

"What is it?"

"That abomination of a temple is still out there. We must destroy it."

Emberly was nearly speechless. He had forgotten about the temple. "Dear Goddess, why?"

"You know exactly why," the bishop said dismissively. "It will take several men, I imagine, and explosives. We should start immediately."

"But..." Emberly struggled. "Could any of you who've been there even find it again? On foot, no less?"

"We must try. Brin will go if he has not lost himself. If not, I will take his place. As for Brother Nor, I doubt we'll ever see him again."

"Arumin, we can't do it." Emberly realized he had forgotten to use the bishop's title. "We shouldn't divide our forces unless it's for something essential. I only wish we could warn the prisoners from Caidfell that the Realm may be coming for them."

Arumin spoke to the heart of his suspicions. "Do you really think the Realm hasn't come for them already? Their troubles are worse than ours. Given their criminal histories, I'm sure they'll turn on us if it benefits them."

Emberly took a breath. "It's out of our hands, regardless. We can only marshal what we have. That's why I pray you will forget about that temple. Next to our lives, it is trivial."

"Captain, you are a failure. You have said it yourself. You have seen the Goddess at work, and yet you make the wrong choices, time and again. Will you keep doing that, even to the end?"

An uproar out in the great hall caught Emberly's ear. Many hostile voices were rising, and as he noticed them, they reached a violent pitch. His eyes met Arumin's and saw the same alarm in them.

Pushing through the curtain, he collided with Robir. His immediate irritation was doused by the private's expression. The man gazed at him with a look of cold fire. He had been eavesdropping.

"Move," Emberly commanded. He shoved past Robir, spinning him around. He felt bright eyes on him as he rushed toward the furor ahead.

47

EMBERLY

EMBERLY ENTERED THE GREAT hall at a run. From the doorway leading to the pyramid's entrance was spilling a mob of his soldiers, including a few posted to guard duty outside. At the center of the throng was Ganet, battered and bruised but alive.

"Quiet!" the captain yelled.

Voices softened. Everyone watched as Emberly approached the Realmsman.

"He came to the entrance and surrendered, sir," someone said.

Ganet's eyes were wide. He spoke to Emberly as though in a reverie. "Good afternoon, Cyril. It seems I have my answer."

"There is no other way." Emberly wanted to ask how Ganet had escaped the outraged crowd that attacked them both, but his men didn't know about that. "What are you doing here?"

Ganet peered at him, and a smile touched his lips. "I don't know yet." He looked around at the room full of people to whom he had made this admission, and his smile grew a little.

Observing the man's fey state, Emberly felt an unwelcome twisting in his heart, as well as a sense of kinship. He wondered if Ganet had also spent the night wandering the city.

Hearing footsteps behind him, Emberly turned. Arumin had entered the room and was approaching, regarding the general severely. Robir entered behind him.

Their presence jostled the captain from his wonderment at Ganet's state. Whatever the truth, things had changed.

"You're an enemy now, General," he told the addled man. His inclination was to speak as he would to a lost child, and he harshened his voice deliberately. "We cannot let you leave."

He spoke to one of the men holding Ganet. "Take him to your room and watch him."

As the soldiers pulled Ganet away, the general seemed to awaken. "No! Cyril! Listen!" He twisted and struggled. The soldiers tightened their grips and forced him toward the hallway.

"We need to talk! Alone!"

"We've talked already," Emberly said, too softly for the general to hear.

"Please!" Ganet's cry held a timbre of desperation. "There's something you need to know!"

Emberly cursed. Then he marched over, grabbed Ganet by the collar, and pulled him toward the company's rooms.

Arumin watched in disbelief. "Emberly, this is pointless." But he followed.

At Ganet's insistence, they chose a room far from the great hall, where they could hope for privacy. When they were alone, Ganet asked pleasantly if he could sit. Emberly expressed vulgarly how little he cared, and the general settled by the wall farthest from the door. The others remained standing, and Ganet looked up at them expectantly.

"First things first," Emberly spat into the silence. "What have you done to my men?"

Ganet's eyebrows bunched in earnest-seeming bewilderment.

"That ale," the captain said. "The swill you've been giving our soldiers. It's some kind of poison, isn't it?"

The general tilted his head back, his confusion growing. "Has it made them ill?"

"No! It's made them barking mad. Haven't you heard about the riot last night?"

"It's wine, Cyril. A strong one, but that's all."

Emberly began to retort, but they had more urgent things to discuss. "What did you want to tell us?" he growled.

Ganet had returned to his daydreams. He looked at the floor.

Arumin scoffed. "For all that's holy, why are you here?"

"I'm a different man than when I last saw you, Cyril," Ganet said. "Something has happened to me, something both great and terrible."

Emberly scuffed the floor with his boot. "Go on."

But the general's mind had taken a different path. "I don't understand why you want a war. You can't win."

The bishop spoke before Emberly could retort. "A goddess protects us. Your power means nothing."

"But she's not here."

"She has ways of helping us, even from far away."

"We know about your Lady, if that's who you mean. Why keep pretending we don't?" Ganet turned his dreamy eyes on Arumin. "Where is she, Bishop? Has she been answering your prayers? Cyril, what about you? Has your divine nursemaid checked on you recently?"

Emberly looked at his boot and thought about putting it into the general's face. "Are you saying you know her whereabouts?"

"I know a number of whereabouts. Those of the woman Shada. Those of the monk Norhim. If you fight us, you will doom them as well as yourself."

Emberly was not surprised to learn that. Yet hearing that his missing people were alive silenced him for a moment.

Arumin had no such trouble. "Enough. You want us to believe that if we surrender, all will be well. I say you're a damned liar! I only wonder that you've risked your life on such a foolish gamble."

The general wrapped his arms around his knees. "Has it occurred to you that I might actually care about you and your people? I told you when we first met, Cyril—I like Ronians."

"Then spare us!" Emberly said. "Let us have our little corner of the universe, and we won't intrude on yours. Isn't that better for everyone?"

"You don't understand. How can I explain the size of it when I haven't fully grasped it myself? Language is still so limited, especially yours."

His eyes were focused, as if to pierce a fog. The others waited.

"Our peoples are not just friends in the making. We are long-lost brothers. The Shining Realm, before we took that name, had a planet and a deity of our own. But ours was unique. He was quite hard on us. He wanted us to be better. During the time of vanishing, he hid away some of the wonders of humanity's golden age, to show us what we could be.

"Now, we seek to gather our species together again. Some, we deem to be soldiers, others builders. Each has its strengths, but all deserve dignity and respect. Ronia is different even than most. You have carved out a place for yourselves. You will have a place among the best of us. As leaders."

"What if we simply refuse?" the captain asked. "What if I tell you that our destiny is not yours to determine?"

"All humans everywhere share the same destiny. We can unite as one or remain bitter, squabbling tribes until some stronger, wiser species puts us out of our misery. You have no right to deny the rest of humanity its chance for final peace. Your only choice is how you will awaken into the holy order. Should you prove less human than we thought, your people will be in the lowest orders—beasts of burden until the end of time."

Emberly thought about his wife and son. For an awful moment, he was unable to recall what they looked like. He interrupted the general's rising incantation. "Why are you only now telling us this? We had no idea what you were planning for us."

Ganet looked sheepish. "Some of us prefer simple domination."

"Ren."

"She and those like her do not really believe in persuasion. A simple choice—that's what she wants. No concessions, no promises. She says that for an enlightened people, the logic of the proposition would be enough." Ganet looked at Emberly then Arumin. "I am not a liar. So I must confess something: I am not supposed to be here. But I could not let you die without telling you everything."

The captain and the bishop looked at each other. Emberly said to Ganet, "Do you mean Ren doesn't know you're here?"

"I am not a liar," Ganet repeated. "I sometimes think she simply enjoys what comes next. And she'll get it." He closed his eyes and said, almost sleepily, "Unless I help you and your missing friends to escape this city."

48

—·—

ROBIR

As the bishop, the captain, and their prisoner vanished down a corridor, leaving the men in the great hall to stare at each other and return, one by one, to their business, Robir felt a shiver pass through him. He thought furiously. Right then was the moment, the one he had known would come, but he didn't know how to begin.

The answer was given to him by a group of men who began to joke among themselves. He heard one of them say Arumin's name, and he moved closer.

Their talk grew louder as they decided that no one who mattered was listening. Lieutenant Iwan was nearby, but he cared little for what occurred outside his own head.

As Robir predicted, the soldiers were amusing themselves with talk of the bishop's fixation on Father Brin. The bishop's proclivities were a secret no one bothered to keep, and not even Robir truly thought the old man's relationship with Brin was a pure one. For older soldiers who most keenly resented Arumin as the Coward of Caid-fell, the two holy men's relationship was an irresistible subject of mockery.

Still, it was Swinburn, one of the younger men in the company, who said one word too many. Mostly seeking the others' approval, he made a joke—loud enough for all to hear—about why the bishop had followed two men into a private meeting.

As the others laughed, Robir glanced around and saw that Iwan was gone. Events had conspired to give him that instant.

He shoved Swinburn from behind. "What's wrong with you?" he asked.

Everyone spun to look at him. He felt that moment in time with a clarity that gave him joy.

He let Swinburn flounder for an answer then cut him off. "Listen to yourselves. That's Huire's man you're talking about."

Sergeant Orund had noticed the disturbance. He stepped between Robir and Swinburn, whose mouth was opening and closing like a fish's. "He was having a laugh, brother. That's all."

"A laugh? About what, Sergeant? What in hell do we have to laugh about right now?" He turned, speaking to them all. "Am I the only one who's realized what's about to happen? Where have the rest of you been? Asleep?"

"You aren't the only one. You're just the only one having a fit about it." Orund laughed, not unkindly, and a few others joined him.

"It's Huire who protects us," Robir said. "She's the reason we're still here. If we make her angry, we're done. She wants us to fight, so we've got to fight."

"Who says otherwise?" Orund pressed.

"You know who," Robir countered. "The one who's led us into pit after pit. Who's been making us fall on our swords ever since Gallobraith. It's the captain."

That silenced everyone for a moment. Orund's reply, when it came, sounded like a quip. "Is this about that bullet you took on Gallobraith, Robir?"

"Of course it's not!" Robir shouted. "That was a scratch next to what others got. You know who I mean: all those brothers of ours who aren't here anymore. Well, maybe they would be if we had a leader who cared more about us than about being a hero."

Looking around again, he could not tell whether he was reaching anyone. Even those who were with him, who had made promises, looked frighteningly neutral.

"And where has he been? Having meetings. Holding talks. Enjoying the hospitality of the enemy."

Perhaps Orund guessed his true intentions. The sergeant's alarm showed in his eyes and voice. "Enough, Private. That's not the whole story you're telling."

"Isn't it, Sergeant? Where's the captain right now?"

He let the question stand for a second then continued, "Where do you think he'll be when the Realm comes? If you think it's with us, you're dreaming."

"Now, hold on." Orund took a step forward, into striking distance. "We won't get anywhere tearing ourselves apart. You can't do this, man. We need you."

"We need each other," Robir said. "That's why we have to cut the captain loose."

Saying it publicly turned the air in his lungs to ice. No one said anything in response, not even Orund, so Robir forged ahead.

"We've got to do what Huire wants," he said. "Arumin knows what that is, whatever his faults. And he's told me. Anyone here who wants to keep his vows and his soul had better come along."

Orund's gaze was cold. "Come along where? What's the plan, Private?"

Men had begun to gather around Robir. Most still had not moved, but at least he wasn't alone.

He raised his voice. It was a risk—he might attract Roark's or Iwan's attention. He hoped they would already be too late to stop him. "The Realm has built a temple somewhere in Om. They made it in mockery of the Goddess and to corrupt us. Its existence is an insult. We cannot let it stand."

Orund's jaw was agape. "You're going to leave? How would you find it? What if the Realm—"

"I know how to find it. And the Realm does not matter to us."

Looking at the men who had gathered around him, his fellow mutineers, Robir counted eight. Most were the faces he had expected, but he saw a few surprises, including—*glory be*—Doctor Staubel.

His group could not stand against the rest if it came to blows, and they were surrounded. He would have to hope that some of the others were not so loyal to Emberly as to fight the mutiny.

"You don't mean any of it!" cried Swinburn, who had collected his senses. His eyes fixed on one of Robir's crew. "You talk about needing us, but you're friends with *that*."

He pointed at Merin, who was close by Robir's side. Merin's face reddened.

"For the love of all that's holy!" Robir cried. "The man was under a spell. Not one of us could have resisted. I say he's a better man than most in this room. Together, we'll go to that horror of a temple and burn it to the ground."

"I can't let you do it," Orund said. He was unarmed, but most of the others were still on his side.

"You will allow it, Sergeant." That was Iwan.

He had entered the room quietly and now walked fearlessly through the crowd to stand with the mutineers. "Go back to your preparations," he said to Orund. "I am ordering you."

The sergeant's face was like a ghost's. He looked from Robir to Iwan then at the men who stood with them. "If you do this, you can never come back."

"We've done it already," Iwan said. "And we shall see."

Heavy footsteps in the hallway drew their attention. Robir guessed it was Hulgar before the man's great bulk emerged from the shadows. Seeing the happenings in the room, he stopped.

"Hulgar," Orund said. "We could use your help here."

Hulgar smacked his lips and said to Robir, "So you did it, then."

"We're going to attack the Shining Realm, Private," Iwan said. "We're tired of waiting."

Hulgar bit his lip. He cradled one of his forearms protectively. On it was a freshly rising patch of burned red skin. "I like the sound of that."

49

— · —

BRIN

BRIN LAY ON THE patch of floor they had covered with blankets and clothing. No one had visited the Realm's secret furnace since he and Ilis came to this room.

He looked around for Ilis, but she was gone. Whenever he did not know where she was, her absence kindled feverish longing in him. She disappeared often, gathering food and supplies from the Realm's stores in the lower levels of the pyramid. She always came back, but he could not accustom himself to this pattern. Each time she left, he was sure she would change her mind and not return.

Brin knew himself well enough to recognize that his heart was prone to extremes. He had reviled Ilis at first, and in some far province of himself, perhaps he still did. But his hatred had been almost entirely eclipsed.

She dominated his mind. He had entirely given up trying to squeeze her for information. He spent most moments obsessing over her and wondering to make her obsessed with him. He hadn't thought he was capable of being in love, but he didn't know what else to call this. He needed her approval, her attention, and her adoration, and she gave him just enough of those things to keep him hoping for more.

His struggle left him little time to wonder what was happening outside their little world. He avoided thinking of Arumin, except to relish how furious and frightened the bishop would be by Brin's disappearance. *He shouldn't have disappeared on me.* Brin feared the bishop's anger far less than others'. He had a way of bringing out the old man's weakness—a weakness Brin despised.

When he heard Ilis enter, he rolled from his back to his belly and rested his chin on his hands. "You there," he said.

She smiled, and all his feelings screamed at him. Something had happened. His innards both demanded that she feel the same way about him and assured him that was impossible.

"What's wrong?" he asked. He could not let his doubts rest, even for a second.

Her smile fell with a blank ease that affirmed his suspicions. "We've been in this room for so long. I needed to escape for a little while."

"That's not all, though."

She looked around as though longing for some alternative to joining him on their mat of blankets. Finding nothing, she sat by him, pushing his legs until he moved them out of her way.

She looked at the floor and asked, "Do you remember what you asked me earlier?"

"When? While...?"

"Yes."

"Not really. I'll bet I said a lot of things." He laughed forcibly, trying to elicit the same from her.

She smiled with a politeness that hurt him. "Yes, and so did I. I'm afraid I got a little carried away."

"I didn't think so. Or, if you did, I didn't mind."

"Well, I did." Her frown deepened. "And you did too."

"It couldn't have been so bad."

"It was, though. Do you really not remember? You asked me to—"

"Look," he said, "I didn't mean any of it. It was all in fun."

"I don't believe you. I could see the difference in your face. I could hear it."

He sighed. Ilis hadn't heard him sigh much yet—Arumin was intimately familiar with the sound. "And what does it matter to you, anyway?"

She cast about for an answer. "Do you really think I'd do that? That I'd hurt you that badly?"

"You might do anything, as far as I know." He sensed regret in her, and this time, his laugh had a cruel edge. "You're not someone who feels bad about things. Or that's what you'd have me believe."

"I've been thinking about something else too." She reached under a blanket on the edge of their little territory and produced his necklace. Seeing the vial and the black powder within it dangling from the hand of another person, Brin felt his heart jump. He grabbed it from her, nearly breaking the chain in his haste.

"I noticed it the first time you undressed," she said.

"Why were you rooting through my things?"

"Brin, I know what it's for. The one who gave it to you was working for us."

"Is that so?"

"You don't believe me?"

He returned the vial and chain to their place around his neck. Sitting up, he curled himself into a ball. "The woman who gave me this expected me to meet the gods themselves." He snorted. "You're too smart to think that way. At any rate, you and your masters mean to keep us here."

"There are plans and fallback plans." She shivered. "I'm stupid for talking about this. There's no way they won't find out."

"Then don't." He turned to look at her, eyes hard. "It will make no difference. We're never getting out of here."

That silenced her for a time. Then she said, "If you had completed your journey and found your gods, would you have used that vial?"

"To kill them?" Brin pursed his lips. "It hardly bears thinking about. The idea of killing the gods is madness, as far as I'm concerned."

"It would have worked—I promise. Would you have used it?"

"What good could it possibly do me to answer that question?"

She sighed. "Fine. I understand. It's just that—you don't even know what it is, do you?"

Indifferent, he shook his head.

"I don't mean what it does but what it *is*. Did anyone tell you?"

"No. And given how things have ended, I can't say I care much."

"Still, it matters, Brin. When you give something like that to someone, they should know what it is and what's being asked of them."

"Nobody asked me anything!" Brin's body shook. "Your woman forced me to take it! She told me I'd be killed if I failed! Then some men attacked us. My head still hurts where they hit me."

Surprised by the force of his reaction, she seemed to turn inward a little. "Well, that's over now. Your part was only to take effect if we failed to stop your company here. We didn't know if your Lady would fight us or how powerful she was."

"You know about her, then?" He snickered. "Of course you do." Then he glared. "Was it your people who tried to kidnap the Lady from the temple in Ronia?"

She nodded. "None of the men we sent returned. Rumor held that the giant—the caretaker—had killed them all, but we were sure they were wrong. Before that, many of us thought the Lady was a fairy tale. Now, we know she is real, and she must be dealt with carefully."

Brin's thoughts had already returned to his own dilemma. "You assigned a man to kill me if I didn't fulfill your task." He tried to sound unafraid. "Is he—"

"He didn't arrive in Om with your company," she said. "From what I hear, your passage through Caidfell was in great doubt. If the company seemed doomed to failure, he may have tried to steal the Lady and return to Ronia. If so, he failed. Or perhaps he never tried and simply died in battle. In any case, he's no danger to you anymore."

Brin could hardly contain his immense relief. He had suspected his assassin was the same man who died while attacking Shada in that tower on Caidfell, but he had never stopped fearing he was wrong until right then. He tried a smile and found it natural enough. "I must congratulate you. I thought I was a scheming bastard, but..."

He lost track of his words, but she would not have let him finish anyway. "Brin," she said with a bitter laugh, "stop."

Her laugh made him angry. "It goes two ways, you know. I got what I wanted from you, believe me."

She shook her head. "You're a human man. Why do you pretend otherwise?"

"If I knew what the hell that meant, I might tell you."

"I mean that the truth is natural to you, and lying isn't. You ought to accept it."

"Who are you to say what I should do? The Shining Realm rattles on about the truth, yet they've got people like you doing their bidding. What does that make you to them?"

"Very little."

"Goddess. What a state of affairs."

She laughed again, much louder, and he jumped. A girlishness in the sound reminded him of when they'd first met. *Was it only days ago?* He laughed, too, and found it less painful than he'd expected.

He said, "So you think I should stop lying. What else would you advise since your own life has turned out so well?"

"Damned if I know. Isn't there anyone who cares about you?"

Brin thought of Arumin, of course, and how the bishop had abandoned him. "No. What I got from you—and you got from me—is all there is to caring."

Maybe Ilis guessed who he was thinking about. "Your bishop is getting old. Can *that* really be all he keeps you around for?"

"He's lonely. There's that, I suppose."

"I mean more than that. He must really care about you, at least a little bit."

Picturing the old man's face, Brin felt poisonous resentment. "There's no one in the entire world like that."

She slapped his arm. "I told you to stop lying."

He smiled then hid his face urgently behind his knees. He kept it there for a while. "So... were you just doing your job, then? I mean... with me?"

"Mostly." She looked at the floor. "But don't think that..." She shook her head and looked at him. "There's nothing wrong with you, Brin."

The comment pricked something deep in him. He glared. "Of course there's not."

She smiled sadly. "Very well, then."

After a moment, she continued, "I've given you my wisdom. Have you got any for me?"

He pressed his face into his knees, which muffled and distorted his voice. "Run away."

She scoffed. "Where?"

"I don't know. Through one of the gateways. There must be hundreds of them around Om."

"My people would find me."

"Stay, then. If you really think you're better off with them."

"You don't know them well enough."

"All those gateways. No one's found the last one yet."

She shifted closer and put an arm around his shoulders. He couldn't help liking it. He wiped his face hard on a sleeve and looked at her. In a moment of dumb courage, he said, "I haven't really gotten all I wanted from you."

She eyed him. "You got all there is. According to you."

He flipped his hands in mild exasperation. "Even if that's all there is, at least it's something. It can still be good. It just depends on us."

Her eyes grew sad. She took her arm away, and its absence left a desolation across his back.

His fear of her leaving rushed back. Forcing himself to speak calmly, he continued, "What I'm saying is it doesn't have to be a tool. It can come from something without going anywhere. People can do it for each other."

Something in those words seemed to make a difference. She turned her face back to him, and he saw a worry there that he relished. Worry made her seem human.

Emboldened, he said, "I'll prove it to you."

Her eyes moved up and down over him. "Are you saying, then, that I'd be doing you a favor?"

"Maybe."

She straightened her legs and rolled her body toward him. "I suppose I could make you put your arguments in writing. You would explain, at length, all the ways you'd serve me. And you'd do it gladly."

"Yes."

"But I'm feeling kind. Perhaps I'll only make you say it aloud, on your knees." Her hand was on his back again. Then she took his hair in her fist and pulled his head back. "And you'll do exactly as I say."

"Yes."

She paused just as her lips were about to touch his. "Don't ask me to do wicked things to you ever again."

"Yes. I won't, if that's what you want. But I'm not afraid to say them—not to you."

She slid on top of him. Soon, he was racking his brain for ways to tell her how badly he wanted her. She stood and told him to undress her. When that was done, she ordered him to his knees.

His chest heaving, he spouted all the things he was thinking—that she was a goddess, that she could have anyone she wanted, and how lucky he was to be chosen.

At the doorway, Robir coughed. His men snickered.

50

— · —

BRIN

SIX OF THEM WERE there. Or maybe seven. They had guns. Brin couldn't count or think straight. His blood sang in his ears like a tea kettle.

"Looks like we didn't need you after all," Robir said. His eyes were still wide at the sight he and his friends had stumbled upon, but his voice was hard.

Brin struggled to sort out what he meant. Words had become unfamiliar sounds.

"No," Lieutenant Iwan replied. He was the only one who didn't look shocked, amused, or even interested by the scene.

"These two were loud enough on their own," someone else said, which set off a fresh round of giggles.

The men advanced, surrounding Brin and Ilis. Brin, whose eyes had been fixed on a place far away, saw only belts and the tops of trousers.

In the moments that followed, many words were directed at the naked couple. From the miasma of their sentiments, sometimes threatening, sometimes mocking, Brin retained only a few snatches:

"Feeling desperate, are you, Father?"

"Didn't nobody teach him how a man does it?"

"Shall I be next, love?"

"The old man'll be jealous, boy."

When the men's attention turned toward Ilis, Robir awakened from his incredulity. "That's enough," he snapped. He turned toward Brin, crouching so that Brin could not avoid his eyes. "Ashamed, are you? Perhaps there's hope for you, then."

Brin's insides clenched. He tried to summon his anger, but it had been scattered and its pieces lost.

Robir went on. "The bishop is down there now, afraid for you." Someone coughed out a laugh, but a look from Robir shut him up. "He's done hardly anything but sit and wait for you to come back."

He looked at the priest in wonderment. "Everything that's happened—you don't know about any of it, do you? Here you've been all along, hiding out with your tramp. What a child."

Then he turned to Ilis. "You're coming with us."

Her face was stone. "Why?"

"You're going to take us for a ride." He extended a hand.

She looked at the hand as if it contained some other answer. Only then did Brin realize how scared she was, and terror washed over him like an ice bath.

She stammered, "No, I—"

Robir's shout made them both flinch. "Do I sound like I'm asking?" He lowered his hand and stood. "Take her."

Private Merin had been standing in the background, separated from the words and actions of his fellows. His eyes regarded Ilis with an unmistakable familiarity. He seized the moment and stepped forward. "Come with me, please." His voice was shaky and achingly cordial.

Brin sent out a silent prayer that he was dreaming.

Ilis didn't even look at Merin. "Wait," she said.

"Now!" Merin cried. It was a flimsy command, likely to collapse under its speaker's lack of assurance. Then he grabbed for her wrist.

She pulled it out of his reach, and another man, larger and rougher, stepped in and shoved Merin out of the way.

That man filled the empty space in front of Ilis. "Don't coddle her, mate. She knows what she's about."

Then the man leaned, took Ilis by the foot, and without a qualm, dragged her like a carcass to the center of the floor. She flailed.

Erupting with inchoate sounds, Brin jumped to his feet and went after them. Robir put a palm on the priest's chest and sent him stumbling back. Then Brin managed to speak. "Stop this! Right now! The Goddess forbids it!"

That drew more laughs.

Robir, however, remained calm. As his men pulled Ilis to her feet, he spoke to Brin with spiteful softness. "Father Brin, you've never cared about Huire or anyone else. It's too late to start."

Struggling, Ilis was overpowered.

Brin surged toward the men who held her, only for Robir to lazily rebuff him again. "Fight me, then!" Brin roared. He pushed toward Ilis once more. "Come on!"

He did not see Robir's knife emerge but only caught a glimmer of its movement. A bolt of lightning, venomous and cold as space, lashed across his cheek from nose to jowl.

A moment of reflection descended on the room. Even Robir's thugs feared breeching some thresholds, and shedding the blood of a holy man gave them pause.

Brin brushed his cheek with quivering fingers. He bent and turned away to consider, in privacy, what the knife had done to him. The wound was too dreadful to explore in depth.

Something about him had been ruined. Watching it die, he suddenly felt free. He spun to face them all. "You're finished! When the bishop finds—"

Robir moved again, and his knife opened Brin's other cheek.

"Stop!" Ilis howled. "I'm coming with you."

Brin panted as warmth ran down his neck and farther down.

Robir looked at him then at her. "If he's finished, then I'm finished," he said, indicating Brin with his blade. When no one moved or answered, he said, "Come on."

Everyone but Brin shuffled toward the doorway. Through the priest's shock, words still came to his lips. "Iwan!" he called as they went. "Don't let him do this."

The lieutenant was in the rear of the group. He had remained coldly removed from the proceedings, and he showed no inclination to answer now.

Brin added, "Iwan! You're an officer!"

Iwan stopped.

Robir saw it. Seeming distressed by even that small degree of cooperation with the priest, he pointedly said, "The others are waiting."

But Iwan's attention had turned to Brin, and it was not easily commanded. "When you face a thing like that"—he nodded at the far wall, at the metal doors and their awesome contents—"you can only die or surrender. I choose death."

No one had anything to add. Brin waited until everyone left.

He knew he should run, find someone, get help. Do something. But in his shock, even simple decisions like placing one foot before the other were too much. He sat on the blankets, bled, and dreamed.

51

SHADA

THE PATH FADED AS Shada and the others neared the edge of the park. Ever since they left the cabin, the woods had hidden the surrounding wall, but Shada could feel it waiting for them. She began glimpsing it through the trees.

She would have asked Jeric where they were going and what they would face there, but Adney's presence made the most innocent words feel like dangerous secrets. Even Delia, whose chattiness had not been dampened even when she witnessed brutal violence, kept her lips shut tight and only occasionally glanced back at Adney, who stalked them like a shadow.

Jeric, who knew the way, walked half a step in front of Shada. Their hands had become fused.

The trees soon cleared ahead to reveal the garden's wall in all its height and unbowed antiquity. Their path reappeared as they approached the forest edge, piecing itself together stone by stone. In the clearing, it met a circular brick floor that surrounded a wide pit.

The bricks were ornately carved and bore the remnants of a once festive variety of paints. The pit was guarded by handrails. She could not yet see its bottom. "What is it?" she asked.

"It was built by whatever king once ruled this place. I'm afraid he must have been quite cruel."

Her heart quickened. Before she could demand more information, they came close enough that she could see for herself what it was.

The pit was deep enough that a man standing inside could not touch its rim even if he jumped. The carvings on the brick continued all the way to the bottom, and the pit's floor was engraved with an army of amused, fierce, and hateful faces.

Several rusted metal loops protruded around from the rim of the pit. Their purpose came to her in grotesque clarity. The loops were meant to hold the chains of whoever was trapped at the bottom. She noticed round metal drains in the floor. Along the walls were alcoves, once blocked by gates now broken or missing, that could have held large animals.

Nor lay at the bottom.

His eyes were closed, and he was unbound. Shada managed not to scream when she saw him. Her first surge of fear receded when she saw him move a little. He was alive, thank the Goddess.

He was dressed in the same plain clothes everyone in the company wore. They looked like rags compared to the clothing she had worn the past couple of days. After what the Ronian company had been through, their clothes were probably rags by any standard.

"They're watching," Jeric whispered before she could speak.

"Why is... this man here?" she asked. The words jangled with multiple, very different inflections. She couldn't let Jeric, or anyone watching, know she knew Nor.

The monk's eyes opened, revealing their expansive whiteness. Jeric nodded as if all was well.

Blinking, Nor turned his head. As his blank eyes passed over Shada, she wanted to hide. She had missed him, of course, but she hadn't realized how much until right then.

She couldn't imagine what he would think, seeing her there, on the other side of the handrail.

She spoke to him, her voice fluttering. "Are you—"

Jeric grabbed her arm and said, "He cannot hear." His voice was soft and calm, but his fingers were a vise. "They will have given him chemicals. He won't be able to see, either. Still, be careful what you say and do."

"Why? What is this?"

Nor raised a hand to his face. His movements were halting, like he was learning how to use his body. He waved the hand in front of his eyes then appeared to accept his blindness with perfect ease. He laid his head back on the stone.

His face changed. Slowly it darkened, tightening and twisting. Before her eyes, it became a mask of agony.

Startled, she gasped. "What's wrong with him?"

Jeric shook his head. "Could be anything. It's sad, really. The medicines, they... take away pretense. Remove the inhibitions."

Shada gasped again. The look on Nor's face gripped her heart and tried to tear it from her chest. If only she could run to him and hold him—like a nursemaid, a mother, anything.

Then she noticed something: a thin chain was fastened to Nor's wrist. It led across the floor and disappeared into one of the drains. Nor did not seem aware of it.

"This is our wedding," Jeric told her.

"I don't understand." She swallowed. "I don't understand... Who is he?"

Jeric's face was grim. "A person who's been found unsuitable. They always find someone."

"What can we do for him?"

He looked at her oddly but accepted the question. "We will watch."

With his warning in mind, she tried to steady her voice. "Watch what? Watch a man suffer?"

He spoke to her with a mixture of sharpness and fear. "I'm surprised you cannot even bear a stranger's pain. How did you survive, growing up where you did?"

"I don't know," she said pleadingly.

Jeric was briefly lost in thought. He breathed heavily, regally. "Shada, what has upset you? Is it this man?"

"I think so, yes."

"There will be many more like this and worse. That will be true no matter how things go on Ronia." He turned to face her full on.

She felt Adney lurking somewhere behind her.

Jeric said, "I must ask you something. This is very important. Give me your hands, please."

She offered them, afraid of how his hands would feel, but he took her by the wrists. When he pressed down with his thumbs, she could hear and feel the thudding progress of her own blood.

He did not bother asking her to look into his eyes. He merely looked into hers, and she was transfixed, like a fowl by an arrow. "Don't look away," he commanded. Having imprisoned her thus, he went on. "Tell me this. Why do you care what happens to this man? If you lie, I will almost certainly know."

The angles were many, the unknowns deep. She fixed on one thing: if she admitted to knowing Nor, she would have to tell Jeric about the company, about everything. If he already knew, telling the truth might save her own skin, but the company would be doomed.

Nor moaned. It was not a sound of bodily pain but seemed to exist beyond the present moment. It was suffering, the memory of suffering, and a vision of the coming suffering of all the world.

She stammered, "I find your ways barbaric, that's all. He is no one to me."

Just by her ear, a voice like an ancient toad croaked, "Liar."

"Adney is right, Shada," Jeric said. He looked very sad.

Something in the pit shifted and clanked. She did not dare look.

Jeric's eyes were ciphers. "Adney told me this morning that a group of Ronians arrived in Om not long after you. We've been expecting one for some time. Adney believes you are part of that party. I told him that could not be. You said you came to Om alone, and I insisted to him that must be the truth. Then he told me that when that party left Ronia, it included a woman meeting your description, a woman with dark markings on her face."

For an instant, Shada's mind reeled, frantic to invent a story. But in the end, she had nothing to say.

Jeric bowed his head. "Shada."

"I had no choice."

"They waited to tell me. Maybe they really don't trust me anymore. Maybe they wanted to test your honesty. In either case..." He shook his head hopelessly.

Nor moaned again. The moan grew into a wail. She had never heard such naked suffering.

She said, "So they brought him here as a test."

"Yes. And you lied."

"Wouldn't you lie, to save people you cared about? Your daughters?"

"Yes. Yes, I would. But that's a weakness, Shada. These past few days have exposed it in me. No wonder I don't live up to my people's hopes."

She grew angry. "What do your people really want? Why do they care so much about one company of Ronians? About me?"

He looked at her stone-faced. "You know why."

She did. "The Lady."

He nodded.

Her mind reeled. "On Caidfell, a man attacked me. He tried to take the Lady. He was one of you, wasn't he?"

"Probably."

"But... your warriors saved us in the market on Ronia."

His eyes widened. "You knew that was us?"

"I saw one of your dead."

He pressed his lips together. "And you said nothing."

"But... why help us? Your people don't like gods. Why save an expedition going to find one?"

"We have our reasons. But things have changed now."

She shook her head. "You really are one of them, aren't you?"

"Why did you lie, Shada? Do you really adore the Lady so much? Has she made your life better?"

Shada wanted to cry. "She has power over me. She's gone now, but she'll come back."

"Then let's talk to her together. The Realm is powerful, Shada. The Lady knows it. If anyone can deal with her, it's us. Maybe we can free you from her."

Feeling tears on her face, Shada shook her head again. "No. It won't work. Whatever you think, she'll be the one making the decisions."

"If she's so deceitful, why were you hoping to bring her master, this Goddess, back to Ronia? What kind of world would you have then?"

Nor began to weep loudly.

That did it. Shada wept with him, despising her own weakness but unable to stop.

Warmth enveloped her hands. Jeric had taken them in his. "Let me try to free you. Be my queen."

Shada sniffed in disbelief. "You still want to marry me?"

"What we have is worth much to me, and I won't give up on it. I want the Realm to be more like you. But a price must be paid, a price in blood."

"What price?"

He looked at the pit, where the weeping was fading, then back at her.

Her blood froze. "No. What? I can't."

"Yes, you can. I believe in you. We'll do it together."

"Do what? Kill him?"

"No. We're going to give him what he wants."

More clattering reverberated from the pit, and she finally looked over. Nor had found the chain and was pulling on it. Some weight on the chain's end pulled it back into the drain whenever he released it. Still, he was gathering it in feeble bunches.

She shivered. "What does he want? What must I do?"

"Join me. Save yourself and me. Give Delia a mother. Give Ronia a queen. Get out from under the Lady's boot. And let this poor man make his own choices."

Nor reached the limit of the chain. The unseen weight on its end caught in the grate at the drain's opening, but he kept pulling.

"We must do just as I said," Jeric replied. "We will watch whatever happens here without interfering. Please, do this small thing."

Nor yanked hard on the chain, but it remained stuck. He used the chain to drag himself into a sitting position then pulled again, bending and shaking with effort. The grate covering the drain snapped from its place. The chain leapt from the hole. On its end was a knife, which sailed over to land close to Nor.

Shada realized what the weapon was for. She held still with great effort. "No! I will not watch this."

"He is paying the price for our past wrongs, Shada, for our lies, yours and mine. That is how pairings work among my people. They must begin in purity. This is why marriage will save us."

She thought of how pitiful Nor's moans had been. They were the sounds of a man in mourning for all things, the sounds of a man who would welcome death as a liberator. *And our marriage would help so many people.*

She could have slapped herself. She hadn't considered it, not really, but even weighing the decision was too much.

"No," she said again.

"You wish to save him?" Jeric's voice was heavy but unsurprised.

"Of course!" Seeing Nor had cast all of her and Jeric's words and deeds in a harsh, unforgiving glare.

"No matter the cost?" Jeric's words fell like boulders. He seemed to not entirely believe it. More than that, he was afraid.

"Yes."

"I cannot leave it at that," he said, running a tense hand through his hair. "I must be sure you understand. Unless we go through with this, you and I won't be redeemed in the eyes of the Realm. I don't know what they will do with us. Delia will go to a new father. And without you there to represent your people's interests when they are invaded, it will likely go badly for them. They will be... reclassified."

"You will conquer us either way."

"That's not true!" His eyes blazed. "You think the Ronians are conquerors? You don't know what a real conquest is yet. This is not a game, Shada. These are lives. Your friends', your fathers', and those of your city. Believe it or not, I understand that."

Shada was speechless. The choice was a precipice, and she was poised on its edge, which burned like a knife. Underneath yawned twin abysses of mass, intolerable suffering. And the choice remained terribly free. No larger imperative would force her hand. The results would be her doing, forever.

It was both a choice and no choice at all.

She moaned and said, "Bring me Nor."

Jeric stared. "You would give up our lives? The futures of two peoples?" Hot anger replaced his sadness.

"Your new world will be a lie. You say your people abhor lies, but you are made of them—lies on top of lies… and murder. Release me and Nor if you can. We will go and share our company's fate."

Jeric dipped his head. His rage had passed in a flash, and his expression was numb. He looked over her shoulder at Adney.

Before he could speak, she blurted, "Come with us!"

He squinted. "What?"

"Escape. Bring your daughters and your wife."

"I know you mean that sincerely. But I would never do it. I have no right to subject my—Oliva—or my daughters to anything of the kind."

"Subject them? You will give them life, real life, at least for a little while."

"They are alive now, you fool!" he cried. Again, he calmed himself quickly. "You don't understand the fate of those who refuse this offer. Any life my daughters might live is better than that."

With a jolt of terror, Shada realized she had forgotten about Nor. Whirling, she cursed in relief when she saw he was still alive, and again in panic when she saw that he was searching around himself, pawing the ground for the prize at the end of the chain.

"Putting that aside," Jeric was saying, "I don't want to leave. The Realm is my mother, and I love it. Someday, whatever you feel now, you will too."

"I'm sorry you think so," Shada replied. "But I'm leaving, as you promised I could. And I'm taking Nor with me."

"I can free Nor. But not you. You and I have been claimed by the Realm."

Shada sighed and nodded.

"As for Nor, we may remove him from the pit, but I cannot give him to you. I've made no promise regarding him. Likely, he will be the first victim of your rebellion—the first to be awakened. Eventually, he will be grateful you saved his life, but it may not be for a long time."

"There has to be something." To her, it was a simple fact. "I must buy his freedom somehow."

"No. Believe it or not, I have no ill will toward him. I would free him outright if the choice was mine—"

"Bloody hell, it is yours!"

He shook his head as if despairing of making her see sense.

"I know!" Seeing that her outburst had startled him, she rushed to explain. "I know something I can give the Shining Realm for my freedom and his. I will be your agent."

His face was blank. Shada looked at him, into his piercing eyes, and lied with every fiber of her being.

"I'll be an agent of the Shining Realm within the Ronian company. I'll betray my Goddess for you. And the Lady. I can talk to the company—"

"It's too late," he interrupted. "Your company, it seems, has already chosen to fight. They will not last the day."

The thought of Nor killing himself scared Shada like she'd never been scared. She could think only of stopping him. To do that, she would lie until she had no soul left. *I won't betray the Goddess, Jeric. I'll betray you.*

She said, "Give me a chance to change their minds. I am the caretaker, the voice of the Lady. I can convince them that Huire wants them to surrender. Or better, that she's abandoned them totally. I can break their will to fight."

Nor had found the knife. As he touched its cutting edge, a peace came over his face. He lay back with it against his chest. He might kill himself at any second. Whatever poison they'd given him would surely make it easier.

Jeric looked at her for an unguessable time. She bounced on her heels, wanting to shake him by the jacket but afraid of shattering the dream in which he was considering her offer.

At last, he said, "If Nor is allowed to leave, you must go separately. To do otherwise would be too much insolence for even me to manage. Nor will go back where my people found him."

"Where is that?" she breathed.

"I don't have the murkiest idea."

She didn't know what it all meant, but she saw little choice. "Yes! Yes, I agree."

"But I don't yet." He reached toward her with both arms. She realized he was asking for her wrists again. "Though I don't think you are lying," he said in completion of something unspoken. "You're not good at that."

"That's a compliment, Jeric. But you know that, of course."

Adney appeared from the edge of sight and slipped in front of her with such speed that she stepped back. Shouldering Jeric aside, he lunged and snatched Shada's hands, which were suddenly and painfully encased in stone. The scarring on his skin extended even to his palms and fingers.

Nor was taking rapid, desperate breaths, preparing himself.

"Jeric, stop Nor!" she cried.

Jeric looked as if he was trying, and failing, to empty himself of all feeling. "Do what Adney wants."

Adney filled her eyes and squeezed harder than Jeric had. How could he feel anything under all his dead skin?

"Look," Adney gargled.

She aimed her eyes at his and felt a trickle of relief. Despite the rest of him, his eyes were like any other man's. Illegible and rarely blinking, they were nonetheless an oasis.

He said, "You will destroy your company from within. Yes?"

She looked dead at him. "Yes."

He stared at her for a time then let go, but he didn't take his eyes off her.

"Save Nor!" she cried to Jeric.

Jeric nodded heavily and turned toward the pit.

Shada looked once more into Adney's eyes, thinking of what she had just sworn to do and what might happen to Jeric when she failed. She shuddered. She had assumed Adney's appearance was the work of some god—that, somewhere out there, an entire people looked like him. That had been a baseless thought. Perhaps someone human had made him who he was.

She heard again Jeric's words: *"I only know what they're like when they come back."*

52

ROBIR

IF THE ROAR OF the mechanical carriage tearing through the streets had not awakened the entire city, Robir was sure the light of their many stolen lanterns would. No one in the carriage except for Ilis knew how to douse the glow of the lanterns or ignite them again, so the carriage's open top shone in the night like a firefly. Robir did not ask Ilis how to operate them because he was embarrassed he had not figured it out.

When they reached the temple and saw its black shape hanging over them, Robir felt a sting of longing for home. For an instant, he fell for the Realm's trick, though he had known it was coming. His hatred was all the darker for it.

"How dare you?" he said softly to Ilis, whom they had forced to drive the carriage.

She didn't answer. The ease and charm she had previously radiated had vanished. He could understand why, given her current predicament, but still he wondered whether anything the people of the Realm said or did amounted to anything but manipulation.

He let her be silent—he preferred it. They swung around to the front of the temple, and the men leapt out as Ilis stopped the carriage. Most of the mutineers had come along, piling into the single available vehicle.

In their hurried search of the pyramid, they captured Lieutenant Roark but were unable to find the captain or, exasperatingly, the bishop. With Emberly still on the loose, the success of their mutiny could be instantly un-done. Had it not been for the bishop's hissed insistence during their previous meeting, Robir might have put off attacking the temple until that detail was sorted. But with the Realm's forces likely to arrive soon, he had made the harried decision to carry out the bishop's command. In doing so, he abandoned the pyramid to the soldiers still loyal to Emberly.

The mutineers who hadn't fit into the carriage, Hulgar among them, were waiting at the archway in the wall out-side the pyramid. With them was the frenzied Roark, who had become so dangerous that Robir considered shooting him.

Robir ordered the men to hold that position and keep the way clear for the carriage's return. He had no idea what else to do with them as they were too few to stay in the pyramid and control the rest of the company. They were in a terrible spot, vulnerable to capture by the Ronians within or the Shining Realm without and with only Roark as a hostage.

But Robir had limited worry to parcel out. Looking up at the temple, he wondered if the lack of visible guards meant something else, maybe worse, was watching over the place.

Merin had assumed guardianship of Ilis, taking a greater interest in her comfort than the others. As the men exited the carriage, he opened the door for her, an oddly placed bit of gallantry.

Robir led the way up the steps. The doors were unlocked. The interior was night within night, and his lantern hardly blemished the darkness. He had expected, if the temple was unguarded, that they would have to round up and drive out vagrants before demolishing the building. The creeping, tarry silence gave him pause.

"Everyone inside. Let's light up the place."

The men entered as he waited by the door. The diverging circles of their light hinted at the size of the space. Finally came Ilis, with Merin at her back.

She stopped without warning at the threshold. Her hands sprang out in either direction as if to brace her body against entering. They didn't quite reach the doorframe, though, before she calmed herself and dropped them. "Are you going to kill me?" she asked steadily.

Robir thought he saw Merin trying to catch his eye, but he paid no attention. "Don't know yet."

Her chest shuddered as she breathed. "Do what you will, I suppose. You have already lost. You are already forgotten."

"It's not about winning, love," Robir replied. At last, he met Merin's gaze, and the other man reluctantly pushed Ilis ahead.

The light of the men's lanterns brushed the temple's altar. Robir was anxious and irritated to see that the soldiers had not removed their shoes before walking on the temple's far-reaching prayer rug. That was an old-fashioned concern, ridiculous under the circumstances. The Goddess would care nothing for this anathema of a temple. Still, the feelings lingered.

They had brought some of the company's gunpowder supply, but Robir didn't know if they had enough to topple the building. The supply was not abundant, and the mutineers had wordlessly decided not to leave the company defenseless against the Shining Realm. Iwan had broken his silence to urge them to bring more, but the others lacked the heart to obey.

The more Robir looked at the temple, the more his doubts grew. The gunpowder flask at his side, even combined with those of his men, felt insignificant pitted against this immensity.

Though he could not yet see the carved hand above the altar, Robir sensed something else about the temple that marred its familiarity. It was the smell. The air in most Ronian temples was touched by the scents of humanity, sour and salty. Here was only cold rock and the tang of recently cut timber.

Yes, it was all wrong. He did not know why he had taken so long to notice. Then he saw the hand, and the perversion was complete.

It was very faint. Seen from the door, even in the light of day, it would look like a mere stain or imperfection in the stone. Had Robir not known what to look for, he might have missed it completely.

"The bishop was right," he told the others. *Who but the old man could have not only noticed it but realized its implications?* Robir marveled at the gall of the Shining Realm. *Do they have any notion, in scorning the gods, what forces of the night they are toying with?*

Someone hissed, and he noticed a motion an instant later. A lump of something darker than the shadows themselves had been waiting just before the altar. It was right in front of them but had somehow seemed a natural part of the scene, so no one had noticed it.

It was too small to be human, he thought at first, but as it rose, it spread. It unfolded like a nightmare, ascending to the size of a tall, shrouded man. All things seemed possible, and Robir's heart quaked at what they might have disturbed.

"Who are you?" he shouted with transparent dread. "What are you doing here?"

A hood was cast back, and he saw the thing's face. His breath stopped, and his horror was not eased. That face had transformed since he had seen it last, losing color and life. Its owner looked bent and old, eyes shining and dead in the lantern light.

"Brother Nor?" Robir asked the demon.

53

NOR

As HIS SIGHT AND hearing began to return, Nor had decided he was grateful for the Shining Realm's potions. The rage and hate they unleashed had been inside him all along, waiting for the right key to turn in their lock. Now they were free, which meant Nor was free too.

By the time his captors left him beside the temple's altar, he felt like a new man. Despair washed over him, and rather than suppressing it as he had so long done, he reveled in it. He enjoyed its taste. He perched by the altar like a bat, seething inside, waiting for a reason to move.

That reason came when the Ronian soldiers arrived. Standing to look over them, he hated them almost as much as he hated himself. He did not dare look closely at any of them for fear that he would want to tear them apart. A smile crept onto his face.

"Brother Nor," Robir repeated. "We thought they'd taken you. Have you been here all along?"

Ignoring the moronic question, Nor thought of how he and Robir had suffered the wraiths' torture on Caidfell. The moment, for all its torment, had also brought a sense of camaraderie. Nor marveled how he could have felt that for such a man, a man who worked for and was paid by an empire as evil as the Shining Realm, but less honest.

Then the monk's eyes fell on something over Robir's shoulder. It was the Realmswoman, Ilis.

Her face was stricken but hard. Nor stared unabashedly, feeling admiration for one who manipulated others and survived so ably. If anyone lived through the coming fight, it would be Ilis.

Robir had followed his gaze. "You've only been gone a couple of days, Brother Nor. Have you forgotten what a woman looks like?" He tried to laugh at his own joke but failed.

No one else laughed, either.

He added, "Well, you're safe for the moment." When Nor again did not deign to answer, the soldier's patience vanished. He snapped at Merin, "Take Ilis back to the door and watch her."

With that distraction removed, he stepped close to the monk and spoke directly to his face. "Brother Nor," he said slowly, "What did they do to you?"

"Never mind that," Nor said, his voice thick from lack of use. He coughed. "Let's go."

Looking relieved to have opened negotiations, Robir shook his head. "We can't leave yet. First, we've got to destroy this monstrosity." He pointed above the altar, where the Shining Realm had carved a massive hand in the Goddess's place.

Nor stared at him then at the hand. "That?" Something in him couldn't believe it—couldn't imagine it.

"Of course," Robir said uneasily. "You see what they did."

Nor spun to face him. The medicine made him feel drunk. His movements were lank and careless. "I do," he said and thought for a moment. "And I rather like it."

The men's eyes widened. Robir looked grave, as if wondering about the monk's sanity. Nor knew he'd never been saner. The Realm had stripped away all the lies and left him with what remained.

The private proceeded. "We've got enough explosives to destroy this temple, we hope. But most of all, we've got to be sure that hand is gone."

Nor sneered. "It'll never work."

Robir scoffed. "Seen a lot of explosions in your time, Brother?"

"They're not like us." The monk smirked. He must speak as if to simpletons. "The Shining Realm. The things they build are different. In fact"—he laughed—"I think they knew you would try this."

Robir's lip curled. "Goddess. What did they do to you?"

"Too much to say. They are animals," Nor admitted. "But still, they are more than that. You can't bring down this temple." He pointed at the ceiling. "It has steel bones. It's how they forge the innards of their buildings."

Robir exchanged glances with the others. Despite his defiance, he paled a little. "Is that true? How do you know?"

Nor didn't bother with the first question. Pondering the second, his smile split into a grin. "I'm not sure." Though Ren must have told him, he couldn't remember when. He wondered if she had taught him other things, scattering information in the corners of his mind for him to stumble over. "You could detonate all your powder and not bring this place down. If it's not magic, it might as well be."

Robir clearly believed him. His face darkened as fear gave way to determination. "You may be right," he told Nor gamely. "But we will destroy that hand. We have enough to blast a part of one wall."

His persistent hopefulness annoyed Nor, who asked, "Are you sure about that?"

"Are you doubting yourself, Brother Nor?"

Nor laughed. It was a villainous cackle, reveling in darkness. "Not anymore. But why aren't you? Why so—"

"No more," Robir cut in. He unslung the flask from his shoulder. "No one needs to hear this."

"You're wrong," Nor replied. "Instead of knocking down that wall, you'd be better off praying to it."

Several men cried out.

Robir's hands formed fists. "You watch yourself."

"I'm serious." Nor looked up again at the hand and had an idea. The idea scared him, but in that fear, he found a wicked, poisonous delight. "I'll show you." Facing the wall, he took to his knees.

Robir must have realized what he was doing. Behind Nor, the private spoke, his voice tight. "I'll kill you."

Nor crossed his arms and bent a little, toward a position of full supplication. As he did, he thought of the Goddess. *Take this, you old bitch.*

The private's voice grew tight. "I mean it."

The others muttered. Killing a holy man was no small thing.

As if to drown out their doubts and his own, Robir shouted, "I'll shoot you in the back!"

Nor stopped short of a complete bow. He stared at the stone floor, tears forming in his eyes. He wondered why. He didn't fear death anymore, at least not enough to let that stop him. After what he had learned, after the things Cadmon had said, part of him would welcome death. But he felt unable to touch his forehead to the ground and complete the pose of worship.

He sat up and stared at the hand on the wall. He felt nothing for it. He had only wanted to pray to it to defy Huire and upset the soldiers. It should mean nothing. But for some reason, even in his drugged, inebriated state, he couldn't quite bring himself to worship... *that*.

As he waited there on his knees, the soldiers shouted. One told another to grab the monk.

"Stay back!" Robir yelled, angrier than he'd yet sounded. Then he said to Nor, "Monk, the sight of you before a heathen altar makes me sick. You've no loyalty to Ronia, but I thought you at least had it to Huire. I'll count to five, and if you're not standing under your own power by then, you'll be dead."

Robir counted, slowly but steadily. For an instant, Nor saw himself through the other's eyes: pathetic, broken, perhaps insane. In that instant, he hated himself more than he had ever hated anything. He wanted to shrivel up and crumble like dry leaves. He wanted to disappear.

"Five," Robir said.

Nor scrambled.

The private fired a second late. The room erupted with sound as Nor scurried, unhurt, into the shadows to one side of the altar. Dizzy from the medicine, he raced along one darkened wall, heading for the doors, managing not to fall.

Behind him, someone cried, "Where'd he go?"

"He's out of his mind!" Robir said. "We'll deal with him in a minute. Let's get the powder ready."

Nor reached the doors to find Merin and Ilis blocking his way. He struck Merin on the chin. The private fell with a wail, and Nor raced past him, leaving Ilis in his wake. Seconds later, he heard a commotion behind himself as the soldiers reached Merin.

"Find them!" Robir screamed, panic in this voice. Ilis must have run also. Belatedly, Nor realized that Ilis was their guide—they probably couldn't find their way back to the pyramid without her.

He had wanted to disappear, to run away and hide from the Ronians, but he hadn't meant to strand them.

As he stumbled through the archway leading from the temple's enclosure into the city, the knowledge of what he had done burned into his mind next to every other thing he had thought and done since the letter had ended his world.

He felt many things at once, none of which fit together: shame and rage, hate and self-loathing. He wanted it all to stop. He wanted to feel nothing. If only whoever gave him that knife earlier had let him finish.

The soldiers caught him before he found another way to escape the pain of being alive. He was slow and stumbling, and they tackled him to the ground, seized him by the arms, and hauled him up. He didn't bother struggling.

They returned to the temple courtyard. As they reached the carriage, Robir burst through the temple doors. "Explosion's coming! Everyone in. We've got to go!"

Once they piled into the intolerably crowded carriage, Robir cursed. "Where's the girl?"

"She got away."

From the back seat, Nor saw Robir put his hands on his face.

"She's the only one who can drive this cursed thing," Robir said.

A moment of quiet, collective despair passed over them as seconds ticked away. Nor briefly felt less alone.

Then Robir recovered. He turned to Nor. "You, traitor!" he spat. "You know the lore of machines."

Nor shook his head. "There isn't a machine like this in all of Ronia."

Robir jumped out of the vehicle, hauling Nor with him. He shoved the monk toward the front of the car. "If you want to live, you'll start this beast now!"

For a moment, Nor pulled his mind from the storm in which it was trapped. He might not have cared what happened to himself, but he could help these men a little. He circled the carriage. With the ease of a man who knew he was guessing, he pulled a knob near one of the front wheels.

"Next, she turned something in front," Merin said.

Nor knelt there, found some moving part, and twisted it. He called to Robir in the driver's seat, "Turn the key in front of you."

Robir did. The carriage gave no sign of life.

"We've got to run," the soldier breathed, desperate.

"Wait!" Merin was squeezed in next to Robir. He pulled roughly on each of a few levers by the wheel.

"Thank Huire for how you stared at that woman," Robir said.

Nor remembered the final step at the same time as the others. When Robir cried, "Turn it again!" Nor was already doing so.

The carriage rumbled gloriously. A storm of shouting arose as Nor jumped in. Robir pushed the pedals by his feet. With a lurch, they were in motion, but the carriage still crawled along. Robir stomped the pedal to no avail. Then Merin pushed a lever, and the carriage tore ahead.

In the temple, the explosion came, a bang followed by a dying rumble. They roared from the gate as if carried on the wave of the blast. They would never know if they had accomplished their mission.

Making one familiar-seeming turn after another, they tried to retrace their route. They became lost almost as soon as they started.

After a few hopeless guesses, Robir halted the car in an empty square of closed-up shops. Then he turned toward Nor and hit him.

He threw himself upon the monk. The others piled on, some cheering while some tried to separate them. He called Nor every name he could think of. Finally, he thrust away the arms trying to restrain him and staggered out of the carriage. "...sold us out!" he was shouting. "You're not a Ronian anymore, if you ever were."

Nor felt barely worse than he had before the beating. He looked up to where, on a normal planet, the sky ought to be. Far away, a moon shone through one of Om's vast windows, lighting the men's faces and leeching their color.

During a pause in Robir's tirade, Nor said, "I met Ilis, you know. The Realm's people come a lot worse than her. She might even escape from them now."

"We needed her to get back, idiot!" Robir howled. "You've doomed us all. Who knows what they'll do when they catch us?"

"I know a little."

"They got to you, did they? A savage like you, it couldn't have been hard. You've always hated Ronia. Well, now, you've got what you want."

"No," Lieutenant Iwan said. He had stepped a short distance away, toward the center of the square. "Look."

They looked where the lieutenant was pointing. In the distance was a vertical column of light, sharp but far enough away to be thin as twine. It was the beam emitted by the pyramid.

54

EMBERLY

IN THE STILL AIR and quiet of the underground tomb, Emberly thought he could hear ancient dust, newly disturbed by their footsteps, settling to the floor.

He asked Ganet, "Are you offering to let us escape this city?"

The general's smile was elfin. "Yes, Cyril. I would give you a chance, at least."

Emberly thought hard. Then he closed his eyes. "Why? Why would you help us, and why now?"

"I'll get to that. Do you accept?"

"No. Assuming we believed you—and we'd be fools to—we have friends here whom we cannot leave without."

"Shada and Nor, yes," Ganet said with a brisk nod. "I can help you find them too. But are you sure that's what you want? The bishop just told me to do what I wished with them."

"It's not just them we're looking for," Arumin said, eyeing the captain.

"Do you mean the Lady?"

"Yes."

"If she has remained with Shada, I might lead you to them both. It could be the death of us, but so could any other course."

"We must leave now, then!" the bishop cried.

The captain breathed deeply. The mere possibility that Ganet was telling the truth tempted him to leap on the man's offer. They could have everything—their missing people, the Lady, and escape. They might even help Ronia against the Shining Realm, for finding the Goddess and gaining her assistance in the war was the only way Emberly could imagine that conflict ending well for Ronia.

But Ganet's state of mind bothered Emberly. The general was being evasive and eerily playful. Perhaps the wreck of the carriage and the attack of the mob had broken his nerves. If so, he might be lying or deluded.

Mind racing, the captain asked, "How can we trust you?"

Ganet peered up at them. "It's simple. Why do you trust your Lady?"

"Faith," the bishop said without hesitation. "At the very bottom, that is why."

"You admit that?"

"I consider it no admission."

"It's more than that, Ganet," Emberly said. "When she came, she knew everything about us and about our Goddess."

"She could have learned those things some other way. What makes you believe so strongly in Huire?"

Arumin's voice rumbled. "Because we know our history."

Ganet nodded. "She existed once, of course. But why do you believe she will return?"

"Faith," Arumin said again.

The general's eyes shifted between them. "There is something I must tell you. It's only fair. When the Realm came to Om, we heard a story. Not long before we arrived, a strange man came to this city. A giant of a man, covered with hair. He had a long snout and fangs. A monster, to hear them tell it.

"He was only passing through, but he was not to be forgotten. Though he was mute, he carried a box that spoke for him. No one understood its language, but they remembered a single word that it said again and again: Ronia.

"The story was strange, but it would have remained a curiosity had not that very man—or one just like him—arrived on Ronia shortly after. We knew at once that the story of the Lady, as the Temple told it, was true. We tried to take her, but she fought back."

The bishop said, "You wanted to destroy her."

"Later, perhaps. First, we wanted to learn about her. And what we learned was that we could not take her by force without destroying her."

Emberly flinched at the word "destroying." *They could destroy the Lady?* A terrifying thought, but when dealing with the Shining Realm, one couldn't dismiss such things out of hand.

Ganet continued, "We would have to win her cooperation by winning Ronia's. So we began preparations on this world, knowing you would return. Here, we would have a few of you alone, and we would make you see sense. We were in a terrible rush to build the temple. But our people in your government delayed the company's departure for as long as they could, and by the time you arrived, we were ready."

Emberly leaned toward him and spoke carefully. "Why now? If you were willing to help us escape, why didn't you mention it before?"

"Things have changed since I saw you last. I wanted to know where you both stood."

"You mean you wanted to know if we could be bought."

"All that I've told you is true." Ganet tilted his head in puzzlement. "Are you sure you won't stay? You've seen so little. Here, on the dusty fringes of civilization, I couldn't give you a proper welcome. If you saw the splendor of the very center—the Shining Realm's home planets—you would understand my regret."

Emberly refused to be led astray. "How would we escape if you let us? How would we find Nor and Shada?"

"As for the second question, I would try. As for the first, I won't say yet."

Emberly's lip twisted in frustration. "What's to stop us from beating it out of you?"

"Only yourself, Cyril. We need that in the Realm."

The captain scoffed. "This is a game. That's all your Shining Realm is: games."

"That's not true at all. We are becoming a perfect system. Each of us, you and I, a cell in the body of an entity spanning the cosmos."

Emberly steeled himself. Ganet's offer of escape had, against his will, kindled a hope of survival in him, but the man might be toying with them. If he was really willing to betray the Shining Realm, something must have been in it for him. "What do you want?"

"You know what I want. Peace. And happiness."

"Well, you've failed."

"If you won't accept my offer, it seems I have. Now, things will be immensely worse for everyone. You will die or be awakened. Your people will suffer. All of you, betrayed by the Lady."

Arumin spat. "Betrayed. Nonsense."

"Didn't you listen to my story? You thought the caretaker killed all of the attackers in the temple that night. But our people saw the aftermath too, and it wasn't true. The Lady herself killed two of them. Their heads were pierced, the wounds impossibly thin and straight. No man could've done it in a fight."

"We knew that already," Arumin said. "My man saw it happen. And I don't blame the Lady a bit. She was in danger."

"But she wasn't in danger when she killed the caretaker."

The bishop stared. "He died of his wounds."

"He survived his wounds. He died because, later, he stopped breathing. No one knew why. Or did they?"

Arumin turned toward the captain. "There's no use listening to this man."

Ganet slapped his palms on the floor. "Please, you must trust me! A Realmsman will tell you the truth though he may take a roundabout path. The truth is that your Lady murdered her own caretaker, a man who had carried her across the universe."

"Why would she do that?" asked Emberly.

Shaking his head sadly, Ganet said, "Because she was finished with him, of course. He was used up, and the Lady had found Shada to take his place. Sooner or later, she will do the same to Shada."

Emberly replied, "I cannot accept that."

"Facts are indifferent to belief. No doubt the giant obeyed the Lady all along because she convinced him that his soul hung in the balance. And now, she's convinced you of the same. So tell me again: where is it that she has promised to lead you?"

Arumin had fallen into a threatening, potentially explosive silence.

Emberly calmly said, "We do not believe you. The bishop is right—you are a liar, Ganet, and I don't care how grave an insult that is."

"Tell me, Bishop, does your Goddess ever come to you in dreams?" The general spoke amiably, as if this were just another turn in the conversation.

Emberly thought he might beat Ganet after all. The man's story was too much to think about, its implications too severe to deal with just now, so he simply dismissed it.

His job now was to pry the information he needed from this madman somehow.

The bishop's face was red. He said quietly, "No."

"My people believe that every dream contains meaning if we have the wisdom to find it. They are not visions from beyond but from within, fragments of the great unconscious. I had a dream last night, but I lack the wisdom to understand it.

"I woke in the night and saw a shadow at the end of my bed. The room was dark, but I felt a presence in the very air, like a low noise. When I touched the light by the bed, I could see that she—my visitor—was quite impossibly beautiful. Wondering how I could see her so plainly, I realized that she herself had begun to glow.

"I knew this was unlike other dreams. She seemed to come closer, though she did not move. Finally, I greeted her and asked who she was. She smiled, but when she heard my question, she seemed to grow sad. She shrank a little into the shadows.

"She was disappointed with me. It clawed at my heart. I only hoped that she would not leave me. I knew who she was—I had merely been scared to admit it. I said, 'Thank you for coming.'

"If my words were adequate, friends...! I can only tell you in the poorest terms who she was. Only a few of my people have seen her like before. She—or he, it doesn't matter—was all of us. She was what we will be. She was the Shining Realm! She was humanity! For the two are the same, though many don't yet know it."

Arumin interrupted. "And you say you have no gods! I've heard mystics from the wilderness whose visions made more sense."

Ganet looked like he'd been slapped, hurt to learn that someone could have heard his words so differently than he did. "Don't let my enthusiasm mislead you. What I've said is entirely reasonable. As humans join together in ever greater numbers, as we find newer and better ways of connecting, how can we fail to create a unified whole? A being capable, with the resources at its disposal, of greater feats than any of us could hope for on our own? Who is to say that such a superbeing, having conquered space, would not discover the secret of journeying across time? There, in my bed, I was perhaps a witness to the very end of all things."

"You had a dream, Ganet," Arumin said.

"What happened next?" Emberly asked, anxious to rein in the general's delirium.

"I cannot convince you of what I experienced, so I will not try. It is something I have long wanted, and perhaps my wanting got the better of me. In any case, she accepted my thanks. Her glow returned, and she asked if I knew why she had come. I admitted that I did not, but thankfully, this did not upset her. She told me that though I had acted faithfully in all of this, the Shining Realm had made a grave error.

"'You must let the Ronians leave,' she said. I was aghast. I still am. I told her, 'But we have long planned for this. We did it all for you.'

"'You have been wrong,' she said, 'terribly wrong.' Then she moved closer, around the side of my bed, and her manner changed. Despite her grim news, her smile remained, and her eyes grew wide. If she were someone else—if the thought were thinkable—she would have seemed seductive. How could such a notion occur to me? Was something wrong that I could not see?

"She said, 'It will go badly for you if you imprison them. Greater forces yet are poised against the Shining Realm.' I replied, 'But you *are* the Realm. Who can be greater than you?'

"She paused there. It was a strange question, I admit. Then she went on: 'None, child. But I am yet to be.' I couldn't help replying: 'But you are here now. That proves that, whatever I do, you will be born one day. Lend us your strength!'

"Then she changed again. It was so fast I barely saw it happen. Her face became red, and the color spread to the rest of her. Her mouth, even her eyelids, quivered. 'You have no idea what I've already done,' she said. 'If you fail me, you will have no part in the world that is coming.'

"She was at my side now, leaning over me like a nurse. I needn't tell you how scared I was. Her mouth hung open, full of jagged, ruined teeth. 'You will free the Ronians. Promise it.'"

Ganet paused and turned his plaintive face to Emberly. "I have never failed like I did then. I did just what she said, giving my word that I would release you and your people. Looking back, I don't know what she really was. The closer she got, the more I doubted her. Her face didn't seem real—close up, it lacked something. Detail, perhaps. But I surrendered because I was afraid. I could feel those teeth ripping into me. Where is the dignity in that?"

He sighed. "She told me she would know if I broke my word, and she vanished. Angry, and half convinced it had been a dream, I came here to convince you to stay. Maybe, if I tried one last time, you would join the Realm of your own will. I saw it as a way around my promise. Childishness."

Emberly's mind had begun to sprint along as the general was telling his story. He spoke cautiously, afraid his heartbeat might be audible in his voice. "And what do you think of your dream now?"

"Why does that matter if you think it was a fantasy?"

Arumin hissed. "Don't be a fool. You know exactly why. We want to find the Lady and escape this city, and your own goddess—or so you say—has commanded you to help us."

"She is not a goddess. Please don't use that word."

Emberly cut in. "But will you obey her?" He fervently hoped that the Lady had been Ganet's mysterious visitor, but he did not trust that hope. The thought that she had been watching over them was too enchanting to rely on. He wished he could listen to Arumin's thoughts.

"I don't know," Ganet replied, his face stark. "May she forgive me if I am wrong, but a man of rational mind cannot believe in visions blindly, especially when a being like the Lady is nearby."

On his first attempt to answer, Emberly gulped instead of speaking. Then he said, "The Lady mostly appears as an old woman."

"But she could assume other forms," said Ganet.

"I suppose."

"If I obey, I may inadvertently do the bidding of a treacherous messenger and her irrelevant goddess. In either case, if my choice is wrong, I could cause untold harm." The general laughed at himself. "There are no answers. What can a mere person do?"

The bishop said, "I'll tell you. You will release us. If the Realm's beliefs are true, the dream was from your goddess, and you should obey. Otherwise, the dream was from Huire, and you've seen that she is dangerous. No matter what, you should obey."

"Or maybe, as you insisted, Bishop, it was a fantasy, the creation of a man clinging to a false hope, who knows he should let it go."

Emberly crouched to look into the general's eyes. "What is your plan for our escape? How can we find Shada and Nor?" If the plan was implausible or a sham, they need not listen to any more.

Ganet still spoke to Arumin. "You were right. If I told my people what I saw—especially if I told Ren—I know what they would think of me. I was the only one to see it. Why did she not appear to many of us at once? Why only to one man in bed, when his memory is least to be trusted?"

His mouth hung open around a partly formed word. Finally, he said, "No, I cannot help you escape. The Shining Realm's will is my own, and it has been from the moment of my birth."

"Listen to me," the bishop snapped. He looked like he might grab the general by the throat. "Someone has spoken to me as well. When you asked to speak to Emberly and me, a voice told me to listen to you. Why was that? What would it be, if not that you should release us?"

"I don't know. Perhaps you are as imaginative as me. I only know that whatever I do, the superbeing will live. That, I believe."

The bishop replied, "You know, don't you, that you are alone and unarmed?

"So I am." Ganet reclined a little. "But I would not recommend trying to detain me. I may not look it, but I am quite capable of defending myself."

"You could fight us," Arumin replied. "But even if you survived it, you would live from then on as a man who broke his word."

The general shrank, curling his shoulders inward, which made him look older. "Broke my word to a phantasm, perhaps."

"Will you take that chance?"

Some agitation had inflicted itself on Emberly's mind from without. In his worry over the general, he had not noticed it until right then. A voice was calling, somewhere in the maze of hallways outside the room. He went to the door and listened.

Hearing the voice's urgency and discerning his own name, he called out to it. The voice stopped, and Emberly shouted again. Soon, one of Emberly's men surged from the darkness.

"You found as deep a hole as you could in this dungeon, sir," the soldier said breathlessly. "But thank the Goddess you weren't closer by."

"What happened?" Emberly demanded.

Then he, Arumin, and Ganet heard the story of Robir's mutiny, such as this man knew it. The soldier spoke with understandable confusion, and a few times, Emberly snapped at him to get on with it. As the captain listened, he felt his blood draining out through his toes.

When the man finished, Emberly did not explode in fury as he might have expected of himself. He only muttered a single black curse, putting into it everything he felt. Then he told the soldier to wait a moment, and they would return to the main level together.

He turned toward Ganet. A certain time was quickly approaching.

Forcing himself to think a little beyond the present, he told the general, "When your army comes, you will order them off."

Ganet replied, "I am incapable of that. I have no value as a hostage, either."

"I thought you were their commander."

"Well, these things only go so far."

"Does she know you're here?" Emberly asked.

The general gave him a smile drained of life. "Ren? Not yet, though she is suspicious of my loyalty."

A sudden lump in Emberly's chest made speaking difficult. The time had come. "If you don't help us... Do you know what I am going to do to you?"

"There will be no need for that." Ganet had sagged so that even his bones seemed to bend. "I will do what you ask."

The captain gaped. He wanted to ask what had changed the general's mind, but he did not want to burst this miraculous bubble.

Nonetheless, Ganet answered the question. He finally replied to Arumin, "I cannot and will not take the chance." He rapped his knuckles on the wall nearby, producing a hollow sound.

55

ORUND

For Sergeant Orund, the years of his life leading to the current day seemed obscure. They were memories, and memories couldn't be trusted. What he could trust was the breathtaking truth of the past hours.

He had always known this moment, or one like it, might come. But he hadn't thought much about how it would feel, which was just as well. He realized that nothing would've prepared him. The world closed and bent around a person, and if he didn't bend to meet it, it would simply break his bones.

He had supposed that, when this moment came, he would fight. Everyone died one way or another, and he had faced death before.

So he was stunned to find himself easily obeying the mutineers' commands word for word. When they announced themselves, several had weapons ready, and the rest had armed themselves with sensible haste.

Had he ordered the loyal men to fight, some would have died, and he was sure enough he would've been among them. And so, facing Robir and Hulgar, he had asked himself, *Now? Like this?*

He had known the answer as surely as if Huire had whispered it to him. Sergeant Feng had followed his lead, and the two of them had watched, now at gunpoint, the capture of Lieutenant Roark and the increasingly frantic search for the captain and the bishop. Once the captain was taken, that would be that. Orund suspected the bishop would be perfectly happy with the change in leadership.

Things soon fell apart. With time short and the captain still missing, Robir had left to attack the temple. Unwilling to leave a handful of his men to stand guard over the whole company, he had taken them all with him, sacrificing his dreams of command to destroy—*What was it? Some kind of unholy statue?*

After they left, Orund had armed and readied the remainder. The mutineers would likely never return from their foolhardy errand, but if they did, the company would be ready. He had sent some of the men to hunt for the captain. That assumed, of course, Emberly was still alive—a more treacherous man than the bishop had probably never lived. Nobody knew what he would try.

The company would be leaving the pyramid soon, if ever. Despite this, Orund had assigned no one to pack the soldiers' equipment and belongings, which was an outward admission that this place would be their tomb.

With the immediate tasks handled, the minutes slowed to an unendurable creep. The sergeant paced back and forth from the pyramid's entrance to the great hall. In the hall, he learned from returning searchers that the pyramid's underground was far bigger than they had guessed. The searchers were moving deeper a level at a time, with no luck so far.

At the pyramid's entrance, sentries pointed out a few of Robir's men hiding outside the arched gate of the pyramid's enclosure. He caught only glimpses of them because they were using the gate as cover from their fellow Ronians in the pyramid. If nothing else, their position told him that the Realm's forces had not yet arrived outside. Hulgar was among them, and Orund suspected Roark was too.

Soon after the sergeant returned to the hall, Father Brin arrived. The young man's entrance shattered the tense monotony, and cries went up from those who realized he was missing. Everyone fell silent when they saw what had been done to him.

The pair of knife cuts on his face looked like the product of sport, a nauseating decoration. The boy had clearly been tortured, and Brin's story, which came out in a trickle, seemed to confirm it.

Orund put his palms over his temples. He was not sure whether to entirely believe what Brin was saying. The thought of Robir, a highly pious man, taking a blade to the face of a priest—one hardly more than a boy—was hard to swallow. But the cuts were there, plain as day, and Brin seemed such a specter of himself that the sergeant could not think he was lying.

"Well," he said when Brin finished, "if Robir comes back, we'll make him pay. But I doubt that he will."

Brin did not seem cheered. "If he doesn't come back, neither will Ilis."

"She's one of the enemy, lad. Maybe you've forgotten. She'll be glad if the Realm catches them. She'll get them caught if she can."

Brin looked around. "Where is the bishop?"

When the sergeant told him Arumin was missing, the priest covered his face. "I've got to help find him."

"No, you don't," Orund answered, taking a tone of command. "I've got enough men out looking. If we don't find the bishop, you've got to take on his role."

A shout echoed down the corridor to the pyramid's entrance. A soldier appeared at a run. Reaching Orund and

Brin, he tried poorly to compose himself. "The mutineers just came inside, Sergeant. They say the Realm is here."

"Hell." Orund told the soldiers within earshot to form up and pounded toward the entrance. Not far inside, he found his own sentries in an uneasy standoff with the five remaining mutineers, who included Hulgar and Dr. Staubel. Both sides kept a wary eye on the archway.

There was not much to tell. The mutineers had seen a company's worth of sky-blue uniforms marching up the road and had beaten an immediate retreat. The street outside the gate was quiet—the locals could hardly fail to notice trouble brewing.

Roark was pressed among the mutineers against one wall of the corridor. His arms were bound behind his back. He stared at the opposite wall, seemingly careless of all else. When the mutineers were out by the gate, Orund had doubted if the company could overrun them without getting Roark killed. But the two groups were crammed together, the traitors were outnumbered, and the balance of power had changed.

Orund said, "Untie the lieutenant."

"Can't do it, Sergeant." That was Hulgar.

"You've lost, Private."

"Found Emberly yet?"

"He'll be back. Robir and the others won't. Best to give up now."

"Who will make me do that?" Hulgar didn't hide the laughter creeping into his voice. "You?"

The sergeant's temper boiled over. "You're damned right I will!" he shouted, putting his hand on his pistol. Fury at the Shining Realm, the bishop, and his own cowardice leapt inside him. Looking at Hulgar's face, he realized just how much he despised the man. "We'll find out how many shots it takes to bring you down. I'll bet it's not as many as you think."

"Don't," said Roark. He was standing straight, with tremendous and unlikely dignity. "There is killing to be done, but I will do it."

"You might," Hulgar said. "Or maybe I'll snap your neck and have it done."

"You do that," Orund said, "and you're dead for sure."

"Here they come!" Staubel yelled.

Orund's heart nearly burst through his chest. He had expected some kind of ultimatum before the Realm attacked. When he realized what Staubel was really talking about, he felt no better.

Down the street outside the wall, the roar of an approaching carriage grew louder with startling speed. It was a hair-raising sound—the metal beast was whining and begging, its innards worked to the verge of death.

"It's Robir," Orund cried in disbelief.

But he could not deny it. No one who knew how to operate one of the Shining Realm's carriages would torture it like that. But whoever was in the carriage was not home yet. The Realmsmen could easily stop them. As the deathly rumble approached the gate, no barrage of gunfire greeted it. None was needed. The soldiers of the Realm appeared suddenly at the gate, blocking the archway in rows three deep.

Their belief that the carriage would stop was mistaken. Most of them jumped or dove out of the way quickly enough, but a couple men bounced off the vehicle's front as it screamed through the gate.

Someone in the Realm started shooting, a noise that drowned out almost everything. Some of the shots missed the carriage and entered the hallway, and Orund heard bullets glancing from the walls. He fell into a crouch as the men around him threw themselves down. As the carriage barreled toward the pyramid's entrance, everyone scrambled backward, thinking it might not stop even for them. Orund glimpsed Robir sitting in the driver's position, eyes wide in horror.

The private halted the vehicle, but not quickly enough. Turning it slightly, he saved the lives of the men in the corridor by driving the carriage into the corner of the entryway. The crash shook the air and resounded in the corridor.

Orund had shut his eyes at the last instant. He opened them to see a tangle of men, thrown forward across the seats, piling from the vehicle. He couldn't believe how many had fit in that little carriage—seven, at least. As they hid behind the vehicle, Orund told his men to return the Realmsmen's fire.

The last person to leave the carriage was Brother Nor. He was so pale and stooped that Orund didn't know him at first glance. The sergeant had hoped never to see Nor again and felt incredulous at the luck that had let him fall in with Robir. As Nor tumbled from the carriage, Orund saw the others take hold of him roughly, as they would a prisoner.

A lull came in the shooting. Robir and his men wasted no time hustling down the corridor toward the great hall.

"There's a lot more coming!" Robir shouted as he passed.

Hulgar and his group followed, taking Roark with them.

Orund looked around at the men that were left. Terror struck him. He knew Robir and the others would try to retake control of the company. He couldn't let that happen, and neither could he leave the entry unguarded with the Realm free to charge in.

He picked two men to stay at the doorway and hold it as best they could. When the attack began in earnest, he ordered, at least one of them was to make it back to the throne room alive, come darkness and damnation, to warn the others. Whoever commanded the company when that happened could organize whatever haphazard defense they might.

As Orund and his men ran into the great hall, Robir punched Nor and knocked him to the ground. As his fellow traitors stood in a circle around him, he spun grandly and announced, "Who hasn't wanted to do that!"

The rest of the company stood watching. Orund was relieved to see that many of them were already armed.

Robir shouted to the heights of the chamber, "Where's Emberly?"

"He'll be back soon," Sergeant Feng said, clenching the barrel of his rifle with bloodless knuckles.

"Well, since he's taking a holiday, someone else ought to be in charge for a while."

"It won't be you," Orund said. "I wouldn't trust you to clean a shitter, not anymore. Now, release the lieutenant."

"Don't see much chance of that."

"You will. We will make you. So will every man in this room who won't take orders from a clown like you."

Orund took a step forward, praying that others would do the same. They did, edging inward to surround the mutineers. Guns bristled on both sides.

"Well," Robir said, eyes darting about, "I've done Huire's work. I'll wager she'll reward me now."

Though Orund expected the private to shoot someone, probably him, the man wasn't ready for his last words yet. "Emberly's betrayed us!" he shouted with startling venom. "He's run off. His friend, the general, showed him a way out. Can't you all see that? How stupid are you?"

"It doesn't have to be this way." Orund took another step forward. "We can all—"

"Will you stop?" Nor interrupted. He was still on the floor. His voice crackled, and he coughed. Raising his head, he looked at Orund. "You're still trying to save them." He sounded as if he couldn't believe it. "There is no saving them."

"Now, you keep your damned mouth shut." As Orund said this, he began to shake with rage. He wished again that Robir had left the monk in whatever pit he'd found him.

"You wandered off too. Carrowy needed you here, and I couldn't find you, and now, he's gone."

The monk's white eyes glistened. "Maybe he'll get away—from the Realm. Anything's better, even if he does away with himself."

Orund slapped him.

He had forgotten that Nor was unbound. The monk rose with a dizzy lunge and attacked him. Several of the others piled on Nor, dragged him back, and threw him down. In front of everyone, they beat him senseless.

"Stop!" Father Brin screamed, suddenly in their midst. He tried to pull someone away from Nor and was rebuffed with an elbow. He found himself in the small space between Orund's men and Robir's.

He straightened, his eyes pits in a bloody mask. When he spoke, Orund heard something of the righteous power that made people listen to the bishop himself. "If you hurt him more, you will regret it."

"Is that so?" Robir asked. His hands touched either side of his belt, finding the sheath of his knife. "Don't you have some regrets of your own to think about?"

Brin shook his head as if wishing the words away. Under his pretense of power, his desperation was unmissable.

Robir saw it. He stepped into Brin and shoved him back a pace.

Voice cracking, Brin said, "We all have the same enemy."

Robir said, "You know what we saw. How would you like that story to get around?"

Brin said tearfully, "Everyone knows who I am."

A few people laughed. Robir replied, "Yes. And you'd better hope you stay in your master's good graces."

"What in Huire's name is this?" When Emberly began that sentence, he was in one of the doorways. When he finished, he was almost to the edge of Orund's crowd, which still surrounded Robir's.

Arumin and Ganet followed him.

Some of the mutineers' guns turned toward the captain, and he stopped.

Robir looked surprised but not flustered. "Didn't think we'd see you again, Emberly. Since you keep stepping out on us, we've decided to make some changes."

Emberly had hardly opened his mouth to answer when Arumin pushed past him. The bishop hurried toward the center of the crowd, then his eyes fell on Brin's mangled face. He stopped in his tracks, and his mouth hung open.

The captain had put the pieces together. He turned his attention to Bishop Arumin. "You're a snake, a worm—that's all you've ever been."

The bishop had eyes for only Brin, who finally and reluctantly met his gaze.

Robir took hold of Brin's collar and shook him. "We found this—"

"You stay away from him!" Arumin proclaimed in an icy hiss.

Robir shook his head as though he had expected this reaction. "He's not worth your trouble, Bishop. Wait until you hear what he—"

"You did this?"

Robir released the priest's collar, protesting, "He betrayed us, Bishop. He tried to stop me from carrying out your orders."

"Damn my orders! How dare you hurt him!"

"He's in one piece," Hulgar said. "Mostly."

While the others were looking elsewhere, Emberly had moved a few steps forward. He had noticed Iwan among the mutineers.

"You're at fault for this, 'Lieutenant.'"

Iwan seemed bemused. "I did what you wouldn't do."

"You're a disgrace." Emberly's eyes passed over the traitors. "Every last one of you."

Staubel said, "Who are you talking to, exactly? I've got a room of sick men losing their minds, and you were nowhere to be found."

"I've done exactly what had to be done."

Robir answered. "Does that include selling us out to your new friend?"

"Friend?" Emberly snarled. He pointed behind himself. "Do you know what I almost did to him?"

Robir glared. "Who are you talking about, Emberly?"

Only then did anyone notice the general was gone.

"He escaped," Emberly said dumbly.

"Imagine that," Robir responded. "Now, what was this deal you made, Captain?"

Emberly turned on him. "If you hadn't torn this company apart—"

Robir cackled. "Are you blaming me for letting your prisoner get away? Nothing's your fault, is it?"

"If you weren't such a jealous, bitter little man—"

"Say that again." Robir raised his gun.

The room erupted. People yelled, guns pointed this way and that.

Emberly marched toward Robir. "I said—"

"Say it again!"

"I said—" Emberly raised his voice over the rest of them. It could've been heard over an artillery barrage. Then, without warning, he closed his mouth. His forward momentum dwindled, and his steps petered to nothing.

Shada stood at the mouth of the hallway leading to the building's entrance. She was bent and out of breath and had clearly been running. She wore an incongruously beautiful dress. The sight of them left her speechless, and the same was true in return.

"Hello," she said at last. "The time to fight—it's over." She paused again and looked at them all. Her eyes fell on Nor. "It's time to—" She blinked slowly, clearing her eyes. "It's time to leave this place... if we can."

56

REN

REN AND HER COMMANDOS moved quickly, arriving at the cabin before Jeric returned. She waited on the terrace.

He appeared among the trees with Adney close behind. She had expected him to plod, consuming as much time with his journey as he could. Instead, his strides were purposeful. She wondered even then if they had made a mistake.

She waited to greet him until he was close enough that she did not have to raise her voice. She invited him to sit in a chair on the terrace, and he did. Adney stood behind him, close enough to look down on the top of his head. Nearby stood a man who looked like Jeric in almost every respect of build, dress, and hair, though they were not exact twins.

For a while, she looked at the old Jeric. His eyes lingered on the man that would replace him, becoming his daughter's father. Then he met her gaze and held it until her own vision grew fuzzy and teary and he became an odd menagerie of poorly defined shapes.

"I don't have much to tell you." She produced a pair of folded pages and a pencil from inside her shapeless garb. Unfolding the papers and pushing out the creases, she prepared to read them aloud.

"Where is my daughter?" he demanded.

She stared.

He looked back with a glare that could have burned down the forest. "You know who I mean. Where is Delia?"

"She is inside. We are keeping her busy."

"She must not know. She must not be hurt." He looked at the new Jeric. "Do you understand me?"

Ren shook her head. "Still, at this late hour." She made a note on the first page. "It's a tendency we must watch out for in the future. Now, where was I?"

"Can't we skip this?"

"And how would you have it, sir?"

He played with his fingers. "I could kill you both. Run and see how far I get. What would all your formalities benefit you once you were dead?"

"They wouldn't," she said. Though she was confident that her face was unperturbed, his words struck an agreeable note in her. A second or two of considerable inner turmoil followed.

After weathering the storm, she continued, "I may regret this, but very well. We will spare ourselves the tedium." She nodded to the new Jeric, who stood, stared at the old Jeric with something resembling pity, and walked toward the cabin.

"Take care of her," called the old Jeric. The words grated out, to the visible agony of the man who produced them.

Ren made a note to make his end quick.

In all honesty, there was little to say. The deal that had freed the two Ronians would never have been approved, yet Jeric had made it of his own volition. The suspicion that generated would live on. Better he had killed himself at once on learning he was capable of such a thing.

"Well, shall we proceed?" Ren asked.

To his credit, the precursor—the man who had once been Jeric—looked at her without a scrap of fear. He stood, stripped off his shirt, and lay on the terrace. Her knife ready to pierce his chest, she stood over him and began to chant.

The scream from the house ruined everything.

Ren sprinted inside, the others at her heels. There, the new Jeric lay panting with a knife in his chest. He screamed again as they entered.

Delia was gone.

Adney raced out the door, but Ren knew he was too late. When he returned, he would be empty-handed. Ren shivered, paling with shock, gazing down at the new Jeric as he died. He was too damaged to be worth saving.

The sight was all wrong. The new replaced the old, always. That simple reversal, so perfectly illustrated before her, turned what might have been a minor setback into a stunning blow to all Ren held dear.

Still shaking, she sat on a nearby chair.

A rumbling caught her attention. Her eyes slowly traced the source: the precursor, now Jeric again, was laughing. It was a deep, easy laugh.

Ren knew what had happened, but she had to say it aloud to believe it. "Your wife."

"My girls are free," Jeric said.

She scrambled for comfort. "We'll find her."

"You can certainly try," he said. Linking his arms behind his back, he strode to the window, the master of the house. "Oliva's a fierce woman."

He tensed a little as she stood, but he kept his eyes on the garden. The ceremony she had anticipated was in ashes. She dashed over and stabbed him.

Again and again she stabbed, a shriek swelling inside her and bursting into the air. He slumped to his knees against the window, forehead on the glass, and died there.

She pulled his head back to check his face and quivered with horror when she found he was still smiling.

57

— · —

SHADA

WHEN SHADA SAW THE company at each other's throats, she'd been stunned. She knew she could not let them fight the Shining Realm. Neither would she convince them to surrender and let the Realm have its way with their bodies and souls.

However, as the company descended into the crypts under the pyramid, she knew another thing even more keenly: she had no idea where to lead them.

After interrupting the impending fight among the soldiers, she said whatever she could think of to stop them. She didn't know how they had come to this, and she didn't have time to find out. She told them they needed to escape the Realm, by death if need be.

She had known no other way to pacify them than to announce grandiosely that the Lady was watching them. Lying with all the assurance she could muster, she claimed the Lady had told her they must stop squabbling and carry on their divine mission. It had seemed impossible that this lie would come back to haunt her as she could see no other option for the company than fighting its way out of the pyramid. They would die, and she would die with them.

But then, as weapons lowered and an uneasy truce descended, Emberly announced that he had learned of an escape route under the pyramid. The bishop, overjoyed to hear of the Lady's presence among them, confirmed that, and the prospect of survival became real.

The group had gathered itself, collecting the sick and wounded and momentarily setting aside memories of the recent, nearly murderous violence, to follow the captain downward. Shada coldly dreaded the moment when someone would turn to her and ask her where the Lady wanted them to go next. She followed along, grateful that her dress concealed her shaking knees.

Whatever happened, she needed to delay as long as possible the revelation that the Lady was not with them. When she revealed that, some would be devastated, and others would not believe her. In any case, they would still be alive and free.

After welcoming her back, a soldier had returned her few possessions to her. He told her that when she went missing, someone had kept them safe for her. She had a feeling it was Nor.

Among her possessions was the Lady's box, where that being had dwelled before taking up residence in Shada's body. Shada had almost forgotten the ugly metal thing existed, and she wished she could have forgotten it completely. It felt unnaturally heavy as she took it up again, her special burden.

The company stopped descending and entered a set of corridors. She stayed near the front of the column. Nor was there, and she edged toward him until their shoulders touched.

"I'm so glad to see you," she said.

He turned his head. He had met her eyes a few times since she returned, and each time, he seemed to remember her presence anew. He smiled. The expression, though artificial, conveyed warmth through the effort he was clearly putting into it.

"What happened here?" she whispered.

"I don't know. Just got here myself."

She couldn't think of anything else to say. She wanted to ask him about the pit, about what he had been thinking when he held the knife, but that would be a cruel conversation to force upon him. Also, it would mean revealing that she had been there and had seen him in that state.

He said nothing else, and she let the interaction die. She remembered when, on Caidfell, she had held his hand for a moment. In her memory, it was soft, a scholar's hand rather than a laborer's, and she wondered how true that recollection was.

The captain entered a large chamber ahead. As his lantern's light filled the room, he started and jumped back.

At the far end of the room, a false section of the wall had been moved to reveal a tunnel. The captain's light hardly touched the subterranean darkness past the threshold, but Shada saw that the ground inside the door was dust and rock.

Next to the opening, waiting, stood a slim middle-aged man.

"Ganet! What are you doing here?" Emberly demanded.

The arrival of the company seemed to shake the man from some grim interaction within himself. "We have a deal."

"We did until you sneaked away."

"You were all about to murder each other. I would have been the first to die. I decided to wait here and see who showed up. I am glad to see your missing friends have returned."

"Why should we trust you now?"

"Because I'm still here, for one thing. And because I will keep telling you the truth: we may not be safe even traveling underground. I was to lead an attack through this very door, taking you all by surprise while you worried about the army outside. I believe I have diverted the soldiers in question, and enough others, to give us safe passage, but I am not who I used to be."

Emberly looked from Ganet to the mouth of night beside him.

"Cyril, I await your decision."

Emberly could give no other answer. "Lead on."

Shada had spent far more time than she cared to in the tapestry of caverns underlying Ronia. She would not have thought she could feel deeper, more buried or suffocated, than she sometimes had there. But the place they entered next was worse—all the more after her days in woods and gardens by the cabin.

The tunnel was narrow and lower than some of the men's heads. They did not have enough lanterns for every-one, so the sergeants distributed them along the column's length in the hope that no one would be entirely blind. The way was not straight, and numerous tunnels, small and large, sprouted from it. As the company passed, steps and voices in those burrows fell silent. The way intersected with larger channels populated with scattered, mostly hu-man shapes, and telling which tunnel on the opposite side was its continuation was often difficult. No soldiers of the

Realm had yet charged out of the darkness, and perhaps that was all they could ask.

Shada thought they would surely ascend to the surface soon. Not until something resembling an hour had passed did another possibility occur to her. Then the sheer enormity of Om pressed down on her, and she imagined how long feeling their way through its floors and walls like rats might take. She swayed with panic.

As she walked, stepping quickly to keep up with the others, she fought a tooth-and-nail battle to keep herself from screaming and sprinting ahead, running one way then another, and clawing at the tunnel ceiling to demand it let her out. She was grateful that her face was nearly invisible to those nearby. She saw Nor's shape ahead and hurried to catch up with him. Someone had found shackles and clamped them on his wrists. Side by side with the monk, though she said nothing to him, she felt that as long as he was calm, she would also be.

After what felt like several hours, the company took a short break. Before leaving the pyramid, they had looted the place for whatever food and drink the Realm had left behind. They realized it might be poisoned, but they had made the unspoken, unanimous decision not to dwell on that.

When they got underway again, the shadows of the endless tunnels seemed to subsume time itself. The larger, noisier areas they occasionally passed through seemed like oases, kingdoms of light and hope.

The boredom and dreariness of the journey reached a point of intolerability then another and another. Each time, Shada's mind reeled with the wish that the tunnel would end or even that a single ray of sunlight would sneak in and glance its way into the bowels of the city. She kept walking. The wish would subside while leaving her misery perfectly intact, and sometime later, the want of light would rise again to unbearable intensity.

When the company's path began to trend downward, she felt herself leaning forward. The entire world seemed to have been picked up, turned on its side, and balanced on its paper-thin edge. After a time, she dared to hope they had reached one of Om's walls and were making their way down to ground level. There, they would finally emerge.

"It shouldn't be hard now," Ganet told Emberly. "There are many sets of stairs and many exits into the desert, or so I've heard."

"You haven't been here before?" Emberly somehow contained this news to a whisper.

"Not this far. Our scouts have, with the locals' help."

"Then how do you know where you're leading us?"

"It's all right, Cyril. People who live here know where they are going. Haven't you learned that yet?"

Then the lanterns began to go out. The one at the end of the column was the first to die, plunging the men at the back of the line into darkness. Their frantic cries brought the column to a stumbling halt, and the lanterns were redistributed. This havoc recurred each time a light died, and the gaps of darkness grew wider. Someone fell while descending a staircase, twisting an ankle and sending others tumbling.

Shada began to navigate more by feel and sound than sight. She put an arm around Nor's, and he did not object. The clink of his shackles let her locate him easily and so was oddly comforting. The company was making more noise, shuffling as they climbed downward, and Shada began to whisper to Nor, telling him what she had been through. The more she talked, though, the more she began to leave out. She did not tell him that the Lady was gone, of course, but neither did she mention the extent of her feelings for Jeric or the intimacy they had achieved. She left her means of escape vague and did not mention seeing Nor in the pit.

If he noticed the holes in her story, he did not mention them. In fact, he didn't talk. She was standing so close and speaking so directly to him that he must have heard her, but she could not tell if he was really listening. Maybe he wished she would stop.

She concluded by saying, even closer to his ear and more softly, that she needed to speak to him privately. It was about the Lady.

He answered, his voice a croak. "I've got something to tell you too. About the Goddess."

She was glad they were speaking to each other.

The tunnels were empty but for the squeaks of vermin. The party was walking mostly in complete darkness. They clung to each other's shoulders and clothing, whispering back and forth to alert each other to obstacles. Once, they heard piteous cries from a soldier who had become separated from the others and found himself alone. The prospect of wandering the underground ways of Om to some unknown fate had reduced him to tears in seconds. It took several minutes of calls and responses to guide him back to the company. No one questioned the necessity of waiting or asked which side the man had taken in the mutiny.

Vertical travel was slower than horizontal travel, and the descent took longer than all that had come before. Shada clung to Nor's arm as to sanity itself. Her mind bobbed, spending much of its time in a stupor, a lower state of sentience, and she rued each return to consciousness.

She didn't know exactly when the first glow of daylight appeared. It was some time after the last lantern had died and the company had been reduced to picking and shuffling forward, a vibrating, mostly thoughtless mass of flesh and bone that radiated heat and fear. Even after the light's presence became obvious, she did not dare believe it was growing brighter. A few of the men whispered feverishly or clutched their neighbors. Most shielded their eyes and waited, thinking of light as an elusive creature that might flee if frightened.

After they stepped one by one from the hole in the wall of Om and descended a treacherous mound of rubble to the desert floor, some of them lay on the ground. Others turned their faces to the sky, eyes shut against the rampant intensity of the sun. The time was close to midday.

Shada released Nor's arm for the first time in perhaps a full day. She stepped back and tried to absorb the torrent from her senses. She had forgotten how overwhelming they could be.

A hand was on her shoulder. It was the captain. "It's time, Shada. Where does the Lady want us to go?"

58

SHADA

BY ASKING SHADA WHERE the Lady wanted them to travel, Emberly might as well have belted her in the stomach. She had known the question was coming, but she would actually have to pick a direction in utter ignorance or admit to everyone that the Goddess was no longer speaking to her at all. She looked dumbfounded at the horizon.

Directly before them, a few minutes' walk away, was an entire city. Minuscule in the shadow of Om, its low, sandy buildings might nonetheless be home to thousands. Past its far outskirts, a number of multihued lumps lay on the horizon like the fingers and thumbs of buried giants. The sight solved her immediate problem—she simply had to lead the company through one of those gateways.

Before she could say a word, Ganet spoke up. "It's this way, Cyril. Through that city."

Emberly glared. "How do you know where we're going?"

"Haven't you learned to listen to me? We must leave immediately. We will be spotted from Om, and they will be after us soon."

Shada touched the captain's arm. "He's right. It is the Lady's will also."

With a last hard stare at Ganet, Emberly relented. The group formed up and set out at once. Everyone was improbably energetic—relief and sunlight had given them new life. They entered the city on a crowded thoroughfare that led in an unwavering line from a great set of doors on the side of Om. Everything was too straightforward for Shada's liking—the Realm would dispatch carriages and catch up with them in short order. When they reached the other side of the city, if the choice fell to her, she would pick the nearest gateway.

In the city, the road took a bend or two. When the front of the column passed the first curve, a cry went up from those in the rear. Hustling back, on the heels of the captain, Shada saw drifting clouds of dust rising from just in front of Om's doors.

"Here they come!" Emberly called.

The column broke into an orderly trot. For all it mattered, though, they might have been crawling on their knees. Glancing back, Shada watched as the company's lead—gained by a day or more of hard travel—was annihilated in a few minutes.

She would never have to face her moment of awful decision. That would have been a relief had the alternative not been so terrifying. She expected Emberly to line up a final stand of some sort before the enemy reached them. They might barely escape the city before they were caught, sparing harm to bystanders, but then they would defend themselves in the open desert, with no time to prepare.

Emberly did no such thing. He kept them moving. Looking ahead, she saw that outside the town was a field of sand-colored stones, mostly standing waist high—a graveyard.

Ganet said something to Emberly.

The captain replied, "That's where we'll go."

The road cut straight through the field of stones, a distance as long again as the city's width. The field continued as far as Shada could see to left and right. If stones were a crop, that place could have fed a planet.

The company did not follow the road across the field. Instead, the captain plunged into the midst of the stones, and the rest followed. Some of the stones stood in rows, but many others, especially those deeper into the field, pressed together in unfurrowed anarchy. A small fraction of them were tombs, buildings large enough to house a corpse or a family of corpses. A few were truly titanic, miniature palaces in their own right. Those fell wherever they wished among the rest, like rocks dropped into a stream.

The nearest of the buildings was too far to reach, so Emberly made for a dense cluster of towering stones nearby. Dozens were there. Some were low, robust monuments of blunt wealth, while others were narrow, tapering to teetering pinnacles.

The forces of the Realm were in plain sight. Three vehicles were in pursuit—hardly the army Shada had expected. Two were motorized carriages of the type she had seen before. The third was much larger, a hulking box.

The vehicles stopped at the spot in the road closest to the fleeing company. There they would have to wait, Shada realized with elation. The stones were too tightly spaced for any of the vehicles to pass between them. The carriages might try to keep the company from escaping the field, driving to whatever edge the Ronians tried to reach, but the soldiers could not enter the field except on foot. Given the small number of attackers, perhaps the company could even attack them directly.

Then the large vehicle turned off the road and plowed across the field toward the Ronians, crushing the stones as it went. It moved with a horrible grinding and popping, steering clear of the more formidable stones, moving more slowly but otherwise unhindered.

The burst of hope that had filled Shada now seemed futile. *If they can do that, what can't they do?*

The company took shelter in the forest of taller monuments and tombs. They arranged themselves defensively, Shada staying in the back and out of the way. She had lost track of Nor, but as she picked a stone to hide behind, she saw that Ganet had picked the next one over. The man's face was an odd mixture of fear and disinterest. He knew how this would end.

Through the stones, she found a mostly unobstructed view of the advancing vehicle. A thin slit like a window crossed its front. On top was a kind of weapon she had never seen before. Far too large to be a rifle, it had several barrels arranged in a circle. Its operator stood behind it, protected by a wide metal plate.

The vehicle stopped a long stone's throw from the grove of monuments where the company waited. No words passed between the two sides. The weapon emitted a thick, live hum, and its barrels spun around each other.

That was the last coherent sight she had for some time. An eruption of sound and motion shook her off her feet. She found herself crouched behind a stone, clenching her head between her arms, trying to cover her eyes and ears and nose all at once. The noise was like hundreds of bombs exploding in her ears, intolerably and without end.

She saw nothing through the sand and smoke, which burned her eyes though she shut them tight. Her lungs, which had never really stopped hurting since Caidfell, felt aflame. She couldn't breathe.

For all she knew, everyone else was dead. She would follow them soon. All she had to do was huddle there a little longer. Or she could stand up or run back and forth—the end would be the same, and it would come at the same time.

A brief respite came. The shooting stopped, though the ringing in her ears tried to tell her otherwise. She cracked her eyes open to see devastation. The nearby stones and monuments were unrecognizable, lumps and protrusions of powdery rock, though most were still standing. The ground was covered with whitish powder and sharp rocks. She wondered that none of the flying chunks of stone had bashed her head in.

As the air cleared a little, she saw a few of her companions. They were gray, dust-covered mounds, crouched against monuments or flat on their bellies. Ganet had not moved, though his face was a mask of grit. He seemed calm, as if he found all this to be sensible enough.

If any blood was on the ground, she couldn't see it under the dust. As she spotted more movement around her, she began to hope that their casualties weren't as bad as she feared. The stones provided ample protection, though they could be chipped away.

More gunfire began, that time of a mundane variety. Bullets from Realmsmen's rifles whirred and snapped. To her right, an explosion drowned out the ringing in Shada's ears. Another blast followed to her left, and that time, she saw what happened. A small dark object came sailing over the monuments from the enemy's direction. The men near it must have seen such things before—they ran and dove before the thing exploded. Through the gaps in the stones before her, she saw the running figures of the enemy.

Explosion followed explosion. None of the bombs landed near Shada, and they didn't seem to be shifting the Ronians from their positions. Then one of the Ronian company cried out, and the pitch of his fear and confusion caused her to risk another glance toward the enemy.

In the short distance between the Realm's vehicle and the cluster of tall stones, she saw a man. His figure was thick and ungainly, and he charged the Ronians in a loping run. As he came closer, she got a better look: he was wearing some sort of heavy armor, and something was strapped around his chest.

She had seen that before, on Ronia. The equipment on the man's chest was a bomb, probably a much larger one than the others—big enough, maybe, to kill all the Ronians at once.

She jumped back from her stone, her legs screaming at her to flee as far from the man as she could. She shouted for someone, anyone to stop him, but her words were muddled as if she had glue in her mouth. As he closed in on the Ronians, she screamed for everyone to run. No one was listening. Maybe they were dazed, deaf, or blind.

But Ganet heard. He peered from behind his stone. What happened next seemed to take no time at all. He fell forward, catching himself on his elbows, and vomited. Out of his mouth spilled a cloud.

The Lady poured out of his throat with blinding speed. She drove through the air toward the armored man. Forming a ball as tight as a massive fist, she struck him.

The impact flung him backward, arms and legs flailing. He hit the ground in an end-over-end roll, stopping in front of the vehicle.

Shada pulled herself into a ball and covered her ears. The blast seemed to shake the planet. When she opened her eyes, she was surprised to see the ground still intact beneath her.

She watched the dust clear. The vehicle had been tossed onto its back, a smoking ruin. The ground around it was scorched. Here and there were blackened forms that might have been the Realm's soldiers or parts of them.

The Lady swept over the ruined stone forest with a hiss—coming toward Shada. The men cheered, their voices warm but shaky and stunned. The Lady glided down, pulling her mass into a thin, serpentine column.

Shada rose to her knees, heart pounding. She raised the Lady's box and pried open its door, expecting the Lady to reside there again.

Instead, the Lady hovered before Shada's eyes. A face formed there, at the tip of her twisting mass—a familiar, matronly smile.

Shada shut her mouth but to no avail. The Lady wrenched her jaws open and entered with an air of graciousness. As before, the Lady left a trail of her mass across Shada's cheek to her ear. Shada heard the familiar, droning whisper: "Not far to go now."

Ganet was staring wide-eyed at Shada. In his face, she saw, among other feelings, relief and pity.

She leaned back against the stone that had sheltered her. With no one but Ganet close enough to hear, she said, "I wish you had stayed away."

The Lady did not respond. Not long before, she would have protested, tried to excuse herself, become angry. But now, nothing.

Shada continued, "You are a cruel, petty fraud. From now on, we are enemies. I will resist you in any way I can."

Nothing.

"I can only hope the Goddess you represent is nothing like you."

The men were starting to gather around her. A few had seen the Lady enter her, and they looked on her with holy reverence. She and the Lady had been two, but now they shared of each other, not quite two and not quite one. Shada would hold on to that last bit of herself if it cost her everything.

As the soldiers' strong hands enclosed hers and helped her to her feet, she noticed that Ganet was gone. She said aloud, "I suppose I will know soon."

59

— • —

EMBERLY

THE ROAD TO THE gateway was not long. Neither could it really be called a road. Emberly saw no sign that any travelers had passed that way in some time, and windblown sand was reclaiming the path in the name of the desert.

The gateway itself was not welcoming. From a distance, Emberly wondered if that was really snow blowing out of it rather than some trick of sand and light. The truth became more certain and malevolent as they approached: the small gray portal led to a place so far away that it had a different sun. Flakes of ice and snow tumbled to their destruction in the heat of this world.

During the attack in the graveyard, more dust had risen from the direction of Om. That cloud was caused by only one carriage, though nobody could say what that carriage contained.

As the company neared the gateway, Emberly judged that, if they hurried, they might reach it before the vehicle reached them. But that would only delay the confrontation—the thing could follow them through. Also, he despised the thought of bringing the madness they had just escaped onto another world. If any chance existed of leaving the Shining Realm on this planet, he would take it.

He placed the men in defensive positions facing the approaching vehicle. Whatever its driver attempted, they would oppose it.

Lieutenant Roark was fighting for his life. He had been found shot and bleeding in the ruins of the graveyard. He was lying away from the road with the other wounded, and the sight of that fearsome, nearly monstrous man in such a state was one of the most frightening things Emberly could remember seeing. The company's dead remained where they had fallen in the graveyard.

The carriage that approached them was enclosed by a roof and windows. It was towing something in its wake—a wagon also enclosed with low walls and a ceiling. In no great hurry, it turned in a tight circle, sweeping in front of the Ronian line, and stopped with its rear facing them.

The driver's door opened, and Ren stepped out. The men deluged her with threats and demands to surrender, but Emberly silenced them with a shout.

Ren joined her hands in front of her. "Thank you, Captain. I hope you will hear what I have to say. I have no intention of fighting you or stopping you from leaving."

Emberly said, "No one here wants to listen to you."

Bishop Arumin muttered, "She'll have explosives, Emberly."

"I have no bomb," Ren answered. "There is no trickery here. If you still care for a fight, our soldiers will arrive soon, but I have come on purely personal business. I must collect a debt."

"What?" Emberly asked.

Several people echoed the question.

"I intend to take Norhim back with me."

"You can't be serious," Emberly said.

"And I have something to offer in return." She walked to the back of the wagon, which faced the Ronians. What had looked like a closed top was actually a large box that filled the wagon's bed. Ren grabbed the handle on the box's closest end.

"Stop!" Emberly cried, taking aim at her.

She stopped but did not move her hand. "I must show you this. If I produce a weapon, or if you even think you see one, feel free to shoot me."

She pushed the handle, sliding a small panel aside and revealing a small slot covered by a dark screen.

"Say hello," she commanded the box.

First, Emberly heard heavy breathing.

Then, a small voice: "Hello? Who is there?"

His heart pounded. A child was inside.

"It's me," Ren replied to the voice.

The breathing became steadier. Comforted, the child reverted to complaining. "I'm cold."

"I'm sorry to hear that, darling. But there is nothing I can do."

One of the Ronians gasped. It was Sergeant Orund, who took a step closer to Ren and the box. "Hello?" he called. His tone was tense and demanding, and the voice did not answer. The sergeant's hands turned to fists. "Say something!"

"I'm scared," the child said.

Orund spat words in twos and threes. "It's not—you can't be—"

Emberly's skin crawled. The sergeant might have been losing his mind.

At last, Orund managed to say to Ren, "You beast! That's him, isn't it? That's Carrowy!"

"It's something not unlike him," the woman said. "His transformation is underway."

"It's a trick, Sergeant," Emberly snapped.

It was hardly even that—the voice in the box was a little boy's.

"Carrowy," Ren said, "speak to your captain."

"Sir... I'm sorry... I just couldn't..." The voice trailed into incoherence, but it didn't matter. By then, Emberly had finally recognized the voice as Carrowy's. The private's voice had changed almost beyond recognition, but not quite.

Nor's shackles clinked, and the monk groaned.

Ren nodded. "This is a trade, Captain. Norhim for Carrowy."

Orund cursed. "And what if you're not alive to make that trade?"

"You can't kill me if you want Carrowy to live. He is at a critical stage. How he is treated now will affect his very survival. If you give me what I want, I will tell you how to keep him alive, though I admit he will never be quite the same."

Arumin began to speak and coughed. His throat sounded dry as he said, "You came all the way out here for Norhim?"

Dipping her head, Ren gave them a little bow. "Why?"

She pointed at Nor. "He lied to me."

Arumin scoffed. "Well, following us may be the last mistake you will ever make. Don't you know the power that protects us? Have you not witnessed what she can do?"

"The Lady will not interfere. She is listening now, and I suspect she can see this." Ren pulled a vial from a pocket. The little glass container was partly filled with a black powder. "She knows the danger she is in. She was scarcely willing to risk herself for all of you together, let alone for one insignificant man."

"That is absurd," the bishop proclaimed.

"Let us proceed and see if I am wrong. Now, as for the liars. We have two here. Why not hand over the one who is most at fault?"

Nor spoke. "She's right, Emberly. Let me go."

"No!" cried Shada, who had remained by the monk's side since they left the graveyard. "You can't."

"Shada, this is my fault. It's the best choice."

"I don't care!" Shada yelled. She placed herself in front of Nor, facing Ren. Had she been an animal, she would have bared her teeth and swung her claws.

"Nonsense," Emberly told Ren. "I will make no bargains with you. I have finished negotiating."

Doctor Staubel had been tending to Roark, whom he had recently nearly helped to murder. He stood in alarm. "We can't let that monster have Carrowy."

"Keep quiet if you want to live," Emberly muttered.

"How about we kill this bitch instead?" Orund added. "We can take care of our own man."

"No!" screamed he who had been Private Carrowy. There was movement in the box and the sound of its occupant sloshing around in a liquid. "Don't hurt her. She is everything—you don't understand. If she goes away, I'll be alone."

"You're never alone, son," said Orund. "She's been lying to you."

"No," the voice said. "She knows the truth, and she's the only one."

The bishop spoke in Emberly's ear. "We have to leave... now."

More dust clouds had risen on the horizon.

"Don't be a fool," Orund told Carrowy. He advanced on the wagon. "We're coming for you. You'll be free in a moment."

Carrowy's howl of fear coincided with Emberly's command to the sergeant. "Stop!"

"Orund," Nor said, "Make him trade!"

"We've got to stop this, Captain," Orund said.

Emberly stared. *Finding the Goddess is what matters now. That will fix everything, make it all worthwhile.*

"No," he said.

The sergeant peered at him, disbelieving. "Of course we do. Do you want to leave him here?"

Emberly turned to the others. Over their shoulders, Rayan watched, telling Emberly to be the leader Rayan knew he could be.

The question was not about Nor or Carrowy. It was about staying here, and that Emberly would not do. He would not be pushed anymore.

"Form up," he said. "Let's go."

After a moment of vast indecision, the company began to move—a step here and there, and then more—toward the gateway. They glanced at each other as if each was making sure the others actually meant to leave Carrowy to the Shining Realm.

Nor screamed and thrashed at his chains. No one seemed to hear him but Shada, who begged him to be silent.

Orund turned from person to person, mouth trembling. He saw another man who hadn't moved—his former enemy. "Iwan! They've all lost their minds. You've got to help me."

Iwan, assessing matters in his distant way, nodded. "Yes, I do." He met Emberly's eye, then he and Orund moved toward Ren, weapons in hand.

Emberly put a bullet in Iwan's back. No one reacted quite as he expected. Orund stooped slowly and covered his head, perhaps unsurprised. Nor suddenly went quiet. The others, who had hardly begun to move, paused, marking the moment.

Iwan was grievously wounded. He lay on his stomach, gasping for breath, trying to push the ground away with his arms and legs, which had lost their strength. Emberly went to him and shot him again.

Ren said, "I see that we don't have a deal."

"Leave this place," Emberly told her, "while you can."

"What a state you are in," she replied. "I must be very candid with you, sir. You were offered friendship and brotherhood, and you declined. Then you ran away from the gift of a quick death."

She spoke loudly and to all of them. Her face had gone white, and her carefully controlled manner had come undone. "You should run as quickly as you can. Our forces will pursue you until you despair. When they find your gods, they will exterminate them. Don't let them capture any of you alive."

"If I ever see you again," Emberly said, "I'll kill you."

Ren watched as they departed. Carrowy whimpered once, setting off a new round of shouting from Nor.

Orund was helped to his feet by Robir, who put an arm over his shoulder and led him away, whispering.

Emberly turned toward the gateway, having made up his mind not to look back. He wondered if he had just poisoned the company and, if so, how much longer they would follow him. An arm fell around his shoulders. It was his brother's.

Walking beside him, Rayan smiled. The curve of his mouth was like the slash of a knife. Emberly was bled dry of words. Nothing was left to say.

To finish the quest, read *Rites of Cataclysm*, the final volume of Liturgy of Worlds! On sale here:

https://books2read.com/ritesofcataclysm

If you enjoyed this book, I would massively appreciate a review wherever you got it or on Goodreads. Even a line or two helps me so much!

Want a free short story set in the Liturgy of Worlds universe? Join my mailing list! Titled "A Monster's War," the story tells of the day the Lady came to Ronia—and it stars her caretaker, beastly warrior that he is. Check out the preview below. Plus, as a list member, you'll get the latest news from me, behind-the-scenes updates, media reviews and recommendations, and more!

Join my newsletter at nathanhartle.com for this free story!

The folk of these realms call him "Beast."

If only they knew he is their savior.

Filled with shame after a cowardly act, a giant warrior with a wolf's face sees one last chance for redemption: he must return a lost goddess to the city of her birth.

If she reaches home, she will remake the world. An age of light will dawn. But she is sick and weak, and she needs a protector.

Only Beast can help. If he triumphs, evil and darkness may disappear forever... and his shame will end. If he fails, he will lose his life and soul. Every step of his quest will be perilous—in these lands, Beast's size and appearance make him feared and hated.

But they also make him mighty.

"A Monster's War" is a quick adventure in the Liturgy of Worlds epic fantasy series.

Preview of A Monster's War

(Beast, the Lady's caretaker, is confronting a gang who have abducted the Lady...)

Beast strode toward the man, his pace steady, not quite promising violence.

Larky stood his ground as his men fled. At the last instant, he fell back, knife drawn, but Beast's arm shot out and grabbed him by the shirt.

Hoisting him off the ground, Beast looked him in the eyes and growled a promise. Larky shouted, and something stung Beast's leg.

A tingle raced like wildfire down to his foot and up to his hip. Something was terribly wrong, and he spun to watch several feathered spikes lodge in his leather breastplate. There stood several of Larky's men, holding thin pipes to their mouths.

For a sliver of an instant, he froze. They had poisoned him. Rather than fight openly, rather than seize combat as a chance to show honor and courage, they had used trickery and deceit. And they had won.

It was the epitome of civilization. He could never win against it. He could not even resist it—not without doing things the only way he knew. He disobeyed his goddess.

With an almighty roar, he charged the men, ready to kill them all...

***

"A Monster's War" is *only* available by signing up for my newsletter. Sign up here: nathanhartle.com

About the Author

Nathan Hartle lives in North Carolina, USA with his amazing wife, son, and two cats who are kind enough to share their house.

Though he's had many, many jobs—travel agent in Bangkok, hostel clerk in Morocco, construction worker in Washington, DC—writing fantasy and science fiction is by far his favorite.

He believes storytelling is a service to others and a sacred act that honors Creation. Good stories let us glimpse eternity.

Keep up with Nathan by following him on Facebook, Goodreads, and BookBub.